'There are love and secrets by the seaside in the feelgood MEET ME AT BEACHCOMBER BAY by the enormously popular Jill Mansell'
Good Housekeeping

'A heartwarming treat from one of my favourite writers'
Katie Fforde

PRAISE FOR

Meet Me at Beachcomber Bay

'Ideal for a summer read on the beach'
paperlovestory

'Must have'
Sunday Express

'A breezy, feel-good romance' *Best*

'We galloped through this funny, bouncy, romantic and brilliantly written yarn. A feel-good gem'
***** *Heat*

'An utter delight – reading Jill is always such a joy'
Veronica Henry

'A wonderful novel, with a
real feel-good factor, some
giggles, and lots of smiles'
brizzlelassbooks

'Upbeat, light hearted,
and a bit of an emotional
rollercoaster . . . a pure 5/5'
whisperingstories

'A warm and witty novel, packed
full of wonderful characters.
Perfect for a lazy summer's day'
fromfirstpagetolast

'A romantic, funny new novel
about love and friendship'
*Ireland's Home
Interiors & Living*

'A beautiful tale that captures us heart and
soul. Another captivating read that would
melt the coldest of hearts'
bytheletterbookreviews

Jill Mansell

is the author of over twenty *Sunday Times* bestsellers including
THE ONE YOU REALLY WANT, TO THE MOON AND BACK
and YOU AND ME, ALWAYS. TAKE A CHANCE ON ME won the
RNA's Romantic Comedy Prize, and in 2015 the RNA presented Jill
with an outstanding achievement award.

Jill's personal favourite amongst her novels is THREE AMAZING
THINGS ABOUT YOU, which is about cystic fibrosis and organ
donation; to her great delight, many people have joined the organ
donor register as a direct result of reading this novel.

Jill started writing fiction while working in the NHS, after she
read a magazine article that inspired her to join a local creative
writing class. Her first book was accepted for publication in 1991
and she is now a full-time novelist. She is one of the few who still
write their books by hand, like a leftover from the dark ages.
She lives in Bristol with her family.

Jill Mansell

Meet Me at Beachcomber Bay

H

REVIEW

First published in Great Britain in 2017 by
HEADLINE REVIEW
An imprint of HEADLINE PUBLISHING GROUP

First published in paperback in Great Britain in 2017 by
HEADLINE REVIEW
An imprint of HEADLINE PUBLISHING GROUP

1

Cataloguing in Publication Data is available from the British Library

ISBN 978 1 4722 4139 9 (A-Format)
ISBN 978 1 4722 0894 1 (B-Format)

Typeset in Bembo Std by Palimpsest Book Production Limited, Falkirk, Stirlingshire

Printed and bound in Great Britain by
CPI Group (UK) Ltd, Croydon, CR0 4YY

Headline's policy is to use papers that are natural, renewable and recyclable
products and made from wood grown in well-managed forests and other controlled sources.
The logging and manufacturing processes are expected to conform to the
environmental regulations of the country of origin.

HEADLINE PUBLISHING GROUP
An Hachette UK Company
Carmelite House
50 Victoria Embankment
London EC4Y 0DZ

www.headline.co.uk
www.hachette.co.uk

For Tina, with all my love.

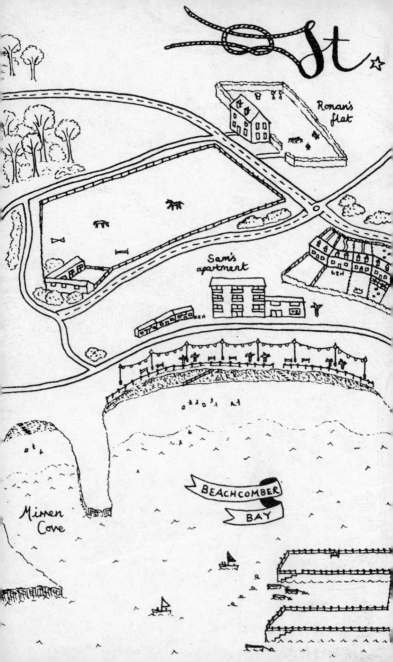

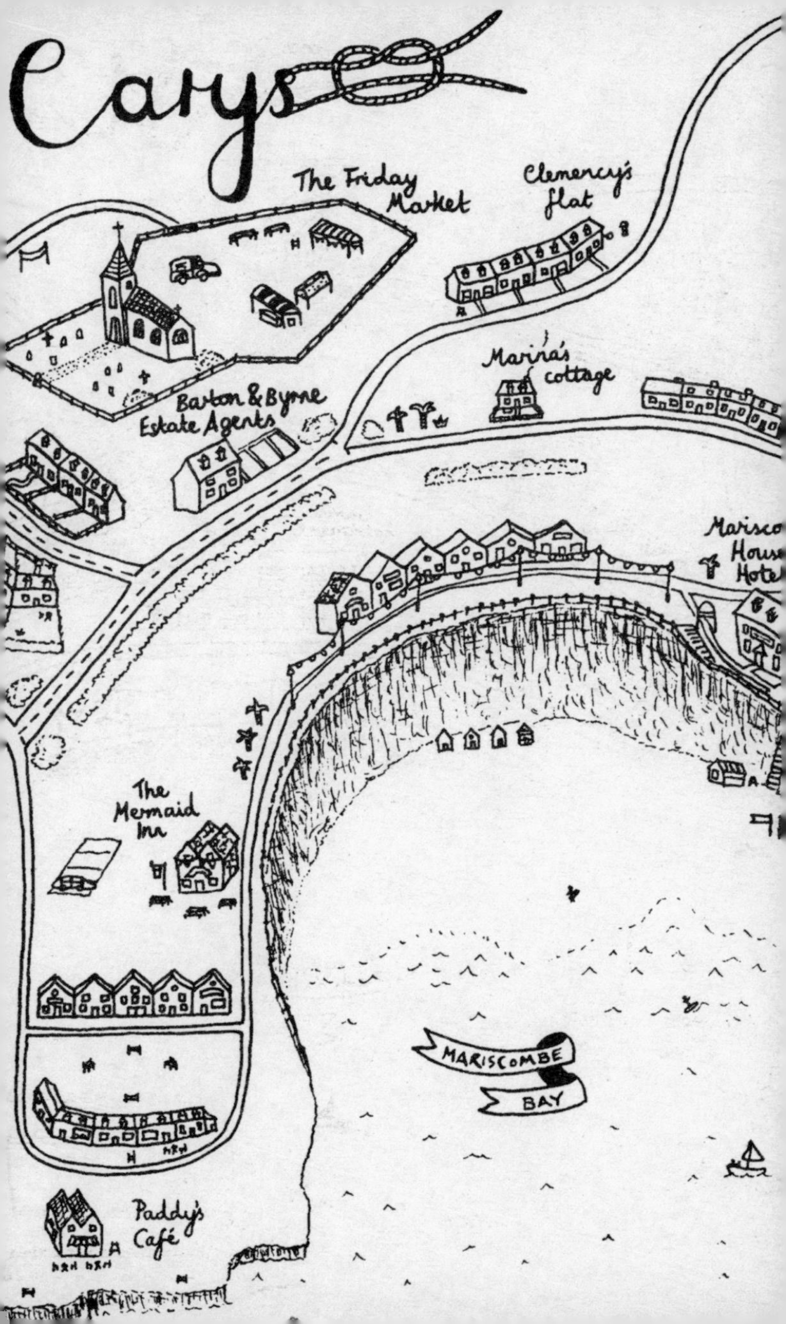
Carys
The Friday Market
Clemency's flat
Marina's cottage
Barton & Byrne Estate Agents
The Mermaid Inn
Paddy's Café
MARISCOMBE
BAY

Chapter 1

Sometimes it only takes a split second for a state of absolute calm to turn to one of horror and panic.

'Oh dear, poor thing.' Clemency turned to watch as a purple-faced businessman in a too-tight suit hurtled across the concourse at Malaga airport in the direction of the departure gates, panting and grunting as he ran and scattering small children in his wake.

The British girl who was working on the Chanel stand in duty-free said, 'Honestly, it's amazing how many people don't bother to pay attention to the boards. Yesterday there was a party of fifteen Spanish guys in one of the bars and they were so busy watching a football match on TV that they ended up missing their flight. Imagine!'

'That's crazy,' Clemency marvelled, trying a purple eyeshadow shot with gold sparkly bits on the back of her hand. *Nice.*

'Oh, we see everything here. So many people don't even turn up at the airport until their flight's about to close.'

'I couldn't do that. I always like to give myself loads of time. Then I know I can really relax,' Clemency said happily, 'and spend ages in duty-free trying out all the make-up.'

Which was why another forty minutes had passed before she finally arrived at the checkout to pay for the new lipstick she'd chosen, because these things took time, and choosing the perfect lipstick was important.

The bored-looking cashier said, 'May I check your boarding pass, please?'

Clemency glanced down at her left hand, the one that should have been clutching her passport. The passport with the boarding pass neatly tucked inside it.

She looked down at the hand and saw that it was clutching instead a handful of perfume card samplers, each one sprayed with a different scent.

And that was the moment absolute calm turned to horror and panic.

'Just in time,' said the female attendant as Clemency hurtled towards the departures desk. 'We were about to close the gate!'

Clemency couldn't speak. She wanted to fall to her knees and gulp air into her burning lungs, but there was no time; she was already being ushered out through the sliding doors and across the tarmac towards the waiting plane. Her drag-along case was banging against her ankles, perspiration was trickling down her spine and her mouth was dry as she struggled up the clanky metal steps, still hyperventilating. Oh God, she could only imagine the colour of her face. She must be *puce*.

The male flight attendant greeted her with a wink. 'Nice of you to decide to join us. Welcome on board.'

You know that little inner surge of triumph you get when you're on a packed-to-the-gills plane and everyone's boarded and the seat next to yours is magically still empty . . . until at the *very* last minute someone else gets on and you realise you won't be enjoying the luxury of having an empty seat beside you after all?

This, Clemency knew, was the feeling currently being experienced by the passenger occupying seat number 45A. As she made her way towards 45B, she could almost hear the thud of disappointment and his accompanying sigh of resignation.

Oh well. His hopes might have been cruelly dashed, but on the upside he had excellent cheekbones and a beautiful mouth. During her flight over here, the guy in the seat next to hers had weighed almost as much as the plane itself and had been eating tuna sandwiches, so this one was already a marked improvement.

Still getting her breath back, Clemency smiled broadly at him. 'I know, I'm sorry, I'd be disappointed too.'

This was the man's cue to relax, to notice that as far as seat-neighbours were concerned he could do an awful lot worse, and to gallantly offer to lift her heavy case into the overhead locker.

Except this didn't happen. Instead he acknowledged her with the briefest of nods before returning his attention to the phone in his hand.

Then again, she had looked better. Maybe a red-faced, perspiring twenty-five-year-old gasping for breath wasn't his cup of tea.

Case stowed and locker closed, Clemency collapsed into her seat, wiped her face and hands with a tissue and examined her left foot where the wheels of her carry-on case had repeatedly bashed against her ankle. She exhaled noisily. 'I can't believe I almost missed my flight! I *always* make sure I leave loads of time so nothing can go wrong. All these years and it's never happened before . . . but I suppose the thing is, something always *can* go wrong. Like today. You can't imagine how I felt when . . . umm . . .'

She trailed to a humiliated halt when she realised the man was determined to ignore her. Nothing, not a flicker; he clearly wasn't interested *at all*.

He might have a beautiful mouth and excellent cheek-bones, but he had no intention of engaging in conversation with the stranger at his side.

Fine. Clemency ostentatiously took out her own phone and began to check her emails. *Because look at me, I'm really busy and important too.*

Half an hour later, once they were flying at 36,000 feet over the Pyrenees, two cabin crew brought the drinks trolley down the aisle, and her travelling companion removed his earbuds in order to speak to them.

'I don't believe it.' Clemency laughed at her own stupidity. 'I'm such an idiot!'

The man turned to look at her. 'Sorry?'

'You! Those things!' She gestured to the earbuds in his right hand. 'I was chatting away to you earlier and you completely ignored me, so I stopped talking because I thought you didn't want to be disturbed. I couldn't see the wires from here because of the way you were sitting and your collar covered them up. But I can't believe I didn't realise the reason you were ignoring me was because you had headphones in.' Giddy with relief, she added, 'Well, I suppose

I was in a bit of a state, what with almost missing the flight . . . my brain felt as if it'd been whizzed up in a blender . . . Ooh dear, sorry, that sounds a bit—'

'Red wine, please,' the man said to the blonde flight attendant.

'Certainly, sir. And you, madam? Would you like something from the trolley?'

It was free. Free wine! Why would anyone say no? Except Clemency had observed on plenty of occasions that some people, for mystifying reasons of their own, did sometimes say no.

Ha, not her, though. She said, 'I'd like white wine, please. Oh . . . is it cold?' Because sometimes it wasn't.

The flight attendant wrinkled her nose conspiratorially and said, 'Not very, I'm afraid.'

'I'll have red, then.' Clemency smiled. 'Nothing worse than lukewarm white wine.' The next moment, seeing that her travelling companion was about to put the buds back into his ears, she added, 'I think I deserve a drink, to celebrate not missing this plane!'

'There you go.' The attendant passed them their mini bottles and plastic glasses, along with two airline-sized packets of cheese biscuits.

'Lovely. Thank you.' Clemency filled her glass, raised it towards the man next to her and said, 'Cheers!'

'Cheers,' murmured the man, before glancing back at his phone.

Sometimes persuading someone to make conversation when they didn't want to became a kind of personal challenge. Before he could plug himself back into his music, Clemency said brightly, 'Doesn't it always feel brilliant, having a glass of wine on a plane?'

5

'It does.' He looked pointedly out of the window.

'I wasn't late getting to the airport, you know,' Clemency told him. 'I had tons of time, which was why I spent ages in duty-free, and it wasn't until I reached the checkout that I discovered I'd put my passport down somewhere and for the life of me I couldn't think where I'd left it. Oh God, that *feeling*, though.' She clenched her free hand and clutched it to her chest at the awful memory. 'My heart was going like a train, I was trying to ask where it might have been handed in, and everyone in the queue behind me was getting annoyed because all they wanted to do was pay for their duty-free . . .'

For the second time Clemency's voice trailed off, giving him the chance to join in and say, 'So what happened next?'

Instead, after an awkward silence that seemed to last longer than Wagner's *Ring* cycle, he replied, 'But you found it.'

'Yes. Yes I did.' Clemency nodded and looked at the buds he was clearly longing to plug back into his ears. Carefully raising the tray in order to get out of her seat before lowering it again and resting her glass of wine on it, she said, 'Excuse me,' and escaped down the aisle.

How embarrassing to realise that whilst you've been merrily going through life thinking you were a perfectly nice travelling companion, the kind of person anyone might enjoy sitting next to, you might have been wrong. That you might, in fact, be the kind of irritating person other people *dread* being trapped with.

Chastened, Clemency stared at her reflection in the mirror above the tiny sink in the toilet cubicle. Oh dear, what a mortifying discovery to make. And that poor man, who had presumably been willing her to shut up and leave him alone instead of wittering on about her stupid passport . . . OK, she wouldn't utter another word from now on, wouldn't even glance at him.

Lesson learnt.

She left the cubicle and made her way back along the aisle. The man in the seat next to hers was gazing out of the window at the great swathes of cloud surrounding them. As Clemency lifted her glass of wine in order to raise the tray and sit back down, he turned and said, 'Want me to hold that for you?'

Hold the front page. He speaks!

But she had no intention of breaking her vow. With a little I'm-fine shake of her head, she put her handbag on the floor in front of her, then went to raise the tray in order to—

Oof . . .

The jolt of the plane was both sudden and dramatic, eliciting shrieks of alarm from several nervous passengers. Having lurched to one side and bounced off the seat in front of her, Clemency ricocheted back and felt rather than saw the contents of the glass hit her chest.

The plane righted itself, the screams and panic subsided and order was restored. From the cockpit, the pilot genially announced over the tannoy, 'Apologies for that spot of turbulence, ladies and gentlemen. If everyone could stay seated for the next couple of minutes and keep their seat belts fastened, we'll just make sure there aren't any more surprises to come.'

Clemency looked down at her pale yellow lacy cotton top, liberally splattered with red wine. The splashes were spreading, joining up into one vast purple splodge across her front. It was, of course, one of her all-time favourite items of clothing, because that was sod's law, wasn't it? You never got a drink thrown over you when you were wearing some ancient falling-to-pieces T-shirt.

'Whoops, poor you,' said one of the air stewards, hurrying down the aisle to check that everyone's seat belt was fastened. 'Sit down.'

'Oh dear,' said the man next to her as she sat.

Clemency glanced at him; he didn't have his earbuds in. She did a tiny shrug and felt the wet material cold against her skin. Urgh.

'I bet you wish you'd stuck with the lukewarm white wine now.'

This was like being in a silent movie. Clemency raised her hand briefly in a doesn't-matter gesture and reached for the riveting airline magazine in the seat pocket in front of her. Time to read about the dazzling tourist attractions of Malaga.

'Are you . . . not speaking to me?'

Ah, so he'd noticed. She turned to look at him, one eyebrow lifted quizzically. 'Sorry?'

'Are you deliberately ignoring me because you thought I was deliberately ignoring you?' There was a hint of amusement in his voice.

'Not at all,' said Clemency. 'I just thought you preferred not to be disturbed. I was respecting your wishes.'

Except it didn't come out like that; it came out as *wishies*. Like fishies.

Oh God . . .

'You were respecting my what?' The corners of his mouth were twitching now. 'My *wishies*?'

8

'Wishes.'

'You said wishies.'

'I was going to say I respected your personal boundaries,' said Clemency, 'but seeing as we were sitting next to each other, I decided at the last minute to change it to wishes.'

'But a bit of it got left behind.' He nodded. 'I like the sound of wishies.'

In an ideal world, she would have produced her own pair of earbuds at this point and fitted them into her ears. But her earbuds were in her big suitcase in the hold of the plane. Instead she said, 'Good,' and returned her attention to the magazine.

'Does this mean you're ignoring me again now?'

And when she looked across once more, he was smiling. With his beautiful mouth.

'What are you saying? That it's fine for you not to speak to me, but I'm not allowed to not-speak to you?'

He inclined his head and replied gravely, 'I'm sorry. I apologise. I didn't mean to be rude earlier, but I clearly was. And now I feel doubly guilty. May I at least offer you half of my drink?' He hadn't poured his wine out; it was still in the mini bottle. When she hesitated, he indicated her ruined top and said, 'May as well risk it. What's the worst that can happen?'

Clemency held out her empty glass. 'Well, the plane could crash.'

Sometimes, just sometimes, you decide you really don't like someone, then they go on to confound you by turning out to be about a million times nicer than you ever suspected.

His name was Sam, he lived in London and he owned

9

and ran an IT company that involved a lot of flying around Europe visiting clients. As soon as they were allowed to unfasten their seat belts, he indicated Clemency's top and said, 'If you give that a soak before the wine dries, there's a chance of saving it, isn't there? Do you have something you can change into?'

She shook her head. 'All my clothes are in my big case. It's OK.'

Sam leant down and unzipped the bag he'd stowed beneath the seat in front of him. He pulled out a navy V-necked sweater and handed it to her. 'Here you go, you can wear this. Don't worry, it's clean. Give your top a rinse in the sink and you might be able to rescue it.'

The sweater was incredibly soft to the touch. It also smelt amazing, Clemency discovered shortly afterwards in the toilet cubicle as she pulled it over her head and pushed the sleeves up in order to rinse her yellow top in the sink.

'Well?' said Sam when she returned.

Clemency dropped the wrung-out top into the sick bag he was holding open for her and tucked it under her seat. 'I think it's beyond help, but we'll see. Thanks for letting me borrow your sweater.' The smell of the soft wool was intoxicating; seriously, she kept wanting to bury her nose in it. Except that would look weird.

Sam's tone was genial. 'Not a problem. It suits you.'

'As soon as we get our cases back, I'll be able to change into something else.' Clemency stroked the wool fondly. 'It's lovely, though. You know, I once nearly died a horrible death because of a sweater like this.'

'How so?' Sam looked quizzical as she took a careful sip of the shared wine.

10

'It belonged to my sister and I borrowed it without asking. She caught me wearing it and tried to wrestle it off me, and I ended up hanging backwards out of my bedroom window with the sleeves tangled round my neck.'

Sam laughed. 'In that case, I promise I won't try to wrestle mine off you.'

'That's a relief.' The rogue thought that such a scenario might actually be quite exciting flitted through Clemency's brain. *Ooh-er.*

'And how old were you when this happened?'

'It was just the other week.' She waited, then broke into a grin. 'No, our wrestling days are behind us now. This was back when we were sixteen.'

Sam's eyebrows rose. 'You were both sixteen? So you're twins?'

Now that they'd turned towards each other and were having a proper conversation, she could see, up close, that his eyes were brown with flecks of gold radiating from their centres and a black outer ring around each iris. His lashes were black too. There were faint violet shadows beneath his eyes and a tiny mole on his right temple. And as for his mouth . . . well, it was still beautiful.

In fact, getting more beautiful by the minute.

Chapter 2

OK, concentrate. Sam had asked her a question and she couldn't just sit here gazing slack-jawed in wonder at his face.

'Not twins.' Clemency gathered herself. 'Well, not even sisters really. We're stepsisters.'

'Ah.' Picking up on her rueful tone, Sam said, 'And which of you is the elder?'

'Belle is. By two months, which she never, *ever* lets me forget. Makes all the difference apparently.'

'I can imagine. And how old were you when your parents got together?'

'Fifteen. It probably sounds funny now, but you can't imagine how traumatic it was at the time.' Clemency shook her head. 'We already knew each other, you see. Went to the same school. And we were just so completely different, we'd never got along together at all. Belle was perfect and organised, and quite show-offy because her dad was this multimillionaire and she'd grown up being given everything she ever wanted. Whereas me and my mum were living in a rented flat above a fish and chip shop where Mum worked sixty hours a week.' She smiled as she said it, because just yesterday, while she'd been staying with her mum and step-father at their glorious villa outside Malaga, they'd jokingly referred to 'the chip shop years'.

Sam said drily, 'I can see that it could be awkward.'

'God, tell me about it. Belle had a huge swimming pool in her back garden. The nearest we had to a garden was our window box. Her dad drove a pale blue Bentley Continental. My mum had a rusty clapped-out Fiesta. Belle used to make fun of my clothes, and me and my friends used to make fun of her and her friends. Then one day my mum sat me down and told me she'd been secretly seeing someone for the last six months and things were getting serious. And I was so *thrilled* for her, because for years I'd been longing for her to meet someone nice. I couldn't understand why she hadn't said anything before.' Clemency paused. 'Until she told me who it was she'd been seeing. And then I couldn't believe it. Nor could Belle, obviously, but for once in her life she wasn't able to get her own way and make it stop. We both prayed they'd realise they'd made a horrible mistake and break up, so that everything could go back to normal. But it just didn't happen, because they were properly in love. The next thing we knew, they'd announced that they were getting married. Is this boring?'

He looked startled. 'What? No!'

'OK, just needed to check.' After last time, she was wary. 'I bored you before. Don't want to do it again.'

Sam shook his head. 'Seriously, that wasn't you, it was me. Now I'm enthralled. Gripped.' He gestured with his left hand. 'Please continue. You can't stop now.'

His voice, beautifully modulated but not off-puttingly

posh, was the kind you'd never tire of listening to. Better still, now that he'd stopped being completely dismissive, it was warm and confiding, with a dash of humour. Clemency felt herself falling under his spell; was he as interested in her as she was in him? It was too soon to tell, but the faint possibility that he might be was sending little zings of anticipation down her spine.

'Well, everyone at school thought it was hilarious, but Belle and I were mortified. Belle was extra angry because she was convinced my mum was only marrying her dad for his money. Which drove me insane, because I knew my mum wasn't like that. And once you'd seen the two of them together, it was obvious how happy they were.' She shrugged. 'So that was that; we ended up having to be bridesmaids in matching dresses, which was a laugh. And after the wedding, me and Mum gave up our flat and moved into their great big house with the swimming pool in the garden and the Bentley on the driveway. Not to mention the stroppy step-sister who went ballistic whenever I borrowed her clothes.'

'Which, let me guess, just made it all the more fun to do.'

'Well of course it did! Because it was such a thrill when I got away with it. Who could resist a challenge like that? And her clothes were so much more expensive than mine,' added Clemency. 'Which made it better still.'

'So you were . . . what, sixteen by then? And both still at school? Weren't the two of you given the same amount of money to buy clothes?'

'Oh yes, we were. Her dad insisted on that. We got the same allowance, but at that age I was going through a surfing craze, so all my money went on wetsuits, traction pads and board wax. Out of the water, everything I wore came from

14

charity shops.' She grinned. 'Which of course meant Belle would rather go out stark naked than wear any of my dreadful clothes. So that was a win-win situation for me.'

Sam said, 'And did you both slightly enjoy having a go at each other?'

Ha, he knew.

'A bit. Sometimes. Me more than her,' Clemency admitted. 'What with us being the interlopers who moved into the house she'd grown up in. You can understand that, I suppose. And it was only for a couple of years, until we both left for university. How about you? Do you live on your own?'

OK, maybe not the subtlest way of asking the question, which presumably accounted for the brief moment of hesitation before Sam said, 'Yes, on my own.' He took a sip of his wine before continuing. 'But you should have seen the house I shared with six other students while I was at university. Actually, you can thank your lucky stars you didn't. What a health hazard that place was. There were real live toadstools growing in the bathroom.'

Clemency felt herself perk up like a meerkat. 'We had water dripping from a light fitting for months in our living room.'

'We used to have competitions to see who could eat the most out-of-date food.' Sam shook his head at the memory of just how gross it had all been.

'We once found a dead mouse in our fridge.'

He smiled. 'You're very competitive, aren't you?'

'Rate yourself for competitiveness,' Clemency said promptly. 'Out of ten.'

'Nine,' said Sam.

'Eleven.' She grinned. 'See? I win.'

15

They flew on, heading back to the UK, talking non-stop. Two more mini bottles of red wine were opened, and Clemency felt their connection deepen. There was an undeniable chemistry between them; at first she'd wondered if it was just on her side, but now she was pretty sure the feeling was mutual. When you found yourself on the receiving end of this much attention and the spark between you was almost palpable, it was kind of a giveaway.

And a very nice giveaway at that. The conversation had swooped and darted from one subject to the next, from teenage adventures to escapades on holiday in their twenties, from the various part-time jobs they'd undertaken over the years to all-time embarrassing moments.

'Mine was pretty awful.' Sam shuddered at the memory. 'I asked a client when her baby was due. She said, "I'm not pregnant, I'm just fat."'

'OK, I can beat that. This guy brought his little daughter into the café where I was working, and I said, "Ooh, is Daddy going to buy you an ice cream?" And the little girl looked all confused and the person with her said, "Actually, I'm her mum."'

Sam almost choked on his drink. '*God.*'

'I know! But . . . short hair, no make-up, jeans and a fleece . . . and in my defence, there was a definite hint of moustache.'

'What did you do?'

Clemency flapped her hand. 'The obvious. Apologised like crazy and told them I was registered blind. Then I served them coffee and ice cream and pretended I was counting out the money by feeling the coins. They sat in the café for thirty minutes, and the whole time I had to

16

make out I was doing everything by touch . . . OK, you can stop laughing now, it wasn't funny at the time. I was eighteen and mortified.'

The captain's voice came over the tannoy. 'Ladies and gentlemen, can you make sure your seat belts are fastened . . . we're now beginning our descent.'

And for the first time in her life Clemency wished a flight could have lasted longer. But hopefully this wouldn't be the last she'd be seeing of this particular travelling companion. Once the plane landed, Sam would be heading into London and she'd be making her way back to Northampton, which wasn't the most ideal of situations. But it wasn't completely ridiculous either. When two people liked each other, a bit of commuting might sometimes need to be factored into the equation. And from Northampton to north London was only . . . what, sixty-odd miles? That was doable.

In her imagination, Clemency realised, she was already picturing them driving to meet each other, or catching trains, the excitement of seeing each other again more than making up for the slight inconvenience involved. And who knew, maybe if things progressed nicely, it might even make sense for her to leave Northampton and search for a job in London . . . unless Sam wanted to move out of the capital to be with her . . .

OK, this was like being a teenager, scribbling your first name and your new boyfriend's surname all over your school exercise books just to see how they'd look together if you got married. Though she didn't even know Sam's surname and couldn't ask him what it was in case he guessed why she wanted to know. Ah, but once they'd managed to retrieve their cases from the luggage carousel, she would give him one of her business cards and hopefully he'd return the compliment.

They landed safely – always a bonus – and made their way through passport control, then waited at baggage reclaim for their cases. Clemency's was one of the first ones to appear on the carousel and she lifted it off with relief.

'OK, don't go anywhere. I'll be two minutes.' Having unzipped her case and rummaged through it, she pulled out a red stripy top and waved it at Sam. 'There's a loo down the corridor – I'll go and change in there, then you can have your sweater back. Oh, and take this as well.' As an apparently careless and casual afterthought, she handed him one of the business cards that had been tucked into a side pocket inside her case. 'Right, I'll be back in no time.'

Then, because Sam was gazing intently at her rather than at the luggage carousel, she added, 'Mind you don't miss your case!'

In the ladies' loo there was a queue for the cubicles. At last it was her turn. Clemency changed out of Sam's top into her own, then gave his sweater one last lingering sniff, committing the scent of it to memory. Although hopefully she would smell it again soon, maybe when they said goodbye to each other a few minutes from now and he gave her a kiss on the cheek.

Or on the mouth . . .

OK, doing it again, stop it. Expertly reversing her cases and manoeuvring them out of the cubicle, Clemency prepared to make her way back to the carousel. Oh, but what if Sam murmured, 'I'm not ready to say goodbye yet. Can I buy you dinner?'

And after that: 'Now I'm definitely not ready to say

goodbye. Do you have to go back to Northampton tonight, or could I persuade you to stay?'

Could he? That was the question. Clemency felt herself quiver with anticipation; she was so clearly able to picture Sam's face and hear his voice as he issued the invitation.

Oh, who was she trying to kid? Of course she would stay. Today, meeting him on the flight, had felt like one of those defining, life-altering events.

If Sam were to ask her to spend the night with him, there was no way in the world she'd say no.

But when she reached the carousel, there was no sign of him.

Which was unexpected, but presumably meant he'd decided to visit the men's loo before making the journey home.

After loitering at a discreet distance for several minutes, Clemency headed over there, pushed open the door and called out, 'Sam, are you in here?'

Silence. Until a man shouted back, 'Yeah, darlin', that's me, I'm Sam. Couldn't come over and give me a hand, could you? Ha ha ha . . .'

She let the door swing shut. All of a sudden the happy-fantasy-that-was-about-to-become-reality appeared to be veering wildly off course. How could Sam have vanished?

Her heart clattering, Clemency made her way through customs. Still no sign of him anywhere. Emerging into the arrivals hall, she searched the sea of faces without success. Hastily she checked her phone to see if he'd texted her, but no. Nothing.

What was going on? This made no sense at all.

Out through the revolving doors she went, because where

else could she search for him in a huge airport? If he'd left a car here and had headed for one of the car parks, she'd never find him, but if he were getting a cab . . .

Except why was she even doing this? She'd given him her business card – if he wanted to be in touch, he had her number. It was just that it was so completely unexpected. Apart from anything else, she still had his navy sweater. And it wasn't just any old sweater; this one was cashmere.

Seconds later, she spotted him. It was only the back of his head, but it was definitely him. Feeling as if she'd been hit in the stomach by a medicine ball, Clemency dragged her cases behind her until she was alongside him. He was waiting in the long queue for a cab, facing directly ahead, jaw visibly tense.

Why? *Why?*

One thing was for sure: she wasn't going to ask.

'Here you go.' She held the sweater in front of him. 'Thanks for letting me borrow it.'

For a split second she glimpsed a world of pain mingled with guilt in his eyes. Then he took the sweater from her and slowly shook his head. 'I'm really sorry.'

Clearly this was the end of the line; the connection between them had been as fleeting as it had been fun. And now it was over, the shortest holiday romance in history.

Clemency said, 'Me too,' and turned away.

He caught up with her twenty seconds later, his hand reaching for her arm to stop her in her tracks.

'OK, I need to explain.' He looked . . . agonised. There was no other word for it.

'You don't have to. It's not rocket science. I'm guessing you have a girlfriend or a fiancée.' He wasn't wearing a wedding ring, but she said it anyway. 'Or a wife.'

'I do.' Sam nodded.

'Girlfriend?'

He exhaled and said evenly, 'Wife.'

Oh. Right. 'And you just forgot to mention her before. Not that there's any reason why you should,' Clemency amended. What had they done, after all, other than sit next to each other and pass the time of day during what would otherwise have been a dull flight?

Except they both knew it had been more, so much more than that.

'I didn't forget.' Sam hesitated, as if searching for the right words. 'I . . . put it to the back of my mind.'

Like thousands of other married men the world over. And women too. It wasn't as if he'd committed some heinous crime. If anything, Clemency envied his wife for having married a man with scruples and enough of a conscience to stay on the straight and narrow.

Lucky old her.

'Oh well, it was nice to meet you anyway.' Crushing disappointment was one thing, but she couldn't be cross. She added on impulse, 'Did you look at my business card?'

'No.' He shook his head and it was clear that he was telling the truth. 'No I didn't.'

Good. 'OK, this is going to sound weird, but can I have it back?' She felt herself flush. 'It's just that I'm . . . um, running a bit low.'

The real reason was so she wouldn't have to spend the next few weeks wondering if he might, against all the odds, be in touch. It would be so much easier to simply remove the possibility that that could happen.

'Sorry, I don't have it. It's in the bin next to the newspaper

21

stand in Arrivals. If you want, I could go back and get it for you . . .'

Of course he'd thrown her card away; why would he even want to keep it? His wife might come across it and wonder what he'd been up to. *God, just for a few seconds, she'd forgotten he had a wife.*

'No, it's fine, doesn't matter.' Clemency looked at him, taking in every detail of his face for the last time. With a brief smile, because she really was leaving now, she said, 'I'm not that desperate.'

'I wish things could have been different.' Sam put his hand out to clasp hers, before stopping himself as if she were radioactive.

Wishing she'd just kept the nice sweater now, Clemency said wryly, 'But they aren't.'

Chapter 3

Three years later

Really, was there anything better than arriving back at the office at the end of a long day and discovering an empty parking space waiting for you right outside?

Well, there probably *wouldn't* be anything better, but right now Clemency couldn't really say, because she'd just missed out on the prize parking space. Having beaten her by mere seconds, Ronan had expertly reversed into it and was now grinning at her as he climbed out of his Audi.

'Too slow, Clem. You snooze, you lose.'

As if she had time for a snooze. Clemency shook her head sorrowfully at him and said, 'If you were a real gentleman, you'd let me take that space.'

'And if I offered it to you, you'd call me a sexist pig. Like the time you had a flat tyre and I offered to change the wheel for you, remember?'

'That was because you assumed I couldn't do it myself.'

'I did assume that, and I was wrong. You're an excellent

23

wheel-changer.' Ronan's smile broadened as he jangled his keys. 'But I'm still not moving.'

'In that case,' said Clemency, 'the ice creams are on you.'

She drove on up the steep winding hill to the crowded car park, squeezed her own car into a tight space between a purple camper van and a dusty black Volvo, then made her way on foot back down the hill to the office.

The Barton and Byrne estate agency had been set up by Gavin Barton over twenty years previously. Seven years ago he'd headhunted Ronan Byrne and taken him on as his whizz-kid sales negotiator, and three years ago they'd become business partners. Gavin was now in his late fifties and keen to reduce his golf handicap. Ronan, now thirty-one, was the energetic one who loved to sell properties and was prepared to put in the hours necessary to keep the company on track.

Two years ago, they'd waved goodbye to a junior sales negotiator who'd soon discovered the job wasn't for him, and had been preparing to advertise for a replacement when Clemency had happened to come home to St Carys for a long weekend to see her mother.

'Did you know Gavin and Ronan are looking to take someone on?' Lizzie, her mum, had mentioned it in passing on her first evening back.

'Hey, there's a job going at Gav's,' said Baz, Clemency's stepfather, when he joined them for dinner a couple of hours later. 'I reckon you'd be good at that.'

'But I've got a job,' Clemency reminded him. 'In Northampton. And I like selling cars.'

'You like selling,' Baz pointed out. 'Houses are exactly the same as cars. They just don't have wheels.'

The next afternoon she bumped into Ronan Byrne in

the Mermaid Inn. When she'd finished giving him a hug – *mmm, muscles* – he said, 'Have you heard we're looking for someone to replace Hugo?'

'I have heard that,' said Clemency. 'And before you ask me, I'm happy where I am.'

'Well that's good, because I wasn't going to ask you.' His eyes glittered with amusement. 'I don't think you'd be up to the job anyway.'

Clemency bridled. 'I can do anything I put my mind to. If I can sell a car, I can sell a house. I sold a Lamborghini last week.'

'No offence.' Ronan's tone was dismissive. 'But selling property is harder than it looks.'

A week later, Gavin called to tell her she had the job. Overjoyed, Clemency said, 'That's fantastic! I didn't think you'd take me on, what with Ronan saying I wasn't up to it. Are you sure he's going to be OK about working with me?'

And Gavin, chuckling into the phone, had replied, 'Darling girl, it was Ronan's idea in the first place. I said you probably wouldn't be interested and he told me to leave it with him.'

A little playful goading was all it had taken. She'd fallen for it, been outwitted by a pro. Not that Clemency had been too bothered; when she'd first been offered the position in Northampton by a friend of her mother's, she'd been flattered and delighted to accept, but after four years, the lure of Cornwall had been proving increasingly hard to resist. As the only saleswoman on the staff of a huge showroom selling high-end cars, she'd loved the job, but had been growing weary of the endless talk about sport, fantasy football teams, more sport and World of Warcraft. Furthermore, what with being between boyfriends at the time, there'd been nothing to keep her in Northampton, and working as an estate agent would be an interesting new challenge.

This was how, along with so many other people who'd grown up living beside the sea, Clemency had found herself realising she wanted to return to St Carys in Cornwall, one of the loveliest holiday destinations in the south-west. And it had turned out to be the best decision she could have made. Her mother and Baz had tried to persuade her to move back into her old bedroom at Polrennick House, but she'd chosen instead to take out a lease on a tiny one-bed flat above a newsagent's. Too small to rent out to holidaymakers, it was also noisy in the early mornings because Meryl, who ran the shop downstairs, liked to clatter around and sing at the top of her voice as she sorted the newspapers and readied the place for the day. But the flat was quirky and cosy, and if you leant right out of the sitting room window, you could just about catch a glimpse of the sea.

'It's OK, here she is now,' Ronan announced as Clemency pushed open the door to the estate agency. 'Panic over.'

He was addressing his mother, Josephine, who rolled her eyes. 'I wasn't panicking, I just didn't want you to eat all the buns before Clem turned up. Hello, my lovely girl, how are you?' Josephine gave Clemency a warm hug. 'Because we both know what he's like, don't we? I wouldn't put it past him. He's eaten five already.'

'You need to guard them with your life. Can you hear that noise?' Clemency patted her rumbling stomach. 'That's because I'm so hungry. I swear I could smell them as I was

26

coming down the hill. Josephine, what would we do without you? You're an angel. Thank you so much.'

When she'd first come to work here, Clemency had thought the best thing about Ronan Byrne was his utter lack of interest in both football and World of Warcraft. It had taken only a couple of weeks to discover that the very best thing about him was actually his mother. Well, his mother and her habit of turning up with baskets of home-cooked food. Born in Barbados, Josephine had come to the UK as a teenager and now ran a small but popular Caribbean restaurant in Newquay. She was both a wonderful cook and a doting mother to her only child. Her belief that he would fade away if she didn't regularly bring essential supplies was shamelessly fostered by Ronan, who adored his mother's food and also knew how much she loved to feed him. Today it was Josephine's famous jerk chicken buns served with spicy lime mayonnaise.

Clemency took a mouthful and feigned a swoon, because the light-as-air bun with its filling of chicken and BBQ jerk sauce was just sublime. She spooned mayo over the rest of the bun and shook her head. 'Best ever.'

Josephine beamed with pride and patted her arm. 'You always say that.'

'Because it's always true.'

'Has he been behaving himself?' Josephine indicated her son with a tilt of her head.

'Always,' said Ronan, before Clemency could reply.

Still addressing Clemency, Josephine said, 'And has he met anyone yet?'

'Mum, I promise you. When it happens, you'll be the first to know.'

Poor Josephine, she was longing for Ronan to settle down. 'You need to try harder,' she said now. 'Find a nice girl, put a ring on her finger, have beautiful babies . . . Don't laugh at me, Ronan, I'm serious.' Her Barbadian accent grew more pronounced as she made her plea. 'You're a good-looking boy, you've got the personality, you could have any girl you want!'

'I know.' Ronan grinned. 'Isn't it great?'

'But you're not so young any more,' Josephine pointed out. 'You're thirty-one. What if you start to lose your looks? Leave it too long and you could seriously regret it, I'm telling you. Like your uncle Maurice . . . Once he turned thirty, he lost it all! His hair dropped out, he grew extra chins and none of the pretty girls would look at him twice any more. You don't want to end up like Uncle Maurice, do you?'

Ronan said, 'Now I'm so depressed, I need to eat another bun.'

Josephine smiled and shook her head at Clemency. 'Tell him he needs to listen to his mother. OK, I must head back. I'll see you both soon. And just remember.' She tapped her son's chest with an admonishing finger. 'I have seventeen nieces and nephews. It wouldn't kill you to give me a grandson.'

She kissed them both goodbye and left the office in a swirl of fuchsia pink. Moments later they heard the toot of her car horn and a squeal of tyres as she drove off.

'Listen to her,' said Ronan. 'She's going to get another speeding ticket, and this time she's not going to be able to charm her way out of it.'

Clemency ate another bun. 'I love your mum.'

'She's not bad,' said Ronan. 'I chose well.'

'Although technically, she chose you.'

Ronan gave Clemency his smouldering, knock-'em-dead look. 'Ah, but only because I wanted her to.'

They worked companionably together at their separate desks, finishing up the paperwork for the day. At 5.30, they closed the office and made their way down to Paddy's Café. This had long been a part of their routine; unless there were viewings or other unavoidable appointments, they called into the café for a drink and an ice cream before heading off to their respective homes. Run by brother-and-sister team Paddy and Dee, it was situated on the quayside, with a cordoned-off seating area at the front affording uninterrupted views of the beach, the boats and the turquoise sea glittering beyond the harbour walls.

Paddy's Café did huge amounts of business during the day, but this was their quieter time, when holidaymakers started to leave the beaches and think about their evening meal. Bagging themselves one of the coveted tables in pole position outside, Clemency waved at Marina, who was busy with one of the artworks she sold from her own corner of the seating area.

'OK,' said Ronan, taking out his wallet. 'My shout. What are you having?'

'Raspberry pavlova ice cream and a cappuccino,' said Clemency. 'Please.'

He went up to the counter to be served by Dee. Clemency sat back to watch as Marina, over at her easel, deftly fitted a family of four into the painting of the stretch of beach beyond the harbour walls. The family were sitting together in front of her, smiling and sunburnt. Marina, who completed

29

the various beach scenes in her own time, was able to add in the characters in just a few minutes, meaning that even small children didn't have time to get wriggly and bored. She used a mixture of watercolour pencils and artist's felt-tip pens, so there was hardly any drying time involved. In less than quarter of an hour, a family could commission and receive a finished piece of art featuring characters that were recognisably them, wearing their own clothes.

The family, Clemency could hear, were down here on holiday from Leeds. They were chattering away to Marina about their joy at having discovered St Carys, asking her if she'd always lived in Cornwall.

Marina shook her head. 'No, I grew up in Oxford, but we always used to come down here on holiday when I was little. I loved it so much. Then a few years ago my husband decided it was time for a divorce. It seemed like a good idea to move away, and I decided the place I'd most like to live was St Carys.' She smiled at the family. 'It was absolutely the best decision I could have made. I've never been happier.'

'So your husband did you a favour,' said the woman with a laugh. 'Getting that divorce turned out to be a good thing.'

'Oh absolutely.' Marina nodded in agreement.

'You'd better watch out.' The woman gave her husband a playful nudge. 'This is giving me ideas.'

Spotting Clemency watching them, Marina winked at her and carried on working. She'd made light of the situation as always; the full story of her divorce was actually far from amusing and pretty traumatic. But that wasn't what strangers wanted to hear while they were having their portraits painted. They were here on holiday, which meant that fun and escapism was the order of the day.

Clemency's phone burst into life. When the name flashed up on the screen, she was tempted to let it go to voicemail.

Except Belle would know she'd done it on purpose.

OK, let's be nice to each other, like proper grown-ups.

'Hi, Belle! How are you?'

'Good, thanks. Now, how are you fixed for tomorrow?'

'Er . . . I'm working tomorrow. Why?'

'I know you're working. I'm asking how you'd be fixed for showing us around a few decent properties. We're talking the luxury end of the market, high spec, sea views, something pretty special.'

'Us?' Clemency's eyebrows rose. 'Is this for you?'

'For my boyfriend. He's interested in buying a holiday home and we're flying down tomorrow morning. If you're busy, it's fine, I can call Rossiter's instead. I just thought, you know, it'd be nice to give you the chance to make a good sale. If you've got anything suitable, that is!'

'I'm sure we can rustle up a few possibilities.' *You see? This is why it's so hard to treat Belle like a normal grown-up.* 'Whereabouts is he wanting to buy?'

'Anywhere in Cornwall. I tell you what, why don't you email me the—'

'I'll email the details of everything that seems like a good fit, and you can let me know which ones he'd like to see. How long will you be down here for? Just tomorrow?'

'Tomorrow and Saturday morning, flying back in the afternoon. He wants to find something and get it sorted in one go. That's the kind of person he is,' Belle explained, the pride evident in her voice. 'Doesn't like to hang around. Once he makes up his mind, that's it.'

'I get it. He's decisive,' said Clemency. 'That's fine, decisive is good. I like that in a client.'

So long as it was one of her properties they were buying.

'Wait until you see him.' Unable to help herself, Belle said, 'Seriously, you're going to be *so* jealous.'

Clemency doubted it. Belle had always had a tendency to go out with noisy, brash public-school types who loved to brag about how wealthy their families were. But to be diplomatic she said, 'Anyone looking to spend plenty of money on a property sounds great to me.'

'OK, send me whatever you have and I'll be in touch. Actually, I'll be seeing what Rossiter's has to offer too. May as well.'

'Silly not to,' Clemency replied, because dissing rival estate agencies was something you never did, no matter how tempting it might be. 'OK, let me get on to that now.'

'How's Ronan? Will he be around?' Belle's tone was elaborately casual.

'Not sure. Possibly. He's right here.' Clemency grinned, because Ronan had returned to the table. 'Do you want to say hello?'

'No, it's fine. We might see him tomorrow. Right, I must dash . . . loads to do . . . Bye-ee!'

And that was it, the phone had already gone dead. Belle always loved to be the first to end a call; it seemed to give her a feeling of one-upmanship.

Chapter 4

'Wild guess,' said Ronan. 'That was Belle.'

'She's coming down tomorrow. *Flying* down tomorrow,' Clemency amended, to let him know that they should both be suitably impressed. 'With her fabulous new boyfriend. I expect she wants to make you jealous.'

When he'd first arrived in St Carys, Belle had developed quite the crush on Ronan; she'd been *very* keen to get to know him better. Her interest in him might not have been returned, but it had certainly provided Clemency with endless hours of entertainment.

'Hmm. Well if she's got herself a boyfriend, I should be safe.' Ronan indicated the notes she'd scribbled on a paper napkin. 'What's he after?'

She told him, and between them they began drawing up a list of potential properties that might fit the bill for Belle's rich new boyfriend. Clemency ate her pavlova ice cream and, when it was all gone, dunked the pointy end of the waffle cone into her cappuccino because she knew it drove Ronan mad when she did that.

He shook his head in disbelief. 'You're revolting.'

Clemency beamed as she bit the soggy end off the cone. 'I know.'

The holidaying family of four left the café with their finished portrait, and Marina packed up her easel and art equipment for the day. She paused at Clemency and Ronan's table and tut-tutted good-naturedly. 'Are you two still working? Mind you don't burn yourselves out.'

'Says the woman who never stops,' Clemency reminded her. 'How many have you sold today?'

'Nine. It's been good.' Marina shifted the large, unwieldy bag on her shoulder. 'It doesn't feel like work when you're having fun, though, does it?'

Ronan indicated the family now heading away from them as they made their way along the beach. 'They seemed really happy with their painting.'

'I know. It's still a thrill.' Marina smiled at him. 'They were lovely people too.'

'And what are you doing tonight?' said Clemency. 'Anything nice?'

'Oh, extremely nice. Poor Alf's still getting over his chest infection, so I'm going to be taking Boo out for a walk. And after that I'm babysitting Ben and Amy.' Marina spread her hands. 'So basically, couldn't be better!'

'You're like Superwoman,' said Ronan. And Clemency smiled because it was true, she was. Alf was Marina's eighty-six-year-old neighbour. Ben and Amy were the hyperactive three-year-old twins who lived with their exhausted parents across the road from Marina's whitewashed cottage on Harris Street. Here at the café, whenever Paddy and Dee needed an extra pair of hands to help out, Marina was always the first to volunteer. Basically, if anyone was ever in need of a lift, a favour or a bit of assistance with an overgrown garden, she was more than happy to oblige. In the five years since she'd moved to St Carys, she'd forged a place for herself in the heart of the community, and her love for the little town and its inhabitants had been returned in full.

'Ah well, how else would I keep myself occupied?' Marina deftly retied the turquoise ribbon that held her auburn hennaed curls away from her face. 'Sit and twiddle my thumbs? Anyway, I only do what I want to do. If someone needs a hand with something, it's nice to be able to help out.'

'There's such a thing as too nice, though.' Ronan shook his head at her. 'Don't go letting people take advantage.'

'Don't worry, I'm not a complete pushover.' Her amber eyes sparkled. 'I'm a better judge of character now than I used to be, thank God!'

She waved goodbye and left the café. Moments later, they watched as she greeted one of the local hoteliers before crouching down to ruffle the ears of his boisterous, waggy-tailed beagle.

'She's probably offering to knit the dog a coat,' Ronan observed.

'Seriously, though, why do bad things happen to good people? Whatever happened to karma?'

'Maybe she's not good. Maybe she's actually a secret agent, a sinister assassin masquerading as a lovable artist.'

Clemency shook her head. 'God, her husband must have been such a bastard to do what he did.'

The next morning, Clemency waited in her car outside the first of the three viewings she'd arranged for Belle and her new boyfriend.

Hopefully he wouldn't be as pernickety as Belle, who had already texted to announce that she'd checked out one of the other shortlisted properties on Google Earth and there was no way they'd want to see it, because who in their right mind would want to live opposite a betting shop?

When in fact a lot of people would find it quite handy.

Oh well, maybe this chap of hers was addicted to gambling and she was just being protective.

Clemency checked her watch; it was now ten past eleven. When she'd called Belle earlier to explain that eleven was the earliest they could begin because she had a viewing with another client at ten, Belle had sighed and said, 'Can't you cancel them?'

Now, presumably, she was being punished for not having done so. Reaching across and flipping open the glove compartment, Clemency took out her secret stash of lemon sherbets and popped one into her mouth. That usually had the sod's-law effect of making people turn up.

And yes, yet again it worked like a charm. Less than twenty seconds later, a black Lexus drew up in front of her and there was Belle, waving at her from her position in the passenger seat.

Clemency smiled despite herself, raised a hand in recognition and bit into the lemon sherbet; from experience she knew it was possible to crunch the outer shell to smithereens and swallow it in under twenty seconds. And since she could do that whilst greeting Belle, no need to wait in the car.

The Lexus was now efficiently parked. Both doors opened. Belle, the first to emerge, was wearing a long, floaty spaghetti-strapped white dress that could well be her way of subliminally suggesting to the new boyfriend that she'd make a stunning bride. Slim brown arms outstretched, she advanced on Clemency. 'It's my little sister!' she cried. 'Come here, you!'

Which didn't always happen; you never knew for sure how you might be greeted by Belle. It tended to depend on who was watching.

Closing her own driver's door, Clemency moved forward for a Hollywood-style hug, crunching the lemon sherbet into glassy splinters en route. Belle clutched her by the elbows and exclaimed, 'Wow, you look so *well*,' which was her way of saying fat.

Luckily Clemency knew she wasn't fat; she was normal. Whereas Belle had been known to point at photos of super-models and remark that they were looking a bit chubby.

They embraced, and Clemency breathed in the expensive scent her stepsister always wore. As she did so, she glanced over Belle's shoulder at the new boyfriend, just as he removed his sunglasses.

Fizzy sherbet and pieces of hard lemon shell collided with a sharp intake of breath and Clemency did one of those convulsive coughs you just couldn't hold down. Before she had a chance to turn her head away, shards of lemon and droplets of sherbety saliva sprayed over Belle's chest.

'Aaarrgh, you are SO GROSS.'

'I'm sorry, I'm sorry, I couldn't help it . . .'

'Have you ever heard of covering your mouth?' squealed Belle.

'You were holding my elbows!' Clemency spluttered, desperately scrabbling in her bag for a tissue and quite unable to look at Belle's boyfriend, who was Sam. Oh God, it was him, it was actually *him*. Starting to cough again in earnest, she backed away and clapped her hands over her mouth, her streaming eyes, her whole face . . .

'Look at my dress,' Belle wailed. 'You're like some kind of animal!'

But Clemency could hardly hear her; it was as if her stepsister were burbling away from inside a box, whilst on top of the box stood a town crier with a giant megaphone bellowing, 'It's Sam, IT'S SAM, *IT'S SAM.*'

'I'm sorry, it was an accident.' Having located a tissue, Clemency wiped her eyes. 'I'm sure we can give it a wash and it'll be fine.'

The last time she'd seen Sam, she'd managed to spill red wine over herself. Coughing and spraying sherbet over someone else was, on balance, probably worse.

Even if the someone else was Belle.

Finally she risked a glance at him and saw that he was looking equally taken aback by the situation.

'It had better be.' Belle was still looking utterly repulsed. 'I only bought this dress last week. Oh well, I suppose I should be used to it by now.' As if getting food sprayed at her by her stepsister was something that happened on a tediously regular basis.

'Anyway. Sorry again,' said Clemency.

'Oh, *fine.*' Belle shook her head with resignation. 'Well, we're here. Sam, this is Clem. Clem, Sam Adams.'

Sam was looking directly at her. Clemency looked back at him. This was the moment during which one of them needed to smile and say, 'Actually, we've met before.' Then they could explain that they'd sat next to each other during a flight, marvel at the coincidence and effortlessly move on with the viewing.

That was all that needed to happen.

The moment paused, hovered in the air between them for a second, then moved on. It was now too late to say it. Sam held out his hand. 'Hello.'

Clemency shook it and heard herself say, 'Hi.'

Like two complete strangers meeting each other for the first time.

'So.' Sam nodded slightly. 'Shall we have a look at this apartment, then?'

'Absolutely.' Taking her cue from him, she jangled the keys in her hand. 'Let's do it. Let's see if we can find you the perfect place.'

Not to be left out, Belle said, 'Plus, let's see if I can wash this gross stuff off the front of my dress.'

The second-floor apartment was decorated in seaside shades of pale green and blue. It was clean and modern, with a huge kitchen and two good-sized bedrooms. When Belle disappeared into the silver and white bathroom to clean the sticky sherbet stains off her dress, she left the door wide open so there was no opportunity for an in-depth private conversation.

But while the taps were running, Clemency murmured, 'So you're not married any more.'

Sam didn't even look at her; he was standing gazing out of the window. Keeping his own voice quiet, he said, 'Clearly not.'

'When she told you she had a stepsister called Clemency, did you wonder if it might be me?'

He shook his head. 'She didn't mention your name. I didn't know.'

The taps stopped running and within seconds Belle

rejoined them, patting the wet patch on her dress with a white hand towel. 'It's come out.'

'Good,' said Sam. 'Panic over.'

She gestured around them. 'What's the verdict on this place, then?'

He shrugged. 'It's great. But I wouldn't say it was . . . you know . . .'

'Love at first sight?' said Belle. Which gave Clemency a bit of a jolt.

Sam didn't miss a beat. 'Something like that.' He tipped his head in agreement. 'And we're in Penzance. Which is stunning, clearly, but that bit further from the airport. OK, we're crossing this one off the list. Where next?'

'The cottage in Perranporth,' said Clemency. 'Um, you've got a ladybird on your shirt . . .' The temptation to reach over and brush it away was almost overwhelming.

Before she could do it, thankfully, Belle flicked the insect off and briefly rested the flat of her hand against Sam's chest, smiling up at him. 'Come on, let's go.'

The cottage in Perranporth, forty minutes away from Penzance, was picturesque and situated on a steep hill.

'Now this is different,' said Sam. 'I do like it. But I'm seeing a problem.'

'I know. Parking,' said Clemency. 'I did warn you.'

'I meant this.' He pointed as a gaggle of tourists paused on the street outside, took several photos of the cottage, then came up to the living-room window and peered right in. The mother of the group, wearing a too-tight purple T-shirt with a picture of Barry Manilow on the front, shielded her eyes from the sun's glare and squashed her nose up against the glass. Spotting Clemency, she gleefully announced, 'Ooh, look at that, there are people inside, I can see them! Coo-eee!'

'She's *waving* at us.' Belle shrank back in horror.

'You could always put up net curtains.' Clemency was struggling to keep a straight face. 'If you were a net-curtainy type of person.'

Drily, Sam replied, 'Which I'm probably not.'

And Clemency felt her stomach do a sudden swooping dive, because he was giving her the look she remembered so vividly from three years ago, the look she'd – much to her own embarrassment – never been able to forget.

Because sometimes it didn't matter how many times you jabbed the delete button, the thing you were trying to remove from your brain simply refused to disappear.

Chapter 5

By two o'clock, they'd arrived in St Carys, where the
third of the shortlisted properties was situated.

'Here we are, then.' Jumping out of the hire car and
shielding her eyes from the sun as she peered up at the third-
floor apartment, Belle said, 'It's like "Goldilocks and the Three
Bears", isn't it? The first place was too boring, the second
place was too interesting. Let's hope this one is going to be
just right.'

Obviously Belle wanted it to be the one Sam chose. Then
he'd be right here in her own home town. Clemency, who
wasn't so sure how she felt about it, was torn. It went against
the grain to *not* want to sell a property, but just seeing Sam
again today had been unsettling. Did she really want him to
buy a place in St Carys? Yet the apartment was stunning.
Once he clapped eyes on it, was there the remotest chance
he'd say no?

Five minutes later, she discovered the answer to that question.
The views were fantastic. Everything about the place was about
as perfect as any potential owner could want. The wraparound
balcony was big enough to throw a party on . . .

Which was apparently what was happening right now, in the penthouse apartment directly above their heads.

In fact it was sounding like quite an *intimate* party. Oh God.

'Listen to them,' Belle exclaimed, slow on the uptake. 'What is going *on* up there?

Sam, who wasn't slow on the uptake, said wryly, 'I think it might be some kind of exercise class.'

As an estate agent, it wasn't the first time Clemency had overheard something she'd have preferred not to overhear during the course of a viewing, but this was without a doubt the loudest.

And appeared to involve the largest number of . . . well, participants.

OK, this was officially awkward.

'Oh!' The penny finally dropped and Belle clapped her hands over her mouth. 'Oh my *God.*'

Overhead, the gasps and shrieks appeared to be escalating. Belle said, 'I don't believe it! Clem, make it *stop.*'

'Seriously?' Clemency looked at her. 'How do I go about doing that?'

'Oh for heaven's sake!' Marching out on to the balcony, Belle bellowed, 'Hey you! Up there! We can all hear you, you know . . . You have to stop making that noise this minute!'

They heard laughter amid the other sounds, followed by the pop of a champagne cork, which sailed over the edge of the balcony. A male voice called out, 'We like it best when we know people are listening.'

'Well you're disgusting,' Belle yelled back, 'and you should all be *ashamed* of yourselves.'

'Don't knock it till you've tried it,' a female voice shouted down to them. 'Come up and join us if you want. Don't be shy! The more the merrier!'

As they were leaving, they encountered the occupier of the flat below the one they'd just viewed. Clemency stopped the middle-aged woman. 'Hi, excuse me . . . do you happen to know if the people in the penthouse apartment are the owners? Or is it let out to holidaymakers?'

Because if they were only going to be staying for a week or two, it wouldn't be a problem after all.

'You mean the Carters?' The middle-aged woman rolled her eyes. 'You're from the estate agents, aren't you? And this is the first time you've heard them having an orgy? Well all I can say is, lucky you. They bought the place in January and they've been inviting their so-called friends around most afternoons ever since.'

'Oh.' Clemency's heart sank.

'The Jeffersons didn't happen to mention that to you, I'm guessing? Thought they wouldn't. Why else do you suppose they're so desperate to move out? God only knows how you're ever going to sell that place. Those new people are a living nightmare.'

Oh dear. The Jeffersons should have told them. Not only had Clemency failed to find Sam a suitable property to buy, they were going to have to drop the price of this one.

'Maybe you could offer any buyers a lifetime's supply of industrial earplugs,' said Sam.

When a problem occurs and people are desperate, they'll call their estate agent at any time of the day or night. At nine o'clock that evening, Clemency emerged from the shower to hear her phone ringing. The initial thought flashing through her brain was that Sam had got hold of her number and was desperate to speak to her about the situation between the two of them.

No, don't even think it. God, though, it was just so weird that at this very moment he was right here in St Carys, less than half a mile away, staying the night with Belle at Polrennick House.

Were they sharing a bed?

OK, *really* stop thinking about it. Dripping water from the shower all over the carpet, Clemency picked up her phone and said, 'Hi, Cissy, everything OK?' because of course it wasn't Sam calling her.

'No,' wailed Cissy Lambert, who was never knowingly underdramatic. 'Everything is *not* OK!'

Maybe she'd just discovered her baby grand piano was going to have to be lifted by crane out of the front window, or the floor tiles in her new house didn't exactly match her favourite shoes.

'Tell me what's wrong.' Clemency adopted the kind of reassuring tone people like Cissy Lambert quite often needed to calm them down when they were on the verge of exchanging contracts and their last-minute nerves were in shreds.

'Oh God, I can't bear it. The sale's fallen through,' Cissy screeched painfully into her ear. 'Those fucking fuckers have only gone and *fucking pulled out.*'

'What?' Belle's voice was crackly over the phone. 'I can't hear you.'

There was a buzz of background noise, of music and

45

voices interspersed with bursts of laughter. Clemency said, 'Where are you?'

'At the Mariscombe Hotel. We're having dinner with Jess and Rob. It's jam-packed here.'

'Look, could I have a word with Sam?'

'Sam? Why?' Not in a suspicious way, just surprised.

'There's another flat he might be interested in.'

'Another flat? Well we wouldn't have time to see it,' said Belle. 'We have to leave St Carys at seven thirty tomorrow morning.'

'How about tonight?'

'Clem, we're having dinner with friends!'

'I know, I know . . .'

'Hang on, Sam wants to speak to you. OK, don't be long, our food's about to arrive. Just tell her it's too late.' Evidently addressing Sam, Belle passed the phone over to him.

Listening, Clemency heard his rhythmic footsteps on the flagstones and the noise of the restaurant receding.

'Right,' said Sam. 'I can hear you now. What's this all about?'

Clemency wasn't accustomed to setting her alarm for 5.30 in the morning, but in fact she was wide awake before it even went off. By six o'clock, showered and dressed in jeans and a grey sweater, she'd left home and headed over on foot to the address she'd given Sam last night. At this time of the morning the sun was nothing more than a bright white blur in a hazy white sky, and there was still a dense mist hovering over the sea. But the temperature was set to rise significantly.

Hers too, it seemed. As she neared the address, her palms grew damp. Always attractive.

He was there ahead of her, leaning against the side of his hire car as he waited for her, and on his own. The butterflies in Clemency's stomach took flight like a swirling flock of birds.

'I didn't know if Belle would be coming with you,' she said.

'At six fifteen in the morning?' He looked amused. 'She decided to go for the extra hour in bed.'

Quelle surprise.

'OK,' said Clemency. 'Well I wouldn't have asked you to view this place if I didn't think it was the perfect fit. Like I told you last night, the vendor's desperate; she's due to complete next week and the buyers have pulled out. The whole chain's on the verge of collapse.' She shrugged. 'You're a cash buyer. It's a stunning property. It was more than you were looking to spend, but Cissy's prepared to accept an offer. Honestly? If I could choose any flat here in St Carys, this is the one I'd go for.'

A flicker of a smile. 'Is that your hard-sell sales pitch?'

'I don't do hard sells. When you view the place for yourself, you'll see what I mean.'

'Why did the buyers pull out?'

'The wife just discovered her husband's been having an affair. So instead of them moving down here from Nottingham, she's filing for divorce.' Clemency held up the keys to the property. 'Want to take a look?'

Sam nodded. 'That's why we're here.'

But it wasn't the only reason they were here. He knew

47

that as well as she did. There was an elephant in the room and Clemency wasn't going to be the one to mention it.

Instead, with a brisk professional nod of her own, she said, 'Let's go.'

The apartment was empty. Cissy was currently in Edinburgh and most of the furniture was already in storage, waiting to be moved into her new house.

It didn't take long to view the open-plan kitchen diner, the two bedrooms, the bathrooms and the spectacular living room. As they stood outside on the wide wraparound balcony and surveyed the view over Beachcomber Bay, the sun finally broke through the early morning haze. The sea was visible now, glittering and palest turquoise. A lone jogger was running along the pristine, just-washed sand with a dog at his heels. Seagulls wheeled lazily overhead, no doubt keeping an eye on the fishing boats chugging into the harbour.

And now the sun was growing stronger, brighter, warming their faces. Sam said, 'Did you arrange for this to happen?'

'You mean for the chain to collapse and the sale of this place to fall through? Yes, of course I did. Just call me Machiavelli.'

He looked at her. 'Actually I was talking about the sun coming out.'

'Oh.' Her stomach tightened. 'Well, that too. Obviously.'

'Thought so.'

'What's the verdict, then?'

'It *is* perfect. Exactly what I wanted. But you already knew that.' Sam paused. 'What are the neighbours like?'

'Scottish. Very fond of bagpipes.' Clemency smiled. 'Don't worry. It's a retired couple below, very charming and very quiet. And a middle-aged divorcee on the ground floor. No orgies, I already checked.'

'Shall we go back inside?'

Clemency allowed him to lead the way. When she'd locked the French windows, he said, 'Are we going to talk about it?'

'About you buying this property? I do hope so.'

'I meant the other thing.'

'Oh. The other thing.' Her heart broke into a gallop. 'We don't have to. Really, it's fine. It was . . . nothing.'

For a couple of seconds Sam didn't say anything; the silence was broken only by the distant swoosh of waves breaking on to the beach, and the cry of a lone seagull overhead.

When he spoke again, his gaze was unwavering and intense. 'But it wasn't nothing, was it?'

Clemency turned, walked through to the kitchen and poured herself a tumbler of water from the tap. She drank half of it and seated herself on one of the high stools around the marble-topped central island. 'It was three years ago. You passed the time by flirting with a stranger. When the flight was over, you remembered you were married and guessed your wife might not be too amused if she found the stranger's card in your pocket. It's actually a sign that you're not a complete bastard,' she said lightly. 'You resisted temptation. You should be proud.'

'I wasn't proud.' Sam shook his head. 'I should never have done it.'

'Well you're divorced now, so it's irrelevant anyway. What happened?' said Clemency. 'Did you do it again and get caught?'

She'd said it in a light-hearted way so he'd know she

49

wasn't bitter, that she understood these things had a habit of happening, especially to men who walked around looking like he did.

There was, after all, only so much beauty a girl could resist.

'Actually,' said Sam, 'she didn't divorce me. She died.'

Chapter 6

When he'd gone out on the evening of his twenty-fifth birthday, Sam had never intended to meet the love of his life. It was meant to be a casual get-together for a motley group of his friends at one of their favourite restaurants, followed by a visit to a club.

What he hadn't banked on was catching the eye of a blonde girl at one of the other tables in the restaurant and liking the look of her enough to keep glancing over in her direction. And each time he did so, as if sensing his attention, she would look up and meet his gaze.

After an hour it was getting ridiculous. They were both doing it and trying so hard not to smile. Leaving his table, ostensibly to pay a visit to the bathroom, Sam walked past her and waited in the corridor outside.

Less than twenty seconds later she joined him, and this time there were no attempts to hide the smiles.

'Happy birthday, dear Sam,' she said, because his friends had sung the rousing chorus to him earlier before clattering their glasses together for a toast.

Sam said, 'It's not shaping up too badly so far.'

'You never know, it could get better.' Reaching up, she murmured, 'Happy birthday to you,' and gave him a kiss on the cheek. Followed by a proper one on the mouth.

Her name was Lisa, she was a nurse at King's College Hospital and she shared a flat with four other nurses in Brixton. Having fulfilled her duty at the works do at the restaurant to celebrate the retirement of one of the doctors in their department, Lisa and two of her friends from King's joined forces with Sam and his friends and spent the next few hours in a club. At the end of the night she kissed him once more and said, 'I'm not coming home with you. If you want to see me again, call me tomorrow and invite me out properly on Saturday night.'

'Fine.' Simultaneously frustrated and impressed, Sam said, 'Give me your number, then.'

'If you *really* want to see me again,' said Lisa, 'you'll track me down without it.'

Was she joking?

'Are you serious?' said Sam.

'Absolutely.' She'd given him a mischievous look. 'I'm deadly serious about finding out if you're serious about wanting to see me again. Because if you aren't, why bother?'

'And do you think I will bother?'

Lisa's eyes sparkled. 'Oh I hope so.'

It hadn't been difficult. He called the restaurant, persuaded them to give him the number of the husband of the doctor whose retirement party it had been, and worked forward from there. Having been passed on to one of Lisa's friends, he found out which ward she worked on and what time her shift ended. That evening, he waited outside the ward for her to appear.

When she saw him, Lisa said, 'So you tracked me down. But did you get my phone number?'

Sam took out his mobile phone and pressed a button. Seconds later, a jaunty tone rang out from inside the yellow raffia bag slung over her shoulder. 'You might want to answer that,' he said.

When she did, he stood just a few feet away from her and said into his phone, 'Hi, this is Sam, I was wondering if you'd like to come out with me on Saturday evening.'

'Thank you.' Her smile broadened as she stepped aside to make room for a patient on a trolley to be pushed into the ward. Speaking into her own phone, she said, 'I'd like that very much.'

It had never been Sam's intention to get married whilst still in his twenties. But sometimes fate took a hand, you met the woman you wanted to spend the rest of your life with, and after a while it seemed like the next logical step, so why wait?

A year after they'd first got together, he and Lisa moved into a tiny flat in Peckham. Six months later, they began making plans for the wedding, to take place on the date of the night they'd first met.

'If we get married on your birthday,' said Lisa, 'you'll never forget our anniversary.'

'Fine, and you aren't allowed to forget it either,' said Sam.

Three months before the wedding, Lisa suffered a week of increasingly severe headaches that culminated in an epileptic seizure at work and admission to hospital. A brain scan confirmed what a physical examination had already given the doctors cause to suspect: there was a large tumour growing in her brain.

And suddenly the future they'd expected to share was no longer the future they found themselves having to face up to. Surgery swiftly followed, as much as possible of the malignant tumour was excised in order to reduce the pressure inside the skull, and Lisa underwent a course of radiotherapy. The tumour was a glioblastoma multiforme, not the kind anyone would choose to have. But Lisa made a good enough recovery to be able to insist that the wedding went ahead.

And for a few more months she was still herself, more or less, albeit weak and tired and with a frustrating struggle to find the right words when she spoke. Eventually the neuro-surgeon informed them that the tumour was on the march again, and Lisa begged him to operate once more to reduce the mass. It was during this risky second bout of surgery that a bleed occurred and significantly more damage was done to her brain. After that, she was confined to her bed on the neurosurgical ward, and the surgeon explained to Sam that all they could do now was make her comfortable.

This was when Sam realised he had to come to terms with the fact that whilst he still loved Lisa, she was no longer the girl he'd fallen in love with. Furthermore, he was on his own. Before, they'd been a team, fighting the tumour together. Now Lisa was – quite literally – the sleeping partner. There was nothing more she could do to help him through the nightmare that lay ahead.

Sam paused, looked at his watch and exhaled; the memories were always with him, but it had been a while since he'd talked about what had happened. He glanced across at Clemency and said, 'Sorry, were you in a hurry to be somewhere?'

'No, not at all.' Clemency was sitting opposite him at the central island in the kitchen. She hadn't uttered a word since he'd begun.

'I wasn't planning on saying all this today.' He shook his head. 'I don't think I've ever spoken about it so much before.'

She looked surprised. 'Really?'

'It's not something I make a habit of. People I've known for a long time already know. New people get the very short version. I don't go into detail. But I needed to tell you everything, to explain why . . . well, that day on the plane.'

'Carry on,' said Clemency. 'I'm listening.'

Sam glanced out of the window at a red speedboat that was bouncing across the water in the bay. When it had disappeared from view, he resumed the story.

'The staff at the hospital thought Lisa would die within months. What usually happens to people in that condition is they catch an infection, like pneumonia, and they're so weak they don't survive. But Lisa didn't catch any kind of infection. And the tumour seemed to have stopped growing, so she just stayed as she was. Which was . . . comatose, without any way of coming back.' His mouth was dry; he took a sip from the glass of water on the marble island before remembering it was Clemency's. 'Sorry. So anyway, I spent my days at work, working. And my nights at the nursing home she'd been moved to by then. I sat with Lisa every evening, and it was a pretty hard thing to do, because I knew how much she'd hate being in that situation if she knew what was going on. But the months went by and nothing changed . . . and after two years she was still there. The ironic thing was, because I didn't have anything else to do with my time, I'd built up my company and turned it into something more successful than we'd ever imagined.' He sat back and raked his hand through his hair. 'One of my work colleagues said, "Every cloud has a silver lining." He didn't seem to realise there aren't enough silver linings in the world to make up for a cloud that big.'

He stopped again and looked at Clemency, who was taking in every word. 'So that's the gist of it. Then three years ago, following a business trip to Spain, I found myself on a plane back to London, sitting next to a girl who'd almost missed her flight.' Every detail of that day was as clear in his mind as if it had happened yesterday. 'I wasn't in the mood for conversation. I tried my best to ignore her. Then the plane hit an air pocket, she ended up covered in red wine and I realised how bloody rude I'd been. Anyway, she was nice enough to forgive me and we got talking. And for the first time in two years, I found myself having a normal conversation . . . the kind where you aren't discussing business plans and things to do with work. Or the fact that your wife's lying in an irreversible coma. It was effortless . . . it felt great . . . it felt like being young, free and single again, just chatting with someone because you wanted to. Because you enjoyed their company and found them attractive. It was like being locked in a dark room for two years then suddenly being let out and seeing the world again, in colour . . .'

Sam stopped speaking. If he hadn't, he knew his voice would be in danger of cracking with emotion; and that was something no one got to hear. He breathed in and out and waited until he'd regained control.

'So that's pretty much it. Now you know why I did what I did. And can I just say, I was never unfaithful to my wife. I never would have been. But meeting you felt like the biggest test in the world, because if I'd been single . . . well, things could have been very different. Because meeting you and talking to you . . . it felt like the first night I met Lisa.'

The silence shimmered in the air between them. Sam shrugged slightly, to indicate that he'd said his piece and now she could speak.

Clemency nodded and rested her forearms on the cool marble worktop. 'I'm so sorry I thought you were divorced.'

'That's OK. You weren't to know.'

'When did she die?'

'Three weeks after I met you. Three weeks and three days,' Sam amended. 'Pneumonia. She was twenty-eight years old.' He gazed for a second out of the window, where the sun was now properly bright. 'The worst part is feeling guilty because you're relieved it's over at last. You can stop waiting for it to happen. And then you think about what you've just thought and you can't quite believe you thought it. I kept trying to tell myself that Lisa would be glad it was over too . . . then I'd have this recurring dream where she was staring at me in horror and saying, "Are you *kidding* me? What kind of husband are you? Did you ever even love me at *all*?" Which was a great dream to have.' He pulled a face.

'Does it still happen?'

'Not for over a year now. The guilt is one of those things you just have to get through.' His phone pinged as a text arrived, and Sam glanced at the screen. 'It's Annabelle, wanting to know when I'll be back.' He tapped in the reply *Soon* and put the phone down once more on the worktop.

'You've told Belle all about what happened to Lisa, though?' said Clemency. 'She knows everything?'

'She knows what happened, that Lisa had a brain tumour and died. And that it took a while.' Sam shrugged. 'That's as much as I said, and we left it there. She hasn't asked any more questions. Lots of people don't,' he explained. 'They assume I'd rather not talk about it.'

'And are they right?' Clemency was watching him, her attention unwavering.

'Probably. It's easier. Well, it depends who you're speaking to. I generally change the subject.'

She nodded slowly. 'And have there been other girls since? Or is Belle the first?'

'Not the first.' He shook his head. 'There was no one for eighteen months, then a couple of disastrous dates. I went out with one girl for a couple of weeks but it didn't feel right. Then two months ago I met Annabelle and things seemed to be going pretty well . . . they *were* going pretty well . . . God, you have no idea what it did to me, seeing you again yesterday, just turning up and here you are . . . and you're Annabelle's *sister*.' When he looked at her again, he could see a pulse beating at the base of her throat.

'It was a shock for me too,' said Clemency, 'finding out you're her boyfriend. And she's—'

This time her phone was the one to burst into life. She pulled it out of her jeans pocket. 'It's Cissy Lambert.'

'Her solicitors have had the search carried out, right? There's nothing else I need to know about this place?'

Clemency nodded. 'Yes, no, it's all legit.'

Was the pulse quickening in her throat? *Was his?* For a second their eyes met and he felt the connection again, the buzz of making a lightning-fast decision combining with an adrenalin rush of quite a different kind.

'You can tell her I'm interested,' he said. They'd already discussed the price he was prepared to pay. 'Make the offer, see what she says.'

Another infinitesimal nod from Clemency. She pressed answer on her phone and said happily, 'Cissy? Fantastic news . . .'

Chapter 7

'Oh I say, look at *you*.'

The potential vendors were a married couple in their forties, a long-suffering husband and his flirtatious wife. Well it didn't take a psychologist to work that out.

'Hi.' Ronan shook her hand, then his, and said, 'I'm Ronan Byrne from Barton and Byrne. I'm here to carry out the valuation.'

The husband muttered, 'Marcia, try not to make a show of yourself.'

'Oh give it a rest, Barry. It's called being friendly.' Marcia's eyes flickered over Ronan from top to toe. 'It's a hard concept for my husband to understand, which explains why he doesn't have any friends. Has anyone ever told you you look like a young Barack Obama?'

'Oh Marcia.' Barry shook his head sorrowfully at Ronan. 'I do apologise.'

'But he *does*. It's a compliment, for crying out loud. The boy's gorgeous!'

Ronan grinned, because he was used to it. 'It's fine. Actually, a few people have mentioned the Barack Obama thing before. You aren't the first.'

'It's the eyes. And that smile.' Marcia batted her lashes playfully at him. 'Ooh, that smile and those teeth!'

'Just ignore her,' said Barry.

'Shut up, Barry, you wouldn't recognise a bit of fun if it came up and bit you on the backside.'

'Right,' said Ronan. 'Shall we get on and take a look around? I can already see it's a beautiful house.'

And it *was* a nice house. It would have been nicer still if the bathroom tiles weren't leopard-print, the kitchen walls hadn't been hand-stencilled with zebra stripes and the living-room ceiling wasn't painted black. At a guess, it meant the property would go for five thousand less than it might otherwise have fetched, but when he discreetly suggested they might want to tone it down with a couple of coats of paint, Marcia wouldn't hear of it. 'But that's what's going to sell the place,' she exclaimed. 'They're the best bits.'

And when he'd finished measuring up the rooms, an asking price had been agreed upon and Ronan was about to leave, she said with a nudge, 'I reckon you should have a quiet word with your mum the next time you see her. It'd be a laugh, wouldn't it, if Barack Obama turned out to be your dad!'

Growing up in Newquay, a lack of self-confidence wasn't something that had ever affected Ronan Byrne. As a mixed-race child in an overwhelmingly white population, he might have found himself picked on or bullied, but it had never happened. As an adopted child, furthermore, he could have been marked out as different and subjected to teasing, but

61

that hadn't materialised either. He'd been lucky; things that had the potential to cause him problems had made him seem excitingly exotic instead.

Essentially, Ronan hadn't encountered any difficulties; if anything, his differentness only made him all the more desirable to know. Everyone longed to be his friend. And as the years went by, during which time he grew from a cheeky, cute little boy into a tall, handsome teenager, all the girls decided they wanted to be his girlfriend.

In this matter Ronan didn't disappoint, but he also took care to keep his social circle wide. He excelled at athletics, was always up for impromptu get-togethers on the beach and loved any kind of party, during which he would dance and chat and flirt with friends old and new. But his adoptive parents, Josephine and Donald, had also instilled in him ambition, enthusiasm and a fierce work ethic, and he worked as hard as he played, always seemingly able to cram thirty hours into each day. Between studying for A levels, working in a local supermarket and doing an early morning paper round, he never stopped. University beckoned, and he'd already received an unconditional offer to study business and management at Manchester. Life was great, and about to get better.

Until, quite out of the blue, it got worse.

OK, no time to think about that now. Work to do, property to sell. Returning to the office at midday on Friday, Ronan pushed open the door and immediately wished he hadn't. *Damn*, should have stopped off at the café instead of coming straight back.

'Ah, here he is,' Gavin exclaimed. 'Perfect timing! Ronan can take you right now.'

Which, under the circumstances, wasn't the best phrase he could have chosen to use.

But Gavin was blissfully unaware of that, thank goodness. He was also clearly anxious to leave, wearing his golfing outfit and with his bag of clubs propped up beside the desk.

'Look, it's OK, I can come back another time . . .'

'Don't be daft, you're here now. Off you go, you two!' Taking a key down from the board, Gavin chucked it over to Ronan, who caught it in his left hand. 'Forty-three Wallis Road. I've got a good feeling about this one.' He winked at Kate Trevelyan as he slung the padded strap of the golf bag over his shoulder. 'Reckon it could be just right for you. Lovely little place.'

Then he waved goodbye to Paula, their secretary, and ushered Ronan and Kate out ahead of him. Ronan, who had blocked Gavin's car in, was left with no choice other than to open the passenger door for Kate.

'Thanks,' she murmured as she climbed in.

'No problem.' It came out far too cheerfully.

Awkward.

When they were both ensconced in the car, Kate said, 'Look, I'm sorry. You weren't there, I checked beforehand, so I thought it was safe to come in.'

'It's fine, it's *fine*.' It wasn't remotely fine. It wasn't often, either, that Ronan's skin prickled with mortification. But he'd been a complete idiot and now he had to endure the uncomfortable consequences.

Like this silence . . .

Thankfully the owner of the property was at home with her two young children and a box full of Lego, so Ronan was able to behave like a normal estate agent showing the property off to a normal client.

'And this is the living room.' Having escorted Kate around the rest of the house, he finally opened the door to where the owner and her boys were kneeling on the carpet surrounded by multicoloured Lego bricks.

'It's lovely,' said Kate.

'Mummy, Mummy, Darren put Lego in my pants!'

'I didn't! It wasn't me! I only did it because you put that carrot stick up my nose. It *hurt*.'

'Sshh,' said their mother. 'Play nicely.'

'Mummy, who's that lady? Is she our postman?'

The mother took a second look at Kate and said in surprise, 'Oh yes, of course it is. Hello, how funny, I didn't recognise you in your normal clothes!'

This was fair enough; when she was working, Kate wore a pale blue cotton shirt and dark blue shorts, with her blond hair tied back in a tight plait. Today her hair was loose and ripply, and she was wearing a red cotton dress scattered with purple stars.

'I know.' She smiled. 'I look a bit different out of uniform.'

'You know who it is, Mummy,' said the older boy. 'It's the slug lady. You know . . . WAAAAHHH.'

Both children collapsed in fits of giggles, clutching their faces in mock-horror and going WAAAAHHH like Kevin in *Home Alone*.

Their mother, mortified, said, 'Boys, *stop* it.'

'Oh I get it now.' Kate's cheeks were flushed. 'I know what this is about.'

The older boy, still creased up with laughter, pointed at her.

'You were outside our house with the letters and you stepped on a big slug and you screamed and jumped in the air and dropped all the letters on the ground and we were watching you from the window and now we call you the slug lady, HA HA HA HA HA HA.'

'It was a *very* big slug,' said Kate, pinker than ever.

'You squashed him dead.' The younger one beamed with ghoulish delight.

'It was an accident,' Kate protested.

'We buried him in the garden after you killed him,' said the older brother. 'We can go outside and say some prayers if you like.'

'Boys,' said their mother, 'she's not going to want to buy our house if you keep this up.'

'Ooh.' The older one's face lit up. 'If you live here, you can put flowers on his grave. And every time you put the flowers down, you can say sorry and cry!'

Kate hadn't told Ronan the full story about her mother and the legacy straight away. Well, there'd been no reason why she should. Ronan only remembered the first time she'd come into the office because she was such a contrast to the previous person who'd delivered their post. Gerald had been six foot five, built like a rugby player and originally from Glasgow. He'd had a huge beard, and a raucous laugh and a great love for those World's Strongest Man competitions that involved contestants dragging lorries along the road with a chain gripped between their teeth.

Kate, who resembled Gerald in no way whatsoever, had taken over his round back in early October when he'd moved to Birmingham. She'd been quiet and efficient, completing her deliveries faster than Gerald simply because she didn't stop to chat to everyone she met along the way. It wasn't until several weeks later, when Ronan had taken the post from her one morning, that he'd seen her pause to study the photos of one of their properties currently for sale.

Joining her at the wall where the photos were displayed, he said, 'Take one of these if you want,' and handed her the details. 'Are you looking for a place to buy?'

Kate nodded quickly. 'I am. But I've never bought anywhere before, so I don't really know what to do or how to choose . . .'

'Well that's why we're here, to help you through it. It's our job to find you the right place. And don't worry,' Ronan added with a reassuring smile. 'When you see it, you'll know. I promise.'

She turned to look up at him. 'Will I really?'

'Oh yes. It's like falling in love.'

The next day, at 5.30, Kate had cycled over to the office and Ronan had driven her to the property that had caught her eye. The cottage, a few miles outside St Carys, was being sold by a lonely old man who'd insisted on sitting them down for cups of stale coffee, slices of cake and a long, rambling story about his years in the army. When they'd finally been able to make their escape, Ronan opened the passenger door to let Kate back into the car.

'I should have warned you about that,' he said as they drove away from the cottage. 'Sometimes people get a bit carried away.'

Kate nodded. 'I get it when I'm delivering letters.'

'Of course you do. So, how about the cottage? It helps to imagine it empty,' he added. 'Take out all the clutter and redecorate it in your mind.'

'I didn't love it,' said Kate.

'No? Well that's OK.' He'd already guessed as much.

'Sorry.'

'Not a problem.' He could see her hands clasped together in her lap. 'Really, it's fine.'

Several seconds later he heard a stifled sob and turned to see tears sliding down Kate's cheeks. 'Hey, what's this about?'

'I can't . . . I just can't . . .' She shook her head, now visibly trembling with the effort of not breaking down completely.

Baffled, Ronan carried on driving, because the lane was twisting and narrow, and there was nowhere to stop. As they approached St Carys, he glanced sideways once more. 'I don't know what to do.'

'You d–don't have to do anything. I'll b–be fine.'

'Of course you're fine. Never better.' Making a decision, he signalled right. 'Look, I can't just drop you back at the office. You're not cycling anywhere like this.'

Ronan's flat was just around the corner. He let Kate out of the car and ushered her inside, privately wondering what he might be getting himself into.

In the flat, he handed her a roll of kitchen paper. 'There you go, nothing but the best for my visitors. I'm going to make us both a cup of tea. The people in the upstairs flat are out at work, so you can cry as much as you want.'

Ten minutes of intensive sobbing later, Kate wiped her reddened eyes with kitchen towel and said, 'I think it's over now. I'm so sorry.'

'Will you stop apologising? Drink your tea,' said Ronan.

'You must think I'm some kind of madwoman.'

'Not at all.' He watched her gulp down the tea and knew by the way she grimaced slightly that he shouldn't have put sugar in. But, being polite, she didn't say so.

'My mum died.' Kate took a deep, shuddery breath. 'Two months ago.'

'Ah, right. I'm sorry.' Now it was his turn to say the words.

'This is the first time I've cried. I kept waiting for it to happen but it just didn't. Everyone said it would come out eventually, but after a while I gave up waiting. I thought maybe I was just immune to crying, that I was one of those people who never . . . does it.'

'But it turns out you do.'

'Seems that way.'

'I lost my dad when I was eighteen,' said Ronan. 'I was the same as you. Everyone else in the family was weeping and wailing, and the more they did it, the more I told myself I needed to be the one who stayed in control. Then a few weeks later, *boom*.' He spread his arms wide. 'It was like a pressure cooker exploding. You should have seen me. What a mess.'

'And did you feel better afterwards?'

'God, yes.'

'Well that's good.' A glimmer of a smile counterbalanced a fresh lone tear trickling down her cheek. 'Something to look forward to, at least.'

Sensing her need to talk, Ronan sent Kate into the bathroom to wash her face and rinse the gritty salt deposits from her eyes. Then he opened a bottle of wine and poured two glasses. When she returned, he patted the seat next to him on the old suede sofa. 'Come on, tell me everything.'

'You'll be bored rigid.' Kate hesitated, clearly not wanting to outstay her welcome.

'If you bore me, I'll just point to the door,' said Ronan. 'But you won't.'

Chapter 8

'We lived in Redland in Bristol,' Kate explained. 'Just me and Mum, in our little terraced house. When Mum got ill, she sold the house in case we needed money to pay for her nursing care and we moved in with my grandparents in Bude. But Mum died six weeks later, much more quickly than any of us had expected. She left everything to me, told me to buy a place of my own and make a good life for myself.'

'So that's what you're doing. Close enough to Bude to stay in touch with your grandparents, far enough away to be independent.'

'Exactly. I'm twenty-six.' She shrugged. 'It makes sense. So yes, that's the plan. The will was straightforward, so it didn't take long to get everything sorted out. The money arrived in my account last week. Except I mentioned at work that I was looking for somewhere to buy, and now word's got around.' Kate shook her head ruefully. 'The thing is, everyone's being really nice and they mean well, but they keep telling me how lucky I am. And I know what they mean, of course I do . . . How many people my age have the chance to buy a property without needing a mortgage? But my mum isn't here and she's the person I love more than anyone else in the world . . . so if it was a choice between her and all the money in the world, I'd rather have my mum back.'

Tears were welling up once more, spilling down her cheeks. Ronan put his arm around her and drew her towards him, touched by her words. 'Hey, of course you'd rather have her back,' he murmured. 'It's hardly been any time at all.'

'I miss her so much. *So much.*' Fat teardrops dripped off her chin and landed on the front of his shirt. 'I keep telling myself I have to act like a grown-up, but I don't *feel* like a grown-up. When something difficult happens, I keep wanting to ask my mum how I should do it. She told me to buy a place that was right for me . . . but how will I know if it's right? What if I make a terrible mistake? This is the money my mum spent her whole life working for. I can't just mess around with it. And I know I've got my grandparents, but I feel so . . . so on my own.'

Ronan nodded without speaking, and continued stroking the back of her neck.

'Thank you,' said Kate, twenty seconds later.

'For what?'

'For not saying you know how I feel. It's what everyone says, and it drives me insane. Yesterday someone said, "Are you still missing your mum?" and when I nodded, they said, "Ooh, I know exactly what you're going through. I lost my cat last year and it was awful – I was in bits for weeks!"'

'There's a special dispensation for those occasions,' Ronan told her. 'You are actually allowed to murder people who say things like that. Instead of arresting you, the police award you a gold medal.'

Kate did an unexpected spluttery laugh. 'Wouldn't that be great?'

'When I'm king of the world, it's the first law I'm going to pass.'

'You could have said it, though. You lost your dad. You've been through it.'

'I only know how I felt,' said Ronan. 'We're all different. And when it happened to me, I still had my mum. I wasn't left on my own like you.'

She nodded, then looked up at him. 'Does it get better? Easier?'

'It does, I promise. Little by little.'

'Thank you. You're being so kind.' Moving forward with him as he reached over for the bottle and refilled their glasses, Kate said, 'Don't you have somewhere else you're meant to be? You can't want to spend a whole evening stuck here with a crying machine.'

'Let me be the one to decide that.' Ronan liked the way she came out with whatever was in her head. He smiled. 'I'm not bored yet.'

To be clear, there had been drink involved. But not huge amounts. As the evening had worn on and a second bottle of wine had been opened, they'd carried on talking. The conversation had ranged in all directions, Kate's tears had dried and the mood had lightened. Somehow, too, it had never seemed necessary for Ronan to remove his arm from her shoulders. His fingers had continued to stroke the back of her neck. Then proximity had turned into kissing . . . lots of kissing . . . and eventually he'd taken her by the hand and led her into the bedroom, and as they'd undressed each other Kate had murmured, 'Sure you're not bored?'

Three hours later, as a glimmer of moonlight shone through the gap at the very top of the curtains, Ronan tilted his head to one side and saw that it was almost midnight. Operation Cheer Up Kate hadn't been pre-planned but it had certainly seemed to do the trick; following an extremely enjoyable hour or so, they'd both fallen asleep.

He glanced across at her. She was breathing deeply and evenly, lying on her side, her bare legs intertwined with his and her left arm resting across his chest. Her lashes cast dark shadows across her cheekbones and her loose blond hair, spread across the pillow, smelt faintly of apple shampoo. Breaking into a slow smile, Ronan marvelled at the way the evening had turned out. Talk about unexpected. And it was even more incredible when you thought how unlikely—

RAP-RAP-RAP.

Ronan froze. *What the hell?* Someone was outside his bedroom window, tapping on the glass. Next to him in the bed, Kate briefly stirred before settling again.

Ten seconds passed, then twenty. Ronan realised he'd been holding his breath. Maybe they'd given up and gone away.

RAP-RAP-RAP-RAP-RAP. Louder this time, and more insistent. Kate's eyes snapped open. 'What's that?'

'Someone's tapping on the window.' His mouth was dry. 'Who?'

'I don't know.' This wasn't true; he was ninety-five per cent certain he knew who was currently standing less than six feet away from them on the other side of the glass.

Much as he'd prefer it to be a burglar, he was pretty sure the midnight visitor was Laura.

Oh God.

RAP-RAP-RAPPITY-RAP.

73

'Don't move,' Ronan whispered.

'If someone's trying to break in, you should probably call the police,' Kate murmured back. 'Then again, if they're trying to break in, they're being very polite about it.' As she said the words, she gave him a knowing look.

Easing himself out of bed, Ronan moved silently through to the living room, located his phone on the floor next to the sofa and returned to the bedroom. As he slid back into bed, he saw the most recent text light up the screen.

The most recent text of very many that had been sent during the last two hours.

Ronan, your car's outside, I know you're at home. Let me in, I need to see you. We need to talk properly.

'Oh no we don't.' He said the words under his breath and gave Kate's hand a squeeze. 'It's OK, she'll go away soon enough.'

Please God . . .

Then they heard her voice, strained with emotion. 'Ronan, you can't do this to me! I love you! Let me *in*.'

All in all, the next minutes surely ranked among the most calamitously awkward of Ronan's life. Since letting Laura into the flat clearly wasn't an option, all he could do was lie there next to Kate and wait it out, while they both listened to his ex-girlfriend cajoling and begging, shouting tearful insults and, most excruciating of all, reading aloud a poem she'd written about their great love for each other.

Despite the fact that the great love existed only in her mind.

Ronan, his eyes closed, felt mortified on Laura's behalf. She'd evidently spent a lot of time on the poem. Even if she had tried to make the word *heaven* rhyme with *leaving*.

'So now my heart is broken, like an egg, And all that's left for me to do is beg. The End.'

Silence followed Laura's recital of the final couplet, while she waited once more for a response. When none came, she said brokenly, 'That's it then, I'm going. I suppose you'll get over this in a few days and find some slapper to sleep with you, and it'll be like you and me never happened. Well, good luck to whoever's in your bed next, because she's going to need it. You'll end up breaking her heart just like you've broken mine.'

Finally, finally it was over. They heard her footsteps receding, then the sound of her car being driven off. Ronan exhaled. 'God, I'm so sorry about that.' He reached for Kate but was too slow; she'd already leapt out of the other side of the bed.

'Don't be sorry. I'm the stupid one for staying here.' In the dim light, he saw that she was trembling as she reached for her discarded clothes and scrambled into them.

'But I thought—'

'No,' Kate blurted out, 'I wasn't thinking straight. I didn't know you had a girlfriend.'

'I don't have a girlfriend.' Even as he heard the words emerging from his mouth, Ronan sensed they weren't sounding good. 'We *were* together, but we broke up.'

She looked at him. 'When did you break up?'

OK, this time he knew for sure she wasn't going to like the answer. 'Well . . . it was yesterday.'

Kate finished zipping herself into her dress. 'Nice. Well done you. That explains why the bed still felt warm.'

Ouch.

'Look, she hasn't slept here for the last fortnight. I was

trying to find a way to break up without hurting her feelings. It took a while.'

'Poor you, it must have been terrible.' Kate located her shoes. 'Yesterday you dumped your girlfriend. Today she wrote you a poem because she's so devastated. But you've already moved on. Which you're perfectly entitled to do, of course. I just wish I'd known, because it makes me feel pretty awful.'

'Oh you mustn't—'

'But I do!' She swiftly intercepted him. 'Laura thought you'd find yourself another slapper to sleep with in a few days. Imagine if she found out it had only taken you a few *hours*.'

'Look, I had no idea this was going to happen,' Ronan protested. 'It wasn't planned.'

Kate shook her head. 'I know, I do understand that. I'm not angry with you, just ashamed of myself. I've never had a one-night stand before, and I'm pretty certain I won't be doing it again.'

'I'm sorry. I thought it was what you wanted. I was trying to help.'

Kate looked at him, her eyes swimming with unshed tears. 'I'm sure you were. How long were you and Laura together?'

'Not long. A couple of months.' Did that make things better?

'And does she live here in St Carys?'

'Yes.'

'Work here?'

'Yes.' Ronan hesitated. 'In the chemist's shop on the Esplanade.'

He saw Kate flinch; she may not have been in St Carys for very long, but there was only one chemist's shop on the Esplanade.

'The pretty brunette or the tall one with the freckles?'

'The . . . er, pretty brunette.'

Kate nodded. 'OK, but she's never going to know about this.' She gestured awkwardly at him, then at herself. 'About us. Is she.'

It was a statement, not a question. Ronan said, 'No.'

'Nobody's going to know about us,' Kate reiterated. 'I mean *nobody*, not a single person. Will you promise me that?'

He experienced a flash of frustration, because it didn't need to be like this. If Laura hadn't turned up, everything could have been so different. It hadn't been planned, but they'd had a nice time, hadn't they? Better than nice. And now she was looking at him as if the mere sight of him were causing her pain.

'You have to promise me,' Kate repeated.

And to think that most girls would be only too delighted to be able to tell their friends they'd slept with him. Ronan sighed; had he really been that out of order? Plenty of men cheated on their girlfriends and didn't think twice about it. At least he'd finished with Laura first.

But it clearly mattered to Kate, so he shrugged and said, 'Fine, I promise.'

That had been over six months ago now, and Ronan had kept his word. Back then, he'd expected the awkwardness between them to last a week, maybe two; he'd had no idea it would carry on this long. But it had only intensified over time, and he still had no idea how to overcome it. Basically

77

because, against all expectations, he hadn't been able to dismiss the attraction he felt towards this girl who had been so disappointed in him.

It really was the most inconvenient situation. Ronan had never experienced anything like it before and he didn't like it one bit. It was as if he'd been turned into a gauche, nerdy teenager incapable of behaving normally in front of a girl he fancied but knew he had absolutely no chance with. And the longer it went on, the worse it seemed to get. Each morning, Kate delivered the post to the office. He wasn't always there when she called in, but often enough. And he wasn't able to ignore her; they had to exchange pleasantries as if everything was completely fine, or suspicions would be aroused. It was so difficult though, like having an illicit affair, with all of the downsides and none of the benefits.

And Kate clearly found the situation as agonisingly uncomfortable as he did, which was why she'd made a point of booking today's viewing with Gavin.

Oh well, it was done now.

'So maybe we'll have to start calling you Slug Lady,' Ronan said as they drove back to the office.

It was a poor attempt at a joke, but she managed a brief smile. 'I could have it tattooed on my arm.'

And there it was, happening again. He instantly found himself recalling that night when he'd lain there in the darkness and felt her bare arm resting across his chest. He could remember every moment of their time together. Details he would normally have forgotten were recalled with Technicolor clarity.

He gave himself a mental shake. 'So, slug graves aside, what's the verdict on the house?'

Kate shook her head sadly. 'It isn't the one. Sorry.'

Still apologising. 'No problem. How many have you seen now?'

'Sixteen.'

She'd been scouring the local property market for something to spend her mum's money on. Clemency had shown her a couple of places, Ronan knew, and she'd also been visiting other estate agents in the area.

'Like we said before, it has to be right, smell right, feel right.' Oh God, he was talking about houses but thinking about *her* . . . He pulled up on double yellows close to the office so she could jump out and pick up her pushbike. 'Don't worry, you'll find the perfect place one day and be glad you waited.'

'I know. Well, thanks anyway.' Kate fumbled to unclip her seat belt.

'Is it starting to get easier?'

'No. Oh. What are you talking about?'

'Being without your mum.'

'Oh, right.' She nodded vigorously. 'I think so. I still miss her, but I'm getting used to it.'

Ronan smiled. 'You'll be fine.'

And when she'd left the car, after yet another clumsy round of goodbyes, he watched her cycle off down the road and wondered if one day he'd be able to look at her and feel fine too.

Chapter 9

Marina had first realised her marriage might be in trouble on the morning of her fortieth birthday, when she opened the card from her husband George and saw that it was a comedy one featuring a picture of a woman with boobs so droopy they peeped out from beneath the hem of her knee-length nightie.

Inside was a voucher from a local private clinic entitling her to a breast augmentation, to be carried out by a surgeon whose client list apparently included stars of stage, screen and reality TV.

And by the look on George's face as he watched her read the punchline inside the card, he was expecting her to be impressed.

'But my boobs don't sag down to my knees,' Marina told him.

'I know they don't. That's just a joke.'

'And this?' She held up the voucher. 'Is this a joke too?'

'No, it's for implants! You can have proper boobs, as big as you like. And a real cleavage. You'll look fantastic.' George made exaggerated curvy gestures with his hands. 'Think of the low-cut dresses you'll be able to wear.'

'But . . . I don't wear low-cut dresses,' said Marina.

'I know you don't. That's because you don't have the figure for it. But once you've got new boobs, you'll want to wear them! There'll be no stopping you!'

Fifteen years they'd been married. From the age of twenty-five through to forty, she'd lived with a man who thought she secretly hankered after a boob job.

'Would *you* like me to have bigger boobs?' she asked George, who looked as baffled as if she'd said, 'Would you like it if we won the Lottery?'

'Of course I would.'

Marina almost wanted to apologise to her boobs, of which she'd always been rather fond. She felt quite protective towards them. They might be on the small side, but they were fine, and they were *hers*. Hopefully they weren't listening in to this conversation; she didn't want them to feel inadequate and get a complex. She looked at George. 'Anything else you think I should get done while I'm there?'

Whereupon George, without missing a beat, said, 'Well Debbie looks fantastic, don't you think? Since she had that facelift?'

Debbie was the sales manager at his furniture showroom. She had been married three times, and was loud and terrifyingly confident. Since last year's facelift, Marina would have described Debbie's facial skin as stretched.

'Or I could have my nose straightened,' she suggested.

Evidently delighted that she was keen to improve herself, George beamed widely. 'You could have that as your Christmas present!'

It had been the initial clue that as a wife she was something of a disappointment. George had always liked to mix

81

socially with people who were keen to show off their wealth, but in the last couple of years he'd gone into overdrive. Having joined the local country club – it was one of the most desirable in Cheshire and had a waiting list that only served to increase its desirability – he'd taken to spending more and more time there.

His new friends regarded themselves as the ultra-smart set, and when they met Marina, they seemed bemused by her love of art. They were nice enough in their own way, but she had so little in common with them. All they seemed to talk about was liposuction and Louboutins and their villas in Puerto Banus. They thought nothing of spending hundreds of pounds on a dry-clean-only swimsuit. One of the wives said, 'Marina, you're so pretty, I don't understand why you won't come along with me to the salon. My beautician's brilliant with a tattoo gun. You could have eyebrows like mine!'

The thing was, Marina was used to having George as her husband. OK, he wasn't perfect, but who was? Marriage was about compromise and tolerance, and loving each other in a comfortable, affectionate way. It was fine for them to have their own interests. It simply wasn't necessary for a couple to be joined at the hip.

Well, those had been her views on marriage at the time.

Gosh, nine years ago now.

Time flies when you're having fun.

The tide had turned and was now going out, the edges of the breaking waves silvery as they were caught by the setting sun. Marina perched on a smooth rock and watched as Boo, her elderly neighbour's springer spaniel, snuffled his way along the shoreline, busily intent on investigating every piece of seaweed left on the wet sand. Boo was fine, so she took out her phone and brought up the email that had arrived an hour earlier, just as she'd been collecting the dog.

It was from George, the first she'd received from him in over two years, though you wouldn't think so to read it.

Hi Marina,

How are things with you? All good, I hope. Everyone says hello and sends their love. I looked at your website earlier and the painting seems to be going well. I always knew it would.

Well, things aren't great with me at the moment, sorry to say. Looks like it's my turn to have health problems. Been pretty miserable, to be honest, and thought it might be nice to come down to Cornwall and pay you a visit. It'll be so good to see you again, Marina. Shall we make it this Saturday? Book a table at the best restaurant in St Carys.

Love, George xx

Marina replaced the phone in her pocket and marvelled at her ex-husband's ability to gloss over the past. But that was George for you; he was the ultimate salesman, Teflon-smooth, always selling himself. Apologies simply weren't in his nature.

The most sensible course of action would be to refuse to see him, she knew that, but the mention of health problems had caught her attention. And George's failure to elaborate was unlike him; she couldn't help but be concerned. As a lifelong hypochondriac, he'd always been one of those people to whom you didn't dare say 'How are you?' unless there was nowhere you needed to be in a hurry. It was just his way.

A light breeze whipped her hennaed curls across her face. Marina brushed them out of her eyes and watched Boo as he cavorted in the shallows with a string of seaweed wrapped around one paw.

It was six years ago now since the diagnosis. The day she'd learnt she had breast cancer might have been traumatic, but it hadn't been the worst day of her life.

That had come along a few weeks later, while she'd been recuperating from the surgery and undergoing chemotherapy. George had arrived home from work, appeared in the bedroom doorway and looked at her for several seconds without speaking.

When he didn't ask how she was, Marina said, 'What's wrong?'

'It's no good, I can't do this. I just can't.'

'You can't do what?'

'*This.*' He gestured towards her. 'I'm not cut out for this kind of thing. It's not fair on you.'

Marina felt a surge of nausea rise up, but this time it was born of a mixture of fear and disbelief. 'I don't know what you're saying.'

George's face reddened. 'You know as well as I do that things haven't been right for some time. And now this has happened. It isn't fair to expect me to have to go through all this business with you. Honestly, a clean break's better for both of us. I'll make an appointment to see my solicitor and he'll put the wheels in motion.'

'The wheels . . .?' Marina said faintly.

'Divorce.'

'Oh.'

'It's for the best,' said George.

'Is it?' Her trembling hand went to her forehead, which was clammy with shock and disbelief.

'Look, it's not my fault you're ill. If I stayed just because you had cancer, what kind of person would that make me? I'll tell you,' George announced with a wag of his index finger. 'It would make me a hypocrite.'

The word ignited a tiny flame of indignation in her brain. He hadn't always been like this, though; the last few years at the country club had changed him for the worse. Emboldened, Marina said, 'So, in sickness and in health, just so long as it isn't the sickness?'

'Oh trust you to twist things to try and make me look bad.' George rolled his eyes. 'That was so long ago. You make those vows when you're getting married. We're talking about divorce now.'

'Well you are.'

'Don't start with the emotional blackmail.' He shook his head and checked his watch. 'I'm not an ogre; it's not as if I'm going to be leaving you homeless and penniless. I'll be moving out tomorrow, by the way.'

'So I'll still have this house?' That was something, at least. Marina realised she was shredding the crumpled tissue in her hand. Her mind was in a whirl.

'No, we'll sell it. The solicitor tells me you're entitled to half, even though I'm the one who's paid the mortgage all these years.'

George had always insisted he didn't want her to work more than part-time, because her job was to look after him. And to think she'd been touched by his thoughtfulness. Because back then, he *had* been kind . . . hadn't he?

'You've already spoken to the solicitor, then.'

'You're getting a bloody good deal, Marina. You should be grateful I'm not the kind who'd rip you off.'

'Who's your solicitor? Arthur?' Arthur was in his late sixties and had done their conveyancing; his office was just down the road.

George shook his head. 'You can have Arthur. I'll be using Jake Hannam.'

If Arthur was a bumbling Labrador, Jake was a wolf. A member of the country club – *of course* – he was in his thirties, wore flashy cufflinks and drove a black Porsche. He was the brother of Giselle, who was at the centre of the smart set and led a complicated social life.

Marina's voice was unsteady. 'Are you having an affair, George?'

'Don't be ridiculous.' He heaved a sorrowful sigh. 'Of course not.'

'OK. Could you pass me that bowl?' She held out a trembling arm. 'I think I'm going to be sick.'

He'd been lying, obviously. It had all been so embarrassing and so predictable. Reaching for the pink frisbee balanced on the rock beside her, Marina waited as Boo raced across the sand towards her, then spun it high into the air for him to try and catch in his mouth. Whilst she'd continued with the punishing, debilitating courses of chemotherapy, George had moved into Giselle's six-bedroom mock-Georgian home, then whisked her off for a holiday on the island of Capri.

Which was, by all accounts, a glorious place to visit.

Lucky them.

A piercing whistle behind her made Marina twist round.

Clemency, in shorts and a T-shirt, was waving at her. Marina waved back.

Out of breath, Clemency jogged over to join her. 'I've done a full circuit of both beaches and the cliffs, and now I need to eat pizza.' She took a swig of water from her almost-empty bottle and collapsed on to the sand.

'Take cover,' Marina warned, because Clemency's arrival had brought Boo charging back up the beach with the frisbee in his mouth. Having been cavorting in the sea, he now shook himself energetically, spraying them both with cold water.

'Oh Boo, you're such a hooligan. Actually, that's really nice.' Clemency seized control of the frisbee and flung it once more, then leant back on her elbows. 'How's Alf?'

'What? Oh, sorry. Much better, thank goodness.' Without even realising it, Marina discovered she'd taken her phone back out of her pocket and was rereading the email from George.

'Everything OK?'

'Fine!'

'Sure?'

Marina hesitated. She was so used to presenting a cheerful face to the world, it was sometimes hard to relax. But this was Clemency she was talking to; she could allow herself to be honest.

'Here.' She passed the phone over. 'I got this.'

She watched as Clemency scanned the lines then turned to stare up at her in disbelief.

'My God, he has a nerve. He walked out on you when you could hardly get out of bed! He abandoned you at the very worst time of your life!' Clemency's eyes glinted in the sunlight. 'And now that things aren't quite perfect for him, he wants to come and see you? I do hope you've told him to fuck off.'

Marina smiled at her indignation. 'I haven't replied yet. That's why I was reading it again.'

'Would you like me to do the honours?'

'It's OK. I think I'm too curious to refuse to see him.'

'You could give him a call, ask him what he's playing at.'

'If George says he's coming down here, he won't take no for an answer. I haven't seen him for over five years,' said Marina. 'If he turns up, I could always shut the door in his face, but I have to admit . . . I do want to know what he wants.'

'And once you've found out, *then* can I push him off a high cliff?'

Amused, Marina threw the frisbee once more. 'Maybe. We'll see.'

'I still can't get over what he did. I don't know how he can live with himself.'

'Maybe he feels bad about it.' Marina shrugged. 'He might be coming here to say sorry.'

'Well if he does, I hope you don't let him off the hook.' Clemency sat up and dusted sand from her tanned legs. 'The trouble with you is, you're too nice. Just remember,' she warned. 'Some things are too horrendous to forgive.'

Chapter 10

On Friday evening, Clemency had just stepped out of the shower when the doorbell rang.

Of course it did. Doorbells always knew. She wrapped a white towel around herself and ran downstairs. For a split second, out of nowhere, the thought flew into her brain that when she pulled open the front door, Sam would be standing there on the doorstep.

Ooh. Hastily wiping the inevitable mascara stains from under her eyes, she mentally readied herself just in case, assumed a flattering pose and opened the door with an expectant smile.

'Hi, surprise! Urgh, you've got a ton of black under your eyes . . . you look like one of the undead!'

'Thanks,' said Clemency as Belle gave her a hug.

'That's OK. Ew, it's like you're all *sweaty.*'

'Well I'm not, I'm all clean.'

'I know! Just teasing. And well done for not coughing all over me this time! Come on, Uncle Fester, let's get you back upstairs before you scare people to death.'

Clemency peered over her shoulder. 'Is Sam not with you?'

'No, just me.' Belle gestured dramatically. 'No one else. I'm all alone!'

'Why? What's happened?' Clemency's heart began to thud against her ribcage. 'Have you and Sam broken up?'

Belle burst out laughing. '*What?* Wow, you're a ray of sunshine – of course we haven't broken up! Why would I want to dump someone like Sam?'

Clemency instantly found herself torn between being discreet and behaving normally. But Belle was her sister, so normal had to win. Flippantly she said, 'I thought maybe he'd dumped you.'

'Er, hello? Look at me.' Belle struck a pose and did a selfie pout. 'Who in their right mind would want to dump this?' She was grinning now, half taking the mickey out of herself but also half meaning it. The way she acknowledged her own vanity was actually one of Belle's more endearing characteristics.

Upstairs in the flat, Clemency threw on a dress and dragged a brush through her wet hair. Returning to the living room, she found Belle peering into the mirror on the wall, trying out her new lipstick.

'What are you doing here?'

'I came to see you!' Belle blew a kiss at her through the mirror. 'Ha, joking. This lipstick's nice, isn't it? I think it probably suits me better than it suits you. No, Sam's in Geneva on business; he's flying back tomorrow. I came on ahead and he'll be arriving tomorrow afternoon. I was planning to have a quiet night in tonight, but then I bumped into Paddy and he said you were off to the Mermaid . . . so I thought I'd come with you. We can go for a drink together! Won't that be nice?'

'Lovely.' *So* transparent. Clemency said, 'Did Paddy happen to mention that I was going with Ronan?'

'I can't remember. Maybe he did mention it, I'm not sure.'

'Except Ronan can't make it now.'

Belle's face fell. 'Oh.'

'Joking,' Clemency said triumphantly.

Ah, a bit of sisterly one-upmanship never went amiss.

Twenty minutes later, they left the flat and made their way over to the Mermaid.

'So you're going to be seeing a bit more of me,' Belle said happily as she perched her Tiffany sunglasses decoratively on top of her head. 'Now that Sam's planning to spend most of his time down here, I'll be keeping him company.'

'Most of his time? I thought he'd just be flying down for the occasional weekend.' This was what Clemency had been mentally bracing herself for.

'No, no.' Belle shook back her hair. 'He's spent the last few years working non-stop. His friends have persuaded him to take the summer off, give himself a break. Well, obviously not a complete break, but he can keep an eye on the business from down here. He deserves a rest after everything he's been through. Did you know he used to be married?'

Did she? Clemency's mind raced once more before settling on the correct answer. She shook her head and said, 'No . . .?' in a mildly enquiring kind of way.

'Oh, I wondered if he'd mentioned it when you showed him the flat on Saturday morning. His wife died. Three years ago, of a brain tumour. She was ill the whole time they were married. Can you imagine? Poor Sam. So sad. Well, sad for him.' Belle beamed. 'But good news for me!'

Oh God. Clemency shook her head. 'That's a terrible thing to say.'

Belle shrugged. 'Just being honest. It's sad that he lost his wife, but life goes on. Sam's still here and he deserves to be happy. And he's going to be happy from now on, because he has me!'

Of all the girls in all the world, he'd had to choose Belle. 'Thank goodness he managed to find someone so compassionate and modest and unassuming,' said Clemency.

'I know.' Belle did an unrepentant shimmy. 'But I mean it. I'm not going to let him go. Sam's everything I ever wanted; he's just perfect. I mean, you must have noticed. He's pretty damn gorgeous.'

'Oh yes, he's got the looks,' said Clemency, because no one could say he hadn't.

'I know! Didn't I tell you on the phone? I said you'd be impressed. But it's not just that,' Belle went on. 'He's the full package. This really could be it, you know. Sam's fantastic. He could be the one. Which is why you're going to be seeing more of me, because there's no way I'd want to leave him down here on his own. That wouldn't be clever. Girls would be swarming all over him like wasps.'

'What about your job?' Even as she asked the question, Clemency realised she already knew the answer.

'Oh, I'm jacking it in. They're just not my kind of people at that place. Anyway, Sam isn't the only one who needs a break.'

No surprises there. No surprise either that Belle hadn't bothered to mention it before. She was brilliant at being interviewed for jobs and excellent at being offered them, but her staying power wasn't the best. She and her flatmates in upmarket Chelsea all appeared to share the same relaxed attitude towards employment, presumably because their families were mega-loaded. Belle's latest attempt at gainful employment had involved working in PR for the company owned by her best friend's father, who really should have known better.

'Why aren't they your kind of people?' said Clemency.

'Oh, they're just so *intense*. No sense of humour. And they're like, really strict about timekeeping.' Belle gestured carelessly with her arm. 'I can't be doing with that sort of hassle. I mean, who needs it?'

Who indeed? At a guess, late nights out had resulted in Belle oversleeping and turning up at work two hours after everyone else. Clemency said, 'And Sam's fine with you not working, is he?'

'Well, yes, good point.' Belle nodded sagely. 'He *is* OK with it, but I don't want him thinking I'm just another trust-fund Tara, so I'll explain that I do a lot of charity work. Which I *do*,' she emphasised. 'So it's completely true. I'm not lying!'

Clemency grinned. Belle's idea of charity work was attending glitzy fund-raising balls at five-star hotels. You wouldn't catch her working behind the counter at the local Oxfam shop.

Two hours later, they were still sitting in the Mermaid's beer garden, gazing out to sea, while Ronan was inside at the bar buying the next round of drinks.

'Well?' said Clemency. 'Go on, you can tell me. Still fancy him?'

'Ronan?' Belle rolled her eyes. 'No I do not.'

'Sure about that?'

'Of course I'm sure. I've got Sam now. He's cancelled out the whole Ronan thing, which was never even a real thing in the first place.'

Ronan materialised behind them. 'Oh thanks a lot. That's my ego crushed then.'

Clemency took her drink from him. 'I think your ego will probably survive. And she only came along tonight because she knew you'd be here.'

'Look,' Belle complained, 'can we stop playing this silly game now? It's really tedious.'

'I like it.' Clemency grinned. It hadn't taken them long to fall back into bickering-sister mode.

'Well it's wearing thin. We aren't teenagers any more. I have a fantastic boyfriend. Unlike you,' said Belle.

'But is he better-looking than me?' Ronan turned to face Clemency. 'Well, *is* he?'

'He's very good-looking,' said Clemency.

'Look!' Belle whipped out her phone. 'I'll show you!'

And she did. Clemency found herself alongside Ronan, gazing at a series of photos of Sam and Belle together.

'He won't let me take selfies of us, he doesn't like it, but I got Tamsin to take these for me. See?' Belle gave Ronan a nudge. 'This is the real reason I wanted to see you tonight. So I could show off my perfect boyfriend and make you think twice about that time you turned me down. Because that's all in the past now, and I've moved on to bigger and better things.'

Clemency was unable to resist it. 'As opposed to Ronan's tiny disappointing thing.'

'Cruel,' Ronan protested, 'and also not true.' He shook his head at Belle. 'She's never seen it, OK? Just so you know. And it's *definitely* not true.'

'Doesn't matter to me.' Belle looked smug. 'I've got Sam.'

'Yes, but if things don't work out . . .'

Belle's eyes were sparkling. 'Don't worry, they will.'

'It doesn't do to be overconfident. If he's that much of a catch, all the girls'll be after him. And now he's going to be down here,' said Ronan. 'Look at Clem, she's still single. What if she makes a play for your boyfriend?' He shrugged, amused. 'You never know, do you? She might steal him off you.'

Clemency's mouth was dry. Thank goodness self-preservation had prevented her from ever telling Ronan the story about the time she'd chatted up the guy on a plane who'd turned out – humiliatingly – to be married. All he was doing now was teasing Belle, blithely unaware of how near the knuckle his remarks were.

But Belle was smiling, confident. 'She wouldn't.'

Ronan said playfully, 'She might.'

'Nope. It'll never happen.' Belle shook her head. 'I know that for a fact.'

'You don't know it for a fact!'

'Ah, but I do. She's my stepsister and sometimes she drives me completely insane, but I know I can trust her. One hundred per cent. And Clem knows she can trust me.' As she said it, Belle slid her arm around Clemency's waist and gave her a squeeze. 'We made a promise, didn't we? To each other.'

Clemency nodded, her mouth still dry. 'We did.'

'How do you know you'll keep it?' Ronan was looking interested.

'Because I made a mistake once. I was a bad, bad girl,' said Belle. 'And I learnt my lesson the hard way.'

It had happened just before they'd turned eighteen. After almost two years of living together in the prickly way of two teenagers who would far rather *not* be under the same roof, Belle had acquired a public-school boyfriend called Giles, who'd come to spend a few days with them at Polrennick House the week before Christmas. Typically loud and confident, he'd made a joke one evening about being fought over by the two sisters. The next morning Clemency had overheard him making a snide comment about her mum having won the Lotto jackpot when she'd hooked up with Belle's father. Later, when she confronted him about it while Belle was upstairs in the shower, Giles had smirked and suggested she was protesting too much. Then on the last day of his stay, aware of her simmering dislike of him and purely for his own entertainment, he told Belle that her stepsister had made a pass at him.

Belle, believing Giles rather than Clemency, had hit the roof. Clemency, outraged at having been accused of something she hadn't done, had been incandescent with fury, firstly at not being believed and secondly because there was no way in the *world* she'd ever make a pass at the spiteful chinless rat-weasel that was Vile Giles.

Giles had left, but the insult-hurling between the two volatile sisters had ricocheted on, and Clemency's mum and Belle's dad had been forced to intervene to prevent the upcoming Christmas celebrations being completely ruined. On the surface, at least, a precarious truce had been called.

Two months later, Clemency had begun seeing Pierre, a nineteen-year-old surf instructor who lived in Bude. Pierre was tall and rangy, with sea-green eyes and tangled blond hair. He was a beautiful specimen, confident and funny. A little bit wild, but charming too, he had won Clemency over completely. She'd been smitten, more so than ever before, and the thought of seeing him brightened each day.

Then at Easter, she went up to Manchester for a week to stay with a friend who'd moved there from Cornwall the previous year. And when she returned, it wasn't quite the happy homecoming she'd anticipated.

The absence of cars on the driveway had told her that Baz and her mum were both out. Hearing music coming from the first floor, Clemency had made her way up the staircase. When she knocked on Belle's bedroom door, Belle opened it and said, 'Oh, it's you.' Then, with a little smirk, she allowed the door to swing wide open and added, 'Oh dear.'

Except there was no *Oh dear* about it, because she'd known which train Clemency had been catching, and exactly what time she'd be back.

In one way, you almost had to admire her exemplary planning skills, because ensuring that Clemency would be home to see Pierre asleep and sprawled across Belle's king-sized bed in just boxer shorts couldn't have been easy.

'Why?' Clemency looked at Belle, who was fastening the belt of her green silk dressing gown around her narrow waist. 'Why would you do this?'

'Ooh, I don't know, maybe because I can?' With an air of triumph, Belle added, 'And because it was so easy. And because now you know how it feels.'

Across the room, Pierre's eyes snapped open and focused on the two sisters. 'Oh shit.'

'Hi, honey.' Clemency addressed him with ice in her voice. 'I'm home.'

On the outside she might appear cool, but inside her heart felt as though it was disintegrating like a digestive dropped in hot tea.

Pierre said, 'Look, it was an accident . . .'

But Clemency was already shaking her head. 'I think you'll find it was deliberate.' She turned back to Belle. 'Do you really like him?'

'He's got a great body.' Belle shrugged. 'We've had fun. But he's not my type.'

'What?' Shocked, Pierre said, 'Why not? What's wrong with me?'

'Seriously?' Clemency counted the reasons on her fingers. 'You didn't have a public-school education, your parents aren't super-wealthy, you ride a moped . . .'

'So the last week hasn't meant anything to you?' Pierre stared at Belle in disbelief.

'Well it meant I got to teach my stepsister a lesson she won't forget in a hurry. So I'd say that makes it worthwhile.' Belle turned to Clemency. 'You can have him back now,' she said flippantly.

'You must be joking. I wouldn't touch him with a bargepole. I never want to see him again.' By some miracle, Clemency managed to hold herself together, though her voice was perilously close to cracking with emotion. 'I wish I never had to see either of you again. God, you deserve each other. The pair of you are just . . . *repulsive*.'

'Are we? *Are we?*' Belle's eyes were glittering. 'Serves you right for making a pass at Giles!'

'Blimey.' Ronan was now shaking his head at the tale they'd recounted between them. 'This is like *EastEnders*. At least you're both still alive. So what happened after that?'

'We had A levels coming up,' said Clemency. 'I wasn't seeing Pierre any more, obviously, so I spent all my time revising. Which is why I ended up doing so well.'

'And I thought it'd be fun to carry on seeing him for a bit longer, just to really rub her nose in it.' Belle pulled a face. 'So I didn't get much revision done at all.'

'With predictable results,' said Clemency. 'It actually made me feel a lot better at the time, knowing she was going to get bad grades.'

Ronan looked from one to the other. 'And were you speaking to each other by then?'

'Are you kidding?' said Clemency. 'No way.'

'Then one day, out of the blue, I got a phone call from Giles,' Belle continued. 'We'd broken up in February and by then it was the beginning of June. He asked me to go and see him, because he had something to tell me. I wasn't really that bothered, but he insisted it was important and told me he was in hospital in Exeter. So then of course I had to go over there, and he was in a right old state.'

'Physically?' said Ronan.

'Well yes, that too. But I'm talking mentally. He was just so ashamed and guilty and sorry. If it hadn't been Giles I'd have thought he was having some kind of religious crisis . . . except it *was* Giles. Anyway, it turned out that the day before, his mum's new cleaner had happened to mention she was psychic and could read auras. Well, Giles let her do his, just for a laugh, and she told him he'd told a lie a few months ago. He laughed, but she said it was a terrible lie and he'd be punished for it. Then she told him the punishment would be very soon, it would teach him a lesson he'd remember for the rest of his life . . . oh, and that holiday in

Mexico he'd been looking forward to? He wouldn't be going on it.'

'Nice,' said Ronan. 'Cheery.'

'Of course Giles thought it was all completely hilarious. Until he went out that same evening to meet up with friends and an old guy in a Datsun lost control and drove up on to the pavement, sending Giles smashing into a wall.' Belle spread her hands. 'Well, that was it. He ended up with two broken legs, a broken arm, three cracked ribs, severe internal bruising . . . and some kind of epiphany. He'd never believed in psychics before, but now he did. And he was convinced the accident was all down to fate, punishing him for his terrible lie. He was crying as he said it. I mean, actually *sobbing*,' she emphasised. 'Then he told me that Clem had never made a pass at him, he'd just made it all up to cause trouble because he knew she didn't like him. And he kept apologising and crying and begging me to forgive him for what he'd done—'

'Even though *I* was the one he'd lied about,' Clemency cut in.

'Anyway, I felt pretty bad too.' Belle shook her hair back. 'Because if Giles hadn't made up that whole story in the first place, I would never have slept with Pierre. So I went home and told Clem, and for the first time in years we sat down and had a proper talk.'

'First time *ever*,' Clemency corrected her. 'We'd never done it before.'

Belle nodded. 'It was a really long talk, too. About boys and family and us being sisters whether we liked it or not. And I knew how I'd felt when I thought Clem had made a play for my boyfriend, so it made me feel extra terrible about doing what I'd done. Anyway, we ended up making a solemn pact. We promised we'd never, ever go near each other's boyfriends – in *that* sense – again. Because we were sisters, and sisters don't do that. It's like people don't do it to their best friends. We weren't best friends, but we were living in the same house, and everything would be so much easier if we could just be nicer to each other and really make an effort to get along.' Belle paused. 'So that was it, we made a pact, we've stuck to it ever since and we always will. My boyfriends are one hundred per cent off-limits to Clem, and hers are off-limits to me. It's actually really nice, isn't it?' She gave Clemency another squeeze. 'Knowing we can trust each other that much.'

'This is weird,' said Ronan. 'Weird but good. All these years, and I've never seen the two of you like this before. You know, relaxed and getting on together.'

'Oh, we have our good moments,' said Belle. 'Don't we?'

'Few and far between,' Clemency admitted. 'But they happen.'

'And there's going to be more of them, because we'll be seeing a lot more of each other once I'm properly back here. And I've got Sam, which makes me *really* happy.' Belle raised her glass. 'Life's never been better.'

'Well that's great,' said Ronan. 'Here's to Giles and his miraculous epiphany.' He clinked his own glass against each of theirs in turn. 'What happened to him, do you know? Did he recover and devote the rest of his life to doing good works?'

'Ha, you're kidding,' said Belle. 'This is Giles we're talking about. He ended up getting involved in a spot of insider trading and did two years in prison for fraud.'

Chapter 11

Marina finished work earlier than usual on Saturday afternoon. George was due to arrive around six and there'd been no mention of him booking himself into a hotel for the night so she needed to get the spare room ready.

As always, she collected Ben and Amy from across the road and brought them back to her cottage for an hour or so, in order to let their mother head off and do the weekly supermarket shop in peace. The three-year-old twins loved coming over to visit, and she enjoyed having them with her, even if coping with their noisy, rambunctious company sometimes felt like trying to herd cats and left her feeling the need to lie down afterwards in a darkened room.

Although with George en route, that most definitely *wouldn't* be happening today.

'Wheeeeee!' screamed Ben, racing along the landing with a pillowcase billowing behind him like a cloak. 'I'm Batman!'

'I'm a ghost,' Amy shouted from beneath her white sheet. She waved her arms. 'Am I scary?'

'Extremely scary,' said Marina. 'In fact, terrifying.'

Delighted, Amy bellowed, 'I'm scary! Wooooooo!' and flapped her arms wildly as she danced around the bedroom.

'OK, let me put the sheet on the bed now,' said Marina. 'And I need the blue towels on the landing to go in the bathroom. Can you be very good and get those for me?'

'I want to get the blue towels,' Ben roared. 'I want to rescue them because I'm Batman.'

'No no NO.' Amy pushed him over as she hurtled past him. 'I do it! Get out my way!'

It took a while, but Marina eventually had the spare room ready. She sat the twins downstairs in front of a cartoon on TV and gave the bathroom a quick once-over, before vacuuming up the trail of biscuit crumbs that had mysteriously appeared on the stairs.

Suzanne, the twins' mum, knocked on the door to collect them.

'Thank you so much,' she told Marina. 'Honestly, you're an angel. I don't know how I'd manage without you.'

Marina smiled. 'It's a joy having them here.'

'Come on, you two.' Suzanne clapped her hands together. 'Let's get home now, give Marina some peace. Pick up your backpacks and say goodbye.'

How Marina loved it when the twins wrapped their bare arms around her neck and gave her a kiss on the cheek. The smell of their baby-fine hair and the warmth of their skin melted her heart.

'I'll see you soon, sweetie.' She straightened the ribbon in Amy's ponytail, then said, 'Oh look at that, your backpack's open, let me close it for you. We don't want your treasures falling out, do we?' Amy was a squirrel who had a collection of shells, postcards, buttons and Sylvanian animals from which she refused to be parted.

The next moment she glimpsed the corner of something inside the Disney backpack. Her heart lurched and she whipped the photograph out, holding it with the picture side pressed to her chest.

'Amy, where did you get this?' It was hard to keep her voice steady, normal-sounding.

Amy instantly looked shifty. 'I found it.'

'Oh darling, you mustn't do that.' Suzanne was mortified. 'I'm *so* sorry, Marina. Amy, you must never take things that don't belong to you. Where did you find it?'

'In a box under the bed. I liked it for a treasure.' The little girl pointed to the back of the photo clutched to Marina's chest.

'It's a special photograph, that's all. Of someone I knew a long time ago. Sorry, sweetheart, but can you always ask me before you take things? I wouldn't like to lose it.' To her horror, Marina heard her own voice go husky. 'You see, grown-ups have treasures too . . . but it's fine, fine . . . my fault for not putting it somewhere safe . . . Did you take anything else from the box?' Straightening up, she slid the photograph between the pages of a nearby book and placed it on the highest shelf in the living room, then checked through the rest of Amy's backpack.

'Amy, say sorry,' prompted Suzanne.

Amy's bottom lip wobbled. 'I liked it. Who was in the picture? I sorry.'

Still shaken but ashamed of her own reaction, Marina said, 'Sweetheart, it's fine, it doesn't matter.'

Only when Suzanne had ushered the twins out of the cottage was Marina able to breathe normally once more.

God, what a close shave that had been. As a rule, no one entered the spare room upstairs, which was why she'd stored the box in there beneath the bed. While she'd been cleaning the bathroom or vacuuming up biscuit crumbs, Amy had found and opened it, and investigated the contents.

Imagine if she hadn't spotted the photo in the little girl's backpack. The thought of it made her feel sick.

She crossed the room, carefully slid the photograph from between the pages of the book and gazed at it for the millionth time. Yes, she'd made digital copies and stored them online — of course she had — but this was the important one, the original. It was, without a doubt, the single most precious item she owned.

She exhaled slowly and headed for the staircase. In an hour or two, George would be arriving on her doorstep. Before he turned up, it was definitely time to find a new and improved hiding place for the box she'd been keeping beneath the spare bed.

Clemency's breath caught in her throat when the door to Barton and Byrne swung open and Sam strode into the office.

'Oh, hello!' Her first panicky thought was that it had been a warm afternoon, the last client had just left a whiff of body odour in the air and she really hoped Sam wouldn't wonder if it was coming from her.

'Hey. How are you? I just called Belle and she's busy at some salon having a mani-pedi, whatever that may be. So I thought I'd drop by on the off chance, see if I can take a quick look at the apartment and do some measuring up.'

'A Moneypenny?' Ronan emerged from the back room. 'Any relation to a vajazzle? Hi, I'm Ronan Byrne.' He shook

Sam's hand. 'And I know who you are, because Belle spent yesterday evening showing us pictures of you on her phone.'

'I've heard about you too.' Amused, Sam turned back to Clemency. 'So would that be possible, do you think?'

'I can give you the key if you like,' said Clemency. 'It's OK, we trust you.'

Sam replied steadily, 'I'd rather do things by the book, if you can spare the time.'

'Of course she can,' said Ronan. 'We'll be closing up soon.' He made a friendly shooing gesture. 'I'll take care of everything here. Go.'

The apartment looked bigger now that it was completely empty. The fast-track purchase had miraculously gone according to plan – which almost *never* happened – and the exchange of contracts and simultaneous completion was on course to take place on Tuesday.

Clemency held the other end of the tape measure as Sam took the dimensions of the windows and relayed them over the phone to a curtain-maker in London. He was wearing jeans and a white polo shirt, and it was lovely being able to watch him unobserved while he was dictating numbers into the phone.

Which, seeing as watching him was all she was ever going to be able to do, was just as well.

Every little helps.

'Thanks,' said Sam when the task was complete. 'And a big thank you for showing me this place last week.'

'Bit of an impulse buy.' Clemency smiled.

'I'm very glad I acted on impulse. I like everything about this flat.' He paused. 'I like everything I've seen about St Carys. It's all good.'

Clemency nodded brightly; she was going to have to get brilliant at this. 'I told you, it's a fantastic place to live.'

For a couple of seconds the silence stretched between them. Then Sam leant against the kitchen worktop and said, 'I wish you weren't Annabelle's sister, though.'

Oh God.

Clemency attempted to conceal her true feelings with flippancy. 'Trust me, over the years I've often wished that. But I am.'

'Look, I need to say this. I can't pretend it didn't occur to me.' His dark eyes were fixed on her, unwavering. 'I really like Annabelle, but it did cross my mind that you and I had that connection, and if things didn't work out between me and Annabelle . . . well then maybe—'

'No,' Clemency blurted out, 'you mustn't think that. It can't happen, it can't *ever* happen.'

'It's OK, I know. She told me why not. I've heard the whole story. She called me last night after your evening in the pub with Ronan.'

'It means a lot to me,' said Clemency, and this time she absolutely meant it. 'It's one of those things I'd never go back on. I just wouldn't.'

'Well that's very . . . honourable.' Sam nodded. 'Good for you.' Wryly he added, 'Bad for me.'

'To be fair, I never thought it'd be an issue. All these years and I've never once been remotely interested in any of Belle's boyfriends.'

A faint smile. 'No? Why not, what were they like?'

'Posh. Loud. Public-school Henrys. Rah-rah, look at me, that kind of thing.'

'I'm not posh,' said Sam.

'You're not her usual type. You're completely different.

She chose well, for once.' Clemency shook her head. 'Annoyingly.'

He sighed. 'This isn't going to be easy.'

Tell me about it. 'I know. But we don't have any choice.'

'Can we do it?' said Sam.

Clemency hoped he didn't know the extent of the effect he was having on her; it was taking every last ounce of her self-control just to sound normal. 'Of course we can do it. I can do it. So can you. We have to.'

'You're right.' He nodded. 'I know. I just wish there was a way to make it easier.'

It was easier for her, Clemency realised, because Sam was already seeing someone else and was therefore off-limits. It was more difficult for him because she was single and unattached.

Flashbacks from last night in the Mermaid distracted her for a moment. A split second later, she understood why her subconscious was tugging at her sleeve, bringing them to her attention. A *zingggg* went through her at the realisation, because this would definitely help. OK, think fast . . . it wouldn't hurt anyone, it'd be easy enough to do, there were no downsides . . .

'Look, I haven't mentioned it before, but there is someone I'm involved with. Well, kind of. It's a . . . developing situation.' Clemency did a you-know-what-I-mean shrug.

'Oh. Right. I didn't realise.' Sam looked taken aback, which was good. 'Annabelle told me you weren't seeing anyone.'

'That's because she doesn't know. I mean, I will tell her,' said Clemency. 'Soon. It's just that we're keeping things low-key for a while, for . . . you know, various reasons. Until the time's right.'

'OK. OK,' Sam murmured. 'Well, that's probably a good thing. Yes, it'll make things easier. Although . . .' His eyebrows creased as a thought occurred. 'Why are you having to keep quiet about it? Is he married?'

'No, no.' Clemency shook her head, amused by the note of disapproval in his voice. 'He's not married. He's my boss.'

'Are you serious? You mean what's-his-name, Gavin? The one who's always playing golf?'

Now that would be a relationship you'd want to keep quiet about. Heroically, Clemency managed not to burst out laughing. Ew, the very thought of having a secret affair with a man who wore checked golfing trousers and was old enough to be your father. Steadily she replied, 'Not Gavin, no. But thanks for thinking it could be him.'

Seriously, though, if you were going to have an imaginary relationship, you'd at least make sure it was with someone gorgeous.

'And it isn't Paula, our secretary, either,' Clemency added. Then she stopped and waited for Sam to say it.

'Right.' He nodded slowly, taking in the news and this time accepting the answer without surprise. 'I see, I get it now. It's Ronan.'

At that moment, a seagull flew down on to the terrace, and noisily rapped his beak against the French window, making them both jump. He eyed them beadily through the glass, clearly waiting to be fed with scraps.

'Yes, it's Ronan,' said Clemency when she'd shooed the bird away. 'Don't mention it to Belle just yet. I'll tell her myself.'

Give me a chance to warn Ronan first.

Chapter 12

'Marina. Let me look at you. Well, this is just . . . amazing. You look so well. *So well.*' George, on the doorstep, spread his arms wide. 'Oh my goodness, come here!'

And Marina, thinking *What am I like?*, discovered she was so British she was incapable of refusing the command and found herself submitting to a hug from the ex-husband she hadn't seen for over five years.

Oh God, the curse of good manners. But a polite hug was one thing. She stepped smartly back before he could give her a kiss on the cheek.

'Hello, George. You probably think I'm looking well because the last time you saw me I had no hair and a face shaped like the moon from steroids.'

George, nothing if not thick-skinned, said, 'But now your hair's grown back. It always was beautiful. And you've found yourself a great little cottage here. Let's have a look at it . . .'

By way of contrast, George's hair had receded, grown thinner and greyer since their last encounter. His nose was thinner too. Fascinated, Marina saw that it was also straighter; it altered his whole face. In addition, his stomach had expanded and he was wearing a designer shirt with a flowery print on the insides of the collar and cuffs, as well as after-shave more suited to a much younger man.

'It's small,' he said, gazing around the living room, 'but you've made it very nice.'

'Thanks. It's small because it was all I could afford after the divorce. What happened to your nose?'

He instantly touched it. 'Oh, sinus problems. I was having trouble breathing.'

Bad Marina thought: *That would be too much to hope for.*

Aloud she said, 'Really? I didn't know those kind of operations could alter the shape like that.'

'Well,' he conceded, 'it was Giselle's idea. I wasn't bothered, but she said why not kill two birds with one stone . . .?'

Marina said innocently, 'How did she manage that? With a cricket bat? And your nose just happened to get in the way?'

George looked at her. He shook his head as if he were disappointed, then heaved a sigh. 'You have every right to be angry. I'm sorry, I can't tell you how sorry I am. I made the worst mistake of my life, and believe me, I've lived to regret it.'

'Oh George, it's not that terrible. It was just a surprise, that's all. Give me an hour or two and I'm sure I'll get used to it.'

'What?' For a moment he looked baffled, then he said, 'I'm not talking about my nose.'

Marina looked surprised. 'No? Oh, OK.'

'I meant Giselle. What she did to us. What she made me do to you.'

The words *passing the buck* sprang to mind.

111

'She was like a witch,' George continued. 'It was as if I'd been hypnotised by her. You have no idea what it was like for me.'

'Careful,' said Marina. 'You'll make me cry.'

'Look, do you have any Scotch? I could really do with a drink.' George sat down heavily on the two-seater sofa and mopped his forehead with a handkerchief. 'I know I've been stupid, and now I'm paying for it. I never really loved her, you know. I was just swept up in the excitement of it all. She knew so many famous people. And do you want to know the truth?' He looked up at Marina as she handed him a tumbler of Scotch. 'The last five years have been hell. Really, the most miserable of my life. Giselle's a nightmare to live with. She spends money like tap water. Anyway, I've learnt my lesson. I should never have done it.'

Since he was clearly waiting for her to say something, Marina murmured, 'Oh dear.'

'And we're not together any more,' George said heavily. 'Ah.'

'She's turfed me out of the house.' He took another slug of Scotch. 'Got that bloody shark of a brother of hers on her side. They're shafting me, of course. And the business is going down the pan.'

'George, if you've come here to ask if I can lend you some money, you've had a wasted journey,' said Marina. 'I don't earn that much. Everything I make during the summer season has to last the whole year—'

'I'm not here asking for money. That's not why I wanted to see you again. I miss you, Marina.' He shook his head. 'I miss you so much. More than you'll ever know. And I'm sorry.'

Outside, seagulls were wheeling and crying overhead.

Inside, there was silence. Marina's throat tightened and the backs of her eyes prickled, because George wasn't the kind of man to whom apologising came naturally.

She'd never expected to hear him say sorry, and now he was saying it.

It actually meant far more to her than she'd thought it would. He was admitting he'd done a bad thing to her, acknowledging his mistake.

'Are you OK?' said George.

She swallowed. 'I'm fine.'

'I'm not homeless, by the way. I've rented an apartment overlooking the golf course. It's a nice place.'

'Well that's good.'

'How about you? Have you missed me?'

'*Missed* you?' Marina stared at her ex-husband in disbelief. 'Why would you even ask me that question?'

'OK, let's leave it for now. I'm blurting everything out without thinking it through. It's just that I'm so happy to see you again. Food,' George announced, pausing to finish his drink. 'I'm hungry, aren't you? Time to go and get something to eat.' He rose to his feet and brushed at the creases in his shirt. 'Have you booked somewhere nice?'

'It's the restaurant at the Mariscombe Hotel, on the other side of St Carys.'

'Good. Now, I want you to relax and enjoy yourself. We're going to have a wonderful time. And don't worry about the bill,' George added magnanimously. 'This is on me.'

By ten in the evening, Marina *was* feeling pleasantly relaxed. Dinner had been delicious, and by unspoken agreement they'd stuck to neutral topics of conversation. She'd told George all about her life down here in St Carys, and

113

in return he'd told her stories about his own friends and work colleagues back in Cheshire. Some of them were people she'd once known, and it had been interesting catching up with their news. Jake Hannam was on his third marriage now, and the nanny his second wife had hired to look after their small children was evidently minus a boyfriend but mysteriously pregnant.

It was a warm night, and after dinner they'd moved out on to the terrace to finish their drinks. There were other people around them but at enough of a distance for their conversation to remain private. George said, 'Did you ever hear anything from . . . you know?' and from his tone of voice, Marina knew at once what he was talking about. She felt her stomach tense up at the unexpected reference. Outwardly calm, she shook her head.

'No, I never did. Anyway, there are things you haven't told me yet. You said something in your email about being unwell.' Apart from being plumper and balder – and the nose, of course – he looked just as he'd looked before. And from the way he'd polished off a rack of lamb with dauphinoise potatoes, followed by a chocolate parfait, not to mention a bottle of Montepulciano, there didn't appear to be much wrong with his appetite.

'Unwell. Yes.' His expression lugubrious, George put down his coffee cup. 'I'm afraid I'm in a pretty bad way. I didn't want to tell you before, but the stress of everything is just making it worse. The doctor says I need to relax and try not to bottle things up.'

'What kind of a bad way?' said Marina.

'Well, put it like this. Now I understand what you went through.'

Jolted, Marina said, 'You've got *cancer?*'

He nodded slowly. 'Yes.'

'Oh George, I'm so sorry!' She clapped a hand over her mouth. 'That's terrible. You poor thing. Where is it?'

'Not just cancer. I have gout, too. People think gout's funny and make jokes about it, but let me tell you, it's bloody painful. And I have back problems as well. I pulled a muscle five weeks ago playing golf and it's still giving me gyp.'

'What kind of cancer is it?' said Marina. Was it present in the bones, in the liver, in the lungs? God, poor George, what an awful ordeal he had ahead of him . . .

'It's a dysplastic nevus.' George reached across the table for his balloon glass of cognac.

She blinked, familiar enough with the term to know at once what it was. 'A . . . what? You mean a mole?'

'It's not a *mole*. It's a dysplastic *nevus*.'

'And have they removed it?'

'They won't remove it. They did a biopsy and apparently it's benign at the moment but could turn malignant at any minute. So I just have to sit and *wait*. Can you imagine how that feels?' George said fiercely. 'It's unbearable. I'm like an unexploded bomb, I could go off at any time. And those incompetent bastards at the hospital don't even care about what it's doing to me. I get headaches every day, you know. It's probably the cancer spreading to my brain. *And* I've been having palpitations . . .'

Oh the joys of the diehard hypochondriac. To think she'd forgotten what he was like, poring and fretting over every symptom, either imagined or real. A dysplastic nevus was a benign mole. The biopsy had evidently confirmed that. And yes, there was always a small risk that one day it might develop malignant cells, but it was far, far more likely that it wouldn't.

Zoning back in, Marina heard the words '. . . but if I'm ill and all on my own, who's going to look after me?'

She looked across the table at her ex-husband. *Seriously? I mean, seriously?*

Aloud, she said, 'Well if it came to that, I suppose you'd have to hire some kind of live-in helper.'

The expression on George's face was so comical that she burst out laughing.

'It's all right for you,' he said finally. 'You can't begin to understand what I'm going through.'

'Of course I can't.' Still smiling, she saw a group of people step out on to the terrace, one of whom looked over and gave her a cheery wave.

'Who's that?' said George.

'The one in the dark suit is Josh Strachan. He owns and runs this hotel. I don't know who the couple holding hands are. Maybe they're guests . . .'

'I meant the one who waved at you.'

'Oh, that's Ronan,' said Marina. 'He's an estate agent here in St Carys. And he's friends with Josh.'

'Word to the wise.' George tapped the side of his new nose. 'Never trust an estate agent. Rip-off merchants, the lot of them. Was he the one who sold you the cottage?'

She shook her head. 'No, he wasn't.'

'What's he doing now?' said George, because Ronan had excused himself from the group and was making his way over towards them.

'No idea.' Marina put down her drink. 'But if you could try not to call him a rip-off merchant, that would be nice.'

116

'Marina, hi! Listen, we were just talking about you.' Ronan's light brown eyes flickered in George's direction. 'Sorry to interrupt, I can see you're off duty, but Josh has been showing that couple around the hotel because their wedding's going to be held here. I sold them their house last year and we've kept in touch. Anyway, they were discussing the arrangements for the reception and I showed them a photo of the painting you did at Jem and Harry's wedding.'

'Oh, right.' Marina was touched that he'd thought of her. 'And did they like it?'

'They loved it. Because it's brilliant.' Ronan grinned. Her lack of salesmanship never failed to entertain him; he was always telling her she should learn to push herself more. 'So I told them all about you and gave them your details so they can get in touch, which I'm pretty sure they will. But seeing as you're here, why don't you let me take you over and introduce you to them now?'

'Oh don't worry. It's fine, really.' Marina shook her head. 'It's kind of you, but I don't want to seem pushy. If they decide they want to use me, they'll do it in their own time.' This was the way she liked to work, by letting the customers be the ones to approach her.

'You'll never make saleswoman of the year.' Ronan looked amused. 'But OK, we'll do it your way. I'll leave you two in peace.'

'Take a cut, will you?' said George.

Ronan raised his eyebrows. 'Sorry?'

'You told the people about Marina's art, so I imagine you'll be expecting a share of the profits?'

'George!' Marina was mortified. 'What are you saying? Of course he doesn't take a share of the profits!'

Oh God, how embarrassing. Luckily Ronan was still smiling, apparently unoffended.

'Don't worry. Just this once I'll make an exception and waive my commission.' He paused. 'Your name's George? You're not . . . *the* George, are you?'

George looked up at him, nonplussed. 'Well, depends what you—'

'Ex-husband George?'

'Yes.' Hastily Marina nodded. 'He is.'

'Really? Well. Interesting. Sorry,' said Ronan, 'when I saw you sitting over here with a man, I assumed you were out on a date.'

Marina's mouth was dry. Before she could react, George said with a hint of belligerence, 'Maybe we are.'

OK, enough was enough.

'No we're not,' Marina said firmly.

'I paid for dinner,' said George.

'This is in no way any kind of a date,' Marina told him. She shook her head at Ronan and added for good measure, 'It's not.'

'OK. Well I'll leave you both to whatever it is you're doing here.' He gave her a ghost of a wink. 'See you!'

They both watched as Ronan made his way back across the terrace. 'Cocky bastard,' said George. 'Who does he think he is anyway?'

'He isn't a cocky bastard,' Marina said patiently. 'He's a lovely lad. Everyone likes him.'

'Not everyone. I don't. And did you see the look he gave me?'

'I wasn't watching.'

'When you said I was your ex-husband. Because I suppose you've told everyone all about me.'

'I didn't tell everyone. Maybe a couple of people,' said Marina. 'If they asked me about my past.'

'And they tell other people.' George knocked back his brandy. 'Nothing like a bit of gossip among the locals to brighten their miserable lives.'

'Mine was the miserable life, before I moved down here. Anyway,' said Marina, 'I didn't know that what happened was supposed to be a secret. They knew I had cancer. They knew I was divorced. If they asked me when those two things took place, I wasn't going to lie about it.'

'You couldn't resist going for the sympathy vote.'

'It was what happened.'

'And now I'm the one who's sick,' said George, 'but you don't see me going on about it. I could have done, though, couldn't I?'

Was it time to leave? He was starting to annoy her now. Marina said wearily, 'Yes, you certainly could.'

They walked back across the small town to her cottage. She showed George to his room and went to bed.

Seven minutes later, he knocked at her bedroom door and said in a plaintive voice, 'Marina, are you awake?'

'No, I'm not.'

'Can I come in?'

'No, you can't.'

'Marina, please.'

'Really, no.'

Silence, but she knew he was still standing there on the landing.

'You said there hadn't been anyone else in your life since we broke up,' said George.

'That is correct.'

'But what if you never do it again? What if no one else comes along? What if you're destined to spend the rest of your life alone, and then you die, and you won't have had sex for years and years?'

Marina considered this. In all honesty, it was a question she'd asked herself many times. Because it was a possibility, of course it was. And a dispiriting one to say the least.

In the darkness, she smiled at the realisation that even if she knew that was going to happen, she still wouldn't be remotely tempted to let her ex-husband into her bed tonight. No way in the world was she going to do that.

Aloud, she called out, 'George?'

'Yes?' He sounded hopeful.

Marina snuggled cosily beneath her deliciously soft duck-down duvet. 'I promise you, if that happens, it's fine by me.'

Chapter 13

Ronan had spent the last forty minutes showing an impressive Victorian double-fronted villa in Perranporth to a pair of incredibly fussy antiques dealers who'd seemed more interested in flirting with him than exploring the property.

'Ronan darling, settle an argument. Reggie thinks you're gay and I say you're not.' Barry clutched his wrist as he asked the question, his eyes as beady as a robin's.

'I'm not gay,' said Ronan.

'Ha! See? I was right.' Barry preened. 'I'm always right.'

'Unless he's just saying that because he doesn't fancy *us*.' Reggie was evidently a poor loser.

'If I were gay, of course I'd fancy you.' Ronan grinned at them and Barry patted his own chest.

'Oh you charmer, I bet you say that to all the boys.'

'Boys? Ha.' Reggie shook his head at his husband. 'You're sixty-three years old.'

'Still young at heart, though,' Barry said happily. 'Still young at heart.'

They'd been together for almost thirty years, Ronan knew,

121

and were utterly devoted to one another. 'So how about this place then?' He gestured to the house. 'Any thoughts?'

'I have thoughts,' said Barry, gazing directly at him. 'Your eyelashes are stupendous.'

'Thanks. And this place?'

'It's not right for us, sadly. Don't be cross. At least we're learning what we don't want.'

'I'm not cross. And I'm not giving up on you.' Ronan smiled at the two of them. 'We'll get there in the end.'

Once Barry and Reggie had driven off with a toot and a wave in their vintage Jaguar, Ronan got into his Audi and headed up the road to Newquay. Since he was in the vicinity, he might as well pay a visit to his mum.

But when he got there, the house was empty. Calling his mother's mobile, he discovered she was at the hairdresser's.

'Don't worry, I'm nearly done,' she said. 'Won't be long. Make yourself a cup of tea and I'll be back in no time.'

'I just hope I don't pass out with hunger before you get here.' Ronan's tone was mournful.

'Don't give me that. There's rum cake in the red tin in the cupboard next to the fridge. And don't eat it all,' Josephine ordered. 'Just have one slice, then you can take the rest back to the office.'

'No need. They don't like rum cake.' Ronan grinned at his mother's audible intake of breath.

'You wicked boy,' she said, scandalised. 'You know it's Clemency's favourite.'

He hung up, made himself a mug of tea in the immaculate kitchen and carried it through – along with a slice of the rum cake – to the living room.

Which was, of course, also immaculate. Although should

122

his mother ever be tempted to sell the house, she'd have some serious paring-down to do.

Whenever a property was about to go on the market, Ronan's advice to the owners was to declutter as much as they could cope with and remove all family photos from view. Potential buyers needed to be able to picture themselves in their new home, he always explained, and photographs of other people and their families were a distraction.

It seemed unlikely, though, that Josephine would ever move, and it was probably just as well, because family was the most important thing in the world to her and she liked to be surrounded by them at all times. The walls were covered with framed photos of her many relatives: brothers and sisters, nephews and nieces. There were also plenty of her and Donald, either just the two of them together or visible amongst the crowd at various raucous family gatherings. But the most popular recipient of the camera's attentions, by far, had always been their adored son.

Ronan's gaze shifted from one oh-so-familiar photo to the next, surveying the various likenesses of himself that had been captured over the years. There he was as a teenager, surfing on Fistral Beach in lime-green board shorts. And there, as a chubby baby, gazing in wonder at an ice-cream cornet. Birthdays, Christmases, all manner of special occasions had been lovingly recorded for posterity . . . trampolining with his cousins in Birmingham, picnicking on the lawn at an aunt's wedding, break-dancing in the kitchen . . . oh yes, his entire life was paraded along these walls for all to see.

And then there were *the* most important photos, in the

very best frames of all, lined up along the mantelpiece and windowsills. From babyhood onwards, here he was, pictured with his mum and dad. Each year, suffused with love and pride, the three of them would line up together, Donald to the left of him and Josephine to the right. Each photo had been taken with great ceremony, then copies made and distributed to the extended family so they could display them too. Following his father's death, it had been just Josephine and himself, but the tradition had continued unabated.

These photos, Ronan knew, meant the world to her. Visitors to the house had always been treated to a guided tour of them. And nothing made his mum happier than when unsuspecting strangers – the TV repairman, the carpet fitter, the Avon lady – enthusiastically announced that you could see the family resemblance between the three of them.

You couldn't, of course; they were just being polite and going along with the easy assumption that one handsome white man plus one strikingly beautiful black woman had between them created one very good-looking mixed-race son.

Ronan remembered the way his mum had almost physically glowed with delight whenever this happened. She'd told the commenters that they were indeed lucky to have such a gorgeous boy. And although it had been pretty embarrassing during his teenage years, he'd got through them and come out the other side, admiring the way Josephine was so unafraid to tell everyone how blessed she'd been to have him in her life.

He still wondered what his biological parents must have

looked like. Of course he did; it was only natural to ask yourself that question, wasn't it? The people who'd arranged the adoption process had done an excellent job of matching him with Josephine and Donald, but growing up, Ronan had still secretly always hankered to know where he'd really come from.

Not enough, though, to risk upsetting Josephine, who he knew would be not so much upset as utterly devastated if she were ever to find out.

There had been a huge story all over the news when he was seventeen years old. A well-loved but famously starchy British actress had been reunited with the son she'd been forced to give up for adoption thirty years earlier. It had had the most extraordinary effect upon her; the starchiness had evaporated practically overnight. Her joy and relief at having him back in her life had transformed the actress completely. It was mother–son love at first sight, over-whelming and all-encompassing, and the nation had rejoiced along with them, delighted for them both and thrilled to have witnessed their happy ending.

Well, most of the nation. Josephine had found it utterly terrifying. More photos appeared, showing the famous actress meeting her son's adoptive parents. In the pictures, they looked terrified and overwhelmed too, trying to put on brave faces but not quite managing to pull it off.

The son, who had recently bought a little terraced house in Swansea across the street from the parents he'd grown up with, then said somewhat tactlessly in an interview that it had been like living a black-and-white life that had suddenly turned into dazzling Technicolor.

Six weeks later, he put the little terraced house on the

market, gave up his office job with the Civil Service and moved into his biological mother's mansion in the Hollywood Hills because her work was based there and they simply couldn't bear to be apart.

Ronan remembered coming home unexpectedly early from school one afternoon and catching his mum weeping over the latest piece about it in the newspaper. Actually, not weeping; that didn't begin to describe it. She was sobbing as if her heart would break.

When she realised with a start that he'd seen her, she let out a wail of despair and covered her face with her hands. Ronan held her and hugged her while she choked back the tears. 'Oh that p-poor woman, I can't bear to think what she's g-g-going through.'

That was when he'd said, 'Mum, it's OK, you're the only one I care about. None of this is ever going to happen to you.'

The storm of crying intensified and Josephine shook her head. 'No, no, I know you must want to . . . it's OK . . .'

But he knew it wasn't OK.

'I'm not interested in finding out who *made* me. I never want to meet them. I love you and Dad and that's it, that's all that matters. You're the only family I need. I swear to you, Mum, you can stop worrying about it, because I'm not going to try and track anyone down. It's never going to happen, I promise.'

And it had been an easy promise to make at the time, because it clearly meant the world to Josephine and she was the only mother he'd ever known. He loved her so much, it was no hardship at all.

Then six months later, when Donald had died, it had

become even more important to keep his word. It was just the two of them now, himself and Josephine. She'd been the best mother anyone could possibly ask for, and no way would Ronan let her down. His love for her outweighed curiosity about his birth mother every time.

And here she was now. As he stood by the window, her yellow Fiat Punto screeched on to the driveway and she emerged in a whirl of emerald green, catching the edge of her long jacket in the car door in her haste to get inside the house.

He greeted her at the front door. 'How you haven't lost your licence for speeding, I'll never know.'

'Hello, darling. That blue shirt suits you! Well, do I look OK?'

'Gorgeous.' Ronan smiled as she showed off the results of her time in the hairdresser's. Having given up on weaves, for the last couple of years Josephine had gone for the Lupita Nyong'o close crop, which suited her perfectly, accentuating as it did the beautiful shape of her head.

'Did you eat all the cake?'

'Not all of it.'

She led the way into the kitchen. 'Take the rest back for the others to share. And there's baked chicken in the fridge, you must have that too. Now, you wouldn't believe all the lovely news I've been hearing in the hairdresser's. Marcy Butler gave birth to a new baby last week – nine pounds six ounces, imagine that! And you remember Barbara's son, the one who almost lost his leg in that motorbike accident last year? He and his wife are having twins!'

'Nightmare,' Ronan teased as she reboiled the kettle and made herself a cup of fiendishly strong tea with two teabags.

'Not a nightmare at all,' his mother scolded. 'It's a gift

from God! Barbara's feet haven't touched the ground since she found out. Everyone was asking after you, by the way. They always do. There's a new stylist called Suzy who's single, if you think you'd be interested. I told her you were on the lookout for a new girlfriend.'

'I'm not on the lookout for a new girlfriend,' said Ronan. 'You're the one on the lookout.'

'Well anyway, she's a beautiful girl. And she'd be up for a date if you gave her a call. *Ow.*' Josephine fanned her mouth. As always, she'd tried to gulp down a mouthful of tea still perilously close to boiling point. 'Too hot.'

Ronan's eyes glittered with amusement. 'Who, her or me?'

Twenty minutes later, as he was preparing to leave, his mother said, 'Oh darling, I meant to ask, could you do me a favour?'

'Let me guess. You want me to phone the new stylist.'

She beamed, taking his teasing in good part. 'That would be very nice, but it's not the favour I was thinking of. I wondered if you could take back a few photos and put them through that lovely whizzy machine you keep at work, brighten them up a bit and make them bigger, like you did with the ones I gave you after Christmas.'

'No problem. I can do that.' Ronan took the slim buff envelope from her; it was simple enough to scan the old photos, adjust the colour and print off glossy new versions on the hi-tech office printer. 'You look after yourself, OK?' He gave her a hug and a kiss. 'I'll see you soon.'

'Oh will you look at that?' Josephine shrank back in dismay as she opened the front door. 'It's raining. Do you want to take an umbrella with you?'

'Mum.' He smiled, because his Audi was parked right

128

outside the house. 'I think I can probably manage to make it to the car.'

The rain worsened as he headed back across town, crawling through the traffic along the congested main road. Playing loud music and singing along, he'd almost driven past the bus stop before he belatedly noticed who was waiting beside it.

Chapter 14

For a split second, their eyes met, then Kate hastily looked away and pretended she hadn't seen him.

Except she had, and she knew he'd seen her. Pulling up twenty yards ahead, Ronan jumped out of the car. 'Kate! Do you want a lift?'

She turned, soaked to the skin by the sudden downpour. 'It's OK, I'm fine.'

Which was ridiculous, seeing as her hair was plastered to her head and her dress stuck to the rest of her. He jogged back along the pavement. 'Look at you. Come on, let me take you home.'

This time their eyes locked and she broke into a reluctant smile. 'Now you're all wet too.'

'What can I say?' Ronan shrugged lightly. 'I'm such a do-gooder.'

In the car, Kate buckled herself into the passenger seat. 'Thanks. I didn't think it was going to rain. And I'd planned to catch the train back, but it was cancelled. I think there was a leaf on the line or something.'

Ronan said, 'Never bet on a fight between a leaf and a

train. The leaf wins every time. What brought you down to Newquay anyway?'

'A friend from Bristol is staying down here for a week. It's my day off, so we met up for lunch at a restaurant overlooking the harbour. We had a lovely time catching up.'

'Sounds good.' He wondered if the friend was male or female.

'The food was fantastic.' Kate patted her stomach. 'I had Coquilles Saint-Jacques and fruits de mer. Lucy had a whole lobster.'

Lucy. Ronan put his foot down as they headed out of the traffic-clogged town. *Hooray for Lucy.*

'What's this?' Kate was pointing to the buff envelope propped up between the gearstick and the dashboard.

'Old photos of me, mainly. I called in to see my mum and she wants some copies made.'

'Oh, I love old photos. Can I see? Is that OK?'

'Only if you promise not to laugh.' For some reason they both seemed more relaxed today. Maybe the awkwardness was evaporating at last. Steering the car along the winding road as they bowled past the turning down to Watergate Bay, Ronan heard rather than saw her reaction to the photographs when she tipped them out of the envelope.

'Oh look at you!'

Her gasp of delight gave him a genuine thrill. He kept his eyes on the road ahead and said modestly, 'I know, I was pretty cute.'

'You certainly were. And so were your parents. Now, which of them do you look most like?'

Ronan didn't reply; he waited to see what she'd say. For some reason it really felt as if it mattered.

After several seconds of close scrutiny, Kate rested the photos on the envelope and shook her head. 'No, I can't tell. Damn, and I'm usually good at resemblances too.'

'Don't worry, you still are.' He broke into a smile. 'I was adopted.'

'Really? That's fantastic. All I could see was how happy you looked together.' She examined the most recent of the photographs once more. 'And it wasn't just for the benefit of the camera. You can tell that too.'

Ronan experienced a surge of pride. 'You're right. I was lucky. Couldn't have asked for better parents.'

'That's so lovely. How brilliant for all of you.' Kate turned sideways in the passenger seat so she could see him properly. 'Tell me about them.'

For the rest of the journey back to Bude, where she lived with her grandparents, Ronan talked about Josephine and Donald and the huge extended family scattered around the UK. They discussed his decision not to attempt to contact his biological mother because whilst it would answer questions in one respect, it was more important not to worry Josephine. 'I haven't missed out on anything. It'd just be interesting to meet an actual blood relative,' Ronan admitted. 'To look at someone and see similarities.'

'You're bound to be curious,' said Kate. 'Maybe it'll happen one day.'

'I know. I can wait.' They were approaching the outskirts of Bude now. 'Lots of people leave it until their adoptive parents are dead before making contact.' He looked pained. 'God, Josephine's only sixty-two, it seems wrong to even think of it, but . . .'

Kate was already nodding. 'I know. You never can tell.'

Exactly. They'd both lost a parent far too soon. Ronan said, 'Anyway, that's what I've always thought I'd do. Wait until it's not going to hurt her. I'm in no hurry. There's plenty of time for all that to happen.'

'Left here,' said Kate. 'Then left again, and we're the one with the blue gate. And I think it's lovely that you don't want to upset your mum.'

'Like I said, I wouldn't do it. She's been amazing. I've had the best parents ever.' Ronan braked and pulled up outside number 77, with its neatly trimmed flower beds and bright hanging baskets decorating the front porch.

'Well they didn't do too badly out of the deal either,' said Kate, 'when they got you.'

The moment the words were out of her mouth, she turned bright red and looked away. Having relaxed to the extent that she'd said something she hadn't meant to say, she was now visibly mortified.

In an effort to defuse the situation, Ronan said, 'Well that goes without saying,' but Kate was too embarrassed to let herself off the hook. She already had her seat belt unfastened and the passenger door open.

'Thank you so much for the lift. It was really kind of you. Thanks again, bye.'

And that was it, she was gone, hurrying through the heavy rain up to the house and disappearing within seconds as the glossy blue front door slammed shut behind her.

OK.

Oh well.

Ronan's phone lit up to signal the arrival of a text from Clemency. *Where are you? What time will you be back at the office?*

133

It was almost 4.30. Tapping his hand in time with the rhythmic swoosh of the windscreen wipers, he looked at the front of the house belonging to Kate's grandparents and saw one of the tweaked net curtains fall back into place.

He sent Clemency a reply. *I'll be there by five.*

'Will you be my boyfriend?'

Ronan looked at Clemency. To be honest, they weren't the words he'd been expecting to hear. 'Excuse me?'

Paula and Gavin had gone home; it was just the two of them in the office. Clemency was sitting on her desk with her bare legs swinging because she'd just painted her toenails with scarlet polish and was encouraging them to dry.

'OK, not my real boyfriend.' She waved her hand dismissively. 'But, you know, if you could bear to fake it for a week or two, I'd really owe you one. And it's not as if you're seeing anyone at the moment, so it wouldn't be putting you out.'

Ronan frowned. 'What's brought this on? Is someone pestering you?'

'No, just driving me nuts.' Clemency pulled a face. 'Seriously, Belle's doing my head in. She's so *smug*, I just can't bear it any more. It's all: oh look, here's me with my perfect gorgeous boyfriend and then there's poor you with nobody at all. She won't stop showing off about it and making out I'm some sad lonely spinster. I swear to God, it feels like we're fifteen again and all I want to do is stuff her head down the loo or wait until she's asleep and chop off all her hair.'

'Did you ever stuff her head down the loo when you were fifteen?'

'Well no, but the urge was pretty strong. And now it's back. But I know I'm not allowed to actually do it, so I thought maybe it's easier to just get myself a boyfriend instead.'

'And you've chosen me to be the one. Can I hazard a guess why?'

'Because if I pick someone boring and average-looking, that'll just make her *more* smug. And because she's always had a thing about you, which means . . . OK, she's got Sam now, but she'll still be a little bit jealous.'

'And?' said Ronan when she paused and waggled her toes. He knew Clemency too well, could read her like a book.

'Well, I did kind of happen to mention to Sam that you and I were seeing each other.'

'Ah.'

'I didn't mean to,' Clemency protested. 'But like I said, Belle has been really unbearable and I said it on the spur of the moment. It just popped out.'

'Oh dear.' Ronan nodded sympathetically. 'So you're going to look pretty silly if I say no now.'

'I am. I will. I'll look like one of those desperate old spinsters who fantasise about men they know they'll never have a chance with. Word will get out and I'll be the laughing stock of St Carys.'

'The whole of Cornwall, probably.'

'So will you do it?'

'Not sure. What's in it for me?'

'Wild sex, obviously.' Clemency raised an eyebrow at him. 'That was a joke.'

'Thank goodness for that. I don't have sex with desperate old spinsters.'

'OK, so are you going to be my fake boyfriend or do I have to find someone else?'

As she had undoubtedly known he would, Ronan said, 'Go on then, we'll give it a whirl. Might be fun.'

'And it'll definitely annoy my sister.' Clemency did a triumphant fist-bump. 'Thanks.'

'Hey, it's not as if anyone's going to be surprised, is it?' Ronan shrugged. For the last two years, as long as they'd been colleagues, people had been asking when he and Clemency were going to get together. It was a standing joke amongst their friends. They were the perfect match, was the general consensus, and everyone wondered why it hadn't happened yet.

'Well that's true enough. We'd better tell your mum, though. It wouldn't be fair to let her get her hopes up – you know she's always wanted us to get together.' Clemency had been tentatively prodding the nail polish on her toes. 'Yay, all dry. We can go now.' Jumping down from the desk, she slid her feet into silver flip-flops. 'We'll start tomorrow, OK? Try not to go out and fall in love with someone else tonight.' She waved her keys at him. 'Just remember, I'm your girl-friend now.'

What was she like? Amused, Ronan said, 'How could I forget?'

Chapter 15

Completion on the purchase of the flat took place at eleven o'clock the next morning. Clemency, who had texted Sam to let him know the money had gone through, spotted his car pulling up outside the office ten minutes later.

'Oh my God, what are you *doing*?' Ronan, who'd been concentrating on his computer screen, jumped a mile and almost sent his coffee cup flying across the room.

'Sorry, Sam's on his way in.' Having flung her arms around him from behind, Clemency planted her freshly lipsticked mouth on Ronan's cheek before realising that was where people who *weren't* boyfriend and girlfriend planted kisses. She did another one at the very corner of his mouth and said, 'Sshh, we're young and in love, don't try to wipe it away, here he comes now. Pretend you haven't noticed. And *please* look besotted . . .'

'With him or with you?'

The door began to open and Clemency rested her cheek lovingly against the side of Ronan's face. She laughed affectionately, as if he'd just said something romantic, then glanced up, let go of Ronan and sprang back.

'Oops, didn't see you there!' She beamed at Sam. 'Sorry about that. Anyway, here you are, I've got the keys all ready for you.'

'Excellent.' Sam nodded briefly.

As she scooped them off the desk and handed them over, Clemency said, 'And congratulations, you've got yourself a fantastic property!'

'Thanks.' Sam's gaze flickered towards Ronan. 'It looks as if congratulations are in order for you too.'

'Oh, right. Yes, early days. But it all seems to be going well so far.' Ronan paused and gave Clemency the kind of look she'd only seen him give other girls before today. She marvelled at his skills. Wow, when he chose to use them, he really was rather impressive.

It also felt quite weird, suddenly finding herself on the receiving end. Anyway, concentrate. She pointed to the corner of Ronan's mouth. 'You've got a bit of lipstick . . .'

'Have I?' Ronan gave her another of Those Smiles. 'You're going to have to keep yourself under control while we're in the office.'

Clemency said flirtily, 'Or I could stop wearing lipstick.' She turned to Sam. 'You haven't told Belle, have you?'

His tone was even. 'You asked me not to.'

'Thanks. I'll do it in the next day or two. It's a sister thing,' she explained. 'She's got you now, so it won't really matter, but Belle always had a bit of a crush on Ronan.'

'She'll be fine,' said Ronan. 'That's all in the past. Belle's got herself sorted out, and you've got me.' He paused, his eyes sparkling as he surveyed Clemency. 'Seriously, I still can't believe how right it feels. We should have done this years ago.'

Phew. He sounded as if he actually meant it.

'Well, I'll be off.' Sam held up the key. 'Thanks for this. I'll see you soon.'

'Definitely,' said Ronan. 'We should all go out together for dinner one night.'

They watched as Sam left, heading off in his car to his brand-new apartment.

'Well?' Ronan spread his hands and looked at Clemency. 'How did I do?'

'Very well. I'm impressed.'

He winked. 'They always say that.'

She tutted. 'You're such a cliché.'

'Hey, I do it with irony. And fun. That's how I get away with it.'

'Why are you looking at me like that?' Clemency regarded him with suspicion; they were on their own now.

'Just practising. This is my seductive expression. We want it to be right, don't we? We need to be believable.'

'You are believable. You're doing great.' There was a box of tissues in her desk drawer; beckoning him closer, Clemency pulled out a tissue and began wiping away the lipstick mark at the corner of his mouth.

'I think I should probably kiss you,' said Ronan.

'Kiss me? Why?' She refolded the tissue and assiduously removed the last remnants of Ruby Crush.

'So we've got it out of the way.'

'But I already kissed you just now. See?' Clemency showed him the crimson-stained tissue.

'That wasn't a kiss.' Ronan turned her to face him properly. 'This is a kiss.'

And there, in the otherwise empty office, he slid his arms

139

around her waist and gave her the kind of proper kiss that was worlds away from her earlier lip-printing one.

Gosh. Yet more skills.

This felt . . . *real*.

Then again, it was a while since she'd last been kissed in any meaningful kind of way; maybe she'd just forgotten how nice proper kissing could be.

'There, done.' Pulling away as his phone began to ring, Ronan said, 'This could be fun after all. Hello? Yes, Mr Arundel, I can come over right away, that's no problem whatsoever.'

It wasn't until he was in the back room collecting his jacket and car keys that Clemency realised the post had been delivered. Instead of coming into the office and leaving it on the main desk as she usually did, Kate had left the collection of letters sticking through the letter box. Which presumably meant she'd glimpsed the two of them enjoying their moment together and had decided to discreetly leave them to it.

Oh well, never mind.

'Right, I'm off to see the Arundels. Wish me luck.'

The Arundels were finicky but very rich. Clemency blew him a jokey kiss. 'You'll be magnificent.'

As he swerved past the desk, Ronan ran a playful index finger down her spine. 'I always am.'

Lugging king-sized bed frames and heavy furniture out of the back of a removals van and up two flights of stairs wasn't Belle's cup of tea. Luckily Sam had hired a couple of muscly men for that task, though there had still been a lot of sweating and grunting involved. Belle had decided her area of expertise lay more in deciding where the paintings should hang on the walls and whereabouts along the worktop the kettle should sit.

After an hour or two of getting in their way, she said, 'Look, why don't I wait until everything's in, then come back and give you a hand with the rest?'

And Sam nodded and said, 'I think that's probably a good idea.'

'I'll see you in a bit.' She gave him a quick kiss. 'Do you have such a thing as a vase?'

Sam pointed to one of the packing crates the men had just lugged up the stairs and left in the corner of the kitchen. 'I think there's one in there.'

'I'll get something to put in it, shall I?'

'Great,' said Sam. 'I've always wanted a goldfish.'

Yesterday's rain had given way to a clear bright day with exuberant clouds dotting the azure sky as if a small child had painted them in. It was a twenty-minute walk into the centre of St Carys, but Belle was in no hurry. She had plenty of time to kill whilst the removals men unloaded the rest of the van.

She stopped for a cold drink at Paddy's Café on the harbour, and watched as Marina Stafford captured the likeness of a dumpy middle-aged couple sporting matching custard-yellow shorts, deftly incorporating them into one of her pre-painted canvases.

Next, she browsed the shops for bits and pieces, picking up a pretty coffee-coloured lace top from the boutique on the Esplanade and a box of the black wine gums she knew Sam liked from the old-fashioned sweet shop next door.

Mustn't forget flowers. She chose a welcome-to-your-new-home card and a huge bunch of cream and green calla lilies, because they were just so elegant and striking and classy.

Like me.

Although they were quite awkward to carry, she realised soon after leaving the florist's shop. Oh well, it wasn't as if they were heavy. She could cope.

Ah, the chemist, that was the next stop. She needed to pick up a couple of things in there, deodorant and insect repellent, and she could do with a new lipstick too, because let's face it, who couldn't always do with a new lipstick?

Inside the shop, she made a beeline for the make-up counter and began happily investigating everything they had. She tried out some of the velvety matte eyeshadow shades, the sheeny highlighter creams, the raspberry lip tint . . . oh dear, that was far too dark, more like magenta.

'No, you're *kidding*.'

'It's true, I swear to God!'

'Wow. I'd say I don't believe it, but . . .'

'Laura, he told me himself. I mean, sorry, I know how much you liked him.'

'Oh, that was ages ago. I'm completely over him now. Still, I never expected this.'

Belle was only half listening to the conversation carrying on over at the counter behind her. Mildly interested, she stroked a sparkly pink eyeshadow on to the back of her hand before realising it was the kind of thing Clemency would wear and putting it down again.

'Although you were in bits at the time, weren't you? After he finished with you?' There was a faint note of relish in the other girl's voice. 'Remember you wrote him that poem?'

Belle wiped the pink eyeshadow off her hand and heard

Laura reply, 'I can't even remember, it's ancient history now.' Except she was saying it in the kind of brittle, offhand way that meant every last detail was engraved across her heart.

'Well anyway, I thought you'd want to know. I was walking up Hope Hill and I bumped into him just as he was getting out of his car, so I told him about Rick's party next Saturday and invited him along. I did it for you!'

'And what did he say?'

'He said thanks, but he was doing something with Clemency on Saturday, and I thought he just meant some boring work event, so I said couldn't she do it with someone else? But he said no, she couldn't, because he was taking her out to dinner that night, so then I said why, what was going on, were he and Clemency a couple now?'

Behind the shoulder-high shelving, Belle's head snapped up. *What? Who?*

'And I'd only said it as a joke,' the girl protested, 'but he said yes, they were. I couldn't believe it!'

'Was *he* joking?' said Laura.

'Not at all. Deadly serious. I *know*,' the other girl exclaimed. 'But when you stop to think about it, they're actually a good match, Ronan and Clemency. You kind of wonder why it's never happened before.'

'Hello?' Laura called over as a powder compact slipped from Belle's hand and landed on the floor with a *crack*. 'Can I help you? Is everything OK over there?'

'Fine, thanks.' But both girls were now peering at her over the shelving. Belle gave up trying to hide behind the bunch of flowers clutched in her left arm.

'Oh, it's you!' Laura said, recognising her through the lilies.

'Hi! So you know all about it, I suppose. When did this start between Ronan and your sister?'

Belle felt as if her brain was being scrambled; she glanced down at the scattering of beige powder on the ground at her feet, then up at the girls' interested faces. 'Oh those two? Not long ago.' She shrugged dismissively, and felt the petals of one of the lilies brush against her ear. 'You know what Ronan's like. Well, we all know what he's like. I shouldn't think it'll last.'

Chapter 16

Much of the beach was busy, but Belle made her way to the quieter section and found a peaceful spot where she could sit and think without being disturbed.

With her bags and the bunch of lilies resting beside her, she wrapped her arms around her knees and surveyed the shoreline of Beachcomber Bay. The tide was receding, and small children with buckets and spades were excitedly searching the clean wet sand for uncovered shells, fascinating pebbles and comical crabs. Two dogs, a golden retriever and a mink-grey whippet, were bounding around together in the shallows.

OK, back to Ronan and Clemency. Well well, when *had* this happened? Had they been hiding it from her last Friday evening at the Mermaid?

And if so, how much longer had they been planning on keeping it a secret?

Plus, how was it making her feel?

This was a tricky one to sort out. Did she feel jealous? *Yes*.

Did she have the right to feel jealous? Probably not, but it didn't make any difference; the emotions were the same either way. Once you had that sibling rivalry thing ingrained in you, it was hard to let it go.

Belle puffed a strand of hair out of her eyes, keeping her arms clasped around her knees in order to hold her skirt in place and remain decent. It was one of those weird beach-etiquette things; if you were wearing a tiny bikini, fine. But if you happened to be dressed in a collared shirt and stripy knee-length skirt, you wouldn't dream of flashing your knickers. Even if they were super-expensive pink silk ones from La Perla.

The dogs were chasing after a ball now, barking with excitement as they cavorted through the waves. A toddler, his face splashed by their antics, let out a wail of protest. An athletic-looking young woman in a slate-grey bikini skipped and swerved to avoid the two dogs as she ran along the shoreline. Seconds later, she passed a group of teenage boys, one of whom wolf-whistled in youthful appreciation. The young woman ignored the whistle and jogged past them, her blond ponytail bouncing jauntily with each step.

Belle closed her eyes and pictured Ronan the first time she'd ever seen him. It had been soon after he'd moved to St Carys in order to take up his new job with Gavin Barton. Word had spread rapidly around town, of course it had, that the new arrival was a twenty-four-year-old with looks, charisma and a decided way with the ladies. Belle, however, had assumed he wouldn't be her type; apart from anything else, he was from a working-class background, and why on earth would she be interested in a boy like that?

Until she'd seen him for the first time a week later, playing a game of pool at the Mermaid, and against all the odds her interest had been piqued, because he was pretty and he exuded fun and sometimes your brain chose not to care about working-class backgrounds and simply thought: *Ooh, he's nice.*

Which had been embarrassing in one way and confusing in another. But at the same time it had been a complete thrill. A fresh challenge was always good.

As an attractive twenty-one-year-old from a wealthy family, Belle had been accustomed to getting any boy she wanted. She'd expected to get Ronan. But it had never happened, which had been both puzzling and annoying. For some reason he hadn't been interested in her. Which had, naturally, had the effect of keeping her interested in *him.*

Belle knew perfectly well that if they'd gone out together for a few weeks, the novelty would have worn off and they'd have drifted apart – because that had been the recurring pattern of her relationships up until then. But it hadn't had a chance to happen, which was why the weird crush had continued unabated. She'd never had the opportunity to get it out of her system.

And now this.

Taking out her phone, she texted Clemency. *Where are you?*

As soon as the text had been sent, she was overcome with impatience and scrambled to her feet. Collecting up her bags, her discarded shoes and the bunch of lilies in their tissue paper wrapping, she dusted the sand off her palms and made her way back up the beach to the stone steps that led to the Esplanade. It was only five minutes from here to the estate agency, so she may as well head over there now.

The text arrived less than thirty seconds later, and she stopped in her tracks, fumbling for the phone she'd tucked into the narrow side pocket of her handbag. In the struggle to reach it, the bag's leather strap slid off her shoulder and the expensive lilies slithered sideways, causing her to double over in order to catch them before they landed head-first in the soft, dry—

Woomph! Something thudded into Belle's side, knocking her off balance and sending her crashing to the ground. She let out a shriek of alarm, the lilies went flying and so did her shoes as she sprawled on the sand. For a split second she thought it was a mugger, about to make off with her bag and everything in it.

'Oh God, I'm sorry, I'm *so* sorry. Are you OK?'

It wasn't a mugger. It was the girl in the slate-grey bikini, who'd careered straight into her. Mortified at how idiotic she must look, Belle said furiously, 'Well that's the stupidest question I ever heard. Do I *look* as if I'm OK?'

'I meant are you hurt?'

Was everyone watching? Were they all laughing at her? Belle stumbled clumsily to her feet, shrinking away as the girl reached out to try and help her up. 'I'm not hurt.'

'Oh thank goodness. Sorry again, it was all my fault.'

Belle glanced at her in disbelief, because of course it was all her fault; who else could possibly be to blame?

'I was timing myself, you see.' The girl tapped a gadget on her left wrist. 'Trying to beat my record. It's harder to run on soft sand, so I checked the coast was clear, then put my head down and just went for it.'

'You didn't see me *at all*?' Still furious, Belle dusted sand off her skirt then watched as the girl hastily retrieved her scattered bags and handed them back to her.

'Of course I saw you, but I thought you were heading

148

for the steps. I thought you'd be long gone by the time I reached this bit; I didn't know you were going to stop dead . . . but of course I should have been looking where I was going. I'm an idiot.' As she handed over the lilies, the girl fixed her steady light-blue gaze on Belle. 'I'm really sorry.'

Belle looked away first and gave the kind of angular, dismissive shrug that signalled their unwelcome encounter was at an end. 'OK. Bye.'

Clemency was on the phone to a client when she saw Belle coming into the office. Once the call was ended, she said, 'Oh how lovely, you shouldn't have!'

'They're not for you.' Belle dumped the lilies on her desk. 'So, how is everything?'

'Fine. The sale went through.' Clemency looked puzzled. 'I gave Sam the keys hours ago. I thought you'd be helping him move into the flat.'

'They don't need me. And I wasn't talking about the flat. I just wondered how everything's going with you and Ronan.'

Unexpected. Clemency hesitated. 'In what way?'

'Well, in the shagging-each-other way, I imagine.'

'Oh.' How on earth had she found out? 'Look, I was going to let you know . . .'

'But didn't.' Belle raised a sceptical eyebrow.

'Did Sam tell you?'

'Are you serious?' This time both eyebrows shot up. '*Sam* knows?'

'I just mentioned it to him,' Clemency hastily explained. 'But I said I'd rather tell you myself. How *did* you find out, then?'

'Oh trust me, you're the talk of the town. Some girl was telling Laura in the chemist's shop.'

'How did *she* know?'

'From what I can gather, Ronan's been spreading the word. And you know what this place is like for gossip,' said Belle. 'Once they start, there's no stopping them. So how long have you two been an item?'

'Not long. Just . . . a couple of weeks.'

'And why didn't you tell me before now?'

Clemency shrugged. 'Probably because I knew you'd be like this.'

'I'm *fine*.' Belle's voice had gone a bit high-pitched. 'It's just . . . I suppose I never thought you'd . . . go there.'

'Look, I know you used to like him, but nothing's ever happened between you two.' Clemency stayed calm, kept her tone gentle. 'He's never been your boyfriend. I'm allowed to go out with him. And now I am.'

'Clearly.' Belle exhaled.

'And you've got Sam.'

Belle nodded. 'I have.'

'Are you not happy with Sam?' Clemency's heart rate began to quicken.

'Of course I'm happy! Sam's the best boyfriend I've ever had. He's *perfect*.'

'That's all right then. And now that you know about me and Ronan, everything's great. So we're all happy!'

Belle hesitated, then nodded, clearly aware that she didn't have a reasonable argument. She managed a brief smile. 'We are.'

Phew, she was mellowing with age. Clemency touched one of the calla lilies and said teasingly, 'Are you sure these aren't for me?'

'Quite sure, thanks. They're for Sam's new flat.'

'Why are they all sandy?'

'Because some blasted jogger crashed into me on the beach, sent me flying. There are so many idiots out there. Clem, it's really hot and my shoes are hurting. Can you give me a lift back to Sam's flat?'

Clemency said, 'I'm on my own, so you'll have to wait until five thirty.'

Belle looked pained. 'Couldn't you just close up half an hour early?' It was what she would do without stopping to think twice about it.

Clemency said, 'You see, this is why you get sacked from jobs and I don't.'

'So pedantic.' Belle wrinkled her nose in disgust. 'Fine then, I'll go and get myself a coffee and come back at five thirty.'

Half an hour later, Belle returned. Her shoes were really pinching now. She waited whilst Clemency closed up, then they left the office. On the way over to Sam's, they passed by her sister's flat and Clemency pulled up outside.

'Oh God.' Belle heaved an impatient sigh; were they ever going to get to Sam's? 'What *now*?'

'Won't be a minute, I just want to pick up my other sunglasses. The lens fell out of my tortoiseshell ones this morning.'

'That's because you buy cheap sunglasses,' said Belle.

Clemency disappeared and Belle waited in the car. Within seconds, the front door adjacent to Clemency's was pulled open and the jogger from the beach emerged. No longer in a bikini, she had showered and washed her hair, and was wearing a fitted delphinium-blue dress. Surprised by the sight of her, and by the transformation, Belle leant forward and inadvertently caught the girl's eye. Recognising Belle in turn, the girl hesitated, then gave a brief nod of acknowledgement before heading off down the street.

A moment later, Clemency was back, wearing her unbroken sunglasses.

'Who's that?' Belle pointed to the figure in blue, now thirty or so metres away.

'Who? Oh, it's Verity.'

'Does she live there?' Belle indicated the front door adjacent to Clemency's.

'She's Meryl's niece. Meryl who runs the newsagent's. Verity's staying with her for the summer. She was down here last summer too . . . Oh, you wouldn't have seen her then, that was when you were in Monte Carlo.' Clemency restarted the car and pulled out. 'Why?'

'She's the one who knocked me over on the beach this afternoon.'

'Really? Oh, but she's nice, though. Proper fitness fanatic. She runs an aerobics class every day, over on Mariscombe Beach.'

'What, with everyone watching? God, how awful.' Belle shuddered. 'How very *Hi-de-Hi!*'

They were overtaking Verity now. Clemency buzzed down her window and waved as they passed her, and Verity waved back.

'Well don't you worry,' Clemency told Belle. 'Verity's class is at seven in the morning, so it's not as if you're ever going to see it.'

Clemency hadn't planned on going in, but Belle said, 'Oh come up, just for five minutes. You can help me with my bags.'

As they were plonked into her arms, Clemency said, 'Just call me Cinderella.'

But once they'd climbed the stairs, the view made it all worthwhile. The glass doors leading on to the balcony were wide open, and Sam was out there, shaking the pale blue seat cushions and placing them on the outdoor sofas. A zing of adrenalin shot down Clemency's spine, because she'd been mentally prepared for seeing Sam, but not for seeing him naked.

OK, *half* naked. He was still wearing his jeans, but the shirt had come off. And her mouth had gone dry, because his tanned torso was every bit as impressive as she'd thought it might be. Oh goodness, what a sight to behold.

'Hi, I'm back! You've been busy!' Heading out to greet him, Belle casually rested the flat of her hand against his bare chest as she planted a kiss on his mouth. 'I bought you some gorgeous flowers as a flat-warming present, but some complete dipstick crashed into me on the beach, which is why they're all battered and sandy. Still, maybe they'll perk up once we stick them in water. Here, smell them, aren't they divine?'

'Thanks.' For a split second, as Clemency watched, he seemed to flinch away from the lilies. The next moment he turned and spotted her. 'Oh, hello.'

'I can't believe the difference,' Belle continued, gazing around at the kitchen and living room. 'All those crates unpacked!'

Sam said wryly, 'It's amazing how much work you can get done if you set your mind to it.'

'Plus you actually stayed around to do the job,' Clemency told him, 'instead of going shopping. That probably helped too.'

'Oh very funny.' Belle rolled her eyes. 'I'm going to put these in water. Did you find the vase?'

'It's under the sink.'

'And is there champagne in the fridge? Shall we have a glass to celebrate?'

'Not for me,' said Clemency. 'I've got the car.'

'I didn't mean you,' Belle replied airily. 'I was talking to Sam.'

'I'll have a Peroni.' As he said it, Sam reached for his discarded shirt and pulled it back on.

'You don't like lilies,' Clemency murmured while Belle was in the kitchen, filling the vase in the sink.

Sam looked at her. 'Not much,' he said in a low voice.

He didn't need to elaborate; she knew why. Just as she could guess his reason for putting on his shirt. She hoped he hadn't noticed the way she'd taken one final glance at his torso before the last couple of buttons had been done up.

Pop went the cork in the kitchen.

'Here we go.' Rejoining them, Belle handed Sam his bottle of Peroni and raised her own fizzing glass. 'Cheers! Here's to the new flat and lots of fun in the sun!' She clinked the glass against Sam's bottle, then mimed a clink with Clemency, whose hand was empty.

Clemency's phone began to ring. 'It's Ronan,' she said.

'Hi,' said Ronan. 'Just wondered, have the Mastertons called back yet? Did they raise their offer on the Port Isaac farmhouse?'

'No . . . no. I won't be long. See you in a bit,' said Clemency.

'What? Why?' He sounded startled. 'Have I forgotten something?'

'I know.' Half turning away and lowering her voice a bit, Clemency said, 'I love you too.'

'Oh, right, I get it now.' Ronan sounded amused. 'Well I love you more, Snugglewuggle.'

'Of course you do. And if you think I'm going to say something like that in front of other people, you can think again. I'll be over soon.'

'Is that a promise?'

'No. Bye!' Clemency ended the call and turned back to the others. 'I must go.'

Sam was taking a gulp of Peroni. He nodded. 'Have fun.'

Belle, accompanying her to the front door, bent her head close to Clemency's. 'Only two weeks and he's already told you he loves you?'

Which, from the note of jealousy in her voice, suggested that Sam had yet to say it to her.

'I think we both realised we're perfect for each other. Sometimes it just happens, doesn't it?' Enjoying this rare moment of sisterly one-upmanship, Clemency gave Belle a parting kiss on the cheek. 'When you know, you know.'

Chapter 17

The sky was layered with clouds, the air temperature had dropped over the course of the last few days and there were fewer people in the sea than there had been for weeks. But once Ronan had made up his mind to go for a swim, he went through with it. He was unstoppable.

'Brrrr.' Clemency shivered, wishing she'd brought something warmer to wear than a thin cotton sweater. 'Rather him than me.'

Marina, as always when she found herself between customers, was painting the view of the beach. She sat back. 'He's such a good swimmer. I do like watching him in the water.' She added with a smile, 'All going well with you two?'

Word had spread. Everyone knew now. Weirdly, most people were delighted they'd got together. To *think* that they'd got together, Clemency amended, because during the course of the last couple of weeks she'd occasionally forgotten it wasn't real. In public, they held hands without a qualm, hugged each other, flirted and generally behaved like a real couple.

'It's going great.' The fact that she was lying to people she liked was the only drawback, but at least it was a harmless lie. Clemency took a sip of hot chocolate. 'Everything's good.'

'You're well matched. It's lovely to see you together. *Whoops*.' Marina grabbed the box canvas as a gust of wind caused it to judder on the easel.

Clemency smiled and watched Ronan power through the swell like a dolphin, with impressive butterfly strokes. He was wearing red board shorts, and his brown shoulders gleamed with each rotation of his arms. She knew just what Marina meant about it being a pleasure to watch someone who swam so well. As she shielded her eyes with her hand, Ronan changed direction and dived head-on into the next wave just before it broke, disappearing from view before popping up again several seconds later. She turned to Marina. 'How about you? Heard any more from that ex-husband of yours?'

'I have, as a matter of fact. He's emailed me a couple of times, telling me how much he misses me and asking if I'd like to go away with him, maybe on a cruise to the Norwegian fjords, seeing as it might be his last chance to have a holiday, what with him being so close to death and all.' Marina sighed. 'Oh dear, I shouldn't make fun of him . . . What if he did die? Imagine how awful I'd feel if—'

'Look at that,' Clemency interrupted, pointing as a figure in a wetsuit roared into the bay on a jet ski. 'What a prat . . . does he think he's in a Bond film?'

'That's so dangerous.' Marina winced as the man narrowly missed the outer edge of the harbour wall and swung the jet ski into a tight circle. The next moment he collided with an early breaking wave and lost his balance, sliding sideways on the seat. Somehow he managed to hang on, rodeo-style, and haul himself back upright before swinging back round in a much wider circle in order to head across the bay.

'Oh God.' Clemency clapped her hand to her mouth as the jet ski accelerated, heading directly for the patch of sea where Ronan was swimming. Why wasn't the rider changing direction? Her heart thudded ominously as she realised he hadn't seen Ronan, didn't know he was there; the swell of the wave had hidden him from view. There was an awful inevitability about the next couple of seconds. Time slowed down as the jet ski bounced across the rough water, zoning in on Ronan like a shark . . .

Then there was no distance between them at all. With barely a judder to show that contact had been made, the jet ski scooted off across the bay with its plume of water fountaining out behind it. And there was Ronan left in its wake, face down in the water and quite still.

The sound of screams filled the air. Clemency pushed back her chair and jumped up as, with a crash, Marina's easel and box canvas went flying. The paint palette clattered to the ground along with Clemency's mug of hot chocolate. Marina, having let out a cry of anguish, was already racing along the harbour wall to the spot on the quay where the distance to Ronan's unmoving figure was shortest. Running behind her, Clemency saw that two speedboats were being launched, but it was too late to stop Marina. Kicking off her deck shoes, she dived off the end of the quay and swam towards Ronan's inert body.

Sick with terror, Clemency watched as she reached him

and turned him over, a cloud of blood spreading through the water around his head. *Oh Jesus, please no.* The urge to dive in was almost overwhelming, but the speedboats had reached him now; there was no room, she'd only be in the way. Together they were working to haul Ronan into the nearest boat, and now – *oh thank goodness* – there were signs of life. Marina had lifted his face out of the water and he'd begun to splutter and choke. But how severe was the damage to his head that had caused all the bleeding?

Having raced back to the harbour wall and half stumbled down the last of the slimy stone steps, Clemency was there to greet them when the boats reached the shore.

'I'm fine, I'm fine.' Ronan didn't look remotely fine, but at least he was able to say it. Blood from the wound at the back of his head was leaking down his body, but with help he was able to step out of the boat on to the sand. One of the GPs from the surgery on the Esplanade had arrived and was already checking him over. Marina, who'd been brought to shore in the other boat, was watching him anxiously, oblivious to the pink bloodstains that covered her own sodden white top and linen trousers.

Reaching her, realising how violently she was trembling, Clemency said, 'Are you OK? You were incredible.'

'I wasn't, I just did it.' Marina was pale and breathing rapidly. 'I thought he was dead.'

Clemency hugged her tightly; for a few seconds they'd both thought he was dead.

'Right,' said the doctor, accustomed to treating injuries sustained whilst surfing in St Carys. 'It looks worse than it is, but we'd better get you along to A and E to be on the safe side. Let them check you over and give you an X-ray.'

'I'll take him,' volunteered one of Ronan's surfing friends. 'My van's a mess anyway, so a bit of blood won't make it any worse.'

'Here.' Someone else produced a blanket.

'Clem?' Ronan beckoned her over. 'I'm OK, I promise. I'll see you later, all right?'

Clemency nodded. 'I'll take Marina home. She's pretty shaken up.'

'Yes. Of course.' Evidently still a bit dazed himself, he looked over at Marina in her bloodstained clothes. 'Marina. Thank you. I can't believe you jumped in like that and saved me. Come here . . .'

And now he was gesturing towards her, but Marina stayed where she was.

'I'm a strong swimmer, that's all. Anyone would have done the same.' Her voice wavered as she added, 'I'm just glad you're all right.'

Ronan was bundled into his friend's van and driven off to the local hospital. Returning to the café, Clemency collected her own bag and Marina's painting equipment from Paddy, who'd righted the table and cleaned up the mess from the spilt paints and hot chocolate. Then they walked together in silence back to Marina's cottage.

Once inside, Clemency saw that Marina was still shivering. 'Have a hot shower. Get yourself warmed up. I'll make you some soup.'

'I don't want soup.'

'OK then, maybe coffee with a dash of brandy in it.'

'That sounds a bit more like it.' This time Marina managed a glimmer of a smile.

'No problem. Now take off those wet clothes,' said

Clemency. 'They need to go in the washing machine if we're going to get the bloodstains out.'

'It really doesn't matter. They didn't cost much.'

'But if we get the blood out, they can be your lucky clothes,' said Clemency. 'You saved Ronan's life.'

For a moment, tears glimmered in Marina's eyes, then she turned and made her way upstairs. Leaving Clemency to think through everything that had happened this afternoon. She felt as if she needed some time to carefully consider each separate detail she'd seen and heard.

And when Marina came back down to the living room twenty minutes later, freshly showered and wrapped in a towelling dressing gown, Clemency knew she had to ask the question that was uppermost in her mind.

'Here you go.' She placed the cup of freshly ground coffee laced with cognac on the table next to Marina's side of the sofa.

'Thank you. Mmm, delicious.' Marina smiled and put the cup back down. 'Better than soup.'

'Can I ask you something?'

'Of course! Is it about the painting?' Marina indicated the half-finished canvas propped up against the wall. 'It's a present for Paddy and Dee, to hang in the café. I thought they might like—'

'It's not about the painting,' Clemency interrupted. 'It's about Ronan.'

'Oh . . .'

Something about the *Oh* . . . made her think she might be right.

'When the jet ski hit him and he was lying in the water, you said something. *Gasped* something. And I didn't understand at first because it didn't make any sense.'

Marina didn't reply. She swallowed audibly and looked down at her hands, clasped together in her lap.

'But you definitely did say it,' Clemency continued. 'I heard you. When it happened, you leapt out of your chair and you said, "*Billy* . . ."'

More silence. Marina remained still. Finally she tilted her face up and back, but the tears slid down anyway.

Gently Clemency said, 'Who's Billy?'

Marina was wiping her eyes with the sleeve of her dressing gown. 'He was my son. My baby boy.'

'And now?'

Marina nodded slowly, with a mixture of fear and relief, and Clemency wondered how it must feel to keep a secret like that for so many years.

'And now,' Marina said simply, 'his name is Ronan.'

Chapter 18

'You have to promise me one thing,' said Marina. 'Ronan must never know.'

Clemency nodded. 'I promise.'

Did she fully understand? 'Seriously. I mean it.'

'I know. Me too. God, though.' Clemency was gazing at her in stunned realisation. 'It's incredible.'

'I can't believe I said his name.' Marina shook her head; in that terrifying split second, she'd heard herself utter the word she hadn't spoken aloud for so many years. The subconscious certainly had its ways of playing tricks on you. But when your son was floating face-down in water, motionless and possibly dead . . . well, clearly anything could be blurted out.

'That's why you dived in,' said Clemency.

'I'd have done the same for anyone,' said Marina. But maybe not so unthinkingly, so blindly, and without the all-encompassing desperation.

'Then afterwards, when Ronan wanted to thank you, he beckoned you over so he could give you a hug. But you wouldn't go, you stayed where you were.' Clemency had evidently slotted all the pieces of the puzzle into place. 'And that's why you wouldn't go to him. Because it would have been too much, too emotional . . . you were scared you might give yourself away.'

This was true. It was exactly why she'd stayed rooted to the spot. Marina nodded, because Clemency had found her out and there was no point in even attempting to deny it. Then she stopped nodding and looked directly at her. 'You're his girlfriend. I know I keep saying this, but you mustn't tell him.'

'And I won't. OK, my secret isn't anywhere near as big as yours,' said Clemency, 'but I'm not really his girlfriend. I just got fed up with Belle being so smug and superior, so I asked Ronan to play along for a couple of weeks.'

'Oh. Really?' Marina smiled briefly. 'That's a shame. I meant it when I said you made a great couple.'

'Well, we're just friends. But you mustn't tell anyone either.' Clemency's eyes sparkled. 'And that makes us even.'

Marina took another sip of cognac-laced coffee. 'So many secrets,' she said ruefully. 'We all have them. We don't mean to, but they just come along and take over our lives. And then we have to learn to live with them, which isn't always easy either. I did a bad thing and the guilt never leaves me, but at the time I couldn't help myself.'

'Oh no, you mustn't think like that,' Clemency blurted out. 'You should never feel guilty about giving a baby up for adoption!'

Marina nodded; along with millions of other people, Clemency had watched the popular TV programmes about long-lost parents and children being reunited. 'I know, I do know that.'

'You did it because you weren't able to look after him,' Clemency rushed to reassure her. 'You wanted him to have a better life. And he *has* had a fantastic life—'

'Actually, when I said I'd done a bad thing, I wasn't talking about giving my son up for adoption,' said Marina.

That stopped Clemency in her tracks. 'No? Oh! You don't have to tell me anything. Really.'

Marina smiled, because obviously Clemency was longing to know. 'It's OK,' she said. 'I want to. We've got this far, you may as well hear the rest.'

How she'd envied the other girls at school, whose parents had been less strict than hers. Her friends were allowed to go to the park together, they were allowed to meet up in the shopping centre on Saturday afternoons. And on Saturday evenings they all went along to the local nightclub, where they danced and gossiped and flirted with boys.

Marina hadn't been allowed to do any of that. Well, she'd still been Mary then. Her mother suffered from her nerves and spent her time in a state of high anxiety, panicking about everything imaginable, whilst her father was an out-and-out bully, who ruled the house and forbade any form of dissent.

It had been kind of ironic, then, that having been banned from going to all the usual places where teenage girls might reasonably encounter members of the opposite sex, she'd met Ellis Ramsay in the local library.

In the reference section, at that. It was a small room, separated from the rest of the library, for people who wanted to work or study in complete silence. She'd gone there because in those pre-internet days, she needed to use the reference books to help with her A levels. Plus it was a lot more restful than studying at home.

She'd noticed him there for several weeks, but no contact had been made between them until the afternoon of the hiccups.

Good old hiccups. The more you tried to suppress them, the louder they got. And the other people in the room all found it utterly infuriating; with each new *hic*, they turned to fix her with unamused glares. Well, all except one of them. The industrious boy who surrounded himself with medical textbooks and was a prodigious note-taker wasn't looking annoyed. He was smiling, mainly with his eyes but a little bit with his mouth too. He had close-cropped black hair, flawless dark brown skin and the whitest of teeth. And when Marina did another *hic*, louder than all the rest, he took a packet of Polos out of his jacket pocket and discreetly rolled one across the wide desk in her direction.

What was it her mother had always told her about accepting sweets from strangers?

Marina had smiled back. He'd shrugged and mouthed, *It might help*. She'd popped the Polo into her mouth, promptly hiccupped again and almost swallowed it whole.

Outside the library, doubled over with laughter, she'd coughed and spluttered and wiped her streaming eyes on the handkerchief he lent her.

'Are you sure you're OK?' he said when they'd both regained control. 'I was all ready to perform the Heimlich manoeuvre if you'd choked on that Polo.'

'I'm fine. Thank you anyway.' Marina went to return his handkerchief, before hesitating and wondering if that was rude. 'Sorry, um . . .'

'It doesn't matter.' He put his hand out to take it, but Marina shook her head.

'No, let me wash it for you. I'll bring it back tomorrow, if you're going to be around then.'

'I have to take my grandmother to a hospital appointment. I won't be here before six.' He had a lovely gentle way of speaking.

Recklessly, Marina said, 'Doesn't matter. I'll wait.'

'What's your name?'

'Mary.'

'Hello, Mary.' He had the most dazzlingly infectious smile. 'It's very nice to meet you. I'm Ellis.'

The next evening she waited outside the library and returned the laundered handkerchief. The way his face lit up when he saw her made her flush with happiness. His full name was Ellis Ramsay, and he was a medical student down in London, staying with his redoubtable Jamaican grandmother up here in Durham during the Easter holidays and revising hard for his end-of-year exams.

Which was good, because it meant she carried on going there every day too, getting far more extra studying in than she would otherwise have done.

It was Mary's first real-life teenage crush, intense and overwhelming, and she felt it would last for ever. When the library closed each evening, they headed over to the local park, sitting on a secluded bench and talking, until one evening her neighbour Mr Williams happened to pass by and give them a long, cold stare. He looked from Ellis to Mary and said, 'Does your father know about this?'

Mary, feeling her face heat up, had replied, 'We're not doing anything wrong,' but inwardly she'd been terrified that Mr Williams would tell her father what he'd seen. From then on, they gave the park a miss and took to walking in the nearby woods instead. And when Ellis kissed her for the first time, it was romantic and beautiful and perfect.

The following week, his grandmother went to a funeral in Cardiff, staying there overnight and for the first time leaving her house empty. Instead of visiting the library, Ellis and Mary crept in through the back door so no one would spot them, and spent the evening together in Ellis's narrow single bed. Ellis only had one condom and they made love twice. But it was OK, it was a safe time of the month.

Ten days later, the time came for him to return to London. Even as they kissed and hugged and said their emotional goodbyes, Mary sensed they were unlikely to see each other again. Like a huge firework display exploding out of nowhere and lighting up the night sky, their dazzling relationship had run its natural course and was fizzling out. If Ellis hadn't been leaving, they would probably have carried on meeting up for a few more weeks, but it was almost easier this way. The mutual infatuation was fading and no harm had been done. She would miss him for a while, but not desperately and not to the point of anguish. They both had exams coming up; it was time now to concentrate on those.

'Except there was something else to concentrate on,' Marina told Clemency. 'I was pregnant.'

'You must have been petrified,' said Clemency.

Petrified was an understatement.

'You can't imagine. It was horrendous. I wanted to run away, but there was nowhere to go.'

'What happened?'

'Well, I did pretty badly in my A levels. I spent a lot of time feeling sick and trying not to throw up. And I wrote a letter to Ellis.' Marina shook her head. 'To let him know.

I didn't have the address of the new place he was living in, down in London, so I put it in a sealed envelope and took it to his grandmother's house. When she wouldn't give me the address, I asked her to send the letter on to him. She told me she would, but I don't know if she ever did. Anyway, I never did hear back from him.'

Clemency shook her head in sympathy. 'You poor thing.'

'Honestly, I felt like a robot. Just getting through each day was an ordeal. But as the weeks passed, it became kind of obvious and my father challenged me. I was five months gone by then, and he hit the roof. That was when they packed me off to stay with my father's cousin in Coventry. I'd brought the worst kind of shame on the family. I was trying to send my mother into an early grave. And no one else must ever find out,' said Marina. 'I'd refused to tell them who the father was, but at some stage while I was away, Mr Williams from next door happened to say something about seeing me in the park that time with Ellis. Except he didn't know his name, just his skin colour. So *that* went down well.'

'Oh God,' Clemency sighed.

'Anyway, I gave birth to Billy and he was just the most beautiful little thing you'd ever seen.' Marina's eyes abruptly swam with hot tears. 'We only had a few days together in the hospital. The adoption was all set to go ahead. I still wish I hadn't let it happen, but back then there just didn't seem to be any other choice. My heart felt as if it was physically breaking.' She paused and swallowed hard. 'On the fifth day, I had to say goodbye to him . . . well, that was the worst day of all. The social worker was very kind; she told me I was doing the right thing, giving Billy a better start in life with a family who'd give him all the love in the world. And I was rocking backwards and forwards, saying they couldn't love him more than I did. But it was too late, they took him away anyway. And that was it. I was sent home to get on with my life as if nothing had ever happened. Except *everything* had happened . . . Oh dear, sorry . . .'

'Don't you dare apologise,' said Clemency.

Marina wiped her leaking eyes and managed a crooked smile. 'That's the worst of it over. It makes me cry every time I think about it. But I'll be fine from now on, I promise.'

'Only if you're sure,' said Clemency.

'OK, let's get on to the next stage. My parents didn't trust me an inch after that. And I put up with the way they treated me because I felt as if I deserved to be punished. Then a year or so later, my father set me up with a work colleague, someone he'd decided would be the right kind of chap to take me off their hands. So I met him, and guess who it turned out to be?'

'George?'

'George.' Marina nodded in agreement. 'I know. Lucky, lucky me. He had a problem with my name, because he'd had a peculiar cousin called Mary. That's why he decided we should change it to Marina.'

'And you married him because your father *told* you to?'

'Believe me, I know how that sounds. I'm not proud of it. But I blamed myself for what had happened, and for making my mother's life miserable. If marrying George went some way towards making up for the other stuff . . . well, maybe it was what I should do.' Marina shrugged. 'So I did.'

'Wow,' said Clemency.

'I also thought if I had another baby it might take my

mind off Billy.' Marina shook her head. 'Except that didn't happen.'

'Must have been hard.'

'I thought it was my punishment for having given Billy away. I felt as if I didn't deserve another baby.'

'Oh Marina, that's so sad. If anything, you deserved it *more*. And did George know about . . . what happened before?'

'He knew I'd had a baby adopted. I told him just before the wedding; it seemed only fair. But that was all, no details.' Marina recalled the evening she'd confided in George; she'd been torn between disappointment and relief when he'd shown no interest whatsoever in either Billy or Ellis and what they'd been like. But he'd been kind to her that night, had given her a hug and told her not to worry, he'd still marry her.

And to think she'd actually been grateful.

God, imagine. Back then, her only experience of marriage had been based on the relationship between her own parents; anything happier shown in movies or on TV had always been roundly derided by her father as fantasy and piffle.

'So anyway,' she continued, 'we got married and stayed married. The years went by. Obviously I never forgot Billy, but I kept telling myself I'd done the right thing and he was living a wonderful life. Before his eighteenth birthday came around, I added my name to the adoption contact register, so that if he were to get in touch with them, they'd be able to tell him straight away that I'd be happy to hear from him. Happy,' she said wryly, 'doesn't begin to describe it. It was what I longed for more than anything in the world. And once he'd turned eighteen, not a day passed when I

171

didn't wonder if it might happen. Every time the phone rang, each time the post came rattling through the letter box . . . I just couldn't help thinking, *Is this it?*'

She paused and took another swallow of the tepid coffee.

'Except it never was,' said Clemency quietly.

'It never was. A year went by, then two years, then a couple more. And all I was able to do was tell myself it could still happen. It just meant I had to be patient and wait a bit longer. As long as it took for Billy to decide he wanted to get in touch.'

Marina stopped, breathed out slowly. 'Until I got ill and realised I may not have as long as it might take.'

Clemency said, 'I just can't imagine.'

'I couldn't handle the idea that I might die without seeing my boy again. It was just unbearable. I know it was selfish, but the thought of never getting to meet him tore me to pieces.' Marina looked down and realised she'd been twisting the end of her dressing gown tie around her fingers. 'And then George buggered off, of course, but compared with the Billy issue, that hardly seemed to matter. The first thing I had to do was get through the treatment. Then I promised myself I'd do whatever it took . . . anything at all, to find Billy again.'

'I still can't work out how you did it,' said Clemency. 'I mean, I'm no expert, but I know the adoption people don't go giving that kind of information out willy-nilly, especially not to the biological parents.'

'You're right, they don't. I begged them to help me. They were sympathetic,' Marina explained, 'but legally there was nothing they could do. So in the end I did it illegally instead.'

Clemency's eyes widened. '*You?* How on earth did you manage that?'

Marina half smiled, remembering how she'd embarked on her search.

'Well I knew I couldn't do it myself, so I started making appointments with all the private detectives I could find in the north of England. I visited each company in turn and pleaded with them to help me. Except they all refused, which was annoying. Private detectives, it turns out, have far more scruples than you'd think. In the end, though, I struck lucky. I told this one guy my story and broke down in tears. Well, it turned out his sister had died before she had a chance to meet the daughter she'd given up for adoption. And he could see how desperate I was. He was lovely, actually. A retired police officer. I promised him that I'd never tell Billy who I was. All I wanted was to see him, to watch him from a distance and know he was all right.'

'And he found Ronan for you,' said Clemency.

'He did. Within a week. It was incredible. Well,' Marina went on ruefully, 'it was illegal too. He'd broken all the rules. That's what I feel guilty about now. I didn't feel guilty back then, of course. It was everything I'd ever wanted, all my dreams come true. He gave me Billy's name, told me where he worked. Three days later I came down to St Carys, walked into the estate agency . . . and there he was. It was the best moment of my life.'

'And you were able to control yourself,' Clemency marvelled. There were tears in her eyes now.

'I was. I knew I had to.' Marina nodded; that knowledge had made keeping control surprisingly easy. 'I felt as if I'd mentally pressed the record button, so I could go through it again in my own time and get emotional then. But while it was happening, I just acted normally and pretended

173

to be interested in buying a property. I told Ronan I'd spent lots of happy summer holidays in St Carys as a child and now I was thinking of moving down here to live. And he was so helpful and charming . . . oh, he was everything you could ask for. Perfect in every way. My boy.' Marina's eyes were shining. 'My wonderful, beautiful boy.'

Clemency had cottoned on. 'So the story about the childhood holidays wasn't true.'

'It wasn't. That was my first visit to St Carys. But not my last.' Drily, Marina said, 'It was like taking some fantastic drug for the first time. Turned out I couldn't give it up. Moving down here seemed like the answer to everything. I'd be getting away from my old life in Cheshire *and* I'd be able to keep on seeing Ronan. So that's it.' She smiled. 'You know the rest. I bought this cottage and built myself a brand-new life, did my best to make myself useful . . . and these last few years have been *so* happy. Seriously, you can't imagine how wonderful they've been. I feel guilty because I did a bad thing and bribed that man to find my boy for me, but I'll never regret it. And I'll always keep my word,' she reiterated. 'Ronan will never ever find out the truth from me.'

'Well I think you're incredible,' said Clemency. 'He's very lucky. Even if he doesn't know it.'

'I'm the lucky one.' Marina spoke with feeling.

'Oh, but imagine if you'd bought the cottage and Ronan had been offered a job in, I don't know, Edinburgh. What if you'd moved down here and he'd left Cornwall?'

'There was always that possibility. It was a risk I had to take. I knew I only had this one shot,' Marina agreed. 'It wasn't as if I could suddenly pop up in the next place he

was living and say, "Ooh, what a coincidence, me again!"'
She shook her head. 'It could still happen. If it does, at least
I'll have had five years of knowing him. It's five years more
than I might have been given. Every day's a bonus.'

'Oh Marina.' Jumping up and coming over to the sofa,
Clemency enveloped her in a long hug. 'And today you
saved his life. How completely amazing is that?'

'I didn't. If I hadn't been there, someone else would have
got to him. Darling, you mustn't tell him.' Marina wondered
how many more times she'd feel compelled to say this.

'Don't worry, you can trust me. I won't breathe a word.'
Drawing back, Clemency looked her steadily in the eye. 'But
can I just say something? If Ronan did know the truth, I
think he'd be so happy. I mean it,' she added. 'Really. If he
ever did find out, I bet he'd be *thrilled*.'

Chapter 19

It was Monday 15 June and Belle was turning over a new leaf.

She didn't even know why. It was one of those weird scenarios where you realised you were startling yourself.

She'd certainly startled Sam, who'd been working away on his laptop in the kitchen when she'd appeared in the doorway at 6.45 in the morning, wearing a black sports vest and Lycra leggings, and extremely white trainers.

He uncrossed his outstretched legs, resting on the stool opposite. 'You're up.'

'I know.' Belle tried to sound casual, as if it weren't *that* extraordinary. 'It's a nice morning, so I thought I'd go for a run.'

Sam surveyed her outfit. 'I had no idea you even owned any running clothes.'

She hadn't owned any; she'd ordered them online the other day, but he didn't need to know that. She gave him a kiss. 'Ah well, there you go,' she said lightly. 'I'm full of surprises!'

It was only a bit of exercise, after all. How hard could it be?

Twenty minutes later, having made her way across to Mariscombe Bay, on the other side of St Carys, Belle saw the group gathering on the beach not far from the surf shop. Amazingly, there were about twenty of them, greeting each other and apparently looking forward to their early morning exercise.

And there was the girl, Verity, setting up a music system and chatting with various members of the class. She was wearing a sunflower-yellow top and stripy yellow and white knee-length Lycra shorts, and Belle wondered suddenly if she should leave. What if Verity recognised her and told her she wasn't welcome? How embarrassing would that be, in front of everyone? Oh God, why had she come here when she could be back at the flat right now, lying in Sam's rumpled king-sized bed?

She was still dithering as Verity pressed a button and dance music spilt out of the speakers. Everyone else was facing the instructor now, preparing to warm up their muscles and get started.

Belle was edging slowly backwards away from the group when Verity looked over and called out, 'Morning! Are you joining us?'

'Um . . . I don't think so.'

'Oh come on, it's only thirty minutes out of your life!'

The fact that Verity was being so nice had to mean she hadn't recognised her yet. Belle patted her non-existent pockets. 'I just came out for a run. I don't have my purse. No money . . .'

'Well that's OK, because you don't need to pay me. There's no charge,' Verity said cheerfully. 'I do this for love, not money. Out of the sheer goodness of my heart.'

And Belle found herself being beckoned over to join the rest of the group. Oh well, like she'd said, it was only thirty minutes.

Couldn't hurt.

Thirty minutes later, Belle knew better. It could hurt and it did hurt. The rest of the class might look like normal people, but they had to be Olympic athletes in disguise. And now they were preparing to leave, chattering happily and looking as if they'd done nothing more to exert themselves than stand in a supermarket checkout queue.

Belle was still gulping air into her shell-shocked lungs, feeling light-headed with exhaustion and wondering if her muscles would ever stop screaming in pain. Her face was flushed, her hair was sticking to her scalp and her little plastic water bottle was empty.

'Hey, well done.' Verity appeared before her, pulling an unopened bottle out of her holdall. She handed it to Belle. 'You need to keep yourself hydrated. Have you ever done an aerobics class before?'

'No, I haven't. It was harder than I thought.' Untwisting the lid, Belle gulped down the chilled water and was embarrassed – but not embarrassed enough to stop – when some of it dribbled down her chin.

'Your muscles will ache tomorrow.' Verity smiled sympathetically. 'And the next day.'

Belle stopped drinking and looked at her. 'Do you remember me?'

'Yes, I do. Over on the other beach. I ran straight into you.'

'I wasn't in the best mood that day,' said Belle. 'I was pretty rude to you. I'm sorry.'

'Oh! Really, it's fine. You had every right to be annoyed.'

'But it was an accident. You didn't do it on purpose. I kind of wanted a chance to, you know, apologise . . .' Belle hesitated as the words stumbled out; making apologies had never been her forte.

'Have you spent the last two weeks feeling a bit guilty about it?' Verity's eyes sparkled.

'Well, yes, I suppose I have.'

'That's actually rather nice to know.' She broke into a slow smile. 'So now it's all done. We've apologised to each other.'

'Yes.' Belle was glad she'd done it now; it was a relief to have it out of the way.

'And you're Clemency's stepsister.'

Erk. 'I am. Have you talked to her about me?'

'No.' A flicker of mischief. 'Why, what would she have said about you if I had?'

'God, I dread to think.'

'Ah well, that's sisters for you. Mine's two years younger than me and she drives me nuts.' Verity brushed away a hovering insect. 'Actually, I asked my aunt about you.'

'Oh, right.' Belle nodded vaguely and wondered if Verity's aunt had forgotten about the time she and Giles had come into the newsagent's. Giles had made fun of one of the other customers, an elderly local lady who'd been chatting away to Meryl about the time she'd almost got four numbers on the Lotto. He'd stood behind the old woman and mimicked her, and Belle had burst out laughing because it had seemed funny at the time. Meryl had given them both an icy glare, and when the old lady had shuffled out and Giles had finished paying for his cigarettes, she had proceeded to tear a strip off him for being so rude. By way of retaliation, Giles had shoplifted a copy of *Take a Break* on the way out, then stuffed it into a bin at the end of the street. He'd said it served Meryl right for being a stroppy cow.

Belle had taken care to avoid the shop ever since.

God, Giles had been such a prize dick.

'So will we be seeing you here again, d'you think?' Verity indicated the beach and the music system.

'I don't know. Maybe.' All the unfamiliar footwork involved in the step routines had been difficult to keep up with. Belle, who hadn't enjoyed the feeling of not being competent, said, 'I prefer running.' It wasn't true, of course, but at least putting one foot in front of the other was pretty foolproof.

'Well if you ever fancy joining me, feel free.' Verity flashed her white smile. 'I can always do with a running mate. You can shout out warnings to people if I'm about to crash into them.'

Belle said, 'I might just do that.'

You never knew, maybe she was about to turn into a fitness fiend after all.

Sam would be impressed.

'You've been for a what?' Clemency boggled. Surely she'd misheard.

'A run along the beach.' Belle was acting as if it were a completely normal thing for her to have done. 'Nothing extreme. Just a couple of kilometres. Maybe three.'

'Crikey, this is new.' Clemency, who jogged a couple

180

of times a week, was impressed. 'Do you do it in high heels?'

'I wear proper running clothes. I'm enjoying it.'

'You're walking a bit funny.'

'That's because I did an aerobics class on Monday and overdid it. My leg muscles are still getting used to all the activity.'

'Wait, an aerobics class? You mean the one on Mariscombe Beach?'

This time Belle had the grace to flush. 'Yes.'

'The one you thought sounded so awful and completely naff? Like something out of *Hi-de-Hi!*?'

'OK, I changed my mind and went along. And yes, you're allowed to look smug. It was pretty good,' Belle admitted.

'So you've forgiven Verity for knocking you over? Well well. What's all this about then, the sudden passion for exercise?'

Belle said airily, 'No reason. I just thought I'd give it a go, get myself a bit healthier.'

Clemency briefly debated whether to carry on with the teasing. Clearly Belle was doing it to impress Sam but would rather die than admit as much.

Instead she said, 'Remember when you went out with that polo player a couple of years back?'

'Francisco? Of course I remember. What about him?'

'Oh, nothing. I just remembered you buying that pair of white jodhpurs.' Clemency looked innocent. 'Wondered if you still had them.'

Belle narrowed her eyes. 'No, I don't. And if you were wanting to borrow them, they wouldn't have fitted you anyway. They were a size eight.'

Ha, miaow. Also, bingo. Clemency was now pretty certain Sam had made some kind of comment about Belle's aversion to exercise. She hugged this snippet of knowledge to herself and heroically didn't utter another word on the subject. They were going out together for dinner, after all; it wouldn't do to have a sister-spat.

And here was Ronan coming to join them now, late because he'd had to drive back from a viewing in Falmouth before stopping off at home to shower and change. Five days on from the incident with the jet ski, he was completely recovered. His X-rays at the hospital had been clear, the scalp injury that had resulted in so much blood being spilt had been repaired with five neat stitches, and the very next morning he'd been back at work. Which was good.

Clemency broke into a smile at the sight of him, because he was wearing the blue shirt she'd told him he should buy when he'd been so set on getting the orange one.

'That colour suits you,' she told him as he greeted her with a kiss. 'Better than the orange.'

'Ah, what can I say?' He grinned. 'You were right and I was wrong.'

'I'm always right,' said Clemency.

Ronan turned to Belle. 'My girlfriend is trying to give me a makeover. What she doesn't know is I bought the orange shirt too.'

It had been just over a fortnight now, and their 'relationship' was still going strong, essentially because Ronan had had neither the time nor the opportunity to meet someone else who might have caught his fancy. In fact he'd been going through an uncharacteristically dry spell for quite a while now. Clemency was glad; it meant they could maintain the pretence and carry on enjoying themselves, and it had put a *very* satisfying stop to all of Belle's sly digs and smugness. Furthermore, it had been Belle's idea that the four of them should get together for dinner this evening at the newly opened restaurant on Silver Street.

And OK, it had seemed like a strange idea at first, but why not? If Sam and Belle were set to become a long-term couple, Clemency told herself, she was just going to have to get used to it.

'Shall we head on down, then?' said Belle. 'Sam had an appointment an hour ago, so he's meeting us there.'

They left the Mermaid and began to make their way down the narrow, winding street. As they reached the first turn in the road, the sound of music drifted up from sea level. By the time they came to the second turn, the music and singing had grown louder. When they reached the final bend, where the road led down to the harbour and the shops along the seafront came into view, Clemency saw that the noise was being made by a lively group of buskers who'd taken up position against the harbour wall, across the street from Paddy's Café.

'Oh listen to that, they sound fantastic!' She clapped her hands in time to the jaunty music. The band comprised a group of four men and a young woman performing an infectiously upbeat song about the joys of a rainy Cornish holiday. They were playing an eclectic assortment of instruments including a guitar, an accordion, a violin and a saxophone. As she sang, the girl thumped out an energetic beat on a red and silver drum slung around her neck. She had bright red dreadlocks, matching crimson lipstick and a killer smile, and was encouraging the audience to clap along.

The rest of the band danced as they sang, a raggle-taggle collective, each with an individual style of their own.

'God,' said Belle, 'look at the state of them. Talk about lowering the tone.'

'I think they're brilliant,' Clemency exclaimed. 'Look, everyone's loving them! Come on, let's go down there.'

The band had gathered quite a crowd; there was a hat on the ground in front of them, and each time money was thrown into it, the band members let out a rousing cheer whilst carrying on playing. Small children were dancing joyfully, old people were nodding along, and everyone was smiling.

Apart from Belle, who was grimacing as if a seagull had just pooed on her shoes.

'But this is St Carys,' she protested. 'And they're begging for money.'

'They're not begging,' said Clemency. 'They're performing. No one has to give them money if they don't want to.'

'Except the one in the top hat would probably slit your throat if you didn't,' said Belle. 'And that guy with the long black hair looks as if he'd give you nits.'

'Hey, come on, loosen up.' Ronan slid a teasing arm around her waist. 'Have a little dance with me!'

'Oh don't!' Belle wailed. 'It's not *funny*. If you encourage them, their friends will follow them down here. Before you know it, St Carys will turn into some scuzzy dumping ground for unwashed hippies!'

Ronan looked amused. 'Really?'

Belle was outraged. 'Yes, *really*. Someone needs to call the police so they can come over here right now and make them stop before—'

'I can see Sam,' Ronan interrupted and Clemency couldn't help it; as always when she heard his name, her heart leapt into her mouth.

But since it wouldn't do to give herself away, she followed the direction of Ronan's gaze and kept the excitement under control.

Chapter 20

Sam, below them and over to the right, was standing at the back of the crowd that had congregated in an ever-widening semicircle around the band of buskers. In contrast with the casually dressed holidaymakers, he was wearing a dark suit, a white shirt and a striped blue tie.

Oh he looked so handsome, so smart. *Like James Bond but better.*

Belle, who clearly thought so too, said with relief, 'There he is. And he's keeping an eye on them, thank God. Maybe he'll report them to the police.'

Even the way Sam stood was perfect. Clemency watched as he smiled at the sight of a small girl in pink dungarees hopping up and down in front of the band. The girl, seeing his smile, beamed and danced faster. And somewhere deep inside her, Clemency felt her ovaries go *ping*.

He'd make a fantastic father.

The violinist, spotting someone he knew in the crowd, let out a whoop and pointed his bow at them. Then the lead singer called out, 'Hey!' and beckoned to a person standing close to Sam.

'Come on then.' Belle was growing impatient. 'Are we going down there?'

'Hang on a second,' said Clemency, because the little girl in the pink dungarees had threaded her way through the crowd and was now running over to Sam, grabbing his hand. And Sam was laughing and loosening his tie with his free hand as she pulled him towards the band . . . and it was becoming apparent that the person the band had recognised who was standing close to Sam was in fact Sam himself.

'Oh for God's sake,' Belle howled. 'What's going on? What are they trying to *do* to him?'

'I think they're making him sing,' said Ronan as a microphone was thrust into Sam's hand.

Clemency knew why her sister was so outraged. Belle had once been publicly humiliated at the circus by a clown who'd honked his horn in her ear and caused her to wet her knickers in fright. 'But they can't do that,' Belle said furiously. 'They just *can't*.'

Except Sam had already started, joining in and seamlessly continuing the song as the rest of the band stamped their feet and whooped with approval. The audience, amazed, began to cheer and applaud as the handsome businessman in the dark suit and tie sang along brilliantly with the other band members, simultaneously standing out and blending in. He had a fantastic voice, knew all the words and was moving to the music in perfect time.

Best of all, Belle couldn't have looked more stunned if he'd been singing naked.

Worst of all, Clemency realised as they made their way down the street to where the band was performing, it had just made her love Sam Adams that little bit more.

And when the song finally ended, for a brief moment he looked directly at her, and she hoped he couldn't read her mind.

Then everyone in the crowd was clapping wildly, the band members were hugging and high-fiving Sam, and Belle was saying in disbelief, 'Am I having some kind of horrible dream here?'

There were cries of *More, more!* but Sam smiled and shook his head, handing the microphone back to the lead singer and bending down to speak briefly to the small girl in dungarees, who flung her arms around his neck and kissed him on the cheek.

'If he catches nits from the guy with long hair,' Ronan murmured in Clemency's ear, 'let's hope for all our sakes he doesn't pass them on to Belle.'

'I don't understand. I just don't understand.' Belle's tone was pained as they made their way along the Esplanade to the restaurant on Silver Street. 'How did you know all the words to that song?'

Sam was keeping a straight face. 'I thought everyone knew the words.'

'No one in the audience had ever heard that song before.'

'Ah. Well in that case maybe it's because I used to be a member of the band.'

Belle pointed an index finger at him accusingly. 'You see, I want to laugh, but I'm actually starting to think you might be serious.'

'You might actually be right.' Sam's eyes glinted with amusement.

'But that doesn't make any sense!' She was gazing at him in horror. 'Really? I mean, *really* really?'

'Afraid so,' Sam said cheerfully. 'So anyway, they've almost finished for the evening. I said I'd meet them later at the Mermaid. But it's OK,' he reassured Belle. 'You don't have to come along with me. I'll be fine on my own.'

When they'd been seated at the restaurant and served drinks, Clemency said, 'Go on then, tell us everything.'

'OK, the band is called Make Your Day and it was set up eight years ago by the girl with the red dreadlocks,' said Sam. 'Her name's Ali and she was my sister-in-law. Sorry,' he amended, 'she still *is* my sister-in-law, because she'll always be Lisa's sister. She was also one of our bridesmaids when we got married.'

'I hope she didn't have red dreadlocks then,' said Belle with a tinkly laugh.

Sam shook his head. 'No, they were blue for the wedding. And the band played at our reception. Anyway, the year before we got married, Lisa and I were just about to head off on a fortnight's camping trip when Ali called us. Two members of the band had gone down with salmonella poisoning and she was desperate. So we cancelled our holiday, learnt the songs and joined the band for two weeks.'

'Wow,' said Clemency.

'Heavens.' Belle looked as if she were about to be dunked in a tank of cockroaches. 'How . . . brave!'

'It was one of the best times of my life.' Sam was smiling at what were clearly fond memories. 'We travelled along the south coast in their purple and silver tour bus. It was fantastic. Making people's day, cheering them up, seeing little kids dancing along to the music and having a ball.' He shrugged. 'What's not to like?'

'Imagine living in a dirty old tour bus, though.' Belle winced. 'Weren't you worried you might catch salmonella too?'

Sam said, 'The bus was clean. Ed and Tommy contracted salmonella after taking their mother out to a Michelin-starred restaurant on her birthday.'

'But loads of places don't allow busking.' Belle swiftly changed tack. 'It's illegal. Didn't you get arrested by the police?'

'They'd generally just tell us to stop. Advise us to move along. We wrote a song for the occasion,' Sam grinned, 'called "Here Comes the Law". We used to launch into it whenever we saw them coming towards us. It went: "Who are these handsome folk, do they want us to play more? Oh no oh no it's time to go, these handsome folk are the law." And then it went into the chorus: "Here comes the law, law, law . . . to give us what for . . ."' He shrugged. 'Well, it made people laugh. Them too, hopefully. They were only doing their job.'

'I love every single thing about this story,' said Ronan.

At the front desk, the manager was informing a group of diners that he was terribly sorry but all the tables were taken and it was always advisable to make a booking in advance. Clemency jumped up and went over to the desk.

Less than a minute later, she returned. 'Come on, I've paid for our drinks. Those people are having our table and we're going to the Mermaid.'

'But . . . but I'm hungry,' Belle protested.

'They serve food at the Mermaid,' Clemency said smoothly. Belle looked as if she'd just swallowed a wasp.

Two hours later, the evening was in full swing. Ali and the rest of the band had arrived just a few minutes after they'd reached the Mermaid. Sam had introduced everyone to each other, then they'd all headed out on to the terrace and sat down together at one long trestle table to eat huge plates of either home-made lasagne or fried chicken and chips. It clearly wasn't Belle's idea of fine dining, but Clemency, watching her, saw that she was doing her best to pretend she didn't mind.

After they'd finished eating, everyone moved back inside. The band produced their instruments, because making music was what they loved most and did best, and an impromptu party began. Locals and tourists alike danced along to the songs sung with guests on the stage. Sam was persuaded to join the band once more, 'Here Comes the Law' proved to be the hit of the evening, and Clemency danced with Ronan whilst keeping a discreet eye on Belle, who was evidently still in a state of shock.

'And that was my sister's favourite song,' Ali announced when the applause had died down after she and Sam had sung a stirring rendition of a song called 'You and Me'. 'I wrote it about the two of us before she met Sam. Her name was Lisa, we both loved her with all our hearts and she died three years ago. But she'll never be forgotten.' She reached for the bottle of beer on the table at the side of the stage and raised it. 'Here's to our beautiful girl Lisa. Thank you. OK, one more song and then we'll take a break.'

Five minutes later, Clemency was out on the terrace getting some fresh air when Ali joined her.

'Hey. It's been a good night, hasn't it?' Perching on the low wall, she kicked off her faded blue flip-flops. 'I'm so glad we came to St Carys.'

Clemency smiled at her. 'Sam is too. Well, we all are.'

'You think? Maybe not quite all.' Ali nodded across the terrace to where Belle was on her phone. 'When I was talking to your sister earlier, she was leaning away from me as if I might be contagious.'

'Oh God, was she? I'm sorry. If it helps,' said Clemency, 'she sometimes does the same to me.'

Ali looked amused. 'Don't worry about it. I've had worse.' Then her tone changed, grew serious. 'Can I ask you a couple of questions?'

Uh oh. What was this about? Clemency braced herself. 'Fire away.'

Chapter 21

'I love Sam to bits. I want him to be happy again.' Ali paused for a moment and gazed out over the ink-dark sea, then turned and looked directly at Clemency. 'I mean, I *really* want him to be happy again. Will your sister make him happy?'

Oof. No beating about the bush.

'She likes him,' Clemency said carefully. 'A lot.'

'Is she right for him, though? Are they suited to each other?'

Clemency shrugged. 'How can we ever know that?'

'Come on, that's the politician's answer.'

'She's my sister. What do you expect me to say?'

'So that means you're going to be discreet.' Ali tossed back her bright red dreadlocks. 'The two of you aren't a bit alike, are you?'

'We're stepsisters, not blood-related.'

'I know. She told me. I just meant do *you* think they're a perfect match? Because Belle's pretty confident that she's the one for Sam.'

'Maybe she's right.'

'How about you?' said Ali. 'Do you like him?'

'*Me?*' Thank goodness it was getting dark. Praying she wasn't blushing, Clemency said, 'I'm with Ronan!'

Ali's eyes sparkled. 'I know that too. I actually meant would you be happy if they stayed together?'

Urgh, even more embarrassing. 'I would. Of course I would.'

'If they got married, that'd make you Sam's next sister-in-law,' said Ali.

'Which means you and me would be sisters-in-law-in-law.'

Ali laughed. 'Fine by me. Maybe this time we'll both be bridesmaids. If someone gets married twice, are you allowed to be their bridesmaid at both weddings?'

'We'll insist on it,' said Clemency. 'And our hair will have to match. What colour shall we have it?'

'Oh I *do* like you,' Ali exclaimed. 'And I know I've had a few ciders and I probably shouldn't be saying this, but I wish Sam was seeing you.' She tilted her head sideways. 'You don't look like her, but you do kind of remind me of Lisa. Feels to me as if you'd make a much better couple.'

Clemency felt her pulse quicken. What a mess this whole situation was. She saw over Ali's shoulder that Belle had finished her phone call and was making her way over.

Touched, she said, 'Thanks. I mean, it's not going to happen. But I'll take it as a compliment anyway.'

'Honestly, this place is a joke,' Belle announced. 'Three taxi companies I've phoned now, and none of them can pick me up before midnight.'

There were only three small taxi companies in St Carys. Belle was accustomed to flagging down black cabs in London, or using Uber to get picked up within minutes.

'Don't you want to stay?' said Clemency.

'I've got a migraine coming on. All this music is doing my head in. No offence,' Belle added, turning to Ali, 'but I've had enough of it for one night. I just want to go home.'

Clemency thought for a moment. 'Wait here. I'll see what I can do.'

'Thanks so much,' said Belle as Ronan held the door open for her.

'No problem.' He waited until she was settled in the passenger seat before going round to the other side. Having not had anything to drink since a glass of wine at the restaurant, he'd agreed to drive Belle home. 'My mum has migraine attacks, so I know what they're like. Has your GP prescribed medication?'

Belle shrugged as they pulled away from the kerb. 'Oh, I haven't been to the doctor – I'll just take a couple of aspirin when I get back. To be honest, my feet are hurting more than my head. These shoes really pinch my toes.'

The shoes also sported five-inch spike heels. Ronan smiled to himself. How many females would accept the offer of a lift home then brazenly admit they'd lied in order to get it? But that was Belle for you; if her shoes were pinching and she wanted to leave, she'd do or say whatever it took to make it happen.

'You don't have a headache, do you?' He spoke without rancour.

'I'd have had one if I'd stayed any longer listening to that racket.' She grinned and gave him a playful nudge. 'Hey, you can't begrudge me a lift. I've saved you from it too.'

The nudge reminded him that whilst she was nowhere near drunk, Belle had had enough alcohol to blur the edges.

As he drove across St Carys, Ronan idly wondered about something that had first crossed his mind a couple of weeks ago.

'So everything's good with you and Sam then?'

Belle nodded complacently. 'Really good.'

Hmm, should he?

Shouldn't he?

Ah, what the hell . . .

'Typical.' He glanced sideways at her. 'All these years and now I've missed my chance. Oh well, never mind. I'm happy for you.'

'What? What do you mean?' Belle swung her head round to look at him.

'Nothing. Forget I said it.'

They'd almost reached the apartment block now. 'What chance?' said Belle.

'Sshh. It doesn't matter. I should have kept quiet.'

'You can't say that then not tell me what you're talking about.'

Ronan pulled up just past the entrance to the building, where trees efficiently shielded the car from view. He switched off the ignition. 'Are you sure you want me to say it?'

'Yes!'

'OK, but only if you promise not to breathe a word. Not to Sam or to Clem. It wouldn't be fair on them. And it isn't as if anything's going to happen, so there's no need for them to know.'

'Know what?' Belle's tone was breathless.

So easy.

'Well, I suppose it's just ironic how your feelings for

196

someone can change so suddenly.' He lowered his voice. 'So . . . completely.'

'You mean you and Clemency?'

Ronan shook his head. 'I'm talking about me and you. All these years and it's finally happened. Ever since you came back, everything feels different. Each time I see you, all I want to do is kiss you. Don't panic, I won't.' He smiled fleetingly and murmured, 'But I can't help wondering what it'd be like.'

Belle's eyes were shining in the darkness. 'You mean we could do it now and no one would ever know?'

Did this mean she was going to go through with it? Ronan breathed in the scent she was wearing and nodded slowly. 'We could give it a try, see how it feels.'

God, I haven't thought this through. What if she tells Sam and he tries to kill me?

'Come here,' whispered Belle, unfastening her seat belt and moving towards him.

Shit, she's actually going to do it . . .

The next moment, she'd shoved her hands hard against his chest. 'You bastard!' she bellowed. 'How dare you? Weren't you listening the other week when we told you about our vow? How can you even *think* I'd do that to my sister after we made our pact?'

'Thanks for that,' said Clemency when Ronan arrived back at the Mermaid. 'How is she?'

'Her five-inch heels were hurting her feet. Her head is fine.'

She rolled her eyes. 'Might have guessed.'

'Hey.' He touched her arm. 'Did you ever wonder how

confident you could be about Belle keeping her side of that solemn vow you two made?'

Puzzled, Clemency said, 'No. Well, maybe a little bit. Why?'

Ronan was glancing around to check that no one else was within earshot. 'You can be confident.'

'Why?'

'I made a play for her and she turned me down.'

Her stomach lurched. 'What? How much of a play?'

'I said I wanted to kiss her, and that no one else would ever know. Me, the one she's been after for years. You should have seen her reaction,' said Ronan. 'She was horrified.' He mimed Belle's expression. '*Outraged.*'

'Oh.'

'Well at least now you know you can trust her, one hundred per cent.' He was looking delighted at his own ingenuity. 'I thought you'd be pleased.'

Clemency didn't know how to feel. The old Belle had nursed her unrequited crush on Ronan for so long. It meant her sister must be even more in love with Sam than she'd thought.

There was a hollow ache of disappointment in her ribcage. Ali had asked her earlier if she'd be happy to have Sam as her brother-in-law. And she'd said yes, but under the circum-stances had that actually been a massive lie?

Plus there was the other thing . . .

'What?' said Ronan as her expression gave her away.

'She's already got Sam, and now she's had you making advances too. She's going to think she's *won.*' Clemency sighed. 'Oh God, she's going to be smug all over again.'

Smug was an understatement. More like insufferable.

'Ah, sorry about that. Didn't think.' He grimaced. 'But

like I said, at least now you know you can trust her. Good news for you,' he added. 'Bad news for me.'

What did that mean? Clemency looked at him, baffled. 'Why is it bad news for you?'

'Hello? She turned me down!' He gestured to himself, did the top-to-toe sweep. 'Wasn't even tempted! I'm clearly not as irresistible as I thought.'

Clemency smiled at his mock dismay, then her heart did its habitual squeeze at the sight of an unmistakable silhouette appearing in the illuminated doorway that led out on to the terrace. Purely to warn Ronan so he didn't say anything to give the game away, she murmured, 'Sam's over there, watching us.'

Ronan promptly drew her to him and kissed her on the mouth, his fingers sliding up through the hair at the nape of her neck.

When Clemency eventually drew back, Sam had disappeared. Slightly out of breath, she said, 'What was that for?'

He frowned. 'Sorry, I thought it was what you wanted me to do. Because of Sam and Belle. Wasn't that what you meant?'

'I *meant* that I didn't want him to overhear what you were saying about Belle.'

'So much rejection.' Ronan heaved a dramatic sigh. 'I don't know how much more I can stand.'

Clemency laughed because he was looking so tortured, so tragic. 'Listen to yourself. Talk about needy.'

'Listen to *you*,' he retaliated. 'Talk about cruel. There's only one person who really loves me, and that's my mother. Nobody else.' He sighed. 'She's the only one.'

He's talking about Josephine. Don't think about Marina, don't even think about her.

Aloud, she said, 'You poor thing.'

'Would you like another kiss?'

Would she? Clemency hesitated, then shook her head. 'Thanks, but no thanks.'

'See? Is it any wonder my self-esteem is in tatters?' Ronan's brown eyes glittered. 'You know what? It's not easy being rejected.'

She patted his arm. 'I'm sure you'll survive.'

'Tell me, am I still slightly irresistible?'

Clemency paused. 'Maybe. A tiny bit.'

Ronan broke into a grin. 'Phew, thank goodness for that.'

Chapter 22

Sometimes it isn't until you've seen something a few times that it permeates your brain and you actually notice it.

The penny dropped while Clemency was in Paddy's Café, sipping her frothy cappuccino and waiting on the phone for a client to decide when he and his wife might be able to view a property.

'Sorry,' said the client. 'We can't manage Tuesday. Berenice has a shopping trip with friends.'

'Not a problem. How about Wednesday?' Clemency tapped her pen against the arm of the chair, idly watching as Marina waved off a pair of happy customers, then stood up in order to have a stretch and ease the muscles in her aching back.

'No can do. Sailing on Wednesday.'

Did Marina have a touch of indigestion?

'Thursday?' said Clemency.

'Hmm, not sure. Berenice usually sees her regression therapist on Thursdays.'

Of course she did. Who wouldn't? Clemency tap-tapped her pen against her knee and watched as a small boy raced along the harbour, hurling himself into his grandfather's outstretched arms and bursting into tears.

'Oh now, what's happened to you?' The grandfather cuddled the boy and ruffled his hair. 'What's all this about?'

'A insect stung me!' The boy let out a wail of fury and pulled up the sleeve of his Superman T-shirt. 'Look, it hurts! There's a *lump*.'

That was when Clemency saw Marina glance over at the boy, quickly look away again, then gently press the flat of her hand against her chest for the second time.

Except it wasn't only the second time, was it? She'd seen Marina do it yesterday too, as well as some other time she couldn't quite place . . . oh, when they'd bumped into each other in the bakery the other afternoon. She'd been buying apple doughnuts and Marina was picking up a cottage loaf, and while they'd briefly chatted in the queue, Marina had made that same almost-unconscious gesture with her hand, the tips of her fingers resting briefly against the upper curve of her right breast.

Her *healthy* breast.

It wasn't an excuse-me-I-have-a-touch-of-indigestion gesture, though. That much Clemency now knew for sure.

The evil insect, meanwhile, had been identified as an ant. The grandfather solemnly assured the small boy that he wouldn't die and if he stopped crying he could have an ice cream worthy of a superhero.

'OK, we'd better not say Thursday to be on the safe side. Maybe Friday would be good,' said the potential client. 'Although it might clash with her hot-stone treatment at the spa.'

Clemency had plenty of experience dealing with irritating

clients. She also had a ton of patience as a rule. But it wasn't limitless. She said pleasantly, 'How about you check with your wife and get back to me when you've found out which dates she can manage? Might be easier all round. Bye!'

Sometimes people were more trouble than they were worth.

'Hi,' said Marina when Clemency joined her. 'How were the apple doughnuts?'

'Awful.' Clemency patted her stomach. 'They were impossible to resist, so I ended up eating all three. Which means an extra couple of hours in the gym to make up for them.'

'Ah, no harm in treating yourself once in a while. You're fine as you are. Anyway, how about that sister of yours?' Marina sounded triumphant. 'She's still going strong! I saw her just this morning, all bright-eyed and bushy-tailed on the beach. Looks like someone lost their bet.'

Clemency smiled. Last week they'd watched Belle jogging past them in full make-up and she'd assured Marina it was a fad that wouldn't last. Marina had said, 'Oh, but it might,' and she'd replied, 'Trust me, I know what Belle's like. Give it a few days and this whole fitness craze'll be out of the window.'

And they'd made a bet on it.

'You were right and I was wrong,' Clemency said now. 'I owe you a drink.' She paused, ready to change the subject, because Belle's fitness regime wasn't currently uppermost in her mind. 'So, how are things with you?'

'Things? All good,' Marina said brightly. 'Oh, did I tell you I'm meeting up with that couple who are getting married at the Mariscombe Hotel? They've commissioned me to do a painting of their wedding!'

'That's great.' It meant even more to Marina, Clemency knew, because Ronan had been the one who'd recommended her to the young couple. She cleared her throat and lowered her voice. 'And how are . . . *you*?'

'I told you, I'm fine.' But this time the suppressed anxiety was visible in the faint lines around Marina's eyes. 'Why are you asking?'

'I've seen you doing this.' Clemency copied the gesture she'd witnessed earlier. 'Something's bothering you. Have you made an appointment to get checked out?'

Marina blanched. 'You saw me do that? How many times?'

'Only a few. Don't worry,' she added as Marina looked at her in dismay, 'you were very discreet. I just happened to spot it.'

'Oh dear, I'm sorry. But I'm sure it's nothing. I'm just being neurotic.'

'You mean you haven't been to see the doctor yet? You will, though, won't you.' This time she wasn't asking a question.

'Yes, of course.' Marina nodded like a small child dutifully promising to tidy her room. 'I'll make an appointment when I get home.'

'Hmm, unconvincing. Why haven't you done it already?'

Marina paused, then her shoulders slumped in defeat. 'Because I'm scared.' Her voice broke as she said the word. 'Petrified. I don't want it to be happening, not again. Not after last time.'

'But you need to get it checked.' Clemency's voice softened.

'I know, of course I know that, but I'd rather it just went away by itself. Right now, I can tell myself it's nothing, just a harmless cyst.' Marina shrugged helplessly. 'Just for the moment, I'd rather think that than know it's something much worse. Because I don't want the cancer to be back . . . I've been through it once and I don't want to have to go through it again.'

Clemency's heart went out to her; as with anything you really didn't want to do, from filling in your tax return to getting your wisdom teeth yanked out, the temptation was to put it off for as long as possible. This time, though, she knew she couldn't allow herself to agree with Marina's impassioned reasoning.

'I understand,' she said, gently but firmly. 'I do understand. But for your own sake, you know you need to find out.'

Arriving back at the office, Clemency spotted Josephine's bright yellow Fiat outside and her empty stomach gave a happy rumble of anticipation.

And . . . *result*. Pushing open the door, she spotted the familiar blue-and-white-striped cool box resting on her desk.

'You know what I love most about your mum?' Clemency said to Ronan, who was tapping a number into his phone. 'Everything. Every single thing in the world. She's a magical cooking angel.' As she popped open the airtight lid, the heavenly scents of Caribbean rum and coconut shrimp with mashed sweet potatoes and grilled pineapple spilt out in all their glory. 'Now *that's* what I call a thing of beauty.'

At that moment the door swung open behind her and Josephine came in, clutching a huge bouquet of pink and cream roses from the florist down the road.

'Oh Josephine, you shouldn't have. Honestly, the food's more than enough, you didn't need to buy me flowers as well!' It was one of those throwaway remarks meant to make people laugh, and usually it did the trick. This time, though, the moment the words were out she wished she hadn't said them. Josephine was trying to smile, but the awkwardness was visible on her face. Clemency said hastily, 'Oh God, I'm sorry, it was meant to be a joke.'

'Darling, don't worry, you didn't know. They're for my friend Margo. Her husband died yesterday. Dear me, I still can't believe it.' Unshed tears sprang into Josephine's brown eyes and she shook her head. 'None of us can believe he's gone. It was so unexpected. Poor Margo, they were such a happy couple. They were on their way to the supermarket,' she explained. 'Just sitting in the car, waiting for the traffic lights on Trenance Road to turn green, and Patrick said he didn't feel very well. And that was it. He died right there in the driver's seat. One minute he was alive and talking about buying a Gressingham duck, the next minute he was gone.'

'Oh Josephine, that's so awful.' Clemency gave her a hug, careful not to squash the roses. She'd heard Josephine talking about Margo before. 'And isn't their daughter getting married in September?'

'She is, she is.' Josephine nodded and gathered herself. 'It's just heartbreaking. They were so excited about the wedding. Now he's never going to walk his daughter down the aisle. He'll never get to meet his grandchildren. He's going to miss out on *everything* . . . Oh well, I suppose these things happen. That's the trouble with life, isn't it? We never know when our time's going to be up.' Pragmatic as always, Josephine straightened her shoulders and gave herself a mental shake. 'Anyway, I'd better get back. The coconut shrimp is

Margo's favourite too, that's why I made an extra-big batch this morning. Not that she'll want to eat, of course, but she needs to keep her strength up.'

Ronan ended his phone call and came over to kiss his mother goodbye. 'Give Margo my condolences and let me know as soon as they have a date set for the funeral. I'll go with you.'

'Thank you, darling.' Josephine smiled and stroked the side of his face. 'You're a good son.'

'I know.'

'You'd be an even better one if you could just find yourself a proper girlfriend and settle down. Maybe give me a grandchild before it's my turn to keel over and die.'

'Here it comes, any excuse for a spot of emotional black-mail.' Ronan grinned. 'You never miss a trick, do you?'

'With a son like you,' said Josephine, 'I need to make the most of every chance I get.'

Chapter 23

'Ah, look at the two of you, don't you make a lovely couple! How long have you been married then?'

Nevil Burrows was ninety-three, and his long-term memory was pin-sharp. His short-term memory, by way of contrast, was very poor, which was why he was selling his two-bedroomed cottage and moving in with his daughter and her family in Porthleven.

Ronan exchanged a glance with Kate; thank goodness he'd warned her in advance about Nevil's ability to retain information.

'No, Mr Burrows, I'm from the estate agency and Kate is one of our clients. She's come to look at your house,' he explained for the second time. 'We aren't married.'

Nevil's overgrown white eyebrows shot up. 'Not married? Oh *dear*. Ah well, I suppose it's the modern way. Times change, don't they? Everyone used to get married in my day.'

'We're not a couple, Mr Burrows. Not . . . together,' Kate elaborated, shaking her head.

'No? Oh that *is* a shame.' Nevil looked disappointed. 'I thought you were married. You look as if you could be!'

Kate smiled. 'Well we aren't. Shall we have a look at your living room?'

'Of course, of course. Come and see! Are you looking for a boyfriend, m'dear? Or do you already have someone in your life?'

Kate flushed. 'I'm single at the moment.'

'Well bless my soul, that *is* bad news. And how about you?' Nevil turned to Ronan. 'Are you single too? Because if you are, you two could get together! How about that for an idea?'

This was the thing about very old people: they quite often liked to blurt out whatever happened to be on their mind, regardless of whether or not it was appropriate. Ronan saw Kate's flush deepen and felt the back of his own neck grow a bit hot. Before he could reply, Kate said hurriedly, 'Ronan has a girlfriend.'

'He does?' Nevil brightened. 'How delightful! Who's Ronan?'

'I'm Ronan, Mr Burrows. Now, this is the living room,' Ronan said firmly, because someone had to get this viewing started.

'Oh now look at that.' Nevil tut-tutted. 'I wonder who left that there?'

That was a frying pan containing an overcooked fried egg, balanced on top of the bookcase.

'Let me take it into the kitchen,' Ronan offered. When he returned to the living room twenty seconds later, Nevil was pointing things out to Kate at the window.

'Oh hello,' he said. 'I was just showing your wife the rose bushes. You both enjoy gardening, do you?'

'Um . . . yes,' said Kate. 'I do.'

'That's good to hear. And we've got a fair-sized lawn here too, plenty of room for the kiddies to run around and play. How many do you have?'

Nevil was looking eagerly at them both. Briefly tempted to invent a couple of children, Ronan told himself he mustn't do that, it would be unethical. He shook his head and said, 'No children,' then saw Nevil's face fall and hastily added, '*yet.*'

'Ah, that's the spirit.' Nodding vigorously, Nevil gave him a saucy nudge. 'Getting plenty of practice in, eh?' He winked at Kate. 'Nothing like a bit of practice to keep things interesting. Need to make the most of it before those kiddies turn up!'

Fifteen minutes later, having viewed the rest of the house, they said their goodbyes. As he waved to them from the front doorstep, Nevil beamed and called out, 'Don't forget now, lots of practice!' Which rather suggested that not *all* his short-term memory was lost.

Ronan glanced at Kate, whose mouth had begun to twitch uncontrollably. Somehow they made it down the garden path and back to the safety of the car before bursting out laughing. Suppressed for so long, the laughter refused to die down; each time it almost happened, a glance from one of them would set the other off again, until they'd succumbed to full-blown hysteria and Ronan had a stitch in his side.

After several minutes, they finally managed to regain some semblance of control.

'Oh God,' Kate gasped, clutching her stomach. 'My muscles ache. That was like doing three hundred sit-ups.'

Ronan shook his head. 'I can't believe we managed to hold out as long as we did.'

'What do I look like? Has my mascara run?' Kate wiped her index fingers beneath her eyes. 'Trust me to be wearing it on the one day this has to happen. It's the first time I've bothered with make-up in weeks.'

'Here, let me.' There was a mirror on the other side of the sun visor, but it evidently hadn't occurred to Kate to look for it. Ronan took a tissue out of the packet he kept in the glove compartment and turned sideways in his seat so he could carefully wipe away the smudges of mascara on her cheeks.

The last time he'd sat in this car facing a female, it had been Belle, and he'd asked if he could kiss her, despite not really wanting to.

And now it was the other way around; this time he couldn't ask the question, despite it being what he wanted to do more than anything in the world.

Presumably, this was him getting his comeuppance. They were so close . . . *so close* . . . but Kate was avoiding his gaze, keeping very still whilst looking upwards.

At least it meant she couldn't see the vein pulsing away in his neck, betraying his accelerated heartbeat.

Slowly and meticulously, Ronan wiped away every last trace of mascara. When it was done, he felt Kate's warm breath on his cheek as she said, 'Thanks.'

God, this feels good. 'No problem.'

Lifting herself up from her seat, she twisted her neck so she could check her reflection in the rear-view mirror. 'You've done an excellent job there.'

Ronan shrugged and said flippantly, 'I've made a lot of girls cry.' *Oh hell, why did I say that?* Hastily he added, 'OK, that's not true. It just came out. I haven't made lots of girls cry.'

'Apart from the ones who stand outside your flat reading poems to you at midnight.'

Damn, he was just digging himself deeper. 'That was a one-off. It hasn't happened since, I promise.'

'Well that has to be a good thing. And you're with Clemency now,' Kate added lightly, 'so let's hope it doesn't happen again.'

At least he knew he wouldn't be making Clem cry. Ronan smiled at the very idea that he could.

'And it's going really well between the two of you, from what I hear.' Kate was watching him, had evidently noted the smile.

'Oh? And what is it you've been hearing?'

'Nothing but good things. People enjoy a happy ending, don't they? They love it that the two of you finally got together. And Clemency's lovely,' said Kate.

'So am I,' Ronan prompted.

'Well of course. Goes without saying.' The colour was back in her cheeks. 'But I'm glad everything's good. You're so well matched. Everyone says it, and I think so too. You and Clemency are perfect together.'

It wasn't the first time Ronan had been told this. It wasn't even the twentieth. And he could see why people would think it: on paper, all the boxes were ticked. He and Clemency had always got along like a house on fire; they were both hard-working extroverts with a shared sense of humour . . . let's face it, they *did* seem like the perfect match.

And they were, but only as friends. Good friends who loved each other's company, never grew bored with teasing each other and knew perfectly well that they were both physically attractive. But they also knew, deep down, that that was as far as it went. If anything, the problem was that they were *too* alike. He and Clemency, Ronan was sure, would be friends for the rest of their lives. But the magical, indescribable chemistry that had sprung up out of nowhere during the one unexpected evening he'd spent with Kate . . . well, that had been something else altogether. It had also been the kind of chemistry he knew he'd never experience with Clem.

For a second he was tempted to tell Kate the truth, to confide that there was actually nothing at all going on between him and Clem; he'd simply been doing her a favour, helping her out.

But no, he mustn't. It wouldn't be fair on Clem, for a start. And what would be the point, anyway? There was no reason to tell Kate and nothing would change if he did.

He'd blown his chances with her and that was that. Time to accept it once and for all and move on.

'We're doing OK.' Ronan smiled and changed the subject. 'How about you and Nevil's cottage? Could you two be a match made in heaven?'

He already knew they weren't. Years of experience had taught him the signs. When clients viewed a property, he was always able to sense when he was witnessing that irrevocable falling-in-love, have-to-have-it moment. Some people became effusive and blurted it out; others went quiet and said barely anything at all, but their body language always gave them away. Ronan loved it when he saw it happen and took it in his stride when it didn't, which was far more often than not.

Like now.

'I don't think so.' Kate was looking apologetic. 'It just didn't feel . . . you know, right. Sorry.'

Every time, she apologised. 'Don't be sorry.' He started the car and said good-naturedly, 'We'll keep on going. I'm not giving up. We'll find you your perfect place in the end.'

Chapter 24

It was hard to concentrate on llamas when your brain kept bounding off in a different direction altogether, like an out-of-control puppy.

'Clem, are you even listening? Concentrate,' Ronan ordered, rapping her on the knuckles with his pen.

'Sorry.' Clemency forced herself back to the situation at hand. She needed to pay attention; it was the final round and they were neck and neck with Rossiter's, their fellow estate agents and deadliest rivals in St Carys. 'What was the question again?'

Ronan shook his head in an I-don't-believe-this fashion. 'The llama belongs to which family of animals?'

Oh God, no clue. Clemency pictured a llama, all elegant and bright-eyed, with fabulous lashes like a supermodel. 'Sheep?'

'I don't think it's sheep.'

'Giraffe, then?'

'Are you serious?'

'It's an educated guess! They both have long necks.'

'But you don't know the answer,' said Ronan.

'No I don't. And neither do you.'

'Listen to them bickering,' a member of the Rossiter's team commented. 'And not even married yet.'

'Five seconds,' warned the quizmaster, causing Ronan to hastily scribble an answer on the square of paper.

Clemency took a glug of red wine. 'What did you put?'

'Sheep.'

'OK, pens down,' ordered the quizmaster. 'And the answer is . . . "camel".'

'Bum.' Clemency sighed and took another swig of wine, because that put them out of the running. Then she saw that Ronan was grinning and waving the square of paper with his answer on it.

He'd written CAMEL.

'You knew all the time.' Clemency narrowed her eyes at him. 'You lied to me.'

He looked smug. 'You weren't paying attention.'

She'd been thinking about Marina. For the last couple of days it had been pretty much impossible to think about anything *but* Marina.

'So that's a point each for table six, table eight and table three,' the quizmaster announced, 'which means we come to the last question of the night and it's as close as it gets between tables six and three. Ooh, I say, the battle of the estate agents. Rossiter's versus Barton and Byrne. Who do we think will win, hmm? OK, stand by for the final question. Here we go . . .'

This time Clemency paid attention.

'What is the name given to a locked case in which decanters can be seen but not used?'

A chorus of groans went up around the room. Ronan said, 'A really bloody annoying case.' He gave Clemency a look to signal he had no clue and murmured, 'Any idea?'

Clemency took the pen from him and wrote TARANTULA on the last square of paper. It wasn't right but it was something like that. Her memory scrabbled around for the word she couldn't quite remember. Talent. No. Tarantella. No. Oh come on, come on . . . She took another glug of wine and drummed her feet against the leg of Ronan's chair.

'Thanks,' said Ronan. 'That's not annoying at all.'

'Sshh, *you're* annoying.' Clemency tapped her fingers on the table. 'I'm trying to think.'

'Try harder.'

'Tarantula. Tarantella. Talent. Tantalise.' *Nearly, nearly.*

The quizmaster called out, 'Five seconds left. If no one has the correct answer, we'll move on to another question—'

'Got it,' Clemency yelped, scribbling on the paper. She waved it in the air and saw the team from Rossiter's throw down their own pens in disgust.

The quizmaster said, 'The correct answer is "tantalus".'

'Yay! We did it!' Ronan was on his feet, pulling her up out of her chair. Clemency found herself being swung around until she was dizzy. The losing contestants applauded; the team from Rossiter's assured them that the prize was rubbish anyway, and added that people who won pub quizzes were geeks.

Unscrewing the top of the bottle of red wine and taking an experimental glug, Clemency sat back down and said with relish, 'Well it tastes all right to me.'

Twenty minutes later, with the re-capped bottle sticking out of her shoulder bag, they left the pub.

'Where are we going?' said Ronan as she steered him left,

217

heading down the narrow cobbled street, rather than right, which would take them back up the hill.

'You're not tired, are you? It's still so warm. Come on, let's visit the beach.' Clemency tucked her arm through his and breathed in the clean, ozoney night-time air.

'What's this about?' Once they'd reached the dry sand, Ronan steadied her as she kicked off her shoes and bent down to pick them up. 'Are you planning to seduce me? Because I'm warning you now, sex on the beach is seriously overrated.'

'It wasn't what I was thinking of doing, but I'll take your word for it. Let's sit down.' Having located a comfortable spot, Clemency sank down on to the warm, powdery sand. 'We can talk. Want a drink?'

'You mean take it in turns to swig wine straight from the bottle? Glamorous.'

'Hello? What am I, some kind of amateur?' Reaching deeper into her bag, Clemency produced two plastic wine glasses wrapped in kitchen paper. 'Ta-daaa!'

Ronan gave her a nudge. 'I always said you were a classy bird. Did you steal those from the pub?'

'Borrowed,' Clemency corrected him. '*Borrowed* them from the pub. I'll take them back tomorrow. Here you go, I'll hold them and you pour.'

When the task had been completed, she clinked her plastic glass against Ronan's. 'Cheers. Here's to us, the world-beating, quiz-winning nerds.'

Ronan looked amused. 'Can I just say a couple of things? One, I have no idea what we're doing here. And two, I do believe you're a wee bit pissed.'

OK, this was true. She had accidentally not eaten anything

before leaving home this evening, and all the thoughts slithering like mercury around her brain had managed to distract her from the fact that the red wine had gone down rather more easily than usual. But it was a good feeling, a cosy feeling, and it wasn't as if she was so far gone she'd be in danger of blurting out anything untoward.

That definitely wouldn't happen, so it was fine.

'We're just relaxing.' Clemency gestured expansively at the inky sky. 'Look, it's a full moon tonight. Isn't it beautiful?'

Ronan looked. 'Well, it's a moon. It's round. It's about as beautiful as any plain white round thing can get.'

She gave him a push. 'Don't be like that. What about the sea? Listen to it, listen to those waves . . .'

'Did I say you were a *little* bit drunk?'

'I'm not drunk. I'm just trying to point out how lucky we are. We have all this and we take it for granted. Don't we? We have our homes and our jobs and our families . . . and of course we love our families . . .'

He laughed. 'Are you including Belle in that statement?'

'Don't make fun of me, I'm being serious.' Clemency tipped her head back and took another glug of wine, careful not to spill any down her chin. 'But we don't know what's going to happen, do we? There's no crystal ball to tell us how long we'll have them for. Like your mum's friend Margo. I mean, can you imagine what she's going through? Isn't it just unbearable? Poor woman, she and her husband had years ahead of them, and now she's on her own. He's gone and he's never coming back. All the things she wanted to say to him . . . she can't say them now.' Clemency shook her head; her own words were starting to get to her. This was so sad it was choking her up.

'I know, but it happens. You can't get upset about it.' Ronan gave her shoulder a consoling squeeze. 'Any two people who get together, one of them nearly always has to die first.'

The dry sand beneath the surface was cooler as she sifted it through her fingers. The gentle *swoosh* of the tiny waves lapping at the shoreline merged with the sound of Taylor Swift singing about trouble walking in. The music grew louder through an open window somewhere behind them, then a voice yelled, 'Turn that bloody racket off,' and it stopped abruptly.

Clemency said, 'What about two people who don't get together?'

Next to her, Ronan tilted his head. 'Meaning?'

OK, she was getting herself into a muddle now. The words weren't coming out quite as she'd planned. She smoothed out the sand at her side and planted the plastic wine glass on it. 'I suppose I'm just wondering about your biological mother. I mean, I know you don't want to upset Josephine, but what if you wait and wait until Josephine isn't around any more, then you look for your other mother and discover it's too late? What if you've left it too long and missed your chance? What if that happens and then you really *really* wish you hadn't waited, because getting to know her would have been so brilliant?'

'Clem, you're assuming my biological mother is someone fantastic and amazing and we'd both be glad we met up. But that's the fairy-tale ending, because that's the kind of person you are. Except what if she isn't like that? She might not be a nice person at all. She could be horrendous.'

'But . . . you can't think like that!'

220

'Why can't I? These meetings don't always work out. Sometimes there's no connection. By putting it off, I could be saving myself from a world of disappointment.'

'But you *wouldn't*—' Hastily Clemency caught herself. 'I mean, I'm sure you wouldn't. I just think you'd regret it if you didn't find out for yourself before it's too late. For your sake and for hers too. I swear to you, you'd be so glad you'd done it, I *know* you would . . .'

Whoops, too far, time to stop now.

'What's going on? Why are you saying it like that? Clem, do you know something you're not telling me?' Ronan had gone very still. The tone of his voice had changed. Belatedly she realised she'd got carried away.

I made a promise, I made a promise. Not another word.

'Of course I don't know anything. How could I?' Fuelled by panic, a surge of adrenalin coursed through her body. Four glasses of wine on an empty stomach, it turned out, was at least two glasses too many. And the way he was looking at her was making her tremble. Oh God, she'd gone too far.

'Why are you saying this now?' In the light of the moon, Ronan's gaze was unwavering.

'Oh come on, we've talked about it before, haven't we? It's what I've always thought! I'm just babbling on about it because your mum's friend lost her husband. Because he was too young to die, but it still happened. And because, like you said, I'm a little bit drunk.' As she said it, Clemency deliberately tipped the contents of her glass into the sand, collected up her shoes and struggled to her feet. 'Come on, let's go. I need my bed.'

★   ★   ★

221

How long had her phone been buzzing before she'd woken up?

Urgh, it was still dark. Who would even be calling at this time? Crawling back to consciousness, Clemency opened her eyes a millimetre further and saw from the alarm clock that it was 3.30 in the morning.

Three thirty. Have a heart.

The buzzing stopped and she groaned with relief, because her phone was somewhere on the floor over on the other side of the bedroom. Out of reach, anyway. Her eyes closed again and she began to drift back to sleep . . .

Something plastic-sounding hit the outside of her bedroom window and clattered to the pavement. Clemency let out a yelp and stumbled out of bed, locating and scooping up her phone along the way.

Seven missed calls. Oh God.

She opened the window and peered out.

'At last,' said Ronan, gazing up at her. He was holding an empty plastic water bottle, which had presumably been his window-knocker of choice. 'Open the door.'

'What are you *doing* here?' Even in her befuddled state, though, Clemency knew.

Patiently Ronan repeated, 'Just open the door.'

The messages on her phone were all from him too, saying much the same thing. Clemency made her way downstairs, unlocked the door and headed back up to the flat with Ronan right behind her.

In her living room, he turned her to face him. 'You know who my mother is, don't you.'

It wasn't a question.

She swallowed and shook her head. 'No.'

'I can't begin to work out *how* you know, but you do.' Ronan continued as if she hadn't spoken. 'Do *I* know her?'

Oh God. 'No.'

His dark-lashed eyes were fixed unwaveringly on hers.

'Is my biological mother one of Josephine's sisters?'

What? Where had that come from? Clemency said, 'No!'

'Is my biological mother Dee from the café?'

'No.'

'Is it Meryl from the newsagent's?'

'No.'

'Is it Marina Stafford?'

'No,' said Clemency.

'*Is* it Marina Stafford?'

Oh God. 'No.'

Silence. She could hear her own heartbeat, her own ragged breaths. It was like being up on some huge stage in front of a rapt audience, being interrogated by Derren Brown.

At 3.30 in the morning and with a hangover.

'OK,' Ronan said at last. He glanced over at the coffee table, where the contents of her make-up bag were scattered. Clemency watched as he reached for her Topshop navy eye pencil and wrote something on the palm of his hand.

Then he held his hand out to her. On it were the words: IS IT MARINA?

Clemency looked at them and couldn't speak. Nor could she bring herself to look away. Beneath the hem of the over-sized T-shirt she wore as a nightie, her knees were twitching with anxiety, and the urge to jump out of the window was scarily strong.

'It's OK, I get it,' said Ronan. 'You aren't allowed to say.'

She closed her eyes for a moment. This was unbearable.

223

'So you aren't able to say yes,' he continued slowly. 'But you haven't said no, either. Which you would have done if I hadn't been right.'

'I can't tell you,' Clemency whispered. 'I promised.'

'I know. I know you did. It's OK, you don't need to say anything. Because I have the answer now. I can tell *you* who my biological mother is.'

Clemency said faintly, 'Can you?'

'Yes, I can. It's Marina.' As he said it, she heard his voice break with emotion. The next moment she flung her arms around him and hugged him hard.

Oh Lord, I'm going to be in so much trouble.

When they finally disentangled themselves, Ronan held her at arm's length and said with a fond smile, 'God, this is amazing. No wonder you wanted me to know.'

Chapter 25

Back in London on Friday for a slew of business meetings, Sam had deliberately arranged a ninety-minute break between appointments. Following a brief but productive lunch with an overseas investor, he jumped into a black cab and came up to the northern edge of Hampstead Heath.

It was busy with tourists, but they were irrelevant. Kenwood House, originally built in the seventeenth century and beautifully restored inside and out, was a magnet for visitors who had seen the stunning building featured in various TV shows and movies. And you could see why it was so popular. Now, gleaming creamy-white in the sunshine, it resembled a vast and elegant wedding cake. In addition, the gardens were well cared for, the views across the parkland sweeping and impressive.

Were you actually allowed to scatter a loved one's ashes in the grounds? Sam still didn't know the answer; some questions, he'd felt, were better left unasked. A couple of weeks after the funeral service, he'd gone ahead and scattered Lisa's ashes here anyway. Discreetly, of course.

What the hell. He hadn't been arrested.

If there were any upsides to knowing you probably didn't have long to live, it was that you could let people know what you wanted to happen when the prophecy was fulfilled.

The week after their small but perfect wedding, they'd come up to the heath for a walk. It had been Lisa's idea, simply because she loved the place so much. As they'd made their way along the paths, through the woodland and around the edge of the lake, she'd stopped every now and again to take photos.

'OK, I give in,' Sam had said at last, watching as she took a careful photograph of the trunk and exposed roots of a centuries-old oak tree. 'What are you doing?'

Lisa had straightened up, sliding her arm around his waist and hooking her thumb through the belt loop on his jeans. 'When I die, this is where I want my ashes scattered.'

Sam remembered that moment so well. Her words had hit him in the chest like a medicine ball. 'You're not going to die.'

But she'd tilted her head and given him that look of hers, the one that said they both knew different.

'Sam, we're all going to die. And the chances are that it'll happen to me before it happens to you. So I'm just helping you out here, letting you know what I'd like you to do with my ashes. If it makes you feel better, you can tell me where you'd want me to scatter yours. Just in case you beat me to it.'

'OK, I'll have a think. But you need to choose exactly where you want them to go. Down here, by the lake?' He gestured to the glittering expanse of water before them. 'Further up the hill? Or in front of the house?'

'All of the above. I don't want them in just one place.'

Lisa smiled her mischievous smile and gave his waist a squeeze. 'I'd rather have a little bit here, a little bit there. Then you can come back whenever you want, do the walk and think of me all the way round. Deal?'

At the time, Sam had told himself they could still have years left together, maybe even decades, before that happened. Because you never knew, did you? People had been known to make miraculous recoveries.

Aloud, because Lisa had clearly made up her mind, he'd said, 'Deal,' and kissed her on the mouth.

Years later, lost in thought, it took a while for Sam to realise that his name was being called. Looking up, he saw a figure striding down the hill towards him.

'Sam! Oh how marvellous, it *is* you. Well this is wonderful. Come here, what a surprise!'

Alice was in her seventies, tall and rangy, super-intelligent and fiercely independent. How extraordinary to see her again. Sam submitted to her warm, bony embrace and said, 'I'm surprised too. I thought you were living in Barbados.'

He knew exactly how long it was since they'd last seen each other. When he and Lisa had moved into their tiny flat in Peckham, Alice had occupied the ground-floor apartment directly beneath them. The garden had been hers but she'd insisted on sharing it with them, had invited them along to her frequent parties and generally been the best neighbour anyone had the right to expect. They had done favours for each other, shared meals, talked for hours. For nine months they'd seen each other almost every day, until Alice's sister, living in Barbados and newly divorced, had invited Alice to move over there and keep her company in her vast beach-front house. Alice had agreed, with the proviso that she would spend her days volunteering in a school, because otherwise she'd be living a life of pointless privilege.

And that had been it in a nutshell; she'd sold off her possessions and moved out of the flat two weeks later.

Three days after that, Lisa had been taken ill, suffering the first symptoms of her brain tumour.

Alice, who had never owned a computer or had an email address, knew nothing about what had happened from then on.

'I still am living in Barbados!' She was surveying him now, her eyes bright. 'I didn't expect to love it out there as much as I do. This is just a flying visit to see my nieces. Anyway, how are things with you? You're looking so well!'

'Thanks. You too.' This was the bit he hated. The inevitable breaking of the news was surely only seconds away.

'And where are you living now? I drove past the flat yesterday and saw an Asian couple carrying their shopping inside, so I knew you'd moved.'

Sam said, 'Actually, I'm down in Cornwall now. St Carys, on the north coast.'

He saw Alice's eyes flicker as she registered his use of *I* rather than *we*.

Here it comes.

'Just you? Are you and Lisa not together any more? Oh that *is* sad . . .'

The temptation was there to leave it at that, to simply nod and agree that it was unfortunate, then to change the subject and leave Alice thinking things just hadn't worked out.

It would be so much easier for them both.

But he couldn't do that. Not to Alice, nor to Lisa.

'Lisa had a brain tumour,' Sam said carefully, and saw Alice's expression change again to one of dismay. 'It wasn't the kind you can recover from. I'm afraid she died.'

'Oh no. No. Not your beautiful girl.' Appalled, Alice rested her hand on his arm and shook her head in disbelief. 'Oh Sam.'

One of the nearby wooden benches at the water's edge was unoccupied; they sat down together and he told Alice what had happened, how the illness had started and played out and eventually ended.

'How cruel. How unfair,' said Alice. 'But you've coped. If you can get through that, you can get through anything.'

'I suppose that's true.' Sam nodded. 'Doesn't always feel like it, I have to say. But I'm still here.'

'What doesn't kill you makes you stronger.' Alice closed her eyes. 'God, darling, I'm so sorry. I can't believe I just said something so trite. Bloody awful clichés, don't they make you want to spit?' She sounded utterly disgusted with herself.

Sam smiled. 'But we all use them. Don't worry about it.'

For several seconds they sat together in peaceful silence. A young couple walking two terriers paused to let them off their leads, and the dogs launched themselves into the lake, chasing after a gaggle of ducks that promptly sailed off out of reach. The terriers turned away, as if pretending they'd had no interest in the ducks anyway, and began splashing around in the shallows instead.

Alice said, 'It's been how long now, since she died?'

'Three years.' He knew what was coming next.

'And?'

Sam shrugged. 'Are we still using clichés?' he said wryly. 'Life goes on.'

'Is that your way of telling me to mind my own business? It's OK, I won't ask. Stopping now.' Alice mimed zipping her mouth shut. 'No more questions, Your Honour.'

'Hey, it's fine.' He gave her a friendly nudge. 'Of course we can talk about it. But don't get your hopes up. I'm afraid we're a long way from a happy ending.'

'You're not seeing anyone?' Alice's tone was sympathetic.

'Oh I am. The trouble is, I'm not sure she's the right one.' In reality he was pretty certain she wasn't. 'And I know I should probably end the relationship, but it's . . . complicated. She's given up her apartment in London, and left her job here too. I didn't *ask* her to move in with me, it just kind of happened. So if I tell her we're over, it's going to be pretty traumatic. Which is why I feel so guilty about doing it.'

'Ah, tricky. I see where you're coming from. And is this the first real relationship since Lisa?'

'There were one or two brief . . . flings.' Sam shrugged. 'Nothing that meant anything.'

'What's this one's name?'

'Annabelle.'

'And what's she like?'

What was Annabelle like? Sam watched as the two terriers splashed their way out of the lake and started chasing each other, barking furiously as they raced to and fro across the grass. For all the world like a pair of bickering siblings . . .

'She's blonde, slim, beautiful. Stunning, in fact,' he amended. 'She's elegant, intelligent, and good company. When we first met, I really liked her, and she liked me. I thought we could possibly make a go of things. OK,' Sam shrugged, because

230

Alice's eyebrows had lifted, 'I know it doesn't sound that romantic, but I thought maybe the feelings would grow. It doesn't always hit you like a thunderbolt.'

'How's the sex?'

'Sorry?'

'Am I being too impertinent? I was just wondering if you're compatible in bed,' said Alice. 'Because it makes a difference, you know.'

Amused by her bluntness, Sam said, 'I do know. And things are fine in that respect. Thanks for asking.'

'*Fine*,' Alice mused, considering the word. 'Not magnificent, then. But not completely disastrous either. Sort of middling.' She saw the look on his face and conceded, 'OK, let's say on the good side of middling.'

Somewhat belatedly, Sam remembered that Alice's sister had once worked as a sex therapist, which must be where she got her eye-popping frankness from. Since he had no intention of discussing that side of things with her, he said, 'Anyway, who knows, the thunderbolt might still come along. Maybe we just need a while longer to get used to each other.'

'Maybe,' Alice said. 'What would you do if you met someone else and it happened? I mean instantly, like it did when you first saw Lisa?'

Sam's abdominal muscles tightened at the memory of that flight back from Malaga. Without stopping to think, he said, 'Actually, that has already happened. But it's not someone I can get involved with.'

'Oh?' Alice looked interested. 'Why not?'

A few yards away, the two terriers had been thrown a stick to retrieve and were now locked in battle. With each of them having grasped one end of the stick in their teeth, they were now growling and writhing as they fought for victory.

'Because she's Annabelle's sister,' Sam told Alice.

'Ah.' She nodded slowly. 'Can you not swap?'

'No. Not possible.'

The male owner of the two dogs waded into the fight, shouting 'Drop! Drop it!' Somehow he managed to free the stick from their clamped jaws. Laughing, he hurled it high into the air once more, and they all watched as it caught in the upper branches of a maple tree. The two terriers charged over to the tree and waited for the stick to fall, not realising it wasn't going to happen.

'See?' The man's girlfriend addressed the dogs like a weary schoolteacher. 'This is what happens when you don't play nicely. Now neither of you has the stick.'

'I'll find them another one,' said her boyfriend.

Next to Sam, Alice was waiting patiently for him to continue. 'Go on then,' she said. 'Tell me about Annabelle's sister. What's she called?'

'Clemency.' You knew you were in deep trouble when even saying the name aloud made you feel like a child on Christmas morning. 'They're stepsisters.'

'Do they get on well together?'

He nodded over at the terriers, now cannoning off each other as they tore across the grass after a disappearing rabbit. 'Kind of like those two.'

'I see. And have you and Clemency slept together?'

Sam choked back laughter; there really was no stopping Alice. 'No, we haven't.'

'That's a shame. What do you think it would be like if you did?'

'Oh, pretty average, I imagine.' He shrugged. 'You know, *middling*.'

'Now you're making fun of me.' Alice's tone was good-natured. 'But sometimes being asked questions by an outsider can be helpful. Does Annabelle know how you feel about her stepsister?'

'No.'

'How about Clemency? Does she know?'

'Kind of,' said Sam. 'Some of it. But not the full extent.'

'And does she feel the same way about you?'

'Kind of.' What could he do but say it again? 'We both know it's there. But nothing's happened. She's seeing someone else too.'

'What's she like?' Alice genuinely wanted to know. 'Tell me everything. Would I like her?'

And in that split second, he was able to picture them so clearly, Clem and Alice perched side by side on the low stone wall in Alice's old garden, gossiping together, making jokes and collapsing with laughter.

If only it could happen.

'You'd love her to bits. You'd want her at all your parties,' said Sam.

'Oh my darling boy.' Alice gave his arm a consoling squeeze. 'If you could just see the look on your face now.'

Chapter 26

One of the things Marina loved most about her work was the way, when potential customers approached her, she could never predict what they might be about to say.

Last week, an elderly man had asked her to paint himself and his wife Maggie into one of her harbour scenes. But Maggie had died just after Christmas, he explained diffidently, so would Marina be able to do it with the aid of photos instead?

'We came here last summer,' he explained as Marina worked on the painting. 'Stayed at the caravan park, we did, and had such a lovely week. Couple of times we sat here in the café and watched you doing this. We both said how much we'd love to have one of your paintings with us in it, but . . . you know how it is. Money was tight and we decided we just couldn't afford it, not on our pensions. So we bought a few postcards instead and pinned them up on the corkboard in our kitchen to remind us of the best holiday we'd ever had.' At this point he brought a hanky out of the breast pocket of his crumpled shirt and wiped his eyes. 'Sorry, I still get a bit . . . you know.'

'You must miss her so much.' Marina's heart went out to him.

'Oh, you've no idea. Every minute of every day.' He gathered himself and managed a smile. 'That's why I wanted to come back, so I could relive last year's holiday. And when I saw you again, that was it. I decided this time I'd get you to do a painting of us. Me and Maggie together, in our favourite place in the world.'

Marina had worked extra hard to make the two of them instantly recognisable in the painting, and the man had been delighted with their smiling likenesses. She'd charged him less than the usual price and he'd disappeared briefly, returning to the café with a bunch of yellow chrysanthemums for her, which had in turn almost succeeded in reducing Marina to tears. As he'd left with the finished painting, the man said simply, 'Thank you. I wish we'd had it done last year, but this is the next best thing. I know my Maggie would approve.'

Marina smiled at the memory. That had been six days ago, and now she was working with quite a different kind of customer, albeit another one who'd seen her before.

'OK, I don't know if you remember me at all.' The thirty-something woman, who'd introduced herself as Tess, was wearing a red and white polka-dot sundress and red sandals. 'Probably not; you must do so many of these. And I don't exactly look the same.'

Intrigued, Marina said, 'What did you look like before?'

'Well, it was two years ago. I was here with my ex-husband, so I wouldn't have been wearing anything like this, for a start. My hair would have been straight and brown, pretty much the same as my clothes. I wouldn't have been wearing any make-up and I very much doubt if you'd have seen me smiling. Oh, and when you painted us, we were wearing matching khaki shirts and trousers. Not shorts, even though it was a warm day, because I didn't have the legs for shorts.'

Marina took a look at them. 'There's absolutely nothing wrong with your legs.'

'I know that now! But back then I was married to a horrible, jealous, controlling man who'd spent several years chiselling away at my self-confidence until I was left feeling about as worthless as a slug.' Tess shrugged. 'Except slugs probably don't feel worthless, do they? They might have really happy lives, up until the moment someone sprinkles salt on them. Maybe I felt as worthless as a salted slug.'

'And now?' said Marina, observing her buoyant manner, bright eyes and ready smile.

'My ex-husband was emotionally abusive and he made my life miserable,' said Tess. 'Luckily I came to my senses and managed to leave him. It wasn't easy, but it was the best thing I could have done. Everything's different now, and I'm happier than I've ever been.'

'That's fantastic.'

'He kept the last painting you did of us. Not that I wanted it anyway.' Tess grimaced. 'But now I'll have my own, with just me in it. And this time you can paint me smiling.' As she said it, she kicked up her heels and struck a jokey pose. 'New painting, new me! *Whoops . . .*'

Her new-found confidence was heart-warming, but it was something she was still getting used to, Marina realised. Having struck her pose and attracted the attention of someone else in the café, Tess promptly looked embarrassed and pretended to be checking her watch instead.

Marina glanced round and identified that the cause of the embarrassment was Ronan. She hid a smile, because this was the effect he tended to have on young women.

'Sorry, I thought for a moment he was looking at me,' Tess murmured as Ronan raised a hand in friendly acknowledgement and mouthed *Hi* at Marina. 'He's very good-looking, isn't he? How do you know him?'

He's my son. Goodness, imagine being able to just say the words out loud. How would that feel?

Marina glanced round again. Ronan was standing at the counter, chatting to Paddy and ordering two coffees, which meant Clemency would be joining him. 'He lives here in St Carys. Works as an estate agent. Yes, he is good-looking.' Recognising the clatter of heels behind them, she continued, 'And that's Clemency, who's an estate agent too.'

'She looks nice. Are they a couple?'

'Yes.' Marina nodded, because as far as everyone else in St Carys was concerned, this was the case.

'I could tell. They look good together.'

'How about you, have you met anyone else yet?'

'No, I'm taking things slowly. Enjoying being single for now. What about you?' said Tess.

By chance, George had called her this morning, ostensibly to ask about the best way to clean the interior of his leather golf bag, but also to angle for an invitation down to St Carys. 'Wouldn't that be a treat for you, love? I could take you out to dinner again at that smart hotel you like. We can have proper champagne!'

He'd been persistent, but she'd managed to put him off. Honestly, once George got an idea into his head, he didn't find it easy to accept no for an answer.

'Much the same,' said Marina. 'I was married, but now I'm enjoying being single too.'

Once Tess had departed, delighted with her painting, Marina collected together her work materials and folded up the wooden easel.

'Right.' Finishing his coffee, Ronan tapped his watch at Clemency. 'It's almost six. We need to get going.' He paused by Marina's table. 'Are you off home too? Let me carry that for you. We're heading the same way.'

'Are you? Oh, thank you, that's so kind.' Her heart expanded with love as Ronan picked up her heavy holdall and the easel. *Such lovely manners.* 'Where are you two off to then?'

'Gull Cottage is going up for sale. You know,' said Clemency, 'the turquoise one on Chantry Lane.'

'Oh, I didn't know that. Gull Cottage has the prettiest garden.' Happily, Marina walked between them as they left the café and made their way up the hill. They continued to chat about their respective days, the upcoming wedding over at the Mariscombe Hotel, the likelihood of the weather staying warm and dry until next weekend. When they reached her cottage, she unlocked the front door and Ronan insisted on carrying her belongings right inside.

Then Clemency stepped in too, closed the front door behind her and said, 'OK, the thing about Gull Cottage being up for sale was kind of a lie.'

'Sorry? I don't get it.' Marina looked at Ronan, then at Clemency, then at Ronan again. Belatedly it dawned on her that she'd been the subject of an ambush. Her heart began to clatter inside her chest, because surely Clemency hadn't arranged all this expecting her to announce to Ronan that she was his mother. *Oh please God, no, don't let it be happening, this is the worst possible way.*

Feeling sick, she turned back to Clemency. 'I d–don't know what you mean.'

'Look, can I just say, I didn't tell him. I may have accidentally dropped the teeniest hint, but I definitely didn't tell him.' Clemency was sounding sort of guilty, sort of excited. She waggled her hands as if it were the kind of accident that could happen to anyone. 'He guessed!'

'Guessed what?' She couldn't be the one to say it, because what if she'd jumped to completely the wrong conclusion and Clemency was actually talking about Gull Cottage not being for sale after all?

'Last night, Clemency was asking me how I'd feel about meeting my biological mother.' Ronan's eyes were bright, his tone conversational. 'And I said what if she wasn't a nice person and I didn't like her, and Clemency said I would like her. She didn't mean she thought I would,' he elaborated. 'It was something she already knew for a fact.'

'I didn't mean to do it,' Clemency pointed out. 'It was an accident. It just slipped out.'

Ronan said gravely, 'There had been drink taken.'

'But I didn't tell him! I stopped myself! Even though it almost *killed* me.' Clemency clapped her hands to her chest. 'And that's when I went home and went to bed, but at stupid o'clock in the morning he appeared outside the flat and threw stuff at my bedroom window until I woke up. Because he'd made a list of possibilities as to who his mother might be, but I kept saying no . . . no . . . no . . .'

'Then I wrote your name on my hand and showed it to

239

her,' said Ronan, 'and when I saw the look on her face, that was when I knew.'

Marina couldn't breathe. Nor could she tear her gaze away from him. 'And how did it make you feel?'

'Honestly? So happy. *So happy.*' He nodded, and she saw the emotion in his eyes. 'Clemency was right. I didn't have to worry any more. I mean it, I couldn't ask for a better person to be my biological mother.'

And then they were hugging each other, and tears of joy and relief were spilling down Marina's cheeks. The physical contact with her baby boy, which she'd longed for but been unable to allow herself to experience until now, was like nothing she'd ever felt before. Never had she felt so happy, so complete.

'I'm sorry.' She spoke the words she'd wanted to say for so long. 'I'm sorry I couldn't keep you . . .'

But Ronan was smiling and shaking his head. 'You don't need to be sorry . . . you know how lucky I've been. I'm just so glad you found me.'

And then the tears gave way to incredulous laughter, because against all the odds it had happened, they'd found each other, and it was just the best feeling in the world.

'Look,' said Clemency. 'I know I should have left you two alone for this, but I couldn't, OK?' In the kitchen doorway she was wiping her eyes too. 'I just couldn't bear to miss it. I'm so happy for you both.'

'I know how worried you are about your mum,' said Marina. 'I know you don't want to upset her. If you'd rather keep it just between us, that's fine by me.'

Ronan shook his head once more. 'It's OK, I've been thinking about it since last night. I'm going to have to tell her. I can't not.'

Chapter 27

The stupid thing was, there was absolutely no shame in buying a cream bun. It was one of life's little luxuries, choux pastry stuffed with fresh cream and topped with icing and glacé cherries. Belle had been happily eyeing up the one in the chiller cabinet that was destined to be taken home and eaten by her . . .

Until ten seconds ago, when out of the corner of her eye she'd glimpsed a flash of neon pink and instantly felt like a drug addict queuing outside a dealer's den for her next wrap.

The bustling open-air market was held every Friday morning in the church hall car park in St Carys, and it was, by and large, a healthy place for healthy types to visit. Yes, there were a few cake and sweet stalls, but the majority sold good healthy food and drinks.

Belle watched surreptitiously as Verity moved among the crowds, pausing at the stall that sold wheatgrass juice. *OK, there's healthy, but there's also too healthy.* She chatted briefly with the bearded man serving the juices before moving on. She was wearing her bright pink Lycra vest with grey leggings and pink and black flip-flops, and her hair was tied back in a high ponytail. She paused at the next stall to taste something in a wooden bowl, and laughed with the elderly lady next to her, who was pulling a face.

'Right then, my lovely, you're next. What can I get you?'

Startled, Belle realised she was being addressed. She glanced at the cream bun and shook her head. 'Sorry, it's OK, changed my mind.'

She headed over to the fruit and veg stall, where Verity was now looking at leeks.

'Hey, how are you?' Verity greeted her with a friendly smile.

'Good, thanks. Just getting a few bits for lunch.' Belle picked up a yellow fruit, gave it an experimental squeeze and realised she had no clue what it was. Actually, it might be a vegetable.

'Me too. So much to choose from, isn't there?' Verity selected three glossy red peppers and put them in a brown paper bag. 'Cooking something nice for that handsome boyfriend of yours?'

They'd bumped into Verity the other afternoon, walking along the beach at low tide. She'd paused and said hello, and Belle had introduced her to Sam, who'd joked, 'So you're the one she sets her alarm for in the morning.'

'Just me,' Belle said now. 'Sam's in Dusseldorf today.' She reached for a bunch of spinach because it made her look like someone who took care of her body.

'Spinach smoothies.' Watching her, Verity gave an approving nod. 'Fantastic. Packed with minerals and iron.'

How did you even make a smoothie out of spinach? Mash it up with milk, something like that? Oh well, she could always chuck it away when she got home.

Belle watched as Verity filled a bag with mangetout, cherry

tomatoes, tenderstem broccoli and red grapes. 'OK, good. Now I need to pick up some extra-virgin olive oil,' Verity said when she'd paid. 'And some blue cheese.'

'Really?' Belle was taken aback. 'Isn't blue cheese full of . . . you know, *fat?*'

'We need fat in our diet.' Verity grinned at her look of shock. 'I eat healthily, but I'm not a complete food Nazi. Did you really think I was?'

Belle looked askance at everything she'd just bought. 'Well, yes.'

Amused, Verity said, 'Well I'm not. I enjoy cooking. Look, do you have to rush off? Because I'd rather cook for two people than one. Come back with me if you'd like to, and have a spot of lunch.'

Thirty minutes later, Belle found herself perched on a stool in the kitchen beneath Clemency's flat, grating fresh Parmesan and chopping tomatoes while Verity deseeded the peppers and cut cloves of garlic into slivers. They talked about their contrasting childhoods – Belle's here in St Carys, Verity's in Bermondsey, in south-east London. They sang along to the songs on the radio. When the lunch was finally ready – baked stuffed peppers, mixed salad, cheese and bacon frittata and a glass of red wine each – they carried everything out into the tiny sun-dappled back garden.

The meal was fantastic: healthy, fresh and utterly delicious. Just as Belle had found herself starting to enjoy the way exercise was making her feel, so she was beginning to realise that providing her body with the right food made a weird kind of sense after all. Talk about a revelation . . .

Five minutes later, the bedroom window of the flat upstairs was flung open and Clemency stuck her head out.

'Afternoon! Is that what I think it is down there?'

That. Was she trying to be funny? Bristling, Belle rolled her eyes. 'I do apologise on behalf of my stepsister. She can be so bloody rude sometimes.'

Verity spluttered with laughter. 'I'm pretty certain she doesn't mean you.' Beckoning to Clemency, she called up, 'It is. You're like a bloodhound. Come on down.'

By the time Clemency reappeared, having made her way through the newsagent's, Verity had piled three slices of frittata on to another plate.

'It's her favourite thing,' she explained to Belle.

'It's amazing. When she's making frittata, I can smell it wafting upstairs. All that cheese and bacon and garlic,' said Clemency. 'Best thing ever.'

'Join us.' Verity pulled out the third wicker chair and patted the cushion on the seat.

'Thanks, but I can't stay long. Got a viewing on Castle Street in twenty minutes. Just water, thanks.' Clemency waved away the offer of wine. 'What's happening here anyway?' She indicated the table, the glasses. 'Am I interrupting a meeting of Joggers Anonymous?'

'Yes,' said Belle.

Verity grinned. 'We just happened to bump into each other at the market. Bonded over the peppers on the fruit and veg stall. I invited Belle back for a bit of lunch and—'

'*BAAAH!*' Belle heard the bellow of alarm escape from her own mouth as the wasp flew straight at her face, attached itself to her fringe and swung its body millimetres from her right eye. Rearing back in her chair, she batted her hands in panic and felt her splayed fingers knock Verity's arm. The wine glass Verity had been holding spun up into the air and landed with a tinkle of shattered glass on the flagstones.

The wasp, supremely unconcerned, flew off.

'Oh God, sorry.' Belle fanned her face. 'I thought it was going to go right in my eye.'

'No problem. Don't move,' said Verity, pushing back her chair. 'I'll get a dustpan and brush.'

By the time she returned, Clemency had picked up the larger pieces of broken glass and was holding them in the palm of her hand. When Verity had finished sweeping up the splinters on the ground, Clemency tipped the rest into the dustpan.

'I'm really sorry,' Belle repeated. 'I'll buy you another one.'

'Hey, no need. We've got loads more. Oops, looks like we have an injury.' Verity pointed to the trickle of blood sliding down towards Clemency's wrist.

'Didn't even realise I'd done it.' Examining her hand, Clemency located the source of the bleeding; a sliver of glass had sliced through the skin separating her second and third fingers. 'Honestly, it's fine, doesn't hurt at all.'

'But you don't want it dripping on your shirt. Let's get you fixed up.'

Clemency dipped a tissue in her glass of water and cleaned the blood off her hand. Belle watched as Verity peeled the backing strips off a narrow waterproof plaster and carefully fixed it into place.

'There you go.' She made sure the edges were securely stuck down. 'All done. Now you can carry on eating.'

'Thanks.' Clemency picked up another slice of frittata. 'One more injury courtesy of my sister. It's OK, we'll just add it to the list.'

'Oh dear.' Verity's eyes were bright. 'Have there been many?'

Belle said, 'It goes both ways. She's been responsible for her fair share.'

'Like the time I tried to throw an empty Coke can over that tree in our garden and I didn't know you were sunbathing on the other side.' As Clemency said it, Meryl emerged from the stockroom behind the newsagent's shop.

'I was lying there minding my own business,' Belle told Verity, 'listening to music on my iPod, when a Coke can landed on my forehead.'

'An empty Coke can.' Clemency shrugged. 'I'm not a monster.'

'It still left a bump and a bruise. And I had a date that night with Miles Mason-Carter.' Belle sighed at the memory. 'He kept calling me Rhino.'

Amused, Meryl rested a hand on Verity's shoulder. 'You did something like that too, remember? The time you tripped over Malcolm, lost your balance and ended up jabbing your stiletto into David's foot? Three days before his triathlon!'

'Oh God, don't remind me.' Verity cringed. 'He wasn't happy.'

'You can hardly blame him. All those months of training, only to end up with a cracked metatarsal and his foot in plaster.'

'Who's David?' said Belle.

Meryl reached over to pinch a cherry tomato from the salad bowl. 'Oh, David was Verity's husband.'

Husband. Belle looked at Verity. 'I didn't know you'd been married.'

Verity shrugged. 'We're divorced now.'

'He was a lovely man,' said Meryl.

'And who was Malcolm?' Clemency chimed in. 'The one you tripped over?'

'Are you picturing some old drunk guy passed out on the ground?' Verity laughed. 'Malcolm was our bulldog. He was lovely too.'

'OK, I need to get over to Castle Street for my viewing. That was fantastic.' Swallowing her last mouthful of frittata, Clemency patted Verity's tanned shoulder. 'Thanks for letting me gatecrash your lunch. And for the first aid.'

'My pleasure.' Verity smiled up at her. 'You're welcome any time.'

Clemency gave Belle a playful nudge. 'Who knows? Keep up all this exercise and you could find yourself doing a triathlon next.'

Irritated, because this was a prime example of Clemency having a dig and trying to make fun of her in front of other people, Belle replied, 'Maybe I will.'

'Seriously, though, it's doing her the world of good.' Clemency turned to Verity and Meryl. 'Belle's always had these mad fads and they never last. I know she's doing this to impress Sam, but she wouldn't have stuck to it if it hadn't been for you. It makes such a difference, doesn't it, having someone to run with. So much easier than going out on your own.' She paused. 'In fact, what time do you two go for your morning jog? Maybe I'll join you.'

Oh for crying out loud . . .

Belle bit her tongue, because this was another annoying habit of Clemency's: blithely inviting herself along to anything that took her fancy, regardless of whether or not she was wanted.

247

Verity, obliged *unlike some people* to be polite, said, 'Of course you can join us. The more the merrier. That'd be great!'

Which meant they were now beaming at each other as if it were all arranged. Seriously, this was *so* unfair. Squaring her shoulders and out-beaming both of them, Belle said to Clemency, 'I'm warning you now, though, we run pretty fast. You probably won't be able to keep up.'

Chapter 28

On Kate's daily delivery round, there were always some people she didn't particularly enjoy spending time with. When Joseph Miller opened the front door to take delighted delivery of his latest eBay purchase, he invariably managed to spray her with a mixture of toast crumbs and saliva. There was angry Mr Arundel, who always wanted to engage her in furious political debate. And poor lonely Mrs Barker, who owned at least twenty cats and whose lime-green bungalow smelt so strongly of cat wee and fish it made Kate's eyes water.

At the other end of the scale were her favourites. Old Bill Berenson, for example, who owned two adorable King Charles spaniels and every morning offered her a chocolate digestive. The Trainer family, whose three-year-old twins loved to wave to her from the living-room window as excitedly as if she were Father Christmas. And Georgina Harman, a now-retired opera singer who still liked to sing to herself as she dusted and polished the many china ornaments in her tiny whitewashed cottage on Hobbler's Lane. Now in her seventies, she was chatty and friendly, and wore fabulous hand-painted silk kaftans. The sound of her singing and the sight of her round smiling face always made Kate's day.

Except she wouldn't be seeing her this morning, because Georgina had told her yesterday that she'd be setting off early to catch the train up to Cheltenham, where she was booked to sing at a wedding.

Now, turning into Hobbler's Lane, Kate dug into her bag for the next handful of post to be popped through letter boxes. There was nothing exciting for Georgina, just a bank statement and a couple of circulars. Reaching the white-walled cottage, she paused to tuck a loose strand of hair behind her ear and—

What was that?

Kate froze, one hand on the fractionally opened letter box. After several seconds she heard it again, the sound of footsteps on parquet flooring.

But these were shoe-wearing footsteps, and Georgina never wore shoes inside her house, only ballet slippers.

Kate hesitated. Unless she was all dressed up for the wedding and about to leave for Cheltenham.

She rang the doorbell. Nothing.

'Georgina,' she called through the letter box. 'Is that you?'

Moments later she heard the creak of a floorboard on the staircase. OK, whoever was in there was heading upstairs. And it certainly wasn't Georgina. Stuffing the post back into her bag, Kate reached into her shirt pocket for her phone. As she looked up, she glimpsed an unfamiliar face at the bedroom window before it ducked out of sight.

Then came the sound of faster footsteps, followed by a noise at the side of the cottage. Kate raced round just as a downstairs side window was flung open.

'Stay where you are!' she yelled. 'I've called the police and they're on their way!'

The boy had a scarf wrapped around the lower half of his face. He launched himself out of the window and tried to push past her in the narrow passage between the high fence and the outside of the cottage. Kate stood her ground, shoved him back and ripped the scarf from his face.

'Fuck off, *bitch*.' The boy was younger than her, probably only twenty, and he spat the words with venom. Luckily, she was used to being sprayed with saliva by Joseph Miller. She grabbed hold of the boy's jacket and grappled with him, refusing to let go whilst he twisted like an eel. Oh God, where were the police? Why hadn't they turned up yet? Belatedly she remembered she hadn't called them, and there was no one else in sight.

She took a deep breath and yelled at the top of her voice, 'HELP, HELP! CALL NINE NINE NINE, I NEED THE POLICE— *OWWW* . . .'

'You *stupid* bitch.' The boy snarled like an animal, slamming her hard against the wall and attempting to prise her fingers off his jacket. 'Will you stop doing that and just fucking *let go*?'

Ronan had just left a valuation in South Street and was making his way back on foot to the office when he heard the shouts for help. Torn between calling 999 and racing in the direction of the voice, he met the gaze of an elderly white-haired woman deadheading roses in her front garden.

'I'll call the police.' Like an undercover agent, the woman threw down her secateurs and whipped a mobile phone out of her bra. 'You go.'

As he ran down South Street, turning right at the bottom into Hobbler's Lane, Ronan wondered if the voice he'd heard did in fact belong to someone he knew, because the thud in his chest was telling him he definitely recognised it.

Moments later, as he rounded the bend in the lane, he saw a dirty white van accelerating away in a cloud of dust and heard the same voice say furiously, 'Oh you *evil* bastard.'

It was her, it was Kate, sprawled on the ground in her uniform with her hair dishevelled and her delivery bag lying nearby. Her shirt sleeve was torn, her shorts were dusty and her tanned knees were grazed. She was clutching a handful of jewellery in one hand.

'Jesus, what happened? Stay still,' Ronan instructed. 'Are you hurt?'

Please don't let her be hurt.

Kate was practically vibrating with anger and a surfeit of adrenalin. 'He'd broken into the house. I heard him inside and told him I'd called the police. Which was completely *stupid* of me, because I should have just gone ahead and done it. So he jumped out of the window and tried to run off, which meant I had to stop him.' She paused, still catching her breath, and turned her head experimentally from side to side. 'I did my best, it felt like we were fighting for ages, but he got away in the end. *Dammit.*'

'Did he hurt you?' repeated Ronan, because she'd been too outraged to reply.

'No.'

'Are you sure? You just said you were fighting for ages.'

'I'm fine. I got this off him.' She held up the gold jewellery. 'It was in his pocket, little toad. Oh look . . .' Sitting up and studying the tangle of bracelets and chains more closely, she paused at an open heart-shaped locket containing two photos, one on each side. 'How gorgeous is this? It must be Georgina when she was young.' Her finger moved to the second photograph. 'Gosh, does he look familiar to you? He's like a young Luciano Pavarotti.'

The police arrived within minutes, and Ronan marvelled at Kate's powers of recall. Fury had given way to calm as she related the story of how she had realised a burglary was in progress and attempted to prevent the burglar's escape.

'Five foot ten, skinny build, grey eyes, short fair hair, scar across his right eyebrow and a mole on his left cheek. Oh, and he had a tattoo that said NAN on his wrist. Really badly done, though. Actually, if you give me a piece of paper, I'll draw him for you.'

Within a few minutes, in the back of the police car, she'd borrowed the officer's notebook and sketched the face of the young burglar. As an afterthought, she wrote down the make, colour and registration number of the van in which he'd escaped.

'Blimey.' The police officer was equally impressed. 'Our job would be a whole lot easier if there were more people like you. Is that definitely the registration?'

'Of course it is,' said Kate. 'Otherwise I wouldn't have written it down.'

The SOCOs had by this time arrived to check out the house and were currently dusting the window frame for prints. The police officer finished taking down Kate's witness statement and contact details. He said, 'I think we ought to get you checked out at the hospital, let them give you a quick once-over.'

'Oh there's no need,' Kate protested, but the officer was firm. 'Just to be on the safe side. We can take you over there ourselves, or . . .'

'Can I do it?' said Ronan, because the officer had glanced across at him. 'Take her, I mean. Not give her a once-over.' Damn, it was happening again; why did he always blurt out stupid things when he was with Kate? He shook his head. 'I can drive her to the hospital and make sure she's seen by the medics.'

'That would be really helpful.' The police officer was clearly relieved to be spared another task.

'What about work?' Kate looked worried.

'No appointments this afternoon.' Ronan smiled at her. 'I'm free.'

When they arrived at A&E, the triage nurse on duty recognised Ronan from his previous visit.

'Hello! How are you? What are you doing back here again?'

'I'm good. It's not me this time.' He indicated Kate beside him, and the nurse said, 'Oh, is this your girlfriend?'

'No,' Kate said hastily. 'We're just . . . friends.' She blushed and fiddled with her hair. 'Nothing else. He gave me a lift here, that's all.'

'Oh, I see. Whoops, my mistake.' The nurse pulled a comical face. 'That's how rumours get started!'

Another nurse, who'd been washing her hands at the sink just outside their cubicle, popped her head around the curtain. 'Marjorie, remember Lizzie Billingham? Married to Baz Billingham, moved over to Spain a few years back? Had a daughter called Clemency? Well, Clemency is Ronan's girlfriend. They work together at Barton and Byrne, the estate agency in St Carys.'

'Oh, right! I remember Clemency. *Lovely* girl,' exclaimed the triage nurse. 'Sorry I got it wrong, but that's so nice to hear. Well done!'

The other nurse said, 'The last time I saw Clemency, she hadn't had a boyfriend for ages, so we were all thrilled when we heard you two were a couple.' She beamed at Ronan. 'I can really see you being perfect together. Clemency's great!'

Which left Ronan with no alternative other than to say, 'I know.'

By some miracle, they'd arrived during a quiet period. Within an hour Kate had been seen by a doctor, checked over and given the all-clear. Her shoulder was a bit sore, but no serious damage had been done.

'Except next time,' the doctor told her, 'maybe call the police first and leave the apprehending to them.'

'That doctor was right, you know,' said Ronan as he drove her back to St Carys. 'It was a crazy thing to do. What if he'd had a knife? You could have been seriously hurt.' Each time he thought of it, the possibilities seemed more horrendous. 'You could have been killed.'

'But he didn't,' Kate said easily, 'and I'm fine.'

'Luckily for you.'

'Ah well, if we stopped to think about things before we did them, the chances are we'd never do anything. Sometimes you just have to act on instinct and go for it . . .' Her voice faltered and trailed away as they both realised that whilst she'd been talking about the burglary, it could equally well apply to last year's ill-fated one-night stand. Hastily Kate said, 'Anyway, let's hope the police catch him. What's the time now? OK, when we get to St Carys, could you drop me back at work? I need to make up for offloading the rest of my round. And then I'll have a quiet night. How about you, are you and Clemency doing something nice this evening?' She flushed. 'I mean, going out anywhere special?'

He was seeing Marina at six o'clock. Ronan wished with all his heart that he could confide in Kate that he was meeting up with his biological mother so they could discuss how he might most painlessly break the news to Josephine.

He wished it almost as much as he longed to tell Kate there was nothing going on between him and Clemency. He'd been yearning to confide in her since before today's chance encounter, if he was being honest, simply because he knew she would understand.

But he mustn't, he just mustn't. And why would Kate be even remotely interested anyway? It was nothing to do with her.

They were approaching St Carys now. Ronan said, 'Nothing exciting. No plans at all.'

At that moment the traffic lights ahead changed to red and his phone pinged to announce the arrival of a text. Having stopped the car and glanced at it, Ronan said drily, 'Up until now,' and indicated that Kate was free to read the message on the screen.

Aaaargh, Belle's just invited us over for dinner at 8 p.m. and I said yes. She's cooking! Sorry!!

Kate looked over at him. 'Looks like you have a plan now. Why's Clem saying sorry?'

Ronan smiled slightly. 'From what I hear, Belle can't cook.'

Chapter 29

The scallops had been overcooked, the garlic burnt and the bacon had tasted weirdly of treacle. And that was just the starter.

There was now a lot of crashing and clattering going on in the kitchen. Clemency called out, 'Everything OK in there?'

'Everything's *fine*.' There was a note of suppressed hysteria in Belle's voice. 'It's all completely under control.'

Clannngggg went something metallic as it hit the sink.

'Are you sure? If you need a hand, just say.'

'I don't need a hand, thank you!'

Clemency couldn't help feeling sorry for Belle, but a tiny part of her was also quite enjoying the fact that the evening was turning out to be harder work than her sister had envisaged. They were Belle's guinea pigs, she now realised. Yesterday, having watched a Channel 4 documentary about perfect wives living enviable lives and throwing flawless dinner parties, Belle had promptly decided this was something she needed to be able to do. Or at least to say she'd done.

Because they might not be married yet, but she was

desperate for Sam to know what an accomplished and impressive wife she *would* make, when the time arrived.

The table was set beautifully, with silver and fine white china, matching crystal glasses and an actual linen tablecloth.

Clemency had already spilt a couple of drops of red wine on it – would she ever learn? – but her side plate was now covering them up.

'Oh for *crying* out loud.' They heard Belle let out a muffled shriek as something ceramic, possibly a small saucepan, clattered to the marble floor.

'Please don't think it was my idea. I promise you, I didn't ask her to do this.' Sam refilled their glasses. 'I didn't *want* her to do this. And I'd have been happy to share the cooking, but she was determined to do it all herself.'

The main course was taking ages to appear. Luckily Sam and Ronan got on well and found it easy to chat to each other. Clemency, watching them together, wondered if she should have invented some plausible reason why she and Ronan couldn't make it tonight. But the truth was, she found it almost impossible to turn down any opportunity to see Sam. Just being able to look at his face, hear his voice and reach out and touch him was like a drug she couldn't resist.

OK, reaching out and touching him wasn't actually on the cards, but she was still allowed to imagine it.

Even if it did make the whole impossible situation that much harder to bear.

'Right!' The kitchen door burst open and Belle appeared, carrying two dinner plates and with her previously immaculate topknot now leaning precariously to one side. 'Sorry about the delay. Here we are . . . no, sit *down*,' she shouted as Clemency jumped up to help her carry everything through. 'I want you all to *relax* and *enjoy* yourselves.'

The chicken was salty, with a bizarre under-taste of stale digestive biscuits. The fondant potatoes were undercooked. The buttered carrots were nice. As Belle finally got her breathing back under control, Sam said, 'This is great. These carrots are fantastic.'

'They are.' Ronan nodded eagerly. 'They're brilliant.'

'Seriously,' Clemency joined in, 'I think these are the best carrots I've ever tasted.'

Belle narrowed her eyes at her. 'Now you're just being sarcastic.'

'I'm not.' Wounded, Clemency put down her fork. 'I said it because they're *nice*.'

'I've spent hours preparing this meal. The least you could do is be polite.'

'It's a fantastic meal,' said Ronan, but Belle was still agitated.

'No it isn't. There's too much salt in the chicken. Oh God, what's *that*?' she wailed, spotting Sam's attempt to hide something under half a potato.

'Nothing,' Sam said firmly, but Belle had already leant across to find out for herself.

'It's just a teabag,' Ronan said helpfully. 'It's fine. Who doesn't love tea?'

'It's a herb bag.' For a moment Belle looked as if she might burst into tears. 'I looked for it earlier in the pan of stock and couldn't find it anywhere, then made the sauce and forgot to fish it out.' Frazzled, she snatched it off the plate and marched out to the kitchen.

Ronan murmured, 'Oh God, is she going to cry?'

'No, I am not going to cry.' Returning to her seat, Belle picked up her knife and fork. 'I'd just like us to have a nice civilised dinner party,' she said in a brittle voice. 'It can't be *that* hard, can it?'

Which, seeing as Sam was currently attempting to cut into an undercooked potato without it skidding off his plate, caused Clemency to struggle with keeping a straight face. When he glanced up and caught her eye, clearly thinking the same, she said hastily, 'I was just thinking, isn't Belle looking fantastic?'

Because when in doubt and you have a vain sister in need of calming down, shower her with compliments.

'It's new.' Joining in, Sam indicated the cobalt-blue dress splashed with cream roses. 'I think it's great.'

'I ordered it online,' said Belle, 'and the colour wasn't quite what I expected. But it had to do, seeing as I didn't have anything else to wear.'

Belle had a hundred other things to wear; more than half the wardrobes in the flat were crammed with her clothes, but for the sake of her sister's precious dinner party, Clemency didn't point this out. Instead, she carried on with the flattery. 'It's not just the dress, though, is it? You're looking incredible. This new exercise regime is really paying off!'

Belle regarded her with suspicion. 'Are you doing it again?'

Oh for God's sake. 'It's the truth! I'm trying to pay you a compliment. The running has really toned you up.' She turned to Ronan and said, 'Don't you think?'

'I do.' Ronan nodded in agreement. 'In fact, you two should go running together. Isn't it more fun that way?'

Clemency opened her mouth to speak, but Belle got in first.

'I already run with Verity.'

Ronan shrugged. 'So? Can't the three of you go together?'

'I did suggest it,' said Clemency. 'But—'

'We run faster than she does,' Belle interrupted. 'She'd just hold us back. The trouble with Clemency is, she eats too much junk, then wonders why she can't fit into size ten jeans. Well it's *true*.' She raised her eyebrows at Clemency. 'You need to cut out the rubbish and start taking a bit more care of yourself. Give the carbs a rest. I'm only saying it for your own good.'

OK, this was Belle at her bitchy best. And after she'd made such an effort to be nice to her too. Clemency considered the options: either respond by saying that if she was going to cut out the rubbish she'd start with this diabolical meal, or be completely saintly and rise above it. The former might result in Belle-in-a-strop tipping dinner over her head. And as for the latter option . . . well, she just wasn't saintly enough for that.

Although maybe she could manage to rise above it if she allowed herself just one teeny dig along the way.

Well, she was only human.

'You're absolutely right. I do eat too much and I don't exercise enough. No one to blame but myself. I'm a hideous mess.' Clemency broke into a grin to show she'd taken the criticism in good part. 'On the upside, I can treat myself to chocolate whenever I want. Anyway,' she turned her attention to Sam, 'it's all thanks to you that Belle's got into this whole fitness thing. She never used to do it before.'

Sam looked amused. 'I gathered that. But why is it thanks to me?'

'Oh, you know.' Clemency speared a piece of chicken

with her fork. 'When you really like your new boyfriend and you're desperate to impress him.'

'OK, *not* true.' Belle rolled her eyes. 'I'm doing it because it's something *I* want to do. For *myself*.'

'Except you forget how long I've known you,' said Clemency. 'You can say that if you want, but we both know better. Taking up new hobbies to impress boyfriends is par for the course. I'm not saying it's a bad thing,' she added with a cheery shrug. 'It's just the way you've always been. It's what you're like.'

Ronan grinned. 'Maybe I should impress Clem by taking up shark-wrestling.'

But while Clemency and Sam were laughing, she caught Belle giving her a long, cool stare.

'What do you think?' Ronan placed his arm around Clemency's shoulders and gave her an affectionate squeeze. 'Should I do it? Will that make you love me more?'

He was doing it for her benefit. This was why they'd come up with this plan in the first place: to make life easier for her because Belle had a boyfriend and she didn't. Responding with a playful wiggle, Clemency said flirtatiously, 'How could it? You're already perfect.'

Which was a bit *ewww*. OK, quite a lot *ewww*.

But Ronan, entering into the spirit, blew her an affectionate kiss and said, 'Not as perfect as you.'

At this point, Belle made a quiet hissing noise like a tiny kettle coming to the boil. Her eyes, fixed on Clemency, were laser-bright. 'And you believe that, do you?'

Still smiling, Clemency shrugged. 'If Ronan says I'm perfect, I'm not going to argue with him, am I? It's fine by me.'

'The thing is, you've been single for a while, and now

you've finally got yourself a boyfriend. But that's no reason to be gullible,' said Belle. 'Just because he says it doesn't mean it's what he thinks.'

'It is, though,' Ronan protested, laughing. 'It's exactly what I think.'

Belle sat back. 'In that case, why did he try to kiss me the other week?' She turned to look at Clemency as she spoke, her tone triumphant.

Ah.

Oh dear. Too late, Clemency realised they'd gone too far. Belle, in her tense and stressed-out state, had taken offence to her minor jibe and retaliated with a far more ruthless one of her own.

At least, it was ruthless as far as she was concerned.

Ronan said, 'I didn't try to kiss you.'

'You see? I knew you'd deny it. Yes you did!'

Oh God, though. How was Sam feeling about this? Would it make him furious? Was he likely to challenge Ronan? Did he already know about it? Clemency glanced across the table and saw that Sam wasn't angry. Which was good.

Then again, there was a hint of pity in his dark eyes, which was less so.

Damn, talk about complicated.

Belle pointed an accusing finger at Ronan. 'You gave me a lift home that evening after we'd had dinner at the Mermaid. You said your feelings towards me had changed and all you wanted to do was kiss me.'

'I told you I wanted to kiss you,' Ronan reminded her. 'I also told you I wouldn't. Sorry,' he shook his head at Sam, 'I shouldn't have said it. On the upside, Belle told me to get lost.'

'Well,' Sam said steadily, 'that's good to know.'

'So there you go, that's how much your boyfriend really loves you.' Having made her point, Belle took a sip of her wine and raised her eyebrows in faux-sympathy at Clemency. 'That's the kind of thing he gets up to behind your back. Oh dear, you must be feeling a bit stupid now, after all that showing off about the two of you being so happy together. Looks like your bad-boy leopard hasn't changed his spots after all.'

OK, enough was enough.

'Well thanks,' said Clemency.

Belle beamed. 'My pleasure. I wonder what else he's been getting up to behind your back? I mean, I had the decency to turn him down, but I bet there are others who haven't.' She tossed a serves-you-right look in Ronan's direction, then turned back to Clemency. 'Oh well, now you know what he's like. Better luck next time!'

What was Sam thinking right now? He knew they argued, but hadn't witnessed one of their full-blown spats before. Having swiftly run through the options currently available to her, Clemency said, 'Except you only told me to upset me, and I don't know if you've noticed, but I'm not upset. Because I already knew. Because I was the one who asked Ronan to do it.'

That got their attention. Belle said, 'What are you even talking about?'

'You always liked Ronan. Now I'm seeing him. I wondered if our pact still meant something to you.' Clemency sat back on her chair. 'So I decided to put it to the test. It was my idea for Ronan to say what he did. And good for you,' she added. 'You passed with flying colours. I was impressed.'

Ronan, whose idea the test had been – albeit purely for curiosity's sake – nodded in agreement.

Clemency glanced at Sam, whose expression was absolutely unreadable. Only he knew why she might have been so keen to find out how Belle would react.

Belle gave Clemency a pitying look. 'Oh bless, of course I believe you asked your boyfriend to make a move on me. You just keep telling yourself that.'

Chapter 30

'You're back again? I don't believe it!' Josephine did a delighted double-take when she opened the front door and saw Ronan on the doorstep. 'What's this about then? Are you on the scrounge for more food?' She hugged him, then stepped back and searched his face. 'Is everything all right? Are *you* OK?'

'Mum, don't worry, everything's great.' As Ronan followed her into the kitchen, his heart began to thud. Yesterday evening, having driven over here to tell her about Marina, he'd found his mum hosting an impromptu supper party for half a dozen members of her book group. Forced to pretend he'd only been passing by, he'd allowed Josephine to give him containers of curried goat and sweet potato stew, then driven home to St Carys with the story untold.

Now he was back and his mum was on her own. This time it was going to happen. All the way over in the car he'd been practising how to tell her.

'Oh, I know what it is!' Her eyes lit up. 'You've met someone! Am I right? Have you met a girl?'

'OK, the thing is, I have *kind of* met someone, but—'

'Oh my goodness! Is it Clem?' Josephine clapped a hand to her chest. '*Is it?* Has all this pretend stuff made you realise you really do like each other after all? You know, I did wonder if it would!'

'Mum, stop. It's not Clem. It's not any kind of girlfriend.' Shit, all his careful pre-planning had gone out of the window and now he'd lost the thread of how he'd meant to say it. He shook his head and pulled out the stool next to the kitchen table. 'Look, maybe you should sit down . . .'

This time he saw the realisation dawn in his mother's eyes. She swallowed and stared at him intently, and Ronan knew that she knew.

'Oh darling, that's why you came and went yesterday. You've been plucking up the courage to tell me. It's OK . . . really, I promise you it's OK, it isn't going to change anything.' Her voice breaking with emotion, Josephine threw her arms around him. 'Why would it change anything? You're still *you*, and I'm never going to stop loving you!'

The relief was overwhelming. Everything was going to be all right. Exhaling, Ronan hugged her back. 'I thought it was going to be more difficult than this. I was so worried you'd be upset.'

'No, no, of course I'm not upset! It's fine, it's fine. As long as you're happy, that's all that matters. Wait till Sheila hears about this. She was the one who thought it could be on the cards. You know, I didn't believe her at first, but she talked me through it, helped me realise it made sense.'

Sheila, one of his mother's oldest friends, lived two streets away, worked as a school secretary and was never happier than when she was solving other people's problems. Ronan felt a rush of affection towards her for having listened to his mum's concerns and reassured her, thus solving his own problem so beautifully.

'I always did like Sheila.' He smiled as he said it.

Josephine stroked his cheek. 'And Sheila will be delighted. She told me it's a special talent of hers. A gift, if you like. Apparently she can always tell.'

OK, this wasn't making a lot of sense. He'd only just found out about Marina, and he hadn't set eyes on Sheila since Christmas.

'Tell what?' he said, but Josephine was already chattering on.

'And credit where it's due, she spotted it in that burly Welsh rugby chap years ago, ages before he came out . . . in fact I think Sheila cottoned on to him before the fellow even knew it himself!'

Ronan held up his hand. 'Mum.'

'What?'

'Mum, I'm not gay.'

'What?' Josephine's eyes widened.

'Why did Sheila think I was gay?'

'Because you go out with so many girls and then finish with them. And now you have this whole pretendy thing going on with Clem. There's a word for that, did you know? She's your beard!' Josephine paused and looked baffled. 'Are you sure you're not gay?'

'I'd tell you if I was, I promise.' The urge to laugh at the misunderstanding was tempered by the realisation that the evening's big confession still lay ahead. Playing for time, Ronan said, 'Is that the only reason Sheila thought it? Because my relationships never last?'

'And because you're so good-looking. That was something

else she said was a dead giveaway. And you iron your own shirts. You always wear nice clothes, like a model in a magazine.' His mother shrugged. 'Once she told me, it all made sense.'

'Well, tell Sheila thanks for the compliments. But I'm straight.'

'So who's this person you've met, then? *Oh.*' And this time Josephine took an involuntary step backwards as the terrifying possibility she'd always dreaded finally occurred to her. 'Oh no . . .'

'It's all right, I promise,' said Ronan, because she was visibly shaking now.

'You promised me before.' The tremor was there in her voice, along with a world of pain. 'You *promised* you wouldn't find her.'

'Mum, I didn't find her. She found me. And everything's OK, I swear to you. It's all fine.' He rested his hands on her narrow shoulders and gazed into her eyes. 'Listen to me. You're my mum and I love you more than anything in the world . . .'

'How could she find you? She isn't allowed to find you!'

'I know, but she was ill. She had cancer and thought she might die. A private detective helped her. It was wrong, and illegal, but she was desperate. That was five years ago,' Ronan continued. 'She found me, but she didn't tell me who she was. Because she didn't want to upset me . . . or you, Mum.'

Tears were sliding down Josephine's cheeks.

'Except she did tell you. Because how else would you have found out?'

'Mum, you don't have to be upset. This is a good thing to have happened. I didn't know she was my biological mother but I already knew and liked her. She's a lovely person, you'll like her too. We've talked about what happened . . . why it happened . . . I've asked all the questions I wanted to ask. And there's no need to worry, because you're still my mum. You'll always be my mum.'

Josephine wiped her eyes. She looked fractionally reassured. 'When did you find out?'

'Recently. Two weeks ago. She had another cancer scare, but it's OK. The all-clear came through on Monday. And she wasn't the one who told me she was my mother,' Ronan explained. 'Clem put two and two together.'

'Clem did? How?'

'When I was swimming in the sea and got knocked out by that jet ski? Remember I told you Marina jumped in and held my face out of the water?' He paused. 'Marina's my biological mother.'

'Marina the artist? The one who paints on the quayside? *That* Marina?'

Ronan nodded.

'I bought some Christmas cards from her in the café last December. The snowy scenes of St Carys. Everyone loved them.' Josephine nodded slowly, remembering and assimilating this information. 'She was really nice.'

Ronan said gently, 'She still is.'

It was four o'clock in the afternoon. Sitting at her usual table in the café, Marina couldn't stop checking her watch and counting down the minutes. Yesterday Ronan had visited Josephine and told her everything. Today, at six

270

o'clock, Josephine would be arriving in St Carys. And there was nothing to worry about, because she'd taken the news well. Everything was going to be absolutely fine. In fact it couldn't have gone better, according to Ronan. He'd said— *Oh God* . . .

Marina jumped, her right hand knocked over the jar in which her brushes were soaking, and a wave of sludge-coloured water landed in her lap. But she barely noticed, because that was definitely Josephine over there in the distance, making her way along the quayside towards her.

'Butterfingers,' Paddy chided, grinning as he appeared with a towel to mop up the worst of the damage.

'Sorry,' said Marina.

'No need to apologise. You're the one looking like you've wet yourself.'

She cleaned up as best she could, all the while watching as Josephine got closer, her long crimson dress billowing behind her in the sea breeze.

And then she was there. The interminable waiting was over. Marina had made no plans what to say, but in the event it became apparent that no words were necessary. Josephine stood in front of her and opened her arms, and Marina went into them.

Goodness knows what Paddy and Dee and all the other customers were thinking.

When the long embrace ended, they held hands and smiled at each other.

'Thank you for my son,' Josephine said simply.

'Thank you for being such a fantastic mum to him,' replied Marina. 'It's made me so happy to know he had you.'

★   ★   ★

When Ronan and Clemency turned up at 5.30, they found them still there, sitting together, having spent the last ninety minutes talking non-stop.

'I got here far too early,' Josephine explained. 'I just couldn't wait.'

'And it's been so lovely.' Marina's stomach was fizzing with the kind of excitement you only felt when absolutely everything was OK. 'I apologised for breaking the rules and finding you, and—'

'I told her I'd have done exactly the same,' Josephine chimed in. She shrugged. 'Think about it; under those circumstances? No question. Anyone would.'

Then they were all hugging each other, and when it was Marina's turn to embrace Clemency, she said, 'This all happened because of you. Thank you.'

'Me and my big mouth. Well, I'm so glad it worked out,' Clemency said fondly. 'It's about time you had good things happen to you. And how brilliant that you're OK too.'

Marina nodded; this was something else that was down to Clemency, who had carried on nagging her until she'd made an appointment and gone along to the local surgery. Her GP had swiftly referred her to the consultant, who had arranged for a needle biopsy to be carried out. Aware of her anxiety, he had phoned Marina yesterday as soon as the results arrived back from the lab. There was no sign of malignancy; the lump had been confirmed as a harmless cyst.

Marina, who'd been looking after the twins across the street, had taken the call then excused herself, locking herself in the bathroom for a couple of minutes in order to be able to burst into tears of relief. This was it; the fear was behind her now. The cancer hadn't recurred. She had her life back, and her beloved son too. This beat winning the Lotto any day of the week.

Moments later, as she'd been wiping her eyes and attempting to get herself back under control, there'd been a thunderous hammering of tiny hands on the other side of the door.

'Get out of the bathroom,' bellowed three-year-old Ben. 'Quick, hurry up! I need to do a POO.'

Chapter 31

The four of them finally left the café and headed up the hill in search of food. Tomorrow night, Josephine was insisting, they must come over to Newquay and eat in her restaurant; she wanted to cook for them all and introduce Marina to her long-serving staff. But this evening, here in St Carys, they were going to enjoy pasta and pizzas at the cheap and cheerful Italian on the Esplanade.

As they approached La Pulcinella, a group who'd eaten earlier were just leaving. A dozen or so of them were milling around on the pavement outside the restaurant, saying their goodbyes. Several were wearing party hats set at jaunty angles.

'Look who's here! Hey, Kate!' Clemency waved, and Marina saw that Kate was busy unfastening the padlock that secured her bike to the ornate railings. Hearing her name, she straightened up and spotted Clemency, then Ronan.

'Oh, hello! I was going to tell you the news tomorrow. Guess what?' Kate was pink-cheeked. 'I had a call from the police this evening, to let me know they've caught our burglar.'

Ronan spread his hands in delight. 'Really? That's *brilliant.*'

'They tracked him down to a caravan site in Dorset, would you believe? And now he's under arrest. I'm so happy.' She grinned at them both, but Marina noticed that her attention was on Ronan. 'They phoned me while we were here in the restaurant, celebrating Julian's birthday. Everyone cheered when I told them. I'm thrilled!'

'Welcome to the club. We're celebrating too.' Clearly unable to help himself, Ronan drew Josephine closer. 'Have you met my mum before? Mum, this is Kate, the burglar-catcher I told you about. Kate, this is my mum, Josephine.'

'Hi,' said Kate with a shy smile, and Marina saw her cheeks flush once more.

Then Ronan reached for Marina's hand, pulling her forward to join them. 'And this is Marina.'

'I know Marina.' Kate's smile broadened. 'I deliver her post.'

'Marina's my biological mother,' said Ronan.

Kate blinked. 'What?'

Standing between them, he beamed with pride. 'I know, isn't it great?'

Two hours later, after a noisy, convivial dinner together, Josephine voiced the question each of the rest of them had thought but not said aloud.

She rested her hand on Ronan's arm. 'So if there's a way of tracking down your biological father, would you be interested in meeting him?'

Ronan looked at her. 'Would you mind? Would it bother you at all?'

'No, sweetheart, it's fine.' Josephine's dark eyes were luminous in the flickering candlelight. 'And I know your dad wouldn't have minded either.'

Ronan patted the small, capable hand that was clutching his arm, then turned to Marina. 'How about you? How would you feel about it?'

She had told him the story, obviously, but full names hadn't been mentioned. Touched by his concern, she said, 'If it's what you want, it's fine by me too. We'll do our best to make it happen.'

'I'd like to give it a go, if you're both sure you're all right with the idea.' His mouth curved up at the corners. 'Seeing as everything's worked out pretty well so far.'

Josephine exclaimed, 'In that case, let's do it!'

'Try, at least.' Ronan was exercising caution. 'He might be dead. He might live in Australia. He might not want to meet me.'

'He isn't dead,' said Marina. 'And he doesn't live in Australia.'

They all looked at her and she responded with a shrug. 'What? Do you think I'm immune from curiosity? I looked him up on the internet years ago.'

'Have you *spoken* to him?' Clemency's eyes were huge.

'No, no, absolutely not.' Marina shook her head hastily. 'Not for thirty-two years. And we don't know if he ever saw my letter to him. He might not remember a thing about me. Which means all of this could come as a shock.'

'It's OK,' said Ronan. 'I know. If he doesn't want anything to do with me, I can handle that.'

'But he might,' said Josephine. 'We won't know until we try. You did tell us he was handsome when he was young.'

She gave Marina a teasing look. 'And you were crazy about each other back then. Who knows, you might see him again and *boom*, all the old feelings could come rushing back!'

'Oh yes, this is *fantastic*.' Getting carried away, Clemency clapped a hand to her chest. 'Anything could happen!' she said delightedly.

Marina picked up her glass and took a glug of wine, feeling suddenly thirty-two years younger. It was hugely embarrassing and she wouldn't have admitted it to a living soul, but this was something that had crossed her mind too. Of course it had, even if the chances were that he was married.

We're all allowed to fantasise, aren't we?

'Come on then, let's look him up now.' Clemency had already cleared a space on the table and pulled her iPad out of her bag with a flourish. 'Name?'

'Ellis Ramsay. Doctor.'

'Dr Ellis Ramsay,' said Clemency as she tapped it into Google. Around the table, only Marina didn't lean in for a closer look. There was no need; she already knew the results off by heart.

There was only one Dr Ellis Ramsay in the UK.

'He's a GP at a primary care centre in Swindon.' Clemency hovered an index finger over the link that said 'Meet the Team' and checked with Ronan. 'Ready?'

'Go ahead.' He nodded and she clicked the link. A grid of eight smiling faces popped up and all eyes instantly zoned in on the one they were here to see.

Some of the smiles were stiff and forced; others were natural. Dr Ellis Ramsay's was somewhere in between. Marina had always thought he looked as if he wanted to smile more broadly but felt he should be reining it in for propriety's sake. She sat back and watched as her son closely studied the features of the father he was seeing for the first time.

'Wow. I do look like him.' Ronan nodded with delighted recognition.

'I told you.' Marina was touched by his response. 'You're an inch or two taller than he was, but otherwise you take after him so much.'

Clemency looked at her. 'That's how you were able to move to St Carys without anyone suspecting a thing. Ronan doesn't look like you at all.'

'Well?' Josephine's voice was soft. 'How does it feel?'

'Weird. But interesting. I'd like to speak to him. Well, that's if he wants to speak to me.' Ronan tilted his head briefly so it was touching hers. 'But he'll never take Dad's place. You do know that, don't you? The two of you were the ones who brought me up.'

Josephine stroked his cheek. 'It's OK. I know.'

'And we'll need to be careful. If he's got a wife and family, he'll have them to consider as well.'

'He might have them,' Clemency looked up, 'but he doesn't live with them.'

Marina stared. 'How on earth do you know that?'

Clemency tilted the screen in her direction. 'Just checked 192.com . . . there, see? This is where he lives, and there's no one else registered on the electoral roll at that address.'

'Good heavens.' Marina marvelled at the things the internet could divulge in a nanosecond.

Josephine looked at her and said, 'You should call the surgery, leave your number with the receptionist and ask him to phone you back.'

The little hairs on the back of Marina's neck quivered at the thought of hearing Ellis's voice again, then having to explain to him why she was getting in touch.

'Or write him a letter,' Josephine added.

Oh phew.

'A letter would be easier.' Marina nodded with relief. 'Much easier. I'll do that.'

Ronan said, 'Will you put in a good word for me? Say flattering things? Tell him I'm nice?'

She smiled, because this was her beautiful boy, who meant the world to her and had made life worth living again. 'Well, I might.'

Chapter 32

'The thing is, we've had a problem getting hold of these parts,' said the photocopier repairman. 'I'll have to put in an order today and come back when we've got it.'

'Right,' said Clemency. 'Well that's OK. Thank goodness we don't run a business that relies on us needing lots of photocopies of things.'

The repairman shot her a suspicious look. 'Are you being sarcastic?'

'Yes.' Clemency gathered up the sizeable pile of papers that had built up waiting for the broken copier to be fixed, and rolled her eyes at Paula. 'Yes, I am. I'll take this lot over to the post office. Wish me luck, I may be gone for some time.'

Thirty minutes later, her misery was further compounded when she heard an old man behind her say in a strong local accent, 'Orright, me bird, couldn't let us jump in an' make a quick copy o' summat, could 'ee?'

Clemency exhaled in frustration, then turned round and saw who was addressing her. The unexpected sight of him took her breath away.

'Did I get you?' said Sam.

Oh, that face, those eyes.

'You got me. You did that so well. I can't believe I fell for it.'

He looked amused. 'What are you doing? Don't tell me your fancy office copier's broken down.'

'And is going to be out of action for days. So I'm stuck with this geriatric one instead.' Clemency gave the modest machine a pat as it slowly scanned the next page and, bit by bit, inched out the copy. 'And yes, every few minutes someone does come up and ask if they could just do their own bit of copying because it looks like I'm going to be here for hours.'

At that moment, a sheet of A4 somewhere inside the machine made an ominous crackling noise and the red error button began to flash.

'And this is why I love my job,' said Clemency.

'Is this the queue?' A tiny lady in her seventies was waving a small envelope. 'Oh dear, not going to be long, are you? I've got a very bad hip, you know.'

Sam swiftly opened up the top half of the machine, pulled out the crumpled sheet of paper and collected together the yet-to-be-copied pages before the tiny lady could send them flying with her pink crocheted shopping bag. He said, 'It's all yours,' and moved out of the way, then beckoned to Clemency. 'Come on, let's go. I've got the car outside.'

Within fifteen minutes they were back at his apartment. In the spare room that he'd turned into an office stood a brand-new printer-copier.

'Not as fast as the one you have at work,' he apologised.

'But fifty times faster than that thing in the post office.

And no queue-jumpers. Seriously, this is fantastic,' said Clemency. 'Thank you so much. You saved me from having a humiliating meltdown in a public place.'

'Happy to help.' He paused. 'Actually, if I do help, we can be finished in twenty minutes. Then maybe we could sit down and have a chat.'

'What kind of a chat?'

'A private one,' said Sam, and Clemency felt her stomach do a loop-the-loop that was part giddiness, part fear.

'What about?'

His mouth did that thing it did when he was being serious. 'Look, we don't get much chance to talk without other people being around. And I think we need to. There are things I need to know. Questions I want to ask, answers I'd like to hear. *Honest* answers . . .'

'OK.' Clemency nodded hurriedly, the loop-the-loop swirling into overdrive. 'We'll talk, that's fine. But can we get this copying out of the way first?'

For the next twenty-five minutes they worked as a super-efficient team, loading the pages and sorting the churned-out printed sheets into their various piles before stapling together the details for each of the properties on sale.

Clemency felt as if she were holding her breath the whole time. Sam's physical proximity was making her overheat; the scent of his aftershave was drilling its way into her subconscious. Fifty years from now, encountering it again would bring her right back to this moment in time. Just as she knew she would remember the angle of his jaw, the exact way he stood, the shape of his hands.

Was he committing her details to memory in the same way? Or was he currently wondering what to have for dinner tonight or reminding himself to attend to various important business details?

Finally the copying, the collating and the stapling was done. In the kitchen, Sam poured them each a glass of iced water and placed the tumblers on the marble-topped island. By unspoken agreement they sat on opposite sides, facing each other.

'Right.' He rested his hands, palms down, on the marble. 'Am I allowed to speak now?'

Clemency nodded. 'Go for it.' Hopefully she sounded more casual than she felt.

'Are you wondering what I'm going to say?'

'I've got a pretty good idea.'

'Are you more wound up than you're letting on?'

Oh God, he knew. *Of course he knows.* Clemency picked up her glass of water. 'Yes.'

Sam smiled briefly. 'Thought so. How are things with you and Ronan?'

'Really good. Great.' She'd guessed he was going to ask *that*.

'You seem happy together.'

'We are.' And this time, thankfully, Sam seemed to believe her.

'OK.' He nodded. 'I need to ask you now, has Annabelle talked to you about me?'

'Kind of. A bit. In what way?'

'Has she discussed how she feels about me? I mean, is she . . . happy?'

'As far as I know, she's very happy. You're her perfect man. I haven't asked a lot of questions.' Clemency shrugged to indicate that under the circumstances he could probably

283

understand why she wouldn't want to; it was agonising to even think of certain aspects of their relationship. 'But from what Belle's said, there are no complaints on her side. Everything's great. She's found the person she wants to spend the rest of her life with. And congratulations, it's you.'

It almost broke her heart to say it, but Sam didn't look overly delighted. He exhaled heavily. 'Right.'

'Meaning?' Clemency prompted, and this time he drummed his fingers on the marble worktop before finally raising his gaze to her.

'OK, well she's probably not going to be thrilled then. But it's not fair to keep this thing going. I need to tell her it's over.'

'Over?' This gave her a jolt. 'Really?'

'It isn't working out. At least not on my side.' Sam spoke soberly. 'I was kind of hoping it might be mutual.'

'Well I don't think it is. I'm pretty sure she's going to be horrified. And upset. Oh God, and hasn't she told you?' Clemency winced at the realisation. 'It's her birthday in two weeks. You can't do it before then.'

'No?' Sam's face fell. 'Are you sure?'

'*So* sure. That would be awful. Did she really not mention her birthday?' Because that wasn't Belle's modus operandi at all; in her world, birthdays were the event of the year. She was more likely to hire a plane to trail a huge banner across the sky.

'Well yes, she has talked about it.' He shrugged helplessly. 'But I thought maybe it'd be better to do it before then, so she could . . . you know, make a fresh start.'

Clemency shook her head. 'Trust me, it wouldn't be a good move. It's never the done thing to finish with your girlfriend just before her birthday. *Especially* when your girl-friend is Belle.'

Sam sighed. 'OK, I guess you're right. I've been out of circulation so long, I'd forgotten the basic rules. So I need to hang on until her birthday, make sure it's a good one, buy her some fantastic presents, then break up with her a few days after that.'

'Pretty much.'

'OK. OK, I can do that.' Distractedly, he tilted his water glass from side to side. 'Although finishing with a girlfriend is something else I'm out of practice with. It's not going to be fun.'

'I think I can pretty much guarantee that,' said Clemency. If there was one thing they both knew about Belle, it was that she didn't take any form of rejection well.

Then her pulse quickened, because Sam's eyes were upon her once more and it felt as if he was looking right into her soul, willing her to understand what he needed to say.

'I didn't ask her to move in here with me. You do know that, don't you? We were still in London when Annabelle just announced one day that she'd sublet her London apart-ment and couldn't wait to be back in St Carys again. She was telling everyone how great it was going to be. And she'd given up her job, too.' He shrugged. 'How could I not let her move in after that? It was already too late to say no.'

'But you liked her. It might have worked out,' Clemency reminded him.

Sam nodded. 'That's what I told myself. I thought maybe it could happen, and I tried my best to make it work.' He spread his hands. 'But it didn't.'

'Right.' *So many emotions.*

'And in case you're wondering, this isn't because of you. Not entirely, at least. It would have happened anyway.'

'OK.' Clemency nodded.

'So you don't have to feel guilty.'

'I wasn't planning on it.' She looked at him, her mouth dry. 'Why didn't it work out?'

But Sam was already shaking his head; he wasn't prepared to talk about Belle behind her back. 'Just . . . a few things. You know when it's not quite right.' He pushed his fingers through his hair, raking it back from his tanned forehead. 'So anyway, that's the plan. I'll wait until after her birthday. Any idea what she'd like, by the way?' His faint smile signalled the irony of the question he was asking her. 'Well, may as well ask, while you're here.'

What did Belle want from Sam for her birthday? A declaration of undying love, undoubtedly. A huge diamond ring at a guess. And a romantic proposal of marriage.

Aloud, Clemency said, 'Why do men always ask other people what they should buy for their wives and girlfriends? It's your job to choose. Just get her something *nice*.'

Sam looked rueful. 'How did I guess you'd say that? Listen, when I do tell her it's over, do you think she'll move back to London? Or stay here?'

'This is Belle we're talking about. Who knows what she'll do?'

'OK.' He thought for a moment, then said in a low voice, 'But in theory, if she did leave St Carys for good, and if at some stage in the future you and Ronan broke up . . . and then, say, a few more months were to pass . . .'

Clemency's stomach muscles tightened and she felt light-headed beneath the intensity of his gaze. Oh God, it was what she wanted more than anything, and the fact that it couldn't happen was unbearable. Sometimes she really wished she didn't have a conscience.

But she did.

'Nothing would change. It really wouldn't.' Her throat ached and her mouth was dry, but she had to make Sam understand. 'It *can't*.'

Chapter 33

Marina's hand was shaking as she stood in front of the mirror and applied her make-up. Not too much, just a dusting of powder over her freckles, a bit of purply-brown eyeshadow and some mascara. Waterproof, to be on the safe side.

She finished with a matte peach lipstick that suited her complexion, and a few squishes of Shay & Blue scent, then checked that her hennaed hair wasn't sticking up at the back.

OK, this was it. In recent weeks her life had changed out of all recognition, and now it was about to take another turn. Three days ago she had written to Ellis Ramsay at his home address. Yesterday morning she had received his reply, which had made her cry. He'd included his phone number and asked her to call him, which she'd done.

And now it was Monday afternoon, and she was about to come face to face with Ellis for the first time in thirty-two years. To top it all, when she'd finally managed to fall asleep last night, she'd dreamt about today's meeting and woken up remembering every last detail.

Which was embarrassing, because in the dream she'd found herself overwhelmingly attracted to Ellis and unable to hide the way she felt. Like an overexcited teenager meeting Harry Styles, she had got completely carried away, squealing with excitement as she hugged him, while he in turn had looked appalled and said with disdain, 'Actually, would you mind not doing that? We hardly know each other. And that dreadful noise you keep making is hurting my ears.'

Talk about mortifying. He'd been so cruel and dismissive, rejecting her at every turn and denouncing her paintings as absolute garbage, yet still she hadn't been able to control her emotions and had kept begging him to give her a kiss . . .

Frankly, it had been a massive relief to wake up.

With a bit of luck, she wouldn't make such a shameful show of herself when the real Ellis turned up.

Oh, but to think that he'd known about the baby, that it hadn't come as a surprise . . .

Four o'clock was the time they'd agreed upon. Marina forced herself not to peer out of the window like a dog waiting for him to appear.

At three minutes to four, the doorbell rang and she jumped a mile.

OK, stay calm on the outside, don't throw yourself at him, and definitely don't squeal.

Then she opened the door and there he was. It was the most extraordinary sensation. Yesterday she'd heard his voice on the phone, and before that she'd known what he looked like from his photograph on the health centre's website, but this was something else altogether. Now he was real.

And smiling, not in the professional having-your-photo-taken way, but properly.

'Mary. Look at you. It's so good to see you again.'

'Ellis.' His eyes, his *eyes*. 'You too.'

He held out his arms, they exchanged a warm embrace and – *thank God* – she didn't squeal like a teenager. Within the space of five seconds, she knew absolutely that the attraction that had once been so overwhelming was no longer there. It had evaporated, disappeared; not a molecule of it remained.

Which was kind of a shame, seeing as they were both single, but it wasn't something you could make happen; that kind of emotion simply couldn't be conjured up out of nowhere.

What was more, it was entirely mutual. They were gazing at each other now, and she could tell Ellis felt the same way. This time they were destined – she hoped – to be friends.

'You're looking wonderful,' he said warmly.

'Not so shabby yourself.' Marina smiled, because for a man in his mid fifties, he was doing impressively well. His hair was just beginning to grey at the temples, and there were lines at the corners of his eyes, but he was still handsome. You could see instantly where Ronan had inherited his looks from.

'Here.' As she put the kettle on in the kitchen, Ellis produced his phone and showed her the text he'd received earlier from his daughter Tia, currently working in a hospital in Chicago.

Dad, I'm so happy for you. This is brilliant. Call me later so I can hear all about it. And say hi to my new big brother from me! xxxxx

'Well I already like the sound of her,' said Marina.

'She's a wonderful girl.' Suffused with pride, he shook his head. 'What can I say? You know how it feels to love your child.'

'I do.'

His expression changed. 'Oh Mary, I'm so sorry you had to go through it on your own.'

'Doesn't matter, you're here now. It wasn't your fault.' She gave him a playful nudge as a reminder. 'And I'm not Mary any more, it's Marina.'

As she'd always half suspected, Ellis's grandmother had never forwarded her letter on to him. Having opened it and read the fateful news, she had made her decision and thrown the letter into the fire. The first Ellis had known about it was eight months ago, when he'd driven up north to visit his grandmother. Now aged ninety-three, increasingly frail and living in a nursing home in Sheffield, she had evidently felt the need to clear her conscience and confess all, before dying a fortnight later.

Poor Ellis, it must have come as a terrible shock at the time.

'Marina. Yes, sorry. I'll get used to it.' He nodded. 'Like I said on the phone, I did try to look you up on the internet after she told me, but the only name I had was Mary Lewis. And I didn't know if you'd gone ahead and had the baby . . . there were so many possible options. If you'd given the child up for adoption and not had any contact since, Tia was worried that my tracking you down would only stir things up and cause you more pain. In the end, we decided to leave it. I told myself you might have had a miscarriage. After so many years, I didn't imagine for a moment that I'd ever hear from you again . . . about a child I wasn't even sure existed . . .' Another shrug and a smile. 'But I have, and he does. It's pretty incredible.'

'Wait till you meet him.' It was Marina's turn to be the proud parent. 'He's pretty incredible too.'

★   ★   ★

What an evening. Seriously, *what* an evening. Ronan gazed around the room, taking in just how completely his life had changed in the last couple of weeks. The past had come roaring into the present, and all the questions he'd never been able to ask before had now been answered. Meeting Ellis Ramsay had felt like meeting his own future self. He'd even chatted via Skype with Tia, his newly discovered half-sister, and together they had marvelled at the similarity of their high cheekbones and broad smiles. Any concerns he might secretly have harboured about meeting unexpected new family members for the first time had dissolved in an instant; their relationship was effortless and comfortable from the word go. It just felt so right.

Best of all, Josephine was fine about it too.

Warmed by this knowledge, Ronan continued to watch as everyone chatted around him. By prior arrangement, Ellis had arrived here at Marina's cottage at four o'clock, to give the two of them a while in which to get reacquainted. He had joined them at five, meeting his biological father for the first time. Then at six o'clock Clemency and his mum had turned up together, and it seemed as if none of them had stopped talking since. The plan had been for everyone to drive over to Josephine's restaurant at seven so she could serve Ellis some of her signature jerk chicken, but it was now 7.45 and they still hadn't left.

Then again, the great advantage of your mum owning the restaurant in question was that it meant they could turn up whenever they liked.

He couldn't be the only one getting really hungry, though.

The doorbell rang and Marina said, 'We're not expecting anyone else, are we? I hope it's not Suzanne from across the road.' Her eyes sparkled as she rose to her feet. 'Because if she wants me to babysit, it's not going to happen this evening.'

She squeezed between Clemency and Ellis and went out into the narrow hallway to see who was there. Out of politeness, the living room fell silent. They heard the front door being opened, followed by Marina's exclamation of surprise.

'Oh my goodness, what are *you* doing here?'

Ronan caught Clemency's eye; surely there weren't any more unexpected relatives about to introduce themselves?

Although if there were, Marina hadn't been expecting it to happen either.

'I told you I was coming to see you.' It was a male voice.

'You definitely didn't,' said Marina.

'I did. I sent you an email this morning. And a text this afternoon.'

Ronan glanced across the living room; he'd already spotted the mobile lying dusty and discarded on the windowsill, long out of battery and waiting forlornly for its owner to get around to charging it up. Other people might be inseparable from their phones, but Marina had more of a laissez-faire attitude towards hers. And today in particular, she'd had more important things to think about.

They heard her say, 'I've been busy, there's been a lot going on . . . I haven't checked my messages since—'

'Look, it's fine. I'm here now and that's all that matters. Marina, listen to me, this is important. I have something to tell you, and this time I'm not taking no for an answer.'

'But—'

'Let me put these down.' From the sudden crackle of cellophane, it was evidently some form of flower-based gift; well, either that or a dead body wrapped in really noisy

293

plastic. 'They cost a fortune, but that's OK because I know they're your favourite. And I bought you Godiva chocolates too. Godiva! Because you love them . . . but not nearly as much as I love you!'

'*What?* Oh, but—'

'Marina, let me speak. No one else can even begin to compare. We've been through so much together . . .'

They all knew who it was by now, and everyone's face was a picture. Clemency had clapped a hand over her mouth in an effort to smother an explosion of laughter. Josephine was indignantly mouthing: *That man has a nerve.* Ellis, who'd heard the story of how George had walked out on Marina whilst she was at her lowest ebb, shook his head in disbelief. And out in the hallway, the man himself was still talking, telling Marina that she couldn't do better than him.

'. . . all those years we were a team. A good team; the *best*. I miss you, Marina, and I know how much you must miss me. That's why you're still single, living alone . . . but there's no *need* to be lonely!'

Ronan only had so much self-control. Having reached his limit, he couldn't resist popping his head around the open living-room door and saying with a look of puzzlement, 'Who says she lives alone?'

Ha, that shut him up. Marina's ex-husband looked like a bullfrog about to be shot.

Chapter 34

'What? What's going on?' George's face turned a deeper shade of purple as he pointed at Ronan. 'I recognise you. You turned up at the hotel when we were there the other week.' He swung back to Marina. 'What the hell's *he* doing here?'

'Hi, my name's Ronan.' Beaming, Ronan moved forward and extended his hand. 'We're just having a bit of a get-together. Why don't you come on in and join us?'

'You don't live here, though.' George was bristling with suspicion. 'You can't be *living* here.'

Ronan said pleasantly, 'Can't I? Come along through to the living room, then we can introduce you to everyone.'

The look of horror on George's face was a joy to witness. As he coaxed the older man down the hallway, Ronan said, 'It's OK, I don't really live here with Marina. And I'm not her toyboy either, in case that's what you were wondering.' Because it might have been fun to tease him, but it was a bit of a *ewww* idea.

'I don't know what's happening.' George was breathing hard, clearly not enjoying the fact that his plans for a romantic reunion had been well and truly scuppered.

'It's not complicated, George,' Marina said easily. 'Ronan's my son.'

Silence. Looking more bullfroggish than ever, George stopped dead in his tracks and stared at her.

Ronan said, 'Surprise!'

George's gaze swung back to him. 'You can't be.'

'I can. I am.'

'You're the one she gave up for adoption? But . . . but how . . .?'

'We found each other,' Ronan said simply. 'Isn't it great? Here, come and meet my mum. Mum, this is George, who used to be married to Marina. George, this is Josephine, my mum.'

'Hello.' Josephine's eyes were bright as she shook George's sausagey hand.

'And this is Ellis,' Ronan continued smoothly. 'My father.' He waited until the next handshake was done and dusted before adding, 'Not my adoptive father; this is the biological one.'

George was breathing even more heavily now as he duly processed this information. His jaw fell open as he pointed first at Marina, then at Ellis. 'You mean you . . . and him . . .'

'Yes.' Marina nodded encouragingly. 'Yes, we did, and together we made Ronan.' She beamed. 'Aren't we lucky?'

George's purple face turned purpler. Beads of sweat dotted his forehead. 'You didn't tell me any of this.'

'You never wanted to hear anything about it,' said Marina. 'When I tried to tell you, you said it was nothing to do with you. You weren't interested.'

'And now you're living here?' George directed the question at Ellis. 'You've moved in with *my wife?*'

'Ex-wife,' Marina reminded him.

'I don't believe this. You've lied to me. And now you have the nerve to do all this behind my back . . .' The rise and fall of his shoulders grew more pronounced as he sucked in lungfuls of air then noisily exhaled. As he stared wildly around the room, he pressed a trembling hand to his chest. 'Oh God, something's happening to me . . . Look at my hands, I can't even feel them . . . I'm so dizzy . . . My lungs . . . I'm going to pass out . . . My head feels as if it's about to *burst*.'

Fear engulfed Marina as George began to stagger and sway. Clem had grabbed his arm and was pulling him towards an empty armchair, but it was too late; his knees gave way and he first stumbled, then slumped to the floor.

'Oh God, please no! What's wrong with him? George!' Falling to her knees, Marina clutched his hand; he was still breathing as if he'd run a marathon. She stared wildly up at Ellis. 'Is he having a heart attack? Is it a stroke? We need to call an ambulance!'

'Let me take a look at him.' Crouching on the other side of George's prone body, Ellis began rapidly and expertly to carry out a series of checks.

'We should call nine nine nine.' Marina was shaking. *Oh God. If he dies, it'll be all my fault.*

'Hang on for just one minute,' Ellis said calmly. 'Now, George, I want you to listen to me. Everything's fine, but we need to slow down your breathing. While I count to twelve, you exhale slowly. Then I'll count to six and you can slowly inhale. Through your nose, not your mouth. Pay attention and concentrate on me, OK? Here we go . . .'

Like magic, within a couple of minutes George's breathing pattern was back to normal.

'There you are, feeling better now? You're absolutely fine,' said Ellis. 'Let's get you up, shall we?'

But as he was being helped into a sitting position, George's eyes rolled and he said weakly, 'I can't, I can't . . . oh Marina, help me . . .' Then his eyelids closed and he slumped back down to the ground.

Marina let out a gasp of fright. 'George! Oh God, what's happening now?'

'Open your eyes, George,' Ellis instructed. Nothing happened, there was no response at all. This time George was unconscious.

The fear was overwhelming. Marina watched as Ellis carried out the series of checks for a second time. Why wasn't he telling them to call for an ambulance . . . was it because he already knew it was too late? Beside herself, she cried out, 'George, wake up! *Please* . . .'

Nothing, not a flicker. He was out cold. In a flash, Marina knew he was going to die.

'Right,' Ellis announced. 'There's nothing else for it. Stand back, everyone – I'm going to have to start mouth-to-mouth resuscitation.'

Oh God, oh God . . .

'What? No you bloody don't.' George's eyelids promptly snapped open and he ducked sideways, raising his hands to fend off Ellis's approach. 'Don't you dare try that with me!'

Ronan said, 'Now that's what I call a miraculous recovery.'

Marina's mouth fell open as she watched George bat away Ellis's efforts to help him up. He scrambled to his feet unaided and furiously brushed himself down.

'You old fraud,' Josephine exclaimed. 'What was all that about then? Trying to win Marina back by going for the sympathy vote?'

'She still loves me, I know she does,' said George. 'Didn't you hear her just now? She was worried sick!'

'Is he really OK?' Marina needed to double-check.

Ellis nodded. 'He's fine. The hyperventilation caused the dizziness and the numbness in his hands and feet. The rest was just . . . well, nothing to worry about.' His tone signalled what he was too professional to say.

'Manipulative and attention-seeking,' Marina supplied. 'I don't know how I fell for it. You'd think I'd have had enough practice by now.' She turned to address her ex-husband. 'I was only worried because I thought you might die and I'd end up getting the blame. Other than that, I'm really not bothered what happens to you.'

'But—'

'George, don't waste your breath.' Which, under the circumstances, was quite funny. But Marina didn't smile; she just shook her head at him. 'Go home, leave me alone and get on with the rest of your life. I don't want to see you again. I have everything I've ever wanted here in St Carys.'

'Marina—'

'No, you're still not listening,' she said firmly. 'This is my family, George. They're all I need. Thanks to these people . . . these *lovely* people . . .' her sweeping gesture encompassed Ronan, Clemency, Josephine and Ellis, 'I've never been happier in my life.'

As he stormed past her out of the cottage, taking the cellophane-wrapped flowers and the Godiva chocolates with him, George hissed, 'I thought you deserved one last chance. Just shows how gullible I am. You always were a selfish bitch.'

The front door slammed hard behind him and Marina experienced a tidal wave of relief. It was over, once and for all; she knew she wouldn't see him again.

Good.

When she returned to the living room, Clemency said with a grin, 'Well I can't imagine why you turned down such a generous offer. What a catch.'

Chapter 35

'What?' said Clemency. 'Why are you looking at me like that?'

'I wondered if we could have a chat.' Even as he said it, Ronan was wondering if this would turn out to be a brilliant idea or the most terrible mistake.

'A chat about what?'

He switched off the car's engine. 'Invite me in for a coffee and I'll tell you.'

It was Thursday evening. They'd been invited earlier to the opening night of an extensively renovated hotel in Bude, and had bumped into two of his ex-girlfriends there. Both were beautiful, desirable and still single. Both had subtly – and separately – indicated to him that if only *he* were still single, they'd definitely be up for a rematch.

'I think I can guess what this is about,' Clemency said when they'd climbed the stairs to her flat.

Could she? Ronan hid a smile, because he seriously doubted it. 'Go on then, tell me what you think.'

'Lauren, tonight. And the blonde girl . . . I've forgotten her name. Julie?'

'Julia.'

Clem nodded. 'Anyway, those two. Both pretty keen on you. I mean, they were trying not to be obvious, but . . .'

'You noticed.'

'Of course I did. I'm good at stuff like that. I mean, how could I not notice other girls being interested in my boyfriend?'

Ronan shrugged and smiled.

'Except you're not my boyfriend,' said Clemency. She studied his face. 'It's OK, I know what you're going to say. I asked you to do me a favour for a couple of weeks, and it's been way longer than that. Poor you, you haven't complained once, but enough's enough. You want your life back. There are girls out there waiting to be slept with.'

'Well . . .'

'It's fine. I understand. Let's face it, these last few weeks can't have been much fun for you. This must be the longest you've ever been celibate!'

Ronan hesitated, then nodded. If she only knew the truth, Clem would die laughing. Since that evening with Kate, there hadn't been anyone at all. It sounded completely crazy, even to him, but that was the way it was. If he couldn't have Kate, he simply wasn't interested in finding anyone else.

Although having said that, the absence of a sex life had been bothering him; he was only human after all. Hence the reason for the conversation they were about to have, any minute now.

Because if he wanted sex but not a relationship, he'd be happier doing it with Clem than with either of the two girls they'd encountered earlier this evening. Or if it came to that, anyone else he knew.

Plus, Clem was in the same sex-free boat.

'It's fine.' Clemency was shaking her head to show she understood. 'Seriously, you've gone above and beyond the call of duty. You've been a fantastic boyfriend and all the girls are going to be thrilled to bits when they find out you're back on the market. We'll just say we broke up because we decided we're better off as friends. And if anyone asks for a review, I promise to give you five stars!'

Ronan exhaled. 'Or we don't have to break up.'

'Meaning what?' Clemency looked puzzled. 'I thought that's what you wanted.'

'And as usual you jumped to conclusions. I like being your boyfriend. I'm just wondering if you'd be interested in . . . well, maybe getting a bit more out of it.'

'You what?'

OK, actually coming out and saying the words was a bit trickier than he'd anticipated. Ronan shrugged pseudo-casually. 'Come on, use your imagination.'

'You mean you want us to be a real couple?' Clemency's eyes were like saucers. 'Like, for *real*?'

'Well, maybe.' He hadn't considered that possibility, but why not? You never knew, it could happen.

'Oh, I get it.' Her expression cleared. 'You're after *sex*.'

Ronan winced. 'God, you're brutal.'

'But am I right?'

'Don't cock your eyebrow at me like that.'

'Am I right, though?' Clemency's eyebrow remained cocked.

'Yes.' *Witch.*

'You're suggesting we should be friends with benefits.'

'Look, it's just an idea. You can always say no. I thought a harmless reciprocal arrangement might be . . . nice.'

'What with neither of us currently having anyone else to do it with.'

'Well, yes. But it's fine, we can forget it.'

Clemency thought for a couple of seconds, then said, 'OK.'

'Does that mean OK, let's forget it? Or OK, we'll give it a whirl?'

Her eyes sparkled. 'We could try it, if you like.'

'Have you thought about this before?' Ronan tilted his head.

'Maybe.'

He smiled. Of course it was something they'd both considered; the issue had just never been raised, that was all. 'Shall we give it a go then?' he said playfully.

'Do you think it'll be weird?'

'Only one way to find out.' Ronan moved closer and drew her towards him; he'd wondered about the weirdness too. But they'd managed the kissing thing without any trouble, so . . .

Less than a minute later, he realised she was shaking. Not with emotion, sadly, but with pent-up laughter.

After a few more seconds, she pulled away and the suppressed hilarity exploded out of her. 'Oh God, I'm sorry, it's just *so* weird . . .' she gasped.

'We haven't even done anything yet.'

'I know, but it's just knowing it's on the cards. It's making me feel all prickly and strange . . .' She held her hand over her mouth and did her best to stifle the next wave of laughter. 'It's like being given a massage and wanting it to stop, but having to let it carry on because it's supposed to be nice.'

'Thanks,' said Ronan. 'That's what I call an ego boost.'

'I'm sorry! Doesn't it feel weird to you too? OK, let's delete that one and go for another take. This time I won't laugh, promise.'

And she didn't; he could feel her valiantly holding it in. This time Ronan was the one who laughed first, because Clem was right, it did feel all kinds of wrong.

'Oh God, why can't we do this?' He leant against the kitchen worktop and rubbed his hands over his face. 'If we could just get past the beginning bit, maybe the rest will be easier.'

When they'd finally composed themselves once more, Clemency drank a glass of water and wiped her mouth with the back of her hand. 'OK, we're giving this one last go, and this time we're going to get it right. So we're going to concentrate *really* hard and neither of us is going to laugh, and even if it feels strange, we just keep going until it *stops* feeling strange.'

'OK,' said Ronan.

'Close your eyes,' Clemency instructed. 'We'll both keep our eyes closed and we won't open them.' She nodded determinedly. 'I think that'll help.'

He smiled briefly and closed his eyes. Maybe she was right; this way he could pretend she was Kate. Good plan.

It's Kate. Honestly it is. Not Clemency. Kate. He kissed her, then stroked the back of her neck and ran his other hand over her shoulder and down her arm . . . except it was no good. How could his brain believe for one second that this was Kate when it knew perfectly well it was Clem?

Who was starting to shake again with the effort of holding in that uncontainable laughter.

And then they were both laughing and holding on to

305

each other, partly because it was the craziest situation and partly with relief that it was over.

'Ah well, we tried.' Clemency wiped her eyes on a torn-off sheet of kitchen roll.

'We gave it our best shot,' Ronan agreed. 'God, though. Who knew it would feel *that* wrong?'

'I know you have a great body,' said Clemency, 'but the thought of seeing you naked was completely freaking me out.'

'Me too, exactly the same.' Ronan's keys were on the worktop; he picked them up and gave her a hug. 'Anyway, at least we gave it a go.'

As she was letting him out of the flat, Clemency said, 'I even tried to pretend you were someone else, the last time. In case it made things easier. But it didn't.' She paused, then said curiously, 'Did you try that too?'

'No.' Ronan shook his head; no *way* was he admitting it.

'Oh. Sorry. I feel bad about it now.'

'Go on then. Who did you pretend I was?'

She looked at him. 'Chris Hemsworth.'

Ronan broke into a teasing grin. 'That'll be why it didn't work. You should have come up with someone better-looking than me.'

Chapter 36

Belle's birthday was still seven days away, but this evening had been the only date her old girlfriends from school could get together. They'd met up at the Mariscombe Hotel for dinner, then moved on to the terrace afterwards to drink, chat and mingle with the other guests and visitors to St Carys.

Now Belle sat back in the taxi and gazed out of the side window as Clemency, next to her, said, 'Well that was a good night. Everyone had fun, didn't they? Nice to bump into Riley again. And isn't Dot amazing?'

'She is.' Distracted by her own thoughts, Belle nodded.

'God, my toes. These shoes are killing me. I don't know how you do it,' said Clemency.

'That's because you always go for cheap ones. If you bought designer, they wouldn't hurt so much.' But Belle smiled as she said it; the difference in their spending habits had been a standing joke between them for years. Impulsively, she reached out to clasp Clemency's hand. 'Thanks for coming tonight. I know they weren't your friends, so I appreciate it.'

'Hey, no problem.' In return, Clemency gave her fingers a squeeze. 'I'm glad you had fun.'

For a moment Belle's throat tightened. On the surface it had certainly looked that way: seven attractive young women laughing and drinking champagne on the terrace of one of the most glamorous hotels in Cornwall.

But had she really had fun?

They reached Clemency's street and the taxi pulled up outside her flat. Clem leant across to give Belle a bit of a wobbly kiss on the cheek. 'Night. Happy pre-birthday. Don't forget to drink a pint of water before you go to sleep.'

'No need.' Belle managed a faint smile as her often exasperating but essentially good-hearted stepsister wrestled with the wrong end of the door handle. 'You're the one who's going to wake up with a hangover.'

The remainder of the journey involved the cab snaking down into the centre of St Carys, then turning right and taking the road along the seafront. As they made their way along the coast road, Belle rested her head against the cool glass of the window and gazed out across Beachcomber Bay. The stars were out, the sea was glassily smooth and dark, and at that moment there were no other cars in sight.

Which didn't, naturally, prevent the upcoming temporary traffic lights from turning red at their approach.

She sat up. 'Couldn't you just go through them?'

'No I can't,' said the taxi driver.

Typical jobsworth. Belle sighed, slumped back in her seat and gazed out at the bay once more. A flicker of movement caught her attention, and for a second she thought it was two seagulls having a tussle on the sand. The next moment she realised it was someone jogging along the beach, the soles of their trainers showing up as flashes of white with each step they took.

It was eleven o'clock; how many people in St Carys would be out running at this time of night?

The traffic lights turned green.

'Stop.' Belle sat upright.

'No,' said the taxi driver. 'Red means stop. Green means go.'

'And the customer is always right.' There was a charge of seven pounds on the meter; Belle handed over a tenner and said, 'Keep the change. I'm getting out here.'

'Where are you going?'

'For a walk.'

'Blimey, in those shoes? Good luck.'

He drove off chuckling to himself, and Belle strode back down the road for all of ten seconds before stopping and kicking off her stilettos, then making her way over to the steps that led down on to the sand. The little white flashes were no longer visible, having been swallowed up by the darkness, but that didn't matter: these stone steps were the only way off the beach.

She reached the bottom, moved past the pebbly section and sat down on a patch of dry sand. In a crystal-embellished shell-pink silk dress from Harvey Nichols that had cost £675.

As she waited, she breathed in the faint mingled scents of ozone, seaweed, and fish and chips from the takeaway up on High View Road. With the sea this calm, the tiny waves breaking on to the beach resembled frilly-edged crochet. And the night was still warm, almost tropically so, with just the merest hint of a breeze to stop it being muggy.

Finally she heard the rhythmic tap-tap of returning

footsteps. As they came nearer, Belle shook back her hair and turned to look in the direction of the sound. Moments later, Verity came into view, saw her and slowed down.

'Hi.' She came and sat beside her. 'You look like a mermaid in that dress.'

'You're out late,' said Belle. 'I was just on my way home when I spotted you down here.'

'Wasn't tired, couldn't sleep.' Verity shrugged. 'Doesn't bother me, though. I like running at night when there's no one else around.'

'Less chance of bumping into people on the beach,' Belle said with a faint smile. 'Carry on if you want to. Don't stop on my account.'

'It's fine, I've done enough. That's a very nice frock you're wearing. And nice shoes you're not wearing.' Verity picked one up and admired it for a couple of seconds. 'Look at that heel. Are they comfortable?'

'No. Agony. I just pretend they don't hurt.'

Verity laughed. 'And where have you been? Out somewhere nice with Sam?'

Belle shook her head. 'Sam's at home. It's my birthday next week, so I met up with some old school friends for the evening. Clem came along too. We had dinner at the Mariscombe Hotel.'

'Sounds fab. Happy birthday for next week!'

'You could have come along,' said Belle. 'I'd have invited you, but I thought it might be a bit strange when it's a group of people you've never met before. Well, apart from Clemency,' she grimaced, 'and you know what she's like.'

Verity said, 'No problem, it's fine. At least you had a great time.'

There it was again, the assumption that everything in her life was wonderful. Belle leant back on her elbows and gazed out to sea, wishing she could say all the things she really wanted to say.

Beside her, Verity murmured, 'Are you OK?'

'Yes.' Belle nodded in a just-about way.

'Sure? Because you have Sam at home waiting for you. But instead, you're sitting here on the sand in a very expensive dress.'

'True.' Another nod.

After a few seconds of silence, Verity said, 'I'm a good listener, if you think it might help to talk about it.'

'Talk about this dress? Well, it's dry-clean only . . .' See? All was not lost; she could still make a joke.

'Not the dress. You and Sam. I mean, I'm no expert, but I'm guessing that's what this is about.'

And the rest. Belle nodded slowly. 'All my life I've wanted the perfect husband. Even when I was at school, it was the one thing I dreamt of: getting married to the best man ever, so we could have children and be the happiest family in the world. OK, I know it sounds like something out of an Enid Blyton book, but I can't help that. It was what I wanted. And now I have Sam, and he *is* everything I ever wanted, but . . . oh, I don't know . . .'

'If it isn't right, and you don't think you can make it right, you should call it a day,' said Verity. 'There's no shame in that.'

'I know, I *know*. But the thing is, I'll never meet a better man than him. Oh God . . . I haven't breathed a word about this to anyone. You won't say anything, will you?'

'Of course I won't. You can trust me.' Verity reached

311

across, her fingers closing around Belle's right wrist. 'I promise.'

Her hand was dry and firm. Belle closed her eyes. Verity was trustworthy, of course she was. She cleared her suddenly constricted throat. 'When I was at school, being obsessed with boys was what all the girls did. So I joined in and was obsessed with them too. Which was fine, but sometimes the way they talked about how they felt made me wonder if I was missing out on something. I just didn't seem to have the same enthusiasm for, you know . . . things, as they did.'

Things. Listen to me. What do I sound like?

Verity nodded. 'You mean sex.'

Oh, the guilt. The guilt and the shame, the terrible shame. Belle nodded; for the first time in her life, she was admitting her most embarrassing secret. 'Yes, that too. It was never as amazing as they all said it was. But if I'd told them that, they'd have laughed at me. Because they laughed at anyone who wasn't like them.' She faltered. 'God, I don't know how to explain it . . . Is there a kind of food you really don't like?'

'Mustard,' Verity answered promptly. 'I hate mustard.'

'So it's like you're telling all your friends that you don't like mustard and they're all looking at you as if you're completely mad, because who in their right mind wouldn't love mustard? And then they start saying there must be something wrong with you . . . but it's no good, it doesn't help, because no matter how many times you try your hardest to make yourself like mustard, it's never going to happen.'

'I know.' Verity nodded to show she understood. 'That's a good way to explain it. Not much fun for you, though.'

'No.'

'Probably not much fun for Sam, either.'

'Oh, don't worry about Sam. He has no idea about any of this,' said Belle. 'I'm a fantastic girlfriend.' *Not to mention a wonderful actress.* It was a point of pride to her that none of the men in her life had ever suspected anything was wrong.

'How about counselling? Ever thought of giving it a go?'

'That wouldn't help.' This much she did know.

'OK.' Verity nodded. 'Well, like I said, this is just between us. Do you feel better for having told someone?'

Was the conversation over? Belle realised she was disappointed; oh God, had she been boring her to tears? Aloud, she said, 'Yes, I do.'

'Good.' Verity was getting to her feet, preparing to leave. 'Happy to help. Now, fancy a swim?'

Belle stared up at her. 'Sorry?'

'You know. That thing where you get in the sea and waggle your arms and legs to stop yourself sinking to the bottom.' In one smooth movement, Verity pulled her black Lycra sports vest over her head and kicked off her trainers. Then she peeled off the matching Lycra shorts. Beneath them, she was wearing her slate-grey bikini.

'Is this a joke? You're asking me to go swimming with you at half past eleven at night?'

'You don't have to say yes,' said Verity.

'It'll be cold.'

'It won't be.'

'How are you going to get dry afterwards?'

Turning, Verity made her way over to the rocks to the left of the steps and retrieved a black sports bag from the shadows. 'Only one towel, I'm afraid. But we can share it.'

'I don't have a swimming costume,' said Belle.

'So is that a no, then?'

Now that her eyes had adjusted to the dim light, Belle could make out the glint of amusement in those light blue eyes. The note of challenge in her voice was barely discernible, but it was there. Belle shook her head; did Verity seriously think she was the type who'd respond to a dare? What were they, ten years old?

'Waaahh!' Belle let out a muffled shriek as she ran into the sea and felt just how cold it was against her ankles, her knees, her thighs . . .

'OK, so I may have lied a bit.' Next to her, Verity spluttered with laughter.

The stomach and chest were always the worst bits. There was only one way to do it. Belle gasped, 'One, two, three . . . go!' and threw herself into the water to get it over with.

A few minutes later, they'd rounded the headland and reached the next cove along the coastline. Behind them, the golden lights of St Carys had slipped from view. This one, Mirren Cove, was tiny and unreachable on foot. Lazily treading water beside her, ten or so metres from the beach, Verity said, 'Look how much brighter the stars are from out here.'

'Amazing.' Belle rolled on to her back and gazed up at them. 'I haven't visited this cove for years.'

'You're a good swimmer.'

'I know.'

Verity laughed. 'Still cold?'

'I've warmed up now.'

'Isn't it magical, the way that happens? Never gets old. Are you worried about your stuff?'

'No.' Belle shook her head. She'd stepped out of her dress and left it in Verity's sports bag, along with her shoes and the tiny pink handbag containing her purse, keys and phone. Hopefully no one would find the bag and make off with it.

'And how are you feeling?' said Verity.

'Not too bad at all, considering I'm bobbing around in the sea in the middle of the night in my bra and pants.'

Verity smiled, her teeth gleaming white in the moonlight.

'I tried to persuade David to come swimming with me one night on our honeymoon. He wasn't impressed, said he'd rather jump off a bridge without a bungee rope.'

'How long were you married?'

'Just over two years.'

The water lapped at Belle's sides as she moved her arms to keep herself afloat. 'Am I allowed to ask what happened?'

'You mean why did we break up? I suppose you could say we weren't that suited to each other.'

'Was it amicable?'

'Not at first, no. But we got there in the end. We've managed to stay friends.'

'Why weren't you suited?' said Belle.

'Well, Dave likes women. A lot.' Verity paused, then said, 'And so do I. Which kind of made being married to each other a bit awkward.'

Belle looked at her. 'You mean . . .?' The rest of the sentence remained stuck in her throat.

'Yes.' The light blue gaze was unflinching. 'But then you already knew that, didn't you?'

Had she? Deep down, had she guessed, had she actually sensed it? Belle heard her own shallow breathing as she digested Verity's words. She also realised that the incoming tide had carried them closer to the shore. Instead of floating horizontally, she put her legs down, encountered sand beneath her feet.

Verity did the same, and they stood facing each other, up to their shoulders in the gently lapping water.

'I didn't know for sure.' Belle's voice faltered as she prepared to say the words she'd never imagined being brave enough to utter aloud. 'But I wondered. And . . . I hoped it might be true.'

Verity said calmly, 'Well done for spotting it. Not always easy, is it?'

Belle shook her head. There was a rising clamour inside her chest; her body was on fire with anticipation. Was this it, was something about to happen at last?

'Have you ever kissed a girl before?' Verity's voice was low.

'No.'

'Would you like to?'

Oh God. 'Yes.'

'Anyone in particular?'

'Maybe.'

And now they were both smiling. Verity's long wet hair was slicked back from her face, the ends fanning out around her in the water. She reached out and rested her hands on Belle's bare shoulders, and the physical contact caused an adrenalin rush so acute that Belle almost forgot to breathe.

Then Verity moved closer, and closer still, until their bodies beneath the water were touching and their mouths above the water finally met.

So soft . . . so beautiful . . . *so right* . . .

As the kiss deepened, hot tears seeped out from beneath Belle's closed eyelids.

Because what was happening now, she knew, threatened to bring a whole world of trouble into her carefully mapped out, oh-so-perfect life.

Chapter 37

Ronan heaved a sigh of relief as he locked up the office. He loved his job, but sometimes the general public drove him nuts. Today had been one of those frustrating Saturdays when they'd been inundated with well-meaning time-wasters, holidaymakers for whom a spot of window-shopping just wasn't enough. Carried away by the thrill of being on holiday, they came piling into Barton and Byrne to take advantage of the free air-conditioning and to collect as many glossy property brochures as they could get away with, so they could take them away, gaze at the colour photos and fantasise about buying themselves a holiday home with glorious sea views in St Carys.

It was a harmless enough daydream, but still annoying when they engaged you in enthusiastic conversation for twenty minutes about desirable properties you all knew perfectly well they were never going to buy.

Anyway, done now. He was free for the rest of the evening and had been invited along to an early barbecue at the cricket club, which would be a laugh and give him a chance to catch up with some of his more boisterous friends.

'Ronan! Hey, just caught you in time!'

Ronan turned to see Terry Ferguson jumping down from his white transit van. His heart sank, not because he didn't like Terry, who worked as a window-fitter, but because Terry never used one word where a couple of hundred would do. In his late thirties, single and desperate to find himself a girlfriend and settle down, his ability to talk for England had seen off a stream of exhausted girls, who complained that he interrupted them constantly and never listened to a single word they said.

'Hi, Terry, how are things with—'

'Great, never better! Have you heard the news?' Terry beamed at him, red-faced and pleased with himself in his green and white checked shirt and ripped work jeans. 'Well I suppose you wouldn't have, seeing as you're the first to know. I'm leaving, mate. Off to Liverpool! Moving in with Deena, can you believe it? Happy days!'

'Wow,' said Ronan. 'Who's Deena?'

'My girlfriend! Come on, you remember, don't you? I told you all about her the other week.'

'Ah yes.' In all honesty, people tended to zone out when they were cornered by Terry, but the gist of it was coming back to Ronan now. 'You met her on Tinder and she works in a call centre, is that the—'

'I met her on Tinder and she *owns* a call centre! But she didn't want men who were only after her for her money, so she pretended she didn't have any, see? But now she trusts me. And I don't even care about that side of things anyway. I'd still love her if she didn't have any money at all!'

'Right.' Ronan nodded. 'And what brings you here now?'

'Selling my place, aren't I! Don't need it no more!

Deena's got a big house and I'm going to use the money from mine to set up my own window-fitting business on the Wirral. So the sooner you can put it on the market, the better. I just want to get my hands on some cash, quick as you like!'

'Right.' Ronan hesitated, wondering how to phrase the next question. 'Look, can I—'

'So could you come and take a look at it now?'

OK, *whoa*. 'Terry. Have you actually met Deena, or is this another one of your email friendships?' The last girlfriend, it had transpired, had been a startlingly buxom beauty who'd required Terry's help in getting hold of the £76 million she'd been bequeathed by her late father, the president of an African country.

'Oh come on, don't start on about that again. This one's the real deal, I swear.'

'And you've seen her, have you? I mean, not just in photos. In real life?'

'Blimey, you're suspicious!' Whipping out his phone, Terry showed Ronan the screen saver, a photo of himself with his arm around a smiling blonde in her thirties. 'We've been meeting up every weekend for the last two months. I *told* you all about her last week.' He shook his head pityingly. 'You need to pay a bit more attention, mate. Sometimes it's like you don't listen to a word I say.'

'Sorry. Look, I'm just worried that you're rushing into things. Putting your home on the market is a big step to—'

'Ronan, what's the matter with you? Call yourself a salesman? I'm doing it,' Terry declared, 'and nobody's going to stop me. You might not know how it feels to fall in love, but *I* do.' He jabbed a finger with pride at his own chest.

320

'And if you're not interested in selling my place, that's no problem at all, mate. I'll just go to Rossiter's instead.'

Ninety minutes later, Ronan called Kate's number. At the thought of speaking to her, as always, his heart quickened. When she answered the phone, he said, 'Hey, good news. I think I've found it.'

'It? You mean *it*?' He could hear the smile in her voice; she knew at once what he was telling her. 'Really?'

'Pretty sure.' And now he was smiling too, although logically this was the last thing he wanted to happen. Once Kate had her own home, he'd no longer be able to take her out on viewings. 'Of course, I could be wrong, but . . .'

'If you think this is the one, I'm excited. What's it like?'

He gave her the basic details of Terry's traditional white-washed terraced cottage on Victoria Street, with its cleanly decorated interior, pretty back garden and – it went without saying – excellent replacement windows.

'There's even a sea view,' he added happily, because he knew this was something Kate had always wanted but thought she probably couldn't afford. 'I told him that if he waited a while he could get more for it, but he's desperate for a quick sale. At this price, it's going to be snapped up, but no one else has seen it yet. I told him I had a possible buyer in mind and he's keen for you to see it as soon as possible.' *Thud-thud* went his pulse. 'So, what are you doing tonight?' For a mad moment it had occurred to him that the cricket club barbecue was being held not far from Terry's cottage . . . maybe after the viewing he could casually suggest to Kate that they drop in for a quick drink and a burger . . .

'Oh I can't do it tonight,' said Kate. 'I'm sorry. My

grandparents are off on holiday to America and our neighbour's giving them a lift up to Heathrow, so I'm babysitting until she gets back.'

'OK.' So much for that fantasy. Except, Ronan belatedly remembered, if he *had* invited Kate along to the barbecue, she'd have wondered why he wasn't taking Clem. 'Well, how about tomorrow then? Say around midday?'

'Tomorrow would be great.' Kate sounded relieved. 'And midday's perfect. Give me the number of the house and I'll meet you there.'

'Or I could drive over and pick you up,' Ronan offered. 'Save you having to come all that way on your bike.'

'Only if you're sure that's OK. I don't want to be a nuisance.'

As if you could be. Aloud, Ronan said, 'No problem. All part of the service. I'll come over just before twelve.'

'This is so exciting.' Kate sounded thrilled. 'I can't wait!'

Well, what a strange night that had been. Kate, who normally slept really well, gave up at seven and got out of bed. She'd dreamt about Ronan – no change there – who'd been showing her around the house, except it was actually a small zoo and there'd been a llama in the kitchen, and when she'd protested about the llama, Ronan had said crossly, 'Has it ever occurred to you that you're too damn fussy? Clem would *love* to live in a place like this.'

Which had woken her with a jolt at two in the morning and prevented her from getting back to sleep again. By five, she had begun to wonder if she was coming down with something; she felt restless and uncomfortable and generally not quite right.

To take her mind off the low-level sensation of weirdness, she jumped into the shower and used her favourite lemon foaming shower gel. She was probably on edge because she knew she'd soon be seeing Ronan.

Seriously, was this stupid crush ever going to fade away?

After having dried her hair and put on a tiny bit of make-up, she was still unable to quell the restless sensation in her chest. At 8.30, she found herself cleaning the oven and scrubbing down the fronts of the kitchen cabinets. By nine o'clock she was prowling around the garage in search of a can of crimson matt emulsion.

By 9.30, the kitchen floor was covered with dust sheets and she was ready to start giving the walls a fresh coat of paint. It wouldn't take long, but it would save her grandfather a job when he returned from Florida.

At ten o'clock, the stomach cramps she'd been doing her best to ignore abruptly grew worse, to the extent that Kate found herself realising she was going to have to postpone the viewing appointment in St Carys.

Oh God, she really didn't want to, but the discomfort was worsening. It was one thing feeling unwell in the privacy of your own home, but she couldn't bear for it to happen in someone else's. And if she'd picked up some kind of stomach bug, she wasn't going to risk being taken ill while she was out with – of all people – Ronan Byrne.

How typical, though, that she had to be feeling like this today of all days, just when he'd found a property that could be perfect . . . ow . . . *ouch*.

Disappointed, Kate climbed down from the stepladder and picked up her phone. She sent an apologetic text to Ronan explaining that she wasn't feeling well enough to view Terry's cottage but suggesting that maybe they could go and see it after work tomorrow instead.

Her phone rang less than a minute later.

'What's wrong?' said Ronan, and just hearing the concern in his voice made her catch her breath.

'I'm OK. It's just . . . stomach cramps.' As she said it, the griping sensation in her abdomen returned and Kate tightened her grip on the edge of the worktop.

'You sound as if you're in pain. You're breathing heavily.'

'I'm fine. Really.'

'Has it happened before?' He hesitated, clearly concerned. 'I mean, is it a regular thing?'

Kate winced. Her periods had always been light and painless. And yes, she and Ronan had once slept together, but it was still embarrassing that he was asking her the question. As the pain intensified, she let out a gasp. 'I don't think so.'

'Do you think it might be appendicitis?'

'I don't know!'

'Well should you call a doctor?'

'Seriously, there's no need.' She wasn't the calling-a-doctor type. 'I'll be fine. I'm just going to . . . *uhh* . . . take things easy and wait for it to pass.'

He still sounded worried. 'OK, but you take care of yourself. Call me if you need anything at all. Are you in bed now?'

Kate blushed and gripped the side of the stepladder. 'I'm just resting on the sofa.'

But by the time she'd hung up, the pain had receded, so she carried on painting, cutting in around the white kitchen units then applying an even coat of deep red to the walls between them. She still felt a bit odd, but the best way to take your mind off something like this was to keep busy.

Until the next wave of pain seized her, just as she was stretching to reach the wall above the fridge freezer.

Letting out a shriek of surprise, Kate made a grab for the top of the stepladder and felt the back of her wrist knock the tin of paint. Wobbling wildly, she lost her balance and knew the worst was about to happen. The next moment the three of them were falling through the air in what felt like cartoonish slow motion: herself, the pot of paint and the stepladder.

Something about the tone of Kate's voice had bothered Ronan after he'd hung up the phone. Was it a gut feeling, or the memory of how she'd been so dismissive of her injuries the other week when she'd single-handedly tackled that burglar? He knew she wasn't the kind to make a fuss.

He was also aware that Kate would most likely think he was mad, but that was just too bad; she was clearly in pain and far too British to get herself checked out, so he'd decided to drive over anyway.

If he was honest, he'd been looking forward to seeing her this morning – so much so that he now found he couldn't bear not to. He'd even washed and ironed his favourite white cotton shirt, the one that was an absolute pig to get the creases out of.

When he reached the house, he rang the doorbell, hoping Kate hadn't fallen asleep on the sofa and he was now waking her up.

No one came to the door, but he heard a faint noise from inside the house. He pressed the doorbell again and heard a weak cry of 'Who is it?'

Bending down, he pushed open the letter box and called out, 'It's me, Ronan. Are you OK?'

And now, with the letter box open, he was able to hear Kate more clearly. 'No, I'm not OK. Can you come round to the back of the house?'

The hairs stood up on the back of his neck; this was no-fuss Kate actually asking for help. He shouted, 'On my way,' and raced round to the side of the building. The high wooden gate was locked, but he climbed the wall and vaulted over the gate. Moments later, he arrived at the back of the property and saw that the kitchen window was open. When he reached the window, his breath caught in his throat at the sight of the bloodbath that greeted him.

'Oh thank goodness you're here.' Kate was lying on her side on the floor, clutching her stomach and clearly in agony. 'I don't know what's h-happ-happening, but something's wrong.'

Ronan clambered in through the window, jumped down from the worktop and knelt beside her, pushing the horizontal stepladder and the upturned paint pot out of the way.

'Is any of this blood or is it all paint?'

'Just paint. I haven't been stabbed.' The floor was splashed and smeared with vampire-red emulsion, as was Kate. Ronan saw the beads of perspiration on her chalk-white forehead and took out his phone.

Once he'd called 999, explained the situation and been reassured by the operator that an ambulance was on its way, his heart rate slowed down slightly. He held Kate's hand and brushed her damp hair away from her face. 'I can't believe you were painting this kitchen.'

'Thought it would distract me.' Kate exhaled with relief

as the latest pain began to recede. '*I* can't believe you drove over here.'

'I'm just glad I did.' The thought of her lying here on her own was unbearable.

She managed a faint smile. 'Me too. Sorry about your clothes.'

Ronan glanced down at his best white shirt, now ruined. 'This old thing? Don't worry, I was going to throw it out anyway.'

And Kate, evidently relieved, nodded and murmured, 'Oh, that's good.'

Just a couple of minutes later, the call handler on the other end of the phone said, 'The ambulance is pulling up outside your address now. Is the front door open so they can get in?'

'Owwww . . .' Kate screwed up her eyes as a fresh onslaught of pain made itself felt.

Please don't die, please don't die. Ronan jumped to his feet, almost slipping in a puddle of paint. 'I'll go and open the door now.'

Chapter 38

'I'm what?' Lying on the narrow stretcher in the back of the ambulance as it headed off to the hospital, Kate blinked up at the wiry female paramedic. 'I can't be. No, that's not right.'

The paramedic said, 'Remember at the house, when I asked you if you were pregnant and you said no? I didn't tell you back then, because your friend clearly didn't know.'

'He wasn't the only one.' Kate realised her teeth were chattering; she appeared to be in shock. 'OK, one of us is hallucinating here, and I really hope it's you. Because I'm definitely not pregnant.'

'Sweetheart, you are. More than that, you're in labour. This baby is coming out.'

'A *baby*? Oh my God, how can I be having a baby? Look at me!' With rising panic, Kate pointed to her stomach. 'Where is it? Where's the *bump*?'

'OK, sshh, calm down now. My sister was the same.' The paramedic gave Kate's stomach a gentle pat. 'Flat as a pancake, she was. It happens to some women. But you've got a tiny bump there, see? You must have noticed it.'

Still wondering if she was trapped in a dream, Kate took another look at the slightly swollen abdomen that had recently been the cause of her having to buy her first ever pair of size 14 jeans. She'd put it down to extra snacks. As bumps went, it wasn't remotely baby-shaped.

'I just thought I was eating more biscuits than usual.' It hadn't occurred to her to wonder why she'd developed such an appetite for custard creams and chocolate digestives.

The paramedic's voice softened. 'You really didn't know?'

'Are you serious? I still can't believe it's true.' Kate shook her head. 'I've carried on having periods.'

'Light or heavy?'

'Well, light. Lighter than usual, I suppose . . .'

'That can happen too.'

'I just put it down to the shock of losing my mum. Oh help, a *baby* . . .'

'On the bright side,' said the paramedic, 'you're being rushed to hospital with terrible stomach pains . . . but at least you're not ill!'

The next tidal wave of pain duly came along. It overtook Kate and she battled through it. When it was over, she wailed, 'Oh God, what's Ronan going to say?'

'Your friend back at the house?' They'd left Ronan to clear up the worst of the mess in the kitchen. 'Is he your boyfriend?'

'No.' Weakly Kate shook her head, unable to even begin to imagine how he might react. 'But he's the father.'

'Well, maybe it won't be so bad once he's over the shock.' The paramedic's tone was encouraging. 'He definitely cares about you; even I could see that.'

'He has a girlfriend.' A tear slid down Kate's cheek. 'She's lovely and they're perfect together. This is the last thing he needs.' She wiped her face and said with a crack in her voice, 'It's going to ruin everything.'

The bloodbath was now a light pink bath. Ronan had bundled the dust sheets into a black bin liner – thankfully they'd absorbed most of the spilt paint – and scrubbed clean as much of the kitchen as he could manage before the emulsion dried. His white shirt was a lost cause and he threw that away too. Luckily there was a line of washing pegged out in the back garden, so he was able to borrow a plain grey T-shirt that presumably belonged to Kate's grandfather. He could get the kitchen floor cleaner still if he spent another hour scrubbing and rinsing the tiles, but getting to the hospital was his priority now. He was worried sick about Kate and needed to know how she was doing. A couple of years back, he'd briefly gone out with a girl who'd owned horses, and had witnessed the terrible panic when one of them had been taken ill with peritonitis. The horse, writhing in agony on the floor of the stable, had almost died. The thought that this could be what Kate was suffering from was making him feel sick with fear.

Pulling on the grey T-shirt, closing the kitchen windows and grabbing his car keys, Ronan pulled the front door shut behind him. In twenty minutes he'd be at the hospital.

Oh God, please let Kate be all right.

The guilt had got to Sam. It was only Sunday, Annabelle's birthday was on Wednesday and he'd already gone way over the top.

Knowing that she'd always wanted to go to Venice, he'd

booked a short trip there for the two of them, partly because the distraction of being there and doing touristy things would be easier than spending time with her here.

He'd also bought far too many presents, chiefly because he couldn't bear the thought of not buying enough and seeing her look disappointed. Plus he couldn't stand the thought of Belle, in the future, saying to anyone who'd listen: 'What a tight bastard; I should have guessed. He gave me rubbish birthday presents, then he dumped me.'

Which was why he now found himself with too many items still needing to be wrapped, and not enough paper with which to do it. But he wanted to get the job done while Belle was out of the way, visiting a friend in Penzance. Which meant he needed to take a trip into the centre of St Carys.

The journey didn't take long, and miraculously there were still a few spaces in the main car park. Sam headed straight for the upmarket shop where he'd bought the first lot of wrapping paper; having paid so much for it, he'd assumed there'd be enough but had been proved wrong. And since he couldn't use less expensive paper for the remaining presents, he'd better buy two more rolls.

'Oh my God, will you look at these! Have you ever seen anything more beautiful in your life?'

Behind him in the shop, two girls were exclaiming over something. Having paid for the wrapping paper, Sam turned to see the shoes that had caught their attention.

'Gorgeous,' the second girl agreed. 'But look at the price.' She screwed up her nose. 'Who'd pay that much for a pair of shoes?'

Whereupon Sam, feeling guilty for having slightly resented

paying so much for two rolls of embossed wrapping paper, immediately thought: *Me. I would.*

Because the shoes were crystal-encrusted, spectacular and stylish, and he was pretty sure Belle would love them.

When the two girls had left the shop, he went over to look at them.

'Aren't they fantastic?' said the saleswoman. 'We've only just started selling these shoes. You can't get anything else like them in Cornwall. Angeline Jolie wears that designer, you know. They're very in demand.'

The name of the designer meant nothing to Sam, but Belle was a big fan of Angelina Jolie.

'Are they for your wife?'

'Girlfriend,' said Sam. 'Except I can't remember what size she is.'

'Well that's absolutely no problem at all.' The saleswoman spoke with the reassuring tones of someone determined that nothing was going to come between her and the sale of a pair of incredibly expensive designer shoes. 'If these don't fit, she can just bring them back and exchange them for another size.'

But was there anything more disappointing than being given something to wear that didn't fit? As he hesitated, a memory flashed into his mind of Belle once mentioning – not without satisfaction – that Clemency had bigger feet than her, which had been great when they'd been younger because it had meant Clem couldn't borrow her shoes.

Sam took out his phone and called Clem's number. 'Hi, what shoe size is Annabelle?'

'Four. Why?'

He smiled and felt himself relax, because it was just so

good to hear her voice. 'Well, I'm thinking of buying her a pair of gloves.'

'OK, I asked for that.' Clem laughed. 'But Belle's pretty fussy when it comes to shoes.'

'I think she'll like these.'

'Are they expensive?'

'Oh yes.'

'They have to be perfect, though. Where are you?'

'In the blue shop on the corner of Cliff Road. The one that sells nice things.' This was the tactful description, anyway.

'Ella's Emporium,' the saleswoman said helpfully. 'You're Sam Adams, aren't you? Hello, I'm Ella!'

'OK,' said Clem on the phone, 'I heard that. Don't let her sell you anything before I get there; the woman's a cold-eyed shark and she won't do refunds, only credit notes. Look, are you in a hurry? Because I can be with you in fifteen minutes.'

Sam said, 'That'd be great. I'll go to Paddy's and get a coffee while I'm waiting.'

He ended the call and turned to Ella. 'Clem's coming down to advise me.'

'Lovely.' The woman's fixed smile indicated that this was a less than ideal scenario. 'I can't wait for her to see them. Although you mustn't let her tell you they're too expensive,' she added with a little laugh. 'I know Clemency, and designer items have never been a priority with her. She's not a bit like Belle!'

This was confirmed twenty minutes later when Clemency arrived at the café, her hair still wet from the shower and her tanned face make-up free. She was wearing a white shirt, frayed and faded black and white stripy jeans, and lime-green flip-flops.

Sam's heart flipped too, at the sight of her.

'Have you changed your mind about finishing with Belle?' she said.

He shook his head. 'No.'

'So you're spending all this money to ease your conscience.'

'Yes.' She was wearing the clean, lemony scent he always associated with her.

'OK, you don't want to buy those shoes.'

'I need to,' said Sam. Didn't she understand?

'No, I mean I've been to see them. I called into the shop on my way here. The ones with the crystals on, right?' He nodded. 'Belle wouldn't wear those. She likes the toes to be pointier than that. And the heels aren't narrow enough. They're beautiful shoes, but not for Belle.'

'Oh,' Sam said wryly. 'Just as well I asked.'

'Sorry. But the good news is, I've seen another pair she'll like far more.'

'In the same place?'

'Better still. Different shop.'

She led the way to Mallory's, at the far end of the Esplanade, and showed him a pair of dove-grey suede stilettos lined with pale lilac leather. The toes were pointed, the heels were narrow, and as soon as he saw them, Sam knew these were the ones Belle would much prefer.

'You're right,' he said, relieved.

Clemency's eyes danced. 'I'm always right.'

The urge to kiss her had never been stronger. For a split second he wondered what would happen if he were to take her in his arms right here in the shop . . .

OK, better not.

The manageress of Mallory's presented him with the glossy

midnight-blue bag containing the shoebox. 'Are these for Belle? She's going to love them.'

Seriously, did everyone know everyone in St Carys?

'Thanks,' said Sam.

Just as well he hadn't kissed Clem.

Outside the shop once more, not wanting her to leave, he took out his keys. 'Can I give you a lift home?'

'Oh don't worry, I can walk. Now that I'm here, I'll pick up a couple of things in the chemist's.'

Sam shrugged. 'I'm in no hurry. Belle's visiting a friend in Penzance, so she's out for the day. I'm happy to wait.' If Clemency happened to be free too, would it be very wrong to invite her to join him at one of the beachfront restaurants for lunch?

'Well if you're sure. It won't take long.'

'And don't worry, I'll wait outside.'

Clemency grinned. 'Is this your way of being discreet, in case I'm buying something really embarrassing? It's OK, I just need conditioner for my hair, and more suncream.'

When they reached the chemist, Sam said, 'And I've just remembered I need razor blades.' Leaving Clemency happily opening bottles and sniffing her way through all the different brands of conditioner, he moved to the front of the shop, to the shelving where the shaving paraphernalia was on display.

Within seconds he heard one of the girls who worked there exclaim, 'Oh my God, you aren't going to *believe* this.'

A second female voice said, 'What is it?'

'Seriously. No way. This is, like, *so* mind-blowing.'

'And you're, like, *so* annoying. You know I hate it when you do this. You aren't even supposed to have your phone switched on.'

'Now you're the one being annoying. Do you want me to tell you or not?'

'Fine, then. If you must.'

The two girls were hidden from view behind the partition separating the pharmacy storage section from the rest of the shop. Sam smiled to himself at the second girl's unconvincing lack of interest; he might not have been living here for long, but in his experience this pair spent all their time gossiping, either about celebrities they'd read about in magazines or people they knew in real life.

'OK, get this. Ronan Byrne? He's only having a baby. And I mean *right now*.'

'Eh? What are you even on about? Has someone just sent you a joke? Is that it, or is there a punchline?'

'No joke! It's true, swear to God, my mum wouldn't make up something like this! Look, she sent me a text . . . They were waiting in a cubicle in A and E because Nan's had another of her turns, and this girl was brought in having a baby. Mum didn't recognise her, but she overheard one of the paramedics saying that Ronan's the father but he doesn't even know it yet . . . Apparently he was with the girl and he's got some terrible mess to clear up, but as soon as that's done he's heading over to the hospital. Oh God,' the voice gasped. 'D'you reckon the terrible mess is *Clemency*?'

'Are you kidding me? Here, let me see that text . . . Blimey! Wonder who it is? Can't be anyone we know, surely.'

'If it was nine months ago,' said the other girl, 'who was Ronan seeing then?'

There was a pause as they both frantically counted backwards. Finally the girl who'd just read the text said slowly, 'Well that would have been me.'

'Jeez. You had a lucky escape there. I mean, I know he's good-looking, but what a nightmare. It's probably someone he doesn't even remember having sex with.'

'Poor Clemency,' said the other girl. 'I can't help feeling sorry for her. She's going to be gutted.'

Chapter 39

'What's going on?' gasped Clemency as Sam confiscated her wire basket and attempted to whisk her out of the shop. Confused, she made a grab for a bottle of L'Oréal conditioner on the shelf. 'I need to buy this!'

The two girls, hearing the kerfuffle, emerged from behind the partition. Their faces fell and the blonde one said, 'Clem! Oh God, you poor thing, we're so *sorry* . . .'

Once they were back outside on the pavement, Clemency looked at Sam. 'What are they sorry about?'

Sam felt sick. He didn't want to be the one to have to tell her, but she needed to know.

'Look, I don't know how to say this. And it might not even be true.'

'Tell me, then!'

'Where's Ronan at the moment?'

'He's out showing someone a new property.' She shook her head, still baffled. 'Why?'

'OK. Well one of those girls in the shop just got a text to say there's someone over at the hospital right now having a baby. And apparently she's saying the father is . . . well, Ronan.'

'*What?*' Bafflement turned to horror. 'No, it can't be!'

'Maybe it isn't him. She might just be saying that. I'm just telling you what I heard,' said Sam.

Clemency whipped out her phone and called Ronan's number. 'What if it's true, though? Oh God.'

'But it would have happened before the two of you got together.' Sam did his best to reassure her. 'It doesn't mean he's cheated on you.'

'No reply,' said Clemency. She was breathing heavily. 'Why isn't he picking up?'

'I think he's on his way to the hospital. OK, all I know is what they said. But it sounds as if he doesn't even know yet.'

Her eyes were huge. 'This is mad.'

'I know, I'm so sorry. What a shock for you.' Sam raised his hands. 'If it's even true.'

'The way Ronan carries on, I suppose it's a miracle it's never happened before.'

'Hey, we don't know that it *has* happened yet.'

Distracted, Clemency said, 'Can you give me a lift back to my flat? I'm going to drive over to the hospital, find out what's going on.'

She was trembling, clearly shaken. 'You mustn't drive. I'll take you,' said Sam.

The moment the door opened and Kate saw Ronan standing there in disbelief, the gas and air was suddenly no longer enough.

Except this time the pain was emotional rather than physical. Plus she was still in a state of shock herself.

'I'm sorry, I'm so sorry. I swear I didn't know!' What on

earth was he thinking as he looked at her lying there with a drip in one arm, a gizmo measuring the contractions strapped to her stomach, and various other monitors beeping away? The last contraction had just receded and she put the gas and air mouthpiece down on the bed, willing him to believe her.

'I can't believe you're having a baby.' Ronan was twisting his car keys over and over in his hands; he shook his head, evidently having done the maths. 'Is . . . is it mine?'

'Yes.' It was so clearly not the answer he wanted to hear.

'But . . . we used condoms. I mean, are you *sure*?'

'I am. It can't be anyone else.' Kate felt her eyes prickle with unshed tears. 'There hasn't been anyone, not for years.'

'Oh God.'

'I know. I'm sorry.' It was hopelessly inadequate, but what else could she say? 'I had no idea.'

'It's OK, it isn't your fault.' Ronan approached the bed and said tentatively, 'Can I . . . touch your stomach?'

Kate nodded and looked down as he rested his hand on the small bump with the strap around it. 'There's not much to see. The baby's lying right at the back, close to my spine. Apparently it happens sometimes, which is why I didn't feel anything before.'

'I know, they told me. One of the doctors explained before I came in. And one of my cousins in Birmingham had the same thing a couple of years ago, didn't realise she was pregnant until a month before the birth.' He moved his hand gently across her stomach and they both felt something.

'What's that?' said Ronan.

'The start of the next contraction.' Kate braced herself. 'Oh here we go . . .'

But somehow, with Ronan at her side and holding her hand, this time it was easier to cope with. She was no longer terrified; labour was something to be dealt with, a challenge to be met. When the pain finally subsided, Ronan said, 'You're doing so well.'

'I still can't believe it's happening. Poor Clemency, she's going to be so upset.'

He looked puzzled. 'Why?'

'Oh God,' Kate said hastily, 'I know it won't make any difference to you two, not at all! But all the same, she's not going to be thrilled.'

One of the midwives came bustling in to check that everything was proceeding smoothly. 'All OK here?'

As if it could possibly be OK. But Kate put on a brave face and managed a ghost of a smile. 'Yes thanks.'

'Well that's good news. Well done. You'll get there.' The midwife's tone was encouraging. 'Once you're over the surprise, I'm sure everything'll turn out fine. Sometimes these little accidents are just meant to be!' She beamed at them both. 'Oh, and a couple of your friends are here. I've told them they can't come in, of course, what with you being a little bit busy at the moment! But they're sitting out in reception and are happy to wait.'

'Who is it?' Kate looked up at Ronan. How would anyone else know she was here?

'Handsome man, tall, brown eyes,' said the midwife. 'And a pretty, curvy girl with long wavy dark hair. Oh, she did tell me her name, it's on the tip of my tongue . . .'

Kate's heart sank as Ronan said, 'Sounds like Clem.'

'That's it,' the midwife exclaimed. 'Of course. Clemency!'

When she'd left them, Kate covered her face. 'This is awful. What's Clemency going to say?'

Ronan squeezed her hand. 'You've just discovered you're about to have a baby and you're more worried about Clem than you are about yourself?'

OK, it sounded ridiculous when he put it like that, but it was true. A tear trickled down Kate's face and she nodded. 'I don't want to cause trouble.'

'You won't.' He was shaking his head at her. 'Listen. Clem and I aren't together. We're not a couple.'

Kate stared. 'You're not? When did you break up?'

'We've never been together. It was never real. We just put on a show because Clem's sister was mocking her for not having a boyfriend. What?' said Ronan, because she was still staring at him.

'Oh, nothing. But . . . that's good, then.'

'We aren't designed to be anything more than friends, me and Clem.' He smiled slightly. 'Does that make you feel better?'

'Much. Everyone thinks you're so perfect together, though.'

'I know they do.' Ronan looked rueful. 'Honestly? Clem's brilliant and I love her to bits, but she's too noisy for me.'

The surge of relief was making Kate want to gabble. Before the next contraction came along, she blurted out, 'But if everyone thought you were a couple, that meant you couldn't see anyone else. Didn't that make things difficult?'

For a couple of seconds the beeps from the various machines were the only sounds in the room. Then Ronan looked away. 'Not difficult at all. Because there was only one girl I wanted to be with, and she wasn't interested in being with me.'

'Oh.' Ridiculously, Kate felt a twist of jealousy. 'Someone local? Anyone I know?' All of a sudden she desperately *needed* to know, because who in their right mind wouldn't want to be with Ronan Byrne? In fact, how *dare* they not be interested in him? And now here came the next contraction, building inexorably and feeling like a giant fist squeezing her stomach from the inside . . .

'Ow . . .' Kate closed her eyes, tilted her head back and reached blindly for Ronan's hand. And he helped her through it, murmuring encouragement, reassuring her that she was doing brilliantly and pressing a blissfully cool damp flannel against her perspiring forehead. Oh God, who knew a cool flannel could feel so good?

When she could speak again, Kate said, 'Who is it?'

Because she liked to torture herself, clearly.

'It is someone you know.' Ronan was gazing down into her eyes, his expression unreadable. 'Actually, it's someone who's having my baby. It's you.' As he said this, his voice quavered with emotion. 'Sorry, I know it's not what you want to hear, but you did ask. And I know what you think of me, but it won't be a problem, I promise. I'm not going to embarrass you. If we're having a baby – and we definitely appear to be having one – well, the least we can do is get along—'

'Wait!' Kate stopped him in his tracks, barely able to believe what she was hearing. 'Are you serious? Do you mean it? Are you really saying it's *me*?'

'It's always been you. Ever since that first night.' Ronan pointed to her stomach, as if she needed any reminder. '*That* night . . .'

Joy was bubbling up inside her. 'So all this time . . . all these months . . . I've been wishing and wishing it could be me, and it *was* me?'

Ronan did a double-take. 'You wanted it to be you? Really? Why didn't you say?'

'Because I didn't imagine you'd want anything more to do with me after what happened.' Kate's skin prickled with shame at the memory – having given him such a hard time that night, she knew now that she'd overreacted. Ronan had ended his brief relationship with Laura beforehand; it wasn't his fault the poor girl had chosen to stand outside his flat reciting her own poetry. 'I mean, why would you?'

'Because you got to me,' Ronan said simply. 'I mean it. I've never felt this way about anyone before. You were everything I'd ever wanted. But I messed up.' Abruptly his dark eyes filled with tears. 'You have no idea . . . Oh God, this is incredible . . . and now we're having a baby . . . an actual *baby*. Come here.'

For the next couple of minutes they kissed and hugged each other, laughing and crying together, until the midwife returned to catch them in mid-kiss and said with a grin, 'Well this is all very romantic, but I have to say your friend Clemency is close to bursting with curiosity out there in the waiting room.' She turned to Ronan. 'So if you wanted to pop out and see her, while I quickly examine Kate, I'm sure she would appreciate it.'

'I suppose I'd better.' Ronan gave Kate's hand a squeeze as he prepared to go and do the necessary deed. 'Wouldn't want her to burst.'

'So this isn't a joke?' said Clemency. 'It's really happening?'

Ronan's face ached from smiling; the last hour had to rank among the most surreal of his life, and now it was also one of the happiest. He gave his aching muscles a rest for a moment and nodded. 'It really is.'

'Wow. And she didn't know she was pregnant?'

'No clue. Complete surprise.'

'What a disaster! I can't believe you're taking it so well. I had no idea you and Kate had even . . . you know, *done* it.' Clemency's tone was accusing. 'You didn't tell me.'

She was incorrigible. Ronan's mouth twitched. 'Believe it or not, I don't tell you everything.'

'And now you're about to have a baby, completely out of the blue. But what I don't get is, you're *smiling.*'

'I've been in love with Kate all this time. I thought she wasn't interested in me. There was a mutual misunderstanding, but it's all sorted out now.' The grin spread over his face once more. 'OK, we didn't plan this, but I really think it's the best thing that could have happened.'

The penny dropped. 'So is that why you were happy to go along with us pretending to be a couple? Because you weren't interested in anyone else if you couldn't have Kate?'

'Spot on. Weird, isn't it?'

'Ha,' said Clemency, 'I did wonder about that. All I can say is, you must have it bad. Oh, I'm so thrilled for you!' She threw her arms around him and he embraced her in return.

'I'm going to have a baby,' said Ronan. 'Imagine.'

'Josephine's going to be over the moon – it's all she's ever wanted! You should call her,' Clemency declared. 'And Marina . . . she'll be thrilled too.'

As she said it, they both heard an escalating scream, the primal cry of a woman in labour with not long to go.

Further up the corridor, the door to Kate's room was pulled open and the midwife popped her head out, beckoning to Ronan. 'Come along now, Dad,' she called cheerfully. 'We're just getting to the good bit! You don't want to miss it, do you?'

Chapter 40

Twenty minutes later, he was there to witness the miracle of his daughter being born. Having slithered into the world, she kicked her tiny legs and let out an indignant wail, and Ronan felt his heart swell with unimaginable amounts of love and pride. From now on, he knew, life would never be the same again.

Until that moment, he'd always thought cutting an umbilical cord would be completely gross, but now he found himself stepping up and doing it with a flourish. Amazing, not gross at all.

'She's a beauty!' exclaimed the midwife, deftly wiping the squalling baby down with a towel before placing her, skin to skin, in Kate's arms.

'Oh my God.' Ronan's eyes were suddenly damp. 'It's a baby. We've made a whole new human being, and she's perfect.'

'And to think when I woke up this morning I was excited because I thought I might be buying a house. Oh, just look at her,' Kate marvelled. 'How can she be so gorgeous?'

'Easy.' Sitting on the edge of the bed, Ronan kissed her. 'She's got you for a mother.'

The midwife said brightly, 'I don't suppose you've got a name yet?'

'No name.' Ronan shook his head. 'No cot, no clothes, no nappies . . . nothing.' In a daze, he looked at his watch and saw that it was almost three o'clock.

Twenty minutes later, mother and baby had been cleaned up and Clemency was briefly allowed into the delivery room.

'Oh!' She hugged Kate, then Ronan, then gazed adoringly at the baby. 'She looks like both of you! Ronan, she has your eyes! And she was in there all this time, hiding from us all! Just like you two have been hiding how you feel about each other.' She shook her head. 'I'm so happy for you both. It's like the best kind of miracle. God, imagine if it happened to me – I wouldn't know what to do. I've never even changed a nappy before!'

Ronan looked at Kate, who said, 'I've never changed a nappy before either.'

He shrugged. 'Nor me.'

Oh well, how hard could it be?

'Wow. Poor you,' Clemency told the solemn-faced baby in Kate's arms. 'Got yourself a couple of learners, by the looks of things. Where are you even going to live, sweetheart? Have they thought about that yet?'

'We'll figure things out as we go along,' said Ronan. 'I'm sure we'll manage. Meanwhile, if you wanted to do us a favour . . .'

'Of course! Anything! Well, so long as it's not changing a nappy.' Clemency reached cautiously for the piece of paper he was holding out to her.

'We've made a bit of a list . . . except there's probably some stuff missing . . . but the shops close soon and anything's better than nothing.'

She nodded. 'OK, no problem. We can definitely do that.'

'Thanks.' Relieved, Ronan took out his phone. 'And meanwhile, I can work out how I'm going to break the news to my mums.'

'We'd better be quick then.' Clemency broke into a grin. 'Because I definitely want to be back here when Josephine turns up.'

A busy out-of-town supermarket on a Sunday afternoon might not be most people's idea of a good time, but Sam was more than happy to be here. Just this morning he'd met up with Clemency to look at overpriced designer stilettos. Now, a few short but eventful hours later, here they were in a designated – and quite new to him – baby and toddler aisle, buying something called Sudocrem. Which sounded delicious but probably wasn't.

And Clemency no longer had a boyfriend.

Well, she hadn't had one before, but he hadn't known that. Now he did.

'OK, nappies.' She was busy consulting the list in her hand, mentally checking off the items they'd thrown into the trolley so far. 'Babygros. Baby wipes. Muslins. Changing mat. Oh, we need little T-shirts! And socks! Sam, which colour? These? Or these?' She held them up to show him, clearly torn. 'Look how gorgeous they are! Shall we get the ones with the ducklings on, or these yellow ones with the stars? How can anyone choose? Let's have both.' She tossed them into the trolley and said happily, 'You can never have too many teeny-tiny socks!'

'Of course you can't.' Sam smiled, because Clemency's excitement was contagious and he really wanted to kiss her.

Better not.

Next to them, a married couple smiled too. The wife, who was buying cans of powdered milk, said, 'Oh, the socks are adorable! Isn't it a treat, though, being able to come out shopping in peace? Our baby always cries non-stop when we bring him in here, so my mum offered to look after him for a couple of hours. I just said to my husband, it feels like we're out on a date!'

And before Clemency had a chance to open her mouth, Sam said, 'Oh yes, that's exactly how it feels.' He rested his arm affectionately on Clemency's shoulder. 'We said that too, didn't we?'

When they arrived back at the hospital an hour later, Clemency felt her hormones go into overdrive. Ronan and Kate were now even more visibly in love with their surprise daughter. The baby was gazing intently up at each of them in turn, imprinting the faces and voices of her parents on her brain.

And Clemency, who never cried, felt unexpectedly emotional, because what they were experiencing was so unique and infinitely precious. During their brief exchange with the couple in the supermarket, Sam had pretended they were new parents too. He'd done it just for fun, and probably hadn't given it another thought since. What he couldn't begin to understand was how it had made her feel. Just for those couple of minutes she'd been able to pretend – to a select audience of two – that it was true.

But it wasn't, was it? And she'd just felt so ambushed with sadness because it never could be.

'This is brilliant.' Ronan was looking through everything they'd brought back with them. 'Seriously, thanks so much.'

'Our pleasure,' said Sam. 'We had fun, didn't we?'

'We did.' Clemency nodded and forced herself to smile. OK, she needed to get a grip. This wasn't about her; it was about Ronan and Kate, and the seismic change that had just rocked their lives.

Ronan was waiting outside in the car park two hours later when Josephine arrived. Once she'd parked and jumped out of the car, he hugged her tightly. 'You just wait until you see her. She's so beautiful. This is the happiest day of my life.'

Josephine held him at arm's length. 'You can't be as happy as me. It's like a miracle. I'm a grandmother!' She paused, then said, 'Is Marina here yet?'

Ronan shook his head. 'No. I phoned her a little while ago and told her what's happened. She's coming over later, at around eight. I wanted you to be the first to meet our daughter. Because you're my mum and I love you . . . well, you know what I'm trying to say.'

Visibly moved, Josephine gazed up at him and managed an emotional smile. Ronan hugged her again, needing her to understand that of course he loved Marina too, but Josephine had been the one who'd raised him, and just between themselves, she would always be the number one granny.

351

Chapter 41

Celebrating her birthday in style had always been Belle's favourite thing. Birthdays were for being spoilt and the centre of attention, for fresh flowers and breakfast champagne, for laughter and fun and the promise of a delicious day ahead.

And so far, she'd been doing an Oscar-worthy job of pretending she was loving every minute. But how much longer could she keep it up, when inside she felt like one of those cans of toy snakes that just sit there and sit there . . .

Until they explode.

'This is so lovely.' She gestured to the bed, covered in opened cards and presents, and discarded wrapping paper. 'You've bought me far too much. These shoes are . . . amazing.'

It just went to show what a perfect boyfriend Sam was; so many men wouldn't have had the first clue that the dove-grey suede stilettos would be her favourites.

'OK, confession time.' Sam's tone was rueful. 'I can't take the credit for those. Clem helped me choose them. In fact, she told me to buy them for you.'

Ah well. 'That's even more impressive, then. Knowing the kind of shoes Clem usually goes for.'

But he had been generous. He'd bought her a set of Tom Ford make-up, a perfect white cashmere sweater and a huge bottle of her favourite scent . . . not to mention the trip to Venice . . .

Oh Venice, and no ordinary hotel either. They were booked into a suite at the Cipriani on Giudecca Island, with its ethereal views over the lagoon. It was somewhere she'd always longed to stay, but it had never happened before now. And knowing that, Sam had arranged the ultimate mini-break because he was a thoughtful person who wanted to give her the best possible gift.

Belle's throat tightened once more. Who wouldn't want to visit Venice and stay at the Cipriani with Sam Adams? Anyone who didn't had to be out of their mind.

Well, either that or . . .

'Hey, you haven't opened all your cards yet.'

She blinked. 'Yes I have.'

'You missed one.' Sam nudged the crumpled duvet to one side to reveal the pale yellow envelope tucked beneath it. He dropped it into her lap. 'There you go. I think that's the last one.'

Belle hesitated, knowing perfectly well who it was from. Wasn't that why she'd tried to push it out of sight?

But she couldn't not open it, could she?

Slowly she unstuck the flap and slid out the card, ducking her head slightly so that her hair fell forwards and Sam couldn't see her face.

It was an ordinary enough birthday card; not a comedy one, just a simple painted view of a beach similar to

353

Mariscombe Bay. Flipping it open, Belle saw what was written inside.

Hope you have a lovely birthday! Verity xx

The words were as innocuous as you could wish for. The tension expanded inside her ribcage as Sam said, 'Who's it from?' and she passed the card over to him. Her skin prickled as she imagined Verity leaning against her, moving closer and murmuring aloud the words written in the card.

And now she was able to hear them with unbearable clarity, as if Verity were here with her right now.

Hope you have a lovely birthday, my darling . . .

'Oh, from Verity. That was nice of her.' Sam added the card to the little pile on the bedside table. 'How about a Bellini, then, to celebrate Venice? Sound good?'

Belle knew she couldn't speak, was physically incapable of uttering a word. The pressure-cooker sensation was building unstoppably inside her chest, her mouth was dry and she was teetering on the brink of saying the unsayable.

Because once it was out there, that was it; there was no going back. She was so afraid of what might be about to happen, but was it really physically possible to carry on living a lie?

'Hey.' Sam rested his hand on hers and leant forward in an effort to see her face. 'What's up?'

Belle shrugged helplessly and managed to croak, 'Nothing.'

'Come on. Are you OK?'

She nodded. 'Yes.' Then the nod became a shake. 'No, not really.'

His expression changed. 'What's wrong? Are you ill?'

Oh God, poor Sam. He'd been through hell with Lisa dying. Belle said hastily, 'I'm fine, it's nothing like that. It's just . . . just . . .'

Sam waited. Outside the bedroom, happy children were laughing excitedly as they made their way down to the beach. Overhead, a seagull let out a mocking cry. Belle raised her gaze to look at Sam, and felt herself begin to tremble.

Did she have the courage to go through with this?

'You can tell me,' Sam said steadily.

'I don't know if I can.'

'Hey. Will you feel better once you've said it?'

'Maybe. Not sure.' She forced herself to hold his gaze. 'I'm scared.'

He shook his head slightly. 'One thing you've never been is a coward.'

Oh if only he knew. A tear rolled down Belle's cheek. 'I am, though.'

'Just say it,' Sam prompted. 'You've started, so you may as well finish.'

The tip of her little finger was resting on the edge of the birthday card from Verity. Taking strength from the contact, Belle mentally braced herself. 'I'm sorry. There's someone else.'

Then she had to close her eyes, because the look of shocked disbelief on Sam's face was just too much to bear.

'You mean there's someone else you think you like? Or someone else you're already seeing?'

'That one. The second one. I'm so sorry.' God, poor Sam,

what must this be like for him? She was about to break his heart and he really didn't deserve it.

'You've been seeing someone else. For how long?'

'Not long. But it's . . . the real thing.'

'You're in love?'

He was putting on a brave face, but how he must be feeling inside didn't bear thinking about. Slowly Belle said, 'Yes.'

Oh please don't let him cry.

He nodded slowly. 'So what you're saying is, you and me are over.'

'I am. But listen, you didn't do anything wrong. It's not you, it's me. You're perfect, Sam . . . please, you mustn't blame yourself. Anyone would be lucky to have you.'

'Thanks.' His jaw was taut but he was holding up emotionally. 'So who is he?'

'What?' Belle's stomach tensed up, because now came the even more difficult bit.

'What's his name?' said Sam. 'Do I know him?'

Was this how it felt to experience extreme stage fright? Belle glanced down at the birthday card, then back at Sam.

'You do know them. But it isn't a he.' And finally the words were tumbling out. 'It's a she, and I love her more than I can say. It's Verity.'

Stunned, Sam took in what Annabelle had just told him. One minute he'd been battling to conceal his joy, because being told their relationship was over was the answer to all his prayers . . .

And now this. Talk about a double whammy.

It was a shock, but it also explained a lot. A hell of a lot,

356

in fact. So many questions that had been inwardly puzzling him for months were now answered.

Of course. It all made complete sense, once you knew the truth.

'Hey,' he said gently, because more tears were now slipping down Annabelle's thin tanned cheeks. 'It's OK, it really is.'

He wanted to laugh with relief, to tell her this was fantastic news and he couldn't be more delighted, but he also knew that wasn't what she'd want to hear. Belle still had her pride; she wouldn't be remotely happy to know he'd been waiting for his chance to escape their relationship.

Besides, this was about her, not him. And it had taken her all her courage to tell him the truth. That was all that mattered for now.

'I'm s-sorry,' hiccuped Annabelle.

'No need.' He passed her a tissue from the box on the bedside table. 'It's fine. Does anyone else know?'

'No one at all.'

'Have there been other girls? I mean, before this?' Even as he asked the question, Sam knew instinctively that there hadn't.

'Never.' She shook her head. 'I was always too scared. I didn't want to be gay. I tried so hard to make the feelings go away.'

'Must have been difficult to do,' said Sam.

'It was. But I put on a good show.' There was the flash of pride in her green eyes. 'Nobody ever guessed. I mean, you never suspected a thing, did you? I know you didn't!'

And again, Sam knew how much it meant to her to hear the right answer. Even though their sex life had never felt entirely right. He hadn't guessed the reason for it, but the emotional distance had always incontrovertibly been there. Sleeping with Annabelle had never been comparable to the easy intimacy he and Lisa had shared. He'd wondered if he might be the one at fault, if maybe losing Lisa had resulted in him inadvertently putting up mental barriers that just needed more time to be brought down.

Now he knew it hadn't been him after all.

Well that was a relief.

Aloud, he said, 'You're right. I didn't suspect a thing.'

'See? I knew it. I was the perfect girlfriend. And I know I keep saying it, but I am sorry.' Impulsively, she took his hand. 'First you had to lose Lisa. And now you've lost me too.'

Sam nodded gravely. 'I'll get over it in time.' Then, terrified that he might burst out laughing, he said, 'You're doing something very brave, you know.'

'I don't feel brave. I'm scared. But I can't live a lie any more.' She searched his face. 'All these years I've felt so ashamed . . . but I shouldn't, should I?'

'Of course not.' He felt incredibly sorry for her, so desperate her whole life to fit in with her friends that she'd denied her own true feelings and sexuality.

'I've always envied people who are brave enough to be themselves, but I was just too terrified to do it because I was convinced my friends wouldn't want to know me any more. Except if they don't, that's their problem, isn't it? Not mine. I need to be me and I want to be happy.' She raised her chin. 'And Verity makes me happier than I've ever been before in my life.'

'Good for you.' Sam gave her a hug. 'You're doing the right thing. I think you're going to be fine.'

She leant back and gazed up at him. 'Sam, you're amazing. You're taking this so well. I've broken your heart and you're being so good about it.'

There was no way he could tell her about his feelings for Clem, not right now. He said, 'I want you to be happy.'

'Thank you. And after you gave me all these lovely presents too. I do feel bad about that.' She looked at him. 'Do you want them back?'

She was stroking the shoebox as she said it. Sam smiled. 'Don't worry, you can keep them. They wouldn't fit me.'

'There's this, too.' She picked up the envelope containing the details of their trip to Venice. 'Could you get your money refunded, do you think?'

'No.'

'Not even through the travel insurance?'

Sam imagined calling the insurance company and explaining that the reason he was unable to go on holiday with his girlfriend was because she'd come out as a lesbian. Then again, presumably the people who worked in insurance claims departments heard all sorts of wild excuses.

He shook his head. 'It doesn't matter.'

'Oh, the Hotel Cipriani though. It's such a waste.' Annabelle gazed longingly at the booking form. 'If I can get a flight for Verity, could I take her with me instead? No, no, I'm sorry, forget it!' She covered her mouth apologetically. 'I can't believe I said that, I'm so thoughtless. As if you haven't suffered enough.'

With great difficulty, Sam managed to keep a straight face. For her sake he had to let Annabelle believe he was at least partly heartbroken. In a brave, stiff-upper-lip, Gregory Peck kind of way, of course.

He shrugged. 'It's your birthday, your trip. You can take whoever you like.'

'You're such a lovely man.' She beamed and exhaled with relief. 'You deserve to be so happy. I really hope you find someone who's perfect for you.'

Sam said, 'Thanks. I hope so too.'

Chapter 42

Josephine smiled to herself; she couldn't stop watching the two of them together. Except it wasn't the two of them, was it? They were three now, a family unit that had come about completely unexpectedly but at the same time in the most perfect way.

Three days ago, out of nowhere, Izzy Byrne had arrived in the world, and all their lives had been changed as a result, dramatically and for ever. It was a magical experience, witnessing the newly created family and the palpable connection between them. Her heart swelling with love for them all, Josephine hung back and watched the way Ronan and Kate were together, and the way they radiated absolute happiness.

The surprise aspect of the birth had meant Kate staying in hospital for three days, but this morning she'd been discharged and now Ronan had brought her to Victoria Street to see Terry's traditional whitewashed cottage for herself.

Initially, of course, the plan had been for Kate to buy the property and live in it alone. Now, if she liked and approved of the cottage, the three of them could be moving in together.

'Well? What do you think?' said Ronan. He was holding the baby in his arms, smoothing the dark fluffy whorls of her hair as he stroked the tiny head. He looked at Kate, who broke into a grin.

'You know what I think. You knew from the first moment you saw this place. It's just perfect.'

'Really?' He looked relieved. 'I mean *really* really?'

Kate gestured around the living room with its sunny aspect and sea view. 'It feels like home already.'

Ronan leant over and kissed her. 'Terry'll be glad too. And it's a cash sale, so we can get it wrapped up in no time. Are you paying attention?' He addressed Izzy as she gazed unblinkingly up at him. 'This is going to be your new home, so you have to approve too. Oh, you do? That's brilliant, great to hear.'

'What's going to happen to your flat?' said Josephine.

'Not sure yet. I was going to sell it, but Kate thinks I should probably rent it out for now, see how things go. I already know a client who might be interested, so I'll give him a call.'

In her pocket, Josephine heard the *ting* that announced the arrival of a new text message on her phone. She looked at the question on the screen: *Does Kate like the cottage?* and deftly typed back: *She loves it. All systems go.*

Then she looked from Ronan to Kate, feeling a leap of excitement in her chest, and said in a voice that was deceptively casual, 'Actually, I know someone else who'd be very interested too.'

Sam arrived back in St Carys on Saturday afternoon. Before leaving with Verity on the afternoon of her birthday, Annabelle had been adamant that she should be the one who spoke to Clemency about the situation. 'I don't want her hearing about it from anyone else,' she'd explained. 'I have to tell her myself. It's important. Promise me you won't say anything until we're back from Venice. I'll do it then, OK?'

And Sam had promised, whilst wondering how she expected him to explain away the fact that he hadn't gone to Venice after all. Until, fortuitously, an urgent meeting with a Swiss client had needed to be arranged, and he'd solved the problem by flying to Zurich for a few days instead.

Easier all round.

An hour after his return, he heard a taxi pull up outside the apartment. From the balcony he watched as Annabelle climbed out, followed by Verity. Annabelle's case was lifted out of the boot and the two women embraced like good friends until the driver had his back to them, when the look between them changed to one of love and lust, and Verity kissed Annabelle – briefly – on the mouth.

Moments later, Verity slid back into the cab and they gazed at each other with naked longing as the vehicle pulled away.

When he opened the front door, Sam said, 'Welcome back. Did you have a good time?'

'The best. The very best.' Annabelle was glowing, happy but still clearly apprehensive. 'Thank you so much. I'm sorry, these last few days must have been awful for you. How have you been, Sam? Bearing up?'

He nodded. 'Oh yes. I'll be fine.'

Her eyes darted past him to check that no one else was in the flat. 'You haven't told anyone, have you? Especially not Clem.'

'I haven't told a soul.'

'She sent me a text asking how the Cipriani was. At least I didn't have to lie about that. I sent her photos so she could see how fantastic it was. Oh God, sorry again.' She shook her head guiltily. 'Now I'm just rubbing salt into the wound. Look, I'm only back to pick up some more clothes and things. I've booked a room at the Mariscombe, just for tonight, then once everything's sorted out here, me and Verity are heading back to London. When we have an address, could you pack up the rest of my stuff and arrange to have it sent up?'

Sam nodded. 'Of course I will.'

'And you promise you won't wreck everything in a fit of jealousy? I won't open the packing boxes and find all my clothes hacked to bits? Oh, it's OK, I know you wouldn't do anything like that.' Annabelle clapped a hand to her chest, almost teary with gratitude. 'You're a good person and in return I did this to you. I broke your heart and I still feel just terrible about it, but you're being amazing because you're *you*. Sam, all I want is for you to be happy again. And it'll happen, I promise. One day it will!'

Sam made a split-second decision. Really, though, wasn't it just *the* most perfect opportunity of all time? If this wasn't the moment to do it, he didn't know when would be.

'What?' said Annabelle. 'Why are you looking at me like that? Oh no, Sam no, *please* don't beg me to take you back . . .'

'So you see, it was just one of those things that hits you out of the blue. Fate sat us next to each other on that plane. I wasn't looking for it or wanting it to happen, but it did. And nothing could ever possibly come of it.' Sam shook his head at the still-vivid memory in his mind. 'I knew that from the word go. I was married. Lisa no longer knew who I was, but she was still my wife. This girl was a complete stranger I knew I'd never see again. And all we did during that plane journey was talk. About other things . . . life . . . whatever. But there was this connection between us. Such an incredible connection . . . seriously, I couldn't even begin to describe it. I'd felt it when I first met Lisa, and now it was happening again. Except it couldn't, because I wasn't free. But she didn't know that, this girl on the plane, because I couldn't bear to tell her. Once we'd landed and were heading our separate ways, she gave me her business card.' He paused, reliving the moment, the expression in Clem's grey eyes indelibly imprinted on his brain. 'I threw it in a bin without looking at it. And when she caught up with me later in the taxi queue, I told her I was married. Then I walked away.'

Annabelle's own eyes were wide. 'Oh Sam. Oh Sam, that's the saddest thing I ever heard. It's like something out of a *film*. And this happened how long ago?'

'Almost three and a half years.'

'When did Lisa die?'

'Three weeks later.'

'And you weren't able to contact the other girl?'

'No. Not that I wanted to, of course. Not back then.'

'Of course not. Oh, but how unbearable. That was it, game over, you had no way of ever finding her. And you never saw her again.' There were tears of sympathy shimmering in Annabelle's eyes.

'I didn't see her again,' said Sam. 'Until earlier this year.'

Annabelle's mouth opened and she sat up a little straighter. 'Really? You mean *she* found *you*? But . . . how?'

'She didn't find me.' Sam felt a muscle begin to twitch

in his jaw. 'It was just a complete coincidence. Like going on holiday and bumping into someone you went to school with fifteen years ago.'

'You didn't tell me about any of this.' She didn't sound angry, merely mystified.

'I know I didn't,' said Sam. 'It seemed easier not to. And nothing happened between us. Again.' He needed to emphasise that. 'I was seeing you, wasn't I?'

'So how was it, meeting up with this other girl again? Were the feelings still there?'

'Kind of.' He paused. 'Well, yes.'

'And how did she feel about you? The same?'

Sam hesitated, then nodded and reiterated, 'But nothing happened. Because neither of us would do that to you.'

'Oh my God, I know who it is! I've just realised!' Clapping her hand over her mouth, Annabelle let out a squeal of triumph. 'It's Sylvie, isn't it? Sylvie Margason!'

Who? A split second later, the mental image came to him. Tall, blonde Sylvie had been at school with Annabelle and now worked as the events manager at Mariscombe House; he'd briefly met her on a couple of occasions and she hadn't attempted to disguise her interest in him.

She was an attractive girl.

But sadly, the wrong girl.

'It's not Sylvie.'

'Oh.'

Encouraged by the fact that she looked disappointed, Sam took a deep breath and said, 'It's Clem.'

Talk about a Trojan horse.

On her way home from work, Clemency had answered

366

a call from Belle, who announced cheerfully, 'Hi, we're back! Are you at home if I pop over in twenty minutes? Might have a little surprise for you!'

Having happily agreed, Clem had reached the flat and jumped into the shower. Now, wrapped in her white cotton dressing gown, she was tugging a brush through her tangled wet hair.

The moment she answered the door and saw the expression on Belle's face, she knew the little surprise wasn't going to be one of those brightly painted Venetian masks you never quite knew what to do with, or a chunky necklace made of Murano glass.

'All this time,' said Belle. 'All this time you've been lying to me. And why am I even surprised? It's pretty much par for the course.'

Erghhh . . .

'What? I don't know what you're talking about.' That was the trouble with a really narrow hallway: you were forced to back away up the stairs and ended up looking defensive. Because of course she knew what her sister was talking about; it couldn't conceivably be anything else.

Although how Belle had got to hear about it, God only knew.

'You and Sam, three and a half years ago, cosying up together on a plane. Surely you haven't forgotten.'

Clemency shook her head. 'There was no cosying. We sat next to each other. That's all.'

'Oh, but I think it meant quite a lot more than that. Sam's told me *all* about it.'

OK, was Sam completely mad? Had he been drunk? Whatever had possessed him to do such a thing?

'All this time,' Belle sounded as if she were chewing ice chips, 'you've been lying to me, keeping this romantic little secret between you, laughing at me behind my back.'

'We haven't been laughing,' Clemency said at once. 'Trust me, it hasn't been funny. And we haven't done anything wrong, either. *All this time*,' she echoed Belle's accusation, 'we've done *nothing*.'

Belle's eyes were like lasers. 'Of course you haven't. Because you're not that sort of girl.'

'Exactly!'

'Except you've never forgiven me for sleeping with Pierre. All these years, it's niggled away at you. I bet you've always secretly wanted to even things up and get back at me for that.'

Oh good grief. 'Because of what you did with Pierre? Do you *seriously* believe that?'

'You know what? This is so typical of you.' Belle's voice rose. 'You've always thought you were better than me . . . more popular than me . . . more fun than me! And when I met Sam, I was so happy because he was perfect and he was *mine* and he wasn't *yours*. But now you've ruined all that, because this whole time, you and Sam have had this so-called amazing connection, this massive secret you've been sharing between you, which means you think he loves you more than he ever loved me.'

'I don't think that,' Clemency protested. Hopefully Belle wasn't about to whip out a portable lie-detector.

'Oh come off it, of course you do. All this time you've been feeling smug, because yet again you've beaten me . . . and it's just *not fair*.'

Clemency's heart was thudding against her ribs; she still

368

couldn't work out why this was happening. Had Sam already ended the relationship? Aloud, she said, 'I haven't beaten you. And nothing's happened between me and Sam, because I wouldn't break my promise. Tell me what went wrong in Venice.'

'Nothing went wrong in Venice! It was perfect!'

'Well it doesn't sound like nothing went wrong. If everything was so perfect, why would Sam have told you about—'

'Because I didn't go to Venice with Sam,' Belle shouted, her fists clenched at her sides.

'What?' Clemency hadn't been expecting that. Stunned, she said, 'So where have you been, then?'

'I went to Venice. Sam went to Zurich.'

'You mean you're not together any more? He finished with you?' OK, mixed feelings now, because if Sam had dumped Belle on her actual birthday, that was a terrible thing to have done. How *could* he have been so cruel?

Belle was studying her intently. 'He really hasn't told you, has he? I thought he might, but he hasn't. Sam didn't finish with me.' She shook her head with a mixture of pride and what seemed like defiance . . . or possibly terror. 'I finished with Sam.'

'But, but . . . *why*?' Was this a joke? Clemency stared at her in disbelief.

'Because I love someone else.'

Someone else.

Talk about surreal. Clemency said, 'Are you serious?' Because how could there possibly *be* someone else? Oh God, unless Belle was talking about Ronan. Please don't let her mean him! Had she flown off to Venice and somehow

369

managed to convince herself that the horror of unexpected fatherhood would send Ronan into her arms instead?

Aloud, she blurted out, 'Ronan's madly in love with Kate!'

Belle's eyebrows went up. 'So? Who cares about them? I'm madly in love with Verity.'

Silence, broken only by the sound of Belle's rapid breathing. She was standing there wide-eyed, looking as if she couldn't quite believe what she'd just said.

Clemency, feeling much the same way, stared back at her. 'Really? You mean . . . *Verity?*'

In case she'd just blurted out the wrong name by mistake.

But Belle was nodding. 'I do. I love her. She's my girlfriend. I was always too scared to say it before, but I'm saying it now. I prefer girls. I'm a lesbian, and don't you dare laugh at me.'

Laugh . . .?

'But I—'

'Don't you *dare.*' Her voice trembling with emotion, Belle pointed an accusing finger directly at her.

My sister is gay. And angry. Clemency spread her arms and said in disbelief, 'Why would I laugh?'

'Oh, I can't possibly imagine why! Maybe because you've spent your whole life laughing at me? Because you've always thought you were superior to me? Because every single tiny thing that's ever gone wrong in my life has been an opportunity for you to make fun of me!' Now that Belle had got started, her voice was spiralling higher and higher. 'Like the time I got chewing gum in my hair at the school concert . . . and the time we were on holiday in Miami and you told me the American abbreviation for condominium was condom . . . and when I dived into the pool at Jacintha's

370

party and my bikini top flew off . . . every single time you laughed at me and made me feel stupid, but this time I'm not going to let it happen!'

Dismayed, Clemency said, 'I would *never* laugh—'

'Shut up, don't lie, it's what you always do,' Belle howled. 'Like two years ago when I went out on that one date with Hugo Mainwaring and he called me a frosty bitch. He told everyone I was frigid and of course you thought it was hilarious. You taunted me about that—'

'How?' demanded Clemency. '*How* did I taunt you?'

'Oh my God, are you seriously pretending you don't remember? Every time you saw me, you'd start singing "Let It Go" . . . or that "Build a Snowman" song . . . or "Love Is an Open Door".'

Seriously, what was she on about? In bewilderment, Clemency said, 'The songs from *Frozen*?'

'Exactly,' Belle spat back. 'You taunted me non-stop, for weeks.'

Frozen . . . frigid . . . Realisation dawned.

Oh for goodness' sake.

'That wasn't me making fun of you,' Clemency cried in disbelief. 'I loved *Frozen*. I sang those songs all the time, whether you were there or not! It drove Ronan so mad in the office, he threatened to tape my mouth shut. I wasn't doing it to taunt you – I was singing them because I couldn't get them out of my head because I loved them so much!'

'Yeah, right, well it's never going to happen again. Because I'm *proud* of who I am.' Belle jabbed a manicured finger at her own chest. 'I'm me, I'm gay and you're not going to make me feel inferior to you any more! Oh, and if you've been thinking this means you can have Sam, think again.

Because I bet you were, weren't you? Were you expecting me to tell you it's fine, help yourself, he's all yours? Well, I'm not going to! Why should I? No way, d'you hear me? You made a promise and I'm holding you to it. *You're not having him.*'

Twenty minutes had passed since Belle had slammed the door on her way out of the flat. Twenty minutes, but it felt more like twenty hours. Lying on the bed, Clemency listened to the sound of her phone buzzing as it squirmed its way, on silent mode, around her glass-topped bedside table.

Picking it up and glancing at the caller ID, Clemency wondered why on earth Belle would think anyone who'd ignored seven calls from their sister might suddenly decide to answer the eighth.

She switched the phone off, dropped it on to the bed and covered her eyes. *Ow*, sore. Actually, really sore . . . they were swollen and puffy and as fragile as a one-ply tissue.

The doorbell started ringing again and she whispered, 'Stop it,' because this was unbearable. When Belle gave up a few minutes later, Clemency let the tears flow once more, despising her own weakness. Out of curiosity, she reached for her phone and switched on the front-facing camera so she could view her own reflection on the screen.

God, talk about a horrific sight. Her eyelids looked even worse than they felt, the whites of her eyes were spectacularly bloodshot and her face was blotchy and tight.

So this was what proper crying did to you. No wonder she didn't go in for it. What a state.

Oh, but once it started, however were you meant to make it stop? Where did all the tears come from? And how many did she have left? If she kept on going and didn't stop, would she eventually wither to a husk, expire from dehydration and—

CRASHHHHH.

The almighty noise came from the bathroom, and Clemency jackknifed up off the bed as a cacophony of glass jars and plastic bottles tumbled off the windowsill and landed in the sink. Which meant either a seagull had flown in through the open window, or . . .

'*Ow*,' squawked Belle amid a fresh round of clattering, and Clemency heard the bathroom door open. The next moment her sister appeared in the bedroom doorway. 'OK, can I just tell you something? Nobody needs forty half-used bottles of shampoo and conditioner and shower gel cluttering up their windowsill. It's just stupid.'

'How did you get into my bathroom?' Clemency demanded.

'I bounced really hard on a trampoline.' Belle paused. 'There's a window cleaner at the end of the road. I made him lend me his ladder.'

'You don't like climbing ladders.'

'I know, but sometimes when people refuse to answer their phones or open their front doors, we aren't left with much choice. You look awful, by the way.'

'I know.'

'I mean it. Really terrible. I look quite pretty when I cry, but you don't at all. You're a *mess*.'

'Thank you,' said Clemency. There wasn't even any point in trying to shoot her stop-it-now hate-rays; her eyelids were too swollen to let the hatred through.

'Now I know why you don't cry,' said Belle.

Clemency shrugged. It wasn't the reason, but it would do.

'I've never even thought about it before, but I can't remember the last time,' Belle went on.

'Don't let it bother you.'

'No, really. You never do. When was it?' Belle frowned, trying to recall the occasion. 'OK, got it. When your grandad died, not long after I first met you. You were really upset about losing him.'

Clemency nodded. 'I was.'

'What about since then?'

'Hasn't happened.'

'Not even once?'

'No.'

'Until today,' said Belle.

Oh God, would she give it a rest? Clemency shrugged. 'Seems that way.'

For several seconds, neither of them spoke. At last Belle said, 'You must really love him.'

It was as if the insides of her eyelids were coated with fine sandpaper; it even hurt to blink. Clemency said, 'You mean Sam?'

'Of course I mean Sam. Who else would we be talking about?'

How could Belle not realise? Incredulous, Clemency shook her head. 'You seriously think that's why I'm upset? I'm not crying about Sam, I'm crying about *you*.'

'Me? Why?'

'Because I can't believe you thought I'd make fun of you. I can't believe you ever thought I was better than you . . . or more popular . . . I mean, we've always had different friends and interests, but neither of us was ever better than the other. OK, sometimes I laughed at you when things went wrong, but you laughed at me too . . . because we're sisters and that's what sisters do.' Fresh tears were now leaking from her eyes, but Clemency didn't attempt to brush them away. 'I used to envy you because you were so thin and blonde and elegant and stylish and you could speak fluent French and you were always so confident . . .'

'Me? *Me?*'

'Yes! All those things!' Clemency's voice cracked with emotion and the effort of saying what she was trying so hard to say. 'You could be annoying too, but I swear on my life that I never deliberately taunted you after Hugo called you frigid . . . apart from anything else, he was a vile, sleazy git. I was only singing those songs because I loved *Frozen*, and that's the absolute truth.' She swallowed the golfball-sized lump in her throat. 'I'm so sorry you were scared to tell me you were gay because you thought I'd make fun of you. I never would have done, but it makes me feel so terrible and ashamed that you thought I might.'

And now her vision was so blurred with tears that all she could see was the vaguest outline of her sister moving towards her; it wasn't until they were holding and hugging each other that she realised Belle was openly sobbing too.

They clung together and wept, and Belle hiccupped, 'I c-can't believe I made you cry . . . I can't b-believe you ever envied me. I mean, I always *wanted* you to be envious, but you never showed it.'

'That's because I knew it was what you wanted.' Sniffing and wiping tears from her jawline, Clemency said with a glimmer of amusement, 'If I'd shown it, that would have meant you'd won.'

Belle managed a watery smile too. 'We were both pretty stubborn.'

'We really were.'

'Obviously you were more stubborn than me. *Évidemment, tu étais plus têtu que moi.*'

'Excuse me?' Clemency shook her head and started to laugh. 'Now you're just showing off.'

They embraced again and Belle murmured in her ear, 'Do you really love him though? Sam?'

Clemency wiped her waterlogged eyes. 'It's OK, nothing will ever happen. I made that promise to you and I'll keep it.'

'I know you will. I trust you.' Belle paused. 'But it's a bit like me owning the world's most beautiful shoes, don't you think, except they're the wrong size? So I'll never wear them, and they'd fit you perfectly, but I won't let you have them because they're mine.'

Clemency felt as if she'd forgotten how to breathe. She could hear the hectic thudding of her pulse in her ears. She stared at Belle, unable to speak.

'Or like me keeping a private jet and never flying anywhere in it,' said Belle.

'I . . . suppose.'

'Or you could say it was like me owning the most stunning diamond necklace, except I can't wear it because I'm allergic to diamonds.' Belle was clutching her by the shoulders now, gazing deep into her eyes. 'It would just be a waste, wouldn't it? The most selfish, terrible, awful waste. You do really love Sam, don't you?'

Clemency nodded. Oh God, she did. So very much.

'And Sam really loves you too,' said Belle.

'Does he?' It came out as a croak.

'He told me the whole story. You should have heard him. And the look on his face when he was talking about you . . . I mean, trust me, it's the real thing.'

Was it?

'And if the way Sam feels about you is anything like the way I feel about Verity,' Belle said softly, 'I don't think something like that should be wasted.' She paused. 'I think you and Sam should be together.'

It took a few seconds for the words to sink in.

Finally Clemency whispered, 'You do? And you're really OK with that?'

Belle nodded and broke into a grin. 'I know, it's come as a surprise to me too. But yes, I really am.'

They hugged once more and Clemency said, 'I think you might be nicer now than you were when you were straight.'

Belle laughed. 'Except I never have been straight.'

'Listen to me,' said Clemency. 'You're my sister and I don't care what else you are. I love you.'

'Oh Clem. I love you too.'

'*Ahem,*' came a deliberately loud cough from across the hallway. When they peered into the bathroom, they saw a middle-aged man's face at the open window.

'Look, I'm glad you two love each other,' said the man, 'and sorry to interrupt, but you did say you were only borrowing it for a couple of minutes. So is it OK now if I take my ladder back?'

Chapter 43

It took a while before Belle would let Clemency leave the flat.

'Seriously, you look awful. If he sees you like this, he's just going to change his mind and say "Actually, d'you mind if we just stay friends?" Lie down,' Belle instructed, 'and I'll make you an ice pack to put on your eyes. You look like you've gone ten rounds with Rocky Balboa.'

For the next fifteen minutes, Clemency was forced to lie on the sofa with half a small bag of frozen peas covering one eye and a packet of Mediterranean rice pressed on the other. 'You should really learn how to cry prettily, you know,' Belle chided. 'Like me.'

Then came the make-up, again applied by Belle because apparently she was so much better at it. 'I don't just chuck it all on in two minutes flat like you do.' Not too much, just enough to cover the shameful blotchiness and distract from the fading pinkness of her eyes.

Finally Clemency was allowed to get dressed. When she presented herself for inspection, Belle cast a critical eye over the flippy red summer dress and silver flip-flops. 'It makes your bum look big.'

'My bum *is* big.'

'I mean, it doesn't do anything to disguise it.'

Her more stylish sister was trying to help. She wasn't going to take offence. Clem smiled and did a playful wiggle. 'Good.'

It wasn't until they were leaving Clemency's flat that Belle said, 'Oh, is it the fifth today? I've just remembered, Sam's got some charity event down in St Austell this evening. Are you going straight over to see him now?'

As if she might choose to stop off at the garage first to get her car MOT'd and valeted, or maybe head over to the supermarket for a spot of food shopping. Clemency said, 'I thought I might.'

'Well you'll need to get to the flat before he sets off. Shall I give him a call and let him know you're on your way?'

Clemency shook her head. 'It's OK, I can be there in five minutes. He won't have left yet, surely.'

Thirty minutes later, she was wishing she'd made the journey on foot. Because if she had, she'd have been there by now. *With Sam.*

Instead, she was stuck in gridlock, caught smack in the middle of traffic that was backed up in all directions thanks to the hapless holidaymaker who'd towed his caravan down a lane that was too narrow for it, then come nose to nose with a tractor that had been trundling in the other direction.

No one could move. There were too many cars behind them now, and no room for anyone to turn round. And to cap it all, Clemency was trapped at the bottom of Fox Hill Lane, where phone signal was as hard to capture as Cornish pixies. Out of her car and leaning against it, she tried again to get through to Sam, then Ronan, then Belle.

Nothing, nada, zilch.

OK, maybe it wasn't a life-threatening situation; she wouldn't actually *die* if she didn't get to see Sam until, say, tomorrow . . . but she still *wanted* to see him, more than anything in the world. The amount of adrenalin swooshing through her body was making her feel sick and light-headed with anticipation. All her carefully applied make-up was melting in the heat and her heart was clamouring inside her chest. Twenty or so yards away, the tractor driver and the owner of the caravan were arguing about whose fault it was that all this had happened. A couple of small children were crying, a carload of surfers were playing loud music and dancing in the lane to pass the time, and holidaymakers leaving the beach and making their way on foot back to their campsite eyed the situation with smug amusement.

The music now blasting out of the surfers' battered purple Renault was 'Don't Worry, Be Happy' and the surfers were bellowing along to it with energetic enthusiasm and complete disregard for the actual tune. Apart from the driver, they were all glugging from bottles of chilled lager, waving them in the air between gulps. One of the boys caught Clemency's eye. 'Cheer up, beautiful lady! It's a perfect day, right? Want a beer?'

She smiled at him and shook her head. 'No thanks.'

'See? You're feeling better already. No need to panic, eh? Don't worry, be happy!'

And she was happy, but the frustration was building and building, because seeing Sam again would make her *so* much happier.

Just to be doing something, Clemency gave her phone a vigorous shake before trying Sam's number once more and for good measure waving it high above her head.

The next moment, unbelievably, it began to ring at Sam's end, then it was picked up and she was just able to make out his voice saying her name.

Oh, his beautiful voice . . .

'Sam! Hang on!' At last, a use for all the adrenalin in her bloodstream. Barefoot, she leapt up on to the bonnet of her car. 'Sam, are you still at home? I'm on my way to see you but I'm stuck in traffic . . . Oh Sam, do you know what Belle said? She doesn't mind about us – she's completely fine about it! This is killing me. I'm trapped in a stupid traffic jam and I'm so desperate to see you!'

'. . . what . . . can't . . . where . . . cutting out . . .'

'Sam, can you hear me? I'm at the bottom of Fox Hill Lane by the turn-off to Beachcomber Bay . . . I was coming to meet you, but I can't leave my car— *oh*.'

The line had gone dead and she'd hardly been able to make out a single word he'd said. Presumably he hadn't been able to hear her either. She tried to redial, but the oh-so-evasive fragment of phone signal had evaporated, drifted off out to sea.

And the bonnet of the car, super-heated by the afternoon sun, was burning the soles of her bare feet. *Ouch.*

One of the small boys in the car behind Clemency's wailed in plaintive tones, 'Mum, I'm hungry.'

'Well you'll just have to wait,' said his mother.

You and me both, thought Clemency.

Oh well, she'd managed without Sam for the last three and a bit years. Another day of waiting wouldn't kill her.

Except knowing her luck, Sam would be seated next to some gorgeous, stunning blonde at the charity event in St Austell and would fall madly in love with her at first sight and there'd be nothing Clemency could do about it, because it would be *too late*.

The charity night was a black-tie affair. Having showered and changed into his dinner suit, Sam had been about to head off to St Austell when his mobile phone had rung.

Clemency's name flashed up and he reversed back into the parking space he'd just been about to pull out of.

Two minutes later, he was pretty much none the wiser. A catastrophically poor connection had meant all he'd been able to hear was 'Sam . . . way . . . stuck . . . Belle . . . trapped . . . desperate . . .' When he'd tried to make her aware that she was cutting out, she'd burbled something about Fox Hill and Beachcomber Bay and coming to meet him, before the call had abruptly ended.

He hadn't been able to call her back – there was no connection at all now – and the few words he'd managed to make out weren't reassuring. He thought she'd sounded excited, but what if it had been distress causing her to shout like that? She'd mentioned Belle, and being trapped. Had Belle gone ballistic and done something to her? Oh God, surely not . . .

But when he tried Belle's number, her phone was turned off.

Then he checked his sat nav and saw that Fox Hill Lane was currently unreachable, with traffic at a standstill all around it.

Had there been some kind of terrible accident? His blood ran cold at the thought. Oh God.

He switched off the ignition and jumped out of the car. It was six o'clock and he'd allowed himself a couple of hours to reach St Austell, but this wasn't a situation he could ignore. If something had happened to Clemency, he needed to get to her fast, and on foot was clearly the way to go.

Please don't let anything bad have happened to her.

The sun was lower in the sky now, but a heavy, shimmering heat still hung in the air; the temperature had to be up in the high twenties. Sam soon encountered the snarled-up traffic. He carried on walking purposefully past sunburnt families loaded down with pushchairs and cool boxes, beach balls and lilos. Since the holidaymakers were all sporting shorts and T-shirts, swimsuits and cotton kaftans, he didn't exactly blend in; no one else was wearing highly polished shoes, a black bow tie and a dinner jacket.

Minutes later, he drew level with a particularly sprawling group complaining about the heat, and got wolf-whistled by a couple of bawdy grannies. 'Ooh, look at 'im, Jean, bit of a fittie, in't 'e?'

'That's what I call a decent body, Marj. Hey, love, not so fast. Stay and 'ave a chat. If you're 'eading to the same campsite as us, you can give me a piggy back if you like!'

Sam, overtaking them at a brisk pace, turned to the two older women. 'Next time, ladies, I promise.'

They cackled with delight and Jean said, 'Young man, we'll hold you to that.'

Ten minutes later, he reached the brow of the hill and paused to take in the view of the traffic-clogged valley ahead of him. Making his way down past the line of cars, he searched for Clemency's but couldn't spot it. The good news, though, was that there didn't appear to have been any kind of accident. OK, if he wasn't able to locate her here on Fox Hill Lane, that must mean she was wanting him to meet her down at Beachcomber Bay.

As he came closer to the dip at the bottom of the hill, Sam heard music and singing. Then a bend in the lane meant he was able to see a group of people who'd previously been obscured from view by a large caravan, and his heart leapt in his chest. Because the people were dancing along to the music, their joie de vivre infectious, and one of them was a girl wearing a red summer dress and silver flip-flops. Her legs were long and tanned, her dark wavy hair flew around her shoulders as she twirled, and even from here, Sam could see that her head was thrown back and she was laughing.

Which was good, because it meant she was all right, nothing terrible had happened. She was happy, she was fine. He felt his shoulders relax and realised just how worried he'd been.

Now all he had to do was find out why she'd called his phone and what she'd been trying to tell him.

As he made his way down the rest of the steep hill, Sam wondered if she'd even heard from Annabelle yet.

Chapter 44

Clemency's eyes were closed, her head tilted back as the blond surfer called Ted swung her round in the road and sang along, wildly off-key, to 'Happy' by Pharrell. The sun warmed her eyelids and she breathed in the mingled scents of wild flowers and grass from the high hedgerows on either side of the lane, as well as the oily tang of tarmac from the road itself.

And she *was* happy, despite having missed her chance to see Sam this evening, because she'd see him tomorrow and in the meantime she could celebrate what would hopefully happen then, now that it was—

'Happy, happy, happy, happy!' bellowed Ted, swinging her arm so vigorously he almost tipped her over. Clemency opened her eyes in order to regain her balance and saw that they were being watched. A small boy, pointing at her, was saying to his father, 'Daddy, why are they dancing? Can we dance too?'

The next moment Clemency's attention was caught by another figure headed her way. In contrast with everyone else, this one was wearing black, and in even more of a contrast the black outfit was a perfectly tailored tuxedo.

It was like looking up and seeing James Bond coming towards you. Except this was even better than James Bond because somehow, unbelievably, it was Sam.

'Hey,' Ted protested when she let go of his hand. 'Don't stop now, we're just getting to the good bit.'

But Clemency had already turned away from the dancers; her attention was fixed on Sam alone. Did he know? Had Belle contacted him to tell him? Oh goodness, her knees were going funny just at the sight of him . . . What was he doing here?

'Hello.' He came to a halt in front of her. 'You're OK, then.'

She breathed in his aftershave. 'Never better. I couldn't hear you on the phone so I thought you probably couldn't hear me.'

'I only managed to make out Fox Hill and Beachcomber Bay. And trapped. I didn't know if you'd had an accident.'

'No.' Clemency greedily drank in the details of his face, the face she'd dreamt about kissing for so long. 'Has Belle spoken to you since then?'

Sam shook his head. 'I tried, but couldn't get through to her either. Why?'

'She told me about you and her, and about Verity. We had a massive row about you and she stormed off. Then she came back and climbed in through my bathroom window and we made up.' Clemency knew she was gabbling; hopefully he was following enough to get the gist. 'And that was when it happened . . . Belle told me that under the circumstances, what with Verity and everything, it didn't seem fair for her to hold me to the pledge we'd made.'

Sam's expression was unreadable. 'You mean . . .?'

'Basically, I can do whatever I like with you. Anything at all.' Just the thought of it made her feel breathless. 'Only if I want to, obviously.'

His dark eyes glittered in the late-afternoon sunlight. 'And if I want you to, of course.'

'If you don't want me to, that's fine.' Clemency found she couldn't tear her gaze from his mouth; his beguiling hint-of-a-smile was utterly hypnotic. 'Really. Not a problem. We'll just forget all about it.'

Sam paused. 'Although, just out of curiosity, what would you like to do with me? You know, given the option?'

OK, it was all very well being flirty and playful and teasing, but sometimes you were just desperate to get all that stuff out of the way.

'I'd do this,' said Clemency, wrapping her arms around his neck and reaching up to kiss him on the mouth. Because it was what she'd been wanting to do for so, *so* long.

She knew people were watching them, but it didn't even matter. It was the most perfect kiss of her life.

'Well,' Sam murmured when they finally came up for air. 'That was worth waiting for.'

Clemency touched the sleeve of his dinner jacket. 'This is very smart. You didn't have to dress up to come and see me.'

'I wanted to look my best.' He took her face in his hands. 'Is this really OK? Are you sure?'

'It's really OK. Isn't that incredible?' Clemency held his gaze. 'Are you glad?'

'What do you think?' Sam bent his head and kissed her again; once, twice, three times.

Not enough times . . .

Behind them she heard the same young boy say, 'Daddy,

why is that lady kissing that man? Is it because it's her birthday?'

'I think it's all my birthdays come at once,' Clemency whispered. 'Are you scared?'

Sam trailed a teasing index finger down the side of her face. 'Scared of what? You? I'll cope.'

'I mean it, though.' It had been bothering her. 'Aren't you scared that after all this waiting, it might not work out?'

'Hey.' He gave her one more reassuring kiss. 'I'm not worried about that at all. I know how I feel about you. I know how I've always felt about you, from day one.'

'Daddy, that lady and that man, are they in love with each other?'

The little boy's father said wryly, 'Seems like they might be . . .'

'Daddy, are they married to each other?'

Clemency was doing her best to keep a straight face. The car closest to them contained a desiccated-looking middle-aged couple with their windows fully wound down. The woman in the passenger seat, addressing the little boy, said in pointed tones, 'Oh I think they look far too happy for that.'

Five minutes later a farmer arrived, tearing across one of the adjacent fields on a cobalt-blue quad bike. He unlocked the gate that led into the field and began waving the backed-up traffic into it. As they waited outside her car for the backlog to clear in the other direction, Clemency kissed Sam again.

Because why wouldn't you?

'Oh my God, I don't believe it!' The female voice behind her sounded faintly familiar. 'Look who Clemency Price is kissing! In broad daylight!'

Clemency, choking with laughter, murmured, 'Who is it?'

'Blonde girl,' Sam murmured in her ear. 'Works in the pharmacy.'

That was it; she'd known she'd recognised the voice. Surreptitiously turning her head, Clemency saw Laura and her friend from the chemist on the Esplanade making their way back to their shared flat on Derring Road after an afternoon on the beach.

'God, and to think we felt sorry for her after Ronan had that baby with the girl from the post office. I mean, she must have been upset about it,' said Laura's friend, 'but that's no excuse to be all over her sister's boyfriend, is it? Talk about shameless!'

'Talk about asking for trouble,' Laura said with more than a hint of relish. 'You know what Belle's like. I'm not kidding; when she finds out about this, she's going to go ballistic.'

The rest of the evening was an exercise in delayed gratification.

Clemency willed everyone to go faster, but it took ages for the backlog of traffic to clear. Eventually all the vehicles were able to turn around in the field and disperse. When she and Sam finally arrived back at his flat, there was no time to waste; as master of ceremonies for the charity event, he couldn't be late. They jumped into his car and drove to St Austell, reaching the hotel with minutes to spare.

In his room, breathless with longing, they looked at each other, then at their watches. *If only . . .*

'No.' Sam shook his head regretfully. 'We can't. Not now.'

The event was due to begin downstairs in less than five

minutes. He was right, they couldn't. It would be such a waste.

Clemency said, 'What time does it finish?'

'One o'clock.'

She nodded. 'That's OK. We can last that long.'

Sam smiled slightly. 'Can we?'

'Definitely.' God knows, it was the last thing she wanted to do, but they'd get through it. 'Everyone's waiting for you downstairs. Just think, five hours from now, we'll have all the time in the world . . .'

Sam broke into a grin and moved towards the door. 'You're right. And it'll be worth waiting for.' He held out his hand and Clemency felt a zing of electricity race through her as she took it. 'Come on, let's go.'

For the rest of the evening, each glance they exchanged raised the anticipation by another notch, ratcheting up the sexual tension until Clemency wondered if everyone else was aware of it too. She felt as if the pair of them had huge neon signs flashing above their heads proclaiming: *Look at us! It's going to happen tonight! Can you tell?!*

It was frustrating, it was thrilling and she was loving every torturous minute of the evening. Better still, she knew Sam was feeling exactly the same way.

And when the riotously successful event finally came to an end at 1.20 in the morning, and they were able to head up the sweeping red-carpeted staircase to their room, it was even more thrilling to know that the best was yet to come.

Chapter 45

Fourteen months later

It was mid September, so the weather could have gone either way. If it had been pouring with rain, the contingency plan was for the wedding to be held in the ballroom of the Mariscombe Hotel. And last week everyone had assumed this would be the case, what with the storms and the howling gales that had swept the south-west of England in general, and St Carys in particular.

But this week, summer had returned with a show of jazz hands and a saucy 'Did you miss me? Well now I'm baaaack!' A brilliant sun shone from a cloudless Mediterranean-blue sky. Basically, the weather couldn't have been more perfect and the contingency plan wouldn't be required. The wedding ceremony could take place outside after all.

In less than ten minutes, actually. *Exciting*. Clemency checked her watch. Everyone was here; all the guests and the main players were gathered on the lawn at the back of the hotel, where the view was of the turquoise sea and Mariscombe beach.

A lump rose in her throat, because everything here in the hotel grounds was looking so beautiful. The gardens were amazing, as always. The white chairs were lined up in front of the stone pergola, beneath which the exchange of vows would take place. And the pergola itself had been dressed with summer flowers, greenery and swathes of white gauze tied with ribbons.

Really, though, who could ever have imagined that this day would arrive?

Instinctively Clemency turned to search for Sam. There he was, chatting to the owners of the hotel. And to think she'd been worried, back when they had first got together, that their relationship might not live up to expectations. She smiled to herself at the memory, which seemed crazy now, because nothing could have been further from the truth. Every single time she looked at Sam, her heart quickened and her brain gave her a gleeful nudge, reminding her of all the different ways she truly loved him.

The last fourteen months had been completely magical, absolutely the happiest of her entire existence. She had no idea what she'd done to deserve him, but that was life, wasn't it? Sometimes wonderful things did happen, out of the blue and for no apparent reason. And what else could you do but go along with it and just be grateful that the person you loved more than anyone else in the world loved you too?

Soon she would be Clemency Price no more, would become Clemency Adams instead, and—

'It's a good job I'm not a mind-reader.' Ronan materialised at her side and handed her a flute of icy champagne. 'I'd hate to know what kind of smutty thoughts are going on in your brain right now.'

'Nothing smutty at all.'

'Rubbish. I saw the way you were eyeing up that man of yours. Lascivious, that's what I'd call it.'

'I was just thinking about the first time we got together. I mean properly,' said Clemency.

It had been, in every respect, a memorable night.

'Well that explains it,' Ronan said with a grin. '*Ow.*'

'Dada!' bellowed Izzy, tugging at his ear with tiny determined fingers.

'Whoops, sorry.' Kate, who was holding Izzy, said to Clemency, 'It's her new thing, grabbing ears and hair. Especially Ronan's! We're thinking of putting her in baby boxing gloves.'

'Or a straitjacket.' Having disentangled his ear lobe from his daughter's grasp, Ronan took her from Kate. 'Be gentle with me, OK? We both have important jobs to do this afternoon and we need to look our best. If you rip my ear off, there'll be blood everywhere and you don't want it on your new dress.'

In response, Izzy clasped his face lovingly between her hands and gave him a sloppy kiss. Clemency and Kate caught each other's eye. Ronan was completely besotted with his baby daughter, and the way he spoke to her always made them smile. Izzy had burst into his life fourteen months ago and turned it upside down, and it had been the best thing that could ever have happened to him. Character-wise, he and Kate were complete opposites who together complemented each other perfectly. Izzy's arrival might have come as a massive shock to all concerned, but any initial worries had soon been allayed when it became apparent how happy they were together.

And so what if Izzy was too young to be a proper brides-maid? In her white cotton dress, with her huge brown eyes and rosebud mouth, she looked completely adorable. Besides, who else would the happy couple choose for the role on such an occasion?

'Shall we try again with the headdress?' murmured Kate. 'You can have a go this time.'

Ronan retrieved the light-as-air circlet of pink and white flowers that had been bought for Izzy to wear. 'Look at this! I love it!' He placed it on his own head and struck a pose. 'Do I look fantastic or what?'

Izzy shrieked with laughter and clapped her outstretched hands in delight, and Clemency took a quick snap of Ronan with her phone, because you never knew when such a photo might come in handy in a blackmaily kind of way.

'Now it's Izzy's turn.' Ronan gently rested the circlet on his daughter's head. 'Oh, you look *beautiful*,' he exclaimed.

Izzy promptly yanked off the headdress, threw it to the ground and bellowed, 'Nooooo!'

'Talk about stubborn.' Ronan grinned and shook his head in defeat. 'Looks like she's made up her mind.'

'I can't think where she gets it from,' said Kate.

More and more people were arriving now, spilling out of the hotel's French doors and making their way across the terrace. Here came Belle and Verity; Clemency watched as they both paused to greet Sam with mutual affection before heading over to join her.

'Hello! You look gorgeous.' Belle gave her an enthusiastic hug. 'That colour's stunning on you.'

'Thank you. You were right.' Clemency smoothed the

violet silk material of the dress her sister had instructed her to buy. 'This is so much better than the green one.'

'Of course it is. Because I'm always right.' But Belle was smiling, and Clemency was struck once again by the transformation in her sister since Verity had come into her life. Belle was so much easier, softer, happier now that she was able to be her real self. And they were getting along together so much better as sisters, which meant she was able to admit that Belle's eye for clothes might be superior to her own, and that asking for style advice might not be the end of the world after all.

Which was why, last week, she'd taken photos of herself trying on two dresses in John Lewis and emailed them to Belle for a decision. Because sometimes Belle did know best.

'You both look fantastic too,' Clemency said honestly, because they did. Belle was wearing a slinky pale apricot frock in matte organza, while Verity was tanned and elegant in a fitted chartreuse dress with contrasting navy high heels.

'And this has to be the most adorable baby in the world.' Verity was busy admiring Izzy in her white dress.

'Don't get too close,' Ronan warned. 'If she grabs your hair, she won't let go.'

'Oh sweetheart!' Bending to pick up the circlet of flowers, Verity offered it to Izzy. 'Did you drop this? Is it yours?'

With one voice, Clemency, Ronan and Kate chorused, 'She won't wear it.'

'Mine, mine!' Izzy made a grab for the circlet, crammed it sideways on to her head and beamed triumphantly up at them.

'How did you *do* that?' marvelled Ronan.

'Just talented,' said Verity.

Belle slid her arm around Verity's waist. 'It's how she persuaded me to sign up for a triathlon. I didn't want to; she just announced it was what we were going to do.'

Verity said modestly, 'It's my special skill.'

'Hello, girls! Can I take some photos, please?' Marina had approached them with her camera. 'Don't worry, nothing formal, just a few quick snaps for me to work from later.'

Marina, happy and healthy – thank goodness – was going to be creating a painting of the wedding and its guests, and had been photographing everyone in order to help her when it came to sitting down and executing the work itself. She snapped away as they all chatted to each other and were joined by other people, new friends and old. Clemency caught up on hotel gossip with Josh Strachan, who co-owned and ran the Mariscombe, and saw across the lawn that Sam had been captured by Marguerite Marshall, the best-selling novelist, who lived in the largest house in St Carys. Resplendent in aubergine velvet and a hat that resembled a huge silver crow's nest, she was telling him all about her latest novel and pronouncing it the best yet, because modesty had never been one of Marguerite's attributes and something she certainly wasn't lacking in was chutzpah.

Come to think of it, had Marguerite actually received an invitation to this wedding, or had she decided she'd like to attend and simply turned up?

Ah well, what did it matter? It was set to be the happiest of occasions, and who would begrudge the appearance of one or two unexpected extra guests among the many gathered here to celebrate the big day?

As Clemency continued to watch, she saw Sam beckon two of the other female guests over and introduce them to

Marguerite. Within seconds the three women were deep in conversation and he deftly made his escape.

Clemency kissed him on the mouth when he reached her. 'Nicely done. I like your ninja moves.'

'Thank you.' Sam's mouth twitched as his hand came to rest on her hip. 'I like yours too.'

'It's nearly three o'clock. People should start taking their seats.'

'Hey, no hurry. They can get there in their own time.' He kissed her again, his mouth seductively cool and minty, and Clemency said, 'Stop it.'

Because one of them had to.

He smiled. 'Are you looking forward to getting married?'

Had she ever looked forward to anything more? Playfully she said, 'So long as I don't get a better offer,' and led him over to the rows of chairs.

At that moment, Josh Strachan tapped a knife against a glass and announced, 'Ladies and gentlemen, if you'd like to take your seats now, the wedding ceremony will begin very shortly.'

It took a while, but eventually everyone was settled. Kate sat next to Clemency with Izzy on her lap, bouncing with excitement and miraculously still wearing the circlet of flowers in her hair. The guests, arrayed in bright colours like a flock of tropical birds, heard the wedding music start up and waited for the bride to emerge from the hotel before making her way slowly towards the covered pergola where her husband-to-be was waiting for her, along with the registrar.

Thirteen weeks from now, Clemency reminded herself, *it'll be me and Sam saying our vows.*

Except then it would be Christmas and they most definitely wouldn't be standing outside beneath a pergola; they'd be in St Carys church, hopefully with the central heating switched up high.

But today's wedding was about to happen. Heads were turning, and Clemency saw happy tears brimming in Kate's eyes as together they watched the bride-to-be approaching them.

'Oh look at her,' whispered Kate. 'Isn't it just the loveliest thing?'

And Clemency could only nod in agreement, because who could argue with that? She watched as her dearest friend Ronan walked his beloved mother Josephine down the aisle between the rows of chairs until they reached the front, where the registrar and Ellis Ramsay waited for her.

Josephine's face was radiant. Having lost her beloved husband Donald so many years earlier, she had never even considered finding another man to replace him. Instead she had thrown herself into her work, running the restaurant they'd started together all that time ago.

And when Ronan had met his biological father, Clemency hadn't been the only one who'd secretly wondered whether Marina and Ellis, seeing as they were both single and had been mad about each other before, might rekindle their relationship.

But it hadn't happened; the spark of attraction between them had been replaced by the enduring glow of genuine affection and friendship. Instead, quite out of the blue, Josephine and Ellis had experienced an emotional connection that had soon progressed to love. Ellis had bought

Ronan's old flat and begun to spend a lot more time down in St Carys, their deepening relationship beautiful to behold.

Now they were taking the ultimate step and getting married.

It was an emotional moment. Ellis's glamorous doctor daughter Tia, over from America for the wedding and sitting in the front row next to her half-brother, was already dabbing her eyes. Ellis's handsome face was a picture as he gazed at Josephine. And as for Josephine, in her stunning amethyst dress and simple gold jacket . . . well, she just glowed.

'Look at the aunties and cousins,' Kate murmured, giving Clemency a nudge. 'They're all crying too.'

They were. Mascara was running and happy tears were being shed at a rate of knots. Clemency murmured, 'We might need to send out for more tissues.'

Izzy had been preoccupied with removing her white shoes. Now, looking up and spotting Josephine beneath the flower-strewn pergola, she let out a shriek of delighted recognition. 'Nanna!'

'Sshh, sweetheart,' said Kate. 'Nanna's getting married.'

'Nanna,' bellowed Izzy, twisting like an eel in an attempt to escape.

'Quiet now.' Kate tried to distract her. 'Look, what have you done with your shoes? Where are they? Shall we put them back on your—'

'NANNA NANNA NANNA,' roared Izzy, sliding off her mother's knee and racing up the aisle, swerving this way and that and dodging random attempts to catch her. She fell over twice before arriving at Josephine's feet, where, her little arms outstretched, she shouted, 'Nanna, *up.*'

Ronan was on his feet now, preparing to scoop her up himself. 'It's OK, I'll take her away for a bit.'

'Oh no, you mustn't. We can't do this without Izzy.' Josephine shooed Ronan back to his seat and bent to lift her adored granddaughter effortlessly into her arms. 'We can't leave you out, gorgeous girl, can we?'

Izzy beamed, waved her hands in the air and yelled one of her favourite words: 'No!'

When everyone had stopped laughing, the registrar began the ceremony with Josephine still holding Izzy. And this time Izzy stayed quiet and appeared to be listening attentively while Josephine and Ellis, facing each other, made their heartfelt vows.

Clemency felt Sam find her hand and squeeze it, and she returned the squeeze with a secret smile. *That'll be us soon.*

At the very end of the ceremony, the registrar announced to Ellis, 'You may kiss the bride.'

And Izzy, recognising another of her favourite words, promptly clasped Josephine's face in her small hands and planted an exuberant kiss just to the left of her grandmother's mouth.

Amid more laughter and applause, Ellis took a step closer to his new wife and said jokily, 'Do you think it could be my turn now?'

Whereupon Izzy, with the circlet of flowers tipping sideways on her head, twisted round and kissed him too.

Chapter 46

Two days after Ellis and Josephine's wedding, Clemency was more than ready to throw her good friend Ronan off the nearest cliff.

'I can't believe you've done this to me,' she wailed. 'I *told* you there wasn't time to stop off at the bank, and you didn't listen. And now you've come the most *ridiculous* long way round and I'm going to miss my flight .... which means it'll be all your fault but I'll be the one who ends up getting the blame!'

'Hey, no need to get your knickers in a twist.' Ronan had the most infuriatingly relaxed attitude towards air travel. 'Don't panic, we'll make it. Most people are so neurotic — they always get there far too early.'

'That's because they want to make sure they catch their planes. I *like* being early.' Clemency's fingers were twisting together in agitation; how could he not understand? 'Then I can relax and not get all stressed out. Oh God, it's three o'clock! They'll start boarding in five minutes! I *knew* I should've got a taxi.'

'Clem, when have I ever made you late for anything?'

401

Was he being deliberately infuriating? 'All the time!'

Ronan grinned. 'It's only Marcel, anyway.'

'Stop being annoying. Just go faster.' Clemency closed her eyes and willed herself to try and calm down. Marcel was an eccentric but extremely wealthy friend of Gavin's who lived in Paris and was keen to increase his property portfolio in Cornwall. He had arranged a series of meetings requiring the presence of a representative from Barton and Byrne. But Gavin was off playing in a golf tournament in Portugal and Ronan couldn't manage to get away either, so the task had fallen to Clemency.

Except the way things were going, there was now every chance she'd miss her stupid flight.

Fifteen minutes later, they reached Exeter airport. Ronan screeched to a halt, Starsky and Hutch style, as close to the entrance as possible and Clemency threw herself out of the car.

'Don't mention it,' Ronan said cheerfully as she hauled her small case off the back seat. 'My pleasure!'

Clemency blew him a kiss. 'You're a nightmare and I'm never letting you give me a lift again.'

God bless online check-in. Thankfully she was able to get through security without any hold-ups. No time for duty-free, of course. With her case rattling along behind her, Clemency raced to the boarding gates. Oh phew, her flight hadn't closed, and there was the plane, waiting on the tarmac. She'd made it after all.

No thanks to Ronan.

OK. Now she could stop hyperventilating and start to relax.

Once she was on the plane, albeit still out of breath, Clemency made her way down the narrow aisle. Her seat number was 23B. And the flight was pretty full, so there was already someone sitting in 23A. Of course there would be.

Then her seat-neighbour lifted his head and Clemency stopped dead in her tracks and did a double-take. Followed by one more take, because how could it possibly be Sam?

I mean, really. How *could* it be him?

'What's going on?' When she reached him, her heart was clattering like a tambourine against her ribs. And Sam, who'd been gazing idly out of the window, now turned his head to look at her.

Politely, he said, 'Sorry?' and removed the buds from his ears. 'Oh, hello! We've met before, haven't we? You look familiar.'

But his dark brown eyes were sparkling, and despite his best efforts, he wasn't quite managing to keep a straight face. Rising to his feet and easing himself out of the seat, he said, 'Here, let me help you with that case.' Then, once it had been safely stowed in the overhead locker, he turned and kissed Clemency on the mouth. 'That's it. I definitely recognise you now. I sat next to you on a flight back from Malaga a few years ago. I never forgot you, you know.'

She smiled. 'I never forgot you either.'

'Glad to hear that.' He gave her another teasing kiss.

'But I still don't know how you did this.' Clemency shook her head in disbelief. When she'd left the flat less than two hours ago, Sam had been wearing jeans and a faded purple polo shirt, and had been working in the kitchen on his laptop.

Now he was wearing a white shirt, charcoal trousers and

403

the soft midnight-blue sweater that he'd lent her on that first fateful flight.

Plus, he was no longer at home in the kitchen. He was in the seat next to hers, on a plane bound for Paris.

'I drove pretty fast,' Sam explained. 'I didn't stop to go to the bank, and I didn't take the long way round. I came straight here, and was first in line when they opened the boarding gate.'

So Ronan had been in on it all along, and the delay had been precision-engineered. She might have known. Clemency's eyes swam with tears of joy, because Sam had planned this whole thing, and it was one more reason why she loved him. Even if, just this once, he'd actually got it a bit wrong.

'This is such a brilliant surprise.' She hesitated, hating to have to break it to him. 'But the thing is, we're not going to have much time together in Paris. I'm so sorry. Marcel has back-to-back meetings planned with his lawyers, his accountants and his company directors. He says I need to be there, sitting in on all of them so everyone knows what's going on.'

The cabin crew were instructing passengers to place their bags beneath the seats in front of them and to securely fasten their seat belts. By the time everyone had finished doing this, they were ready for take-off.

'Oh dear, how can I say this?' Sam beckoned her closer. 'Marcel's in Mexico. There is no business deal. There are no meetings. Sorry about that. For the next two days, it's just you and me, and the Hôtel Plaza Athénée.'

'No work? Just us? In Paris?' As the plane began to reverse out of the boarding bay, Clemency reached for Sam's warm hand. It felt, as it always did, so good and so right. There were no guarantees in this life, but all she could hope was that they'd be able to carry on holding hands for the next fifty years. Because even when she and Sam were very old and incredibly wrinkly, she knew she would still love him with every fibre of her being. She smiled again. 'Now I'm even more glad I didn't miss the flight.'

'All we have to do is wait for this plane to get up in the air so they can bring the drinks trolley round. Then we can have a couple of glasses of wine to celebrate.' After glancing at her pale blue cotton dress, Sam said, 'We should probably stick to white this time.'

'Or we could live dangerously,' Clemency gave his fingers a squeeze. 'And have red.'

Jill Mansell

books straight through your letterbox...

You And Me, Always	£7.99
Three Amazing Things About You	£7.99
The Unpredictable Consequences of Love	£7.99
Don't Want To Miss A Thing	£8.99
A Walk In The Park	£8.99
To The Moon And Back	£8.99
Take A Chance On Me	£8.99
Rumour Has It	£8.99
An Offer You Can't Refuse	£8.99
Thinking Of You	£8.99
Making Your Mind Up	£8.99
The One You Really Want	£8.99
Falling For You	£8.99
Nadia Knows Best	£8.99
Staying At Daisy's	£8.99
Millie's Fling	£8.99
Good At Games	£8.99
Miranda's Big Mistake	£8.99
Head Over Heels	£8.99
Mixed Doubles	£8.99
Perfect Timing	£8.99
Fast Friends	£8.99
Solo	£8.99
Kiss	£8.99
Sheer Mischief	£8.99
Open House	£8.99
Two's Company	£8.99

Simply call 01235 827 702 or visit our website
www.headline.co.uk to order.